PRESCHOOL CONNECTIONS

Child-Centered Theme Activities for Every Month

by Sarah Felstiner and Annalisa Suid
illustrated by Marilynn G. Barr

Dedicated to:
Mary, John, Alek, & Scobie—S.F.

Mom, Dad, & Greg—A.S.

Thanks to:
The staff, parents, and children of Bing Nursery School
Palo Alto Children's Library
Kepler's Bookstore
and Hobees

Publisher: Roberta Suid
Design: Jeffrey Goldman
Copy Editor: Carol Whiteley
Production & Typesetting: Santa Monica Press

For a complete catalog, please write to the address below:
P.O. Box 1680, Palo Alto, CA 94302

ISBN
1-878279-72-6
Printed in the United States of America
987654321

CONTENTS

Introduction

Preschool Connections is a theme-unit book designed to take you through the school year, from September to June, with a special summer school bonus section at the end.

Each of the twelve chapters focuses on one theme and includes art projects, storytime suggestions, original flannel board tales, discovery activities, and snacks, plus a selection of songs, Mother Goose rhymes, games, and more. A cooperative classroom project highlights each month's theme.

You will also find reproducible patterns for use with the activities and flannel boards, and letters to go home to families.

Incorporated into the themes in *Preschool Connections* are important skills and concepts for children to master. Children will work with various creative media (Art), sing original songs and golden oldies (Songs), build small and large motor skills (Games), explore science and the natural world (Discovery), encounter new and familiar tales (Storytime), and create and enjoy a variety of healthy recipes (Snacks). By interrelating these skills through unifying themes, you will make the activities come alive for every child in your class.

Preschool Connections is based on the "project approach" to teaching and learning. By forming the activities around a central theme or idea, you can create an integrated curriculum that facilitates and encourages children's learning. Classroom work becomes part of an ongoing project, rather than isolated experiences. Though each activity is valuable and enjoyable on its own, it gains more meaning by being connected to the curriculum theme.

The themes in *Preschool Connections* are flexible, and each has many possibilities for branching into other ideas and concepts. As you follow the children's interests, you'll find that each theme flows easily into the next month's and builds on the skills learned along the way. Because of the connections between the themes, you have the opportunity to stay with a theme longer than a month—some themes could take you through an entire year. This flexibility allows you to follow the curriculum you've planned, while being responsive to the needs and tempo of the children.

You may also find that the children's interests lead you in a particular direction, perhaps to activities in another chapter in the book. For example, your study of oceans could spark children's interests in water and weather, in boats and transportation, in whales and endangered species, in land and the earth, or in the sky and outer space.

Everything is connected in the mind of the preschooler: music, art, science, movement, food, stories, and life. Let your children lead you through the themes in this book, and in the world around them. If you provide them with the opportunity for experiences, they will show you the preschool connections.

HOW TO USE THIS BOOK

Here are some general hints and suggestions to lead you through the sections that appear in each chapter of this book. Of course, your own instincts and experience—as well as your knowledge of the individual children in your classroom—should be your primary guide, but we hope these tips will be helpful.

Art

Currently, there is much debate among educators as to how much teachers should guide children's artistic experiences. Some feel children must have free reign to create and imagine without adult intervention, while others wish to offer more structure and supervision. The art activities in this book will allow you to proceed in a way that's comfortable for you and matches your teaching style—most projects include options to make the activities work for the varying skill levels that exist in any group of young children.

Our primary goal is to provide children with the opportunity to practice and master basic skills that they will need to create freely. Therefore, we feel it is appropriate to offer guidance regarding techniques (how to hold a marker, how to wipe the excess paint off a brush, etc.), and express appreciation for whatever children create. Remember that process and product are *both* important and valuable.

Storytime

- *Featured Picture Book*

These activities provide a natural art extension to use with the featured picture book in each chapter. By looking more closely at a book, children will enhance their reading and learning experience. If possible, have several copies of the book available for children to examine, and encourage parents to buy or check out copies for reading at home.

- *More Picture Books*

In each chapter, we have provided a collection of classics and new favorites that relate to the topic of the month. These can be read aloud to small groups, or prominently displayed for "research" by the children. Tying reading material into a theme of interest is an ideal way to encourage emerging literacy.

Flannel Board

Many of these original stories, rhymes, and songs are updated retellings of well-known tales. You may enjoy reading the originals with your class before showing them these whimsical versions. The highlighted words in the text correspond to patterns representing characters, objects, or settings in the story. These patterns can be duplicated, enlarged, colored, or laminated to suit your needs.

If you use a flannel board (large felt-covered board displayed vertically) for your circle time, we recommend duplicating and coloring the patterns, then attaching a small piece of felt to the backs with glue, so that they will stick to the board. You can also tape duplicated patterns to Popsicle sticks to make fun puppets for children to use when reenacting the story after hearing it. And children can cut out and color duplicated patterns. These are all excellent ways for children to revisit the stories and become more familiar with the month's topic.

Discovery

Children are natural scientists—always asking questions and gathering information. The activities in this section provide hands-on opportunities for your class to explore some of the concepts and phenomena associated with the topic in each chapter. We have provided suggestions for water table set-ups, new creations to build at the sand table, and fun ways to observe the great outdoors. You will also find ideas for field trips and in-house speakers.

Class Project

This activity encourages you and your class to work on a "culminating event" that brings together many of the skills and activities worked on during the month. These projects (displays, parades, murals, and more) are all intended to foster cooperation while reinforcing the concepts and ideas your class has been studying.

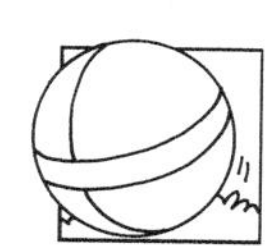

Games

This section includes a wide variety of games: movement, board, card, guessing, and so on. You will also find suggested ways for children to interact and have fun while learning more about the month's subject. Some of the activities in this section are new versions of old games, such as "Fish, Fish, Shark!" (for a new form of "Duck, Duck, Goose") and "Go Fish" which uses pictorial representations instead of numerals. Other games, such as "Dragon Tag," are borrowed from other cultures. And certain classic games have been incorporated into themes in original ways, such as playing "Mother, May I?" during "Family" month.

Dramatic Play

Here you will find a plethora of ideas for adding spice to your dress-up/ make-believe corner through the use of theme-related props and creative rearrangement of furniture, dividers, bookshelves, and so on.

Songs

These pages include original songs (set to familiar tunes) as well as lists of old favorites that fit with the chapter's theme. You are welcome to duplicate the words to these songs so that parents and children can sing them at home, too.

Mother Goose

These classic poems and rhymes have long been a part of growing up. We have included both familiar poems, such as "Peas Porridge Hot," as well as some that are less well-known, such as, "Sleep, Baby, Sleep." Read them aloud to your class, and help the children learn and remember their favorites.

Snacks

Healthy snacks are an important part of every child's day. These treats will be especially popular because they relate to the topic that your class is studying. Serve them on special occasions, or have parent volunteers prepare them in class as a cooking project with the children.

Letter Home

Communication between you and your children's parents is vital to a warm relationship with the children in your class. These letters will make it easy for you to keep parents aware of your classroom activities and encourage their participation. Just duplicate and distribute each letter, or include parts of it in your own parent newsletter.

September: Me!

Your children are each unique and special! By recognizing each child as an individual you will teach all of the children tolerance. Exciting and creative activities, such as "Paper People" (p. 10) and "Walk of Fame" (p. 11), will help children learn about themselves, their appearance, background, feelings, and more. The activities will help them discover new things about their friends, family, and the world around them. Introduce this unit by reading *A Magic Eye for Ida* by Kay Chorao (The Seabury Press, 1973) and making "Magic Eyes" (p. 17).

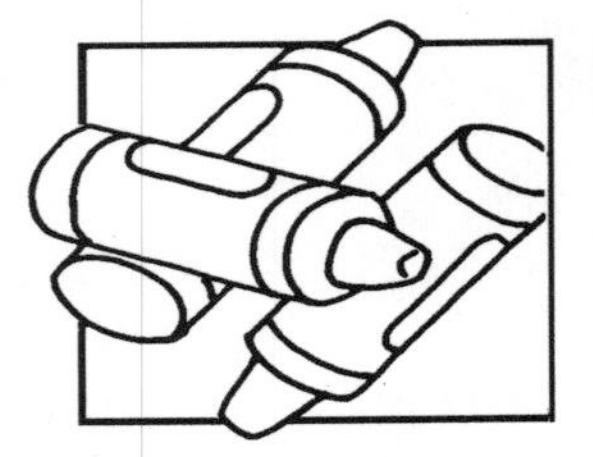

ME!
Art Activities

PAPER PEOPLE

These pictures can represent how children see themselves now, or how they would like to be in the future.

Materials:
Large sheets of butcher paper, scissors, people-colored art materials (markers, crayons, tempera paint), brushes, glue, fabric scraps, ribbons, buttons, yarn, other decorations

Directions:
1. Trace around each child on a large sheet of paper. Older children will be able to pair off and trace each other.
2. Let children decorate their self-portraits with markers, crayons, or paint. They can draw their favorite outfit, or create a new outfit from fabric scraps. Yarn and ribbon work well for hair.
3. Once the paper people dry, have children cut around the outlines.
4. Post the paper people on bulletin boards or the walls and play a matching game: Have children walk around the classroom and try to match the pictures with their friends.
5. At the end of the game, add correct name tags to the paper people to reinforce name recognition.
6. Children may want to draw accessories for their paper portraits, for example, a picture of their pet, their teddy bear, or their favorite book.

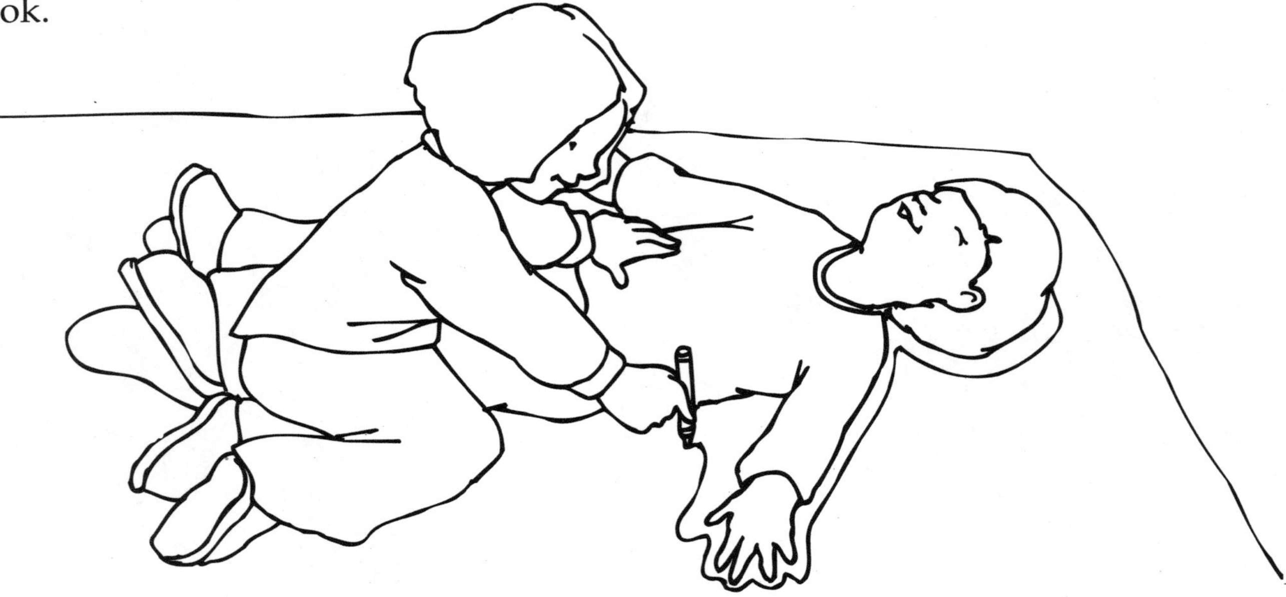

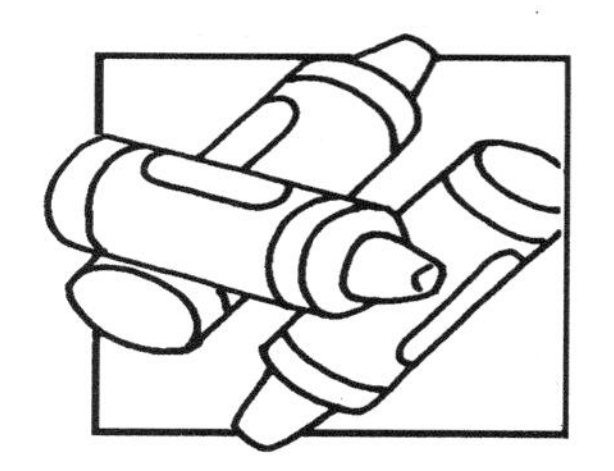

ME!

Art Activities

WALK OF FAME

This project will bring the star-studded streets of Hollywood to your classroom! Your young celebrities can put their handprints in a star, just like the actors and actresses in Hollywood.

Materials:
One Walk of Fame pattern (p. 12) per child, colorful finger paints, brushes, non-toxic markers

Directions:
1. Show children how to use brushes to paint their hands with finger paint and then make prints in the center of the stars on the pattern.
2. Help children write their names in the boxes below the stars.
3. After the papers dry, post them on a "Walk of Fame" bulletin board or as a border around the classroom.
4. Include a discussion of "What I Want to Be When I Grow Up." Invite speakers from a variety of professions to talk with your students. Children can then draw a picture or symbol of their possible future profession on their star.

Walk of Fame

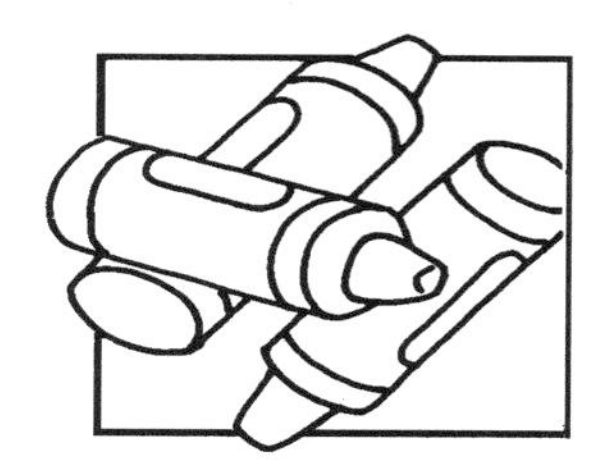

ME!
Art Activities

UNBIRTHDAY CAKE

The Mad Hatter, White Rabbit, Alice, and other friends celebrated their Unbirthdays together in Wonderland. Your class can celebrate their unbirthdays, too. This activity makes any day a celebration, and reinforces learning birthdays and the months of the year.

Materials:

Construction paper, crayons, scissors, glue, decorations (glitter, sequins, fabric scraps, ribbon scraps), one cake pattern (p. 14) per child

Directions:

1. Let children create their fantasy birthday cake from construction paper, crayons, and decorations.
2. Help children write their own birth date on the birthday cake pattern to post next to their birthday cake picture.
3. Make a "Birthday Wall" with a year-long calendar in the center marked with each child's birthday. If you use a month-to-month calendar, place each month's cakes next to the calendar.
4. If desired, you can listen to, and sing, the song from Disney's Alice in Wonderland, "A Very Merry Unbirthday to You."

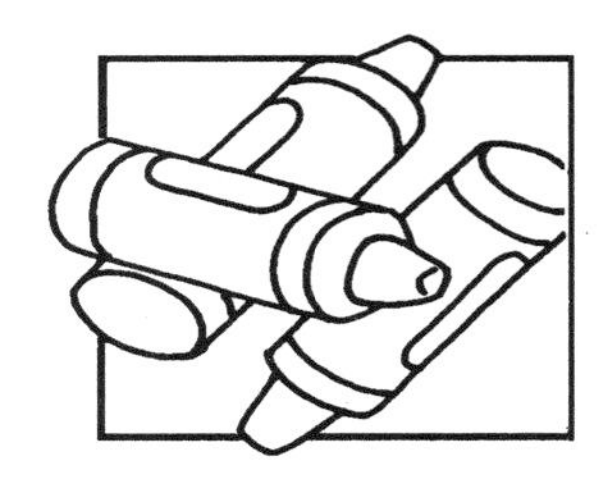

ME!
Art Activities

THE REAL ME

"Mirror, mirror on the wall. . . ." In this activity, each child gets to feel like the fairest one of all, while building his or her observational drawing skills.

Materials:
Mirrors, construction paper, crayons (in people colors), non-toxic markers (in people colors), colored pencils

Directions:
1. Have children look at themselves in the mirrors.
2. Provide paper and an assortment of drawing materials for children to use to create self-portraits. Help them by asking questions as they draw or look in the mirror. Examples: "What color is your hair?" "Is it curly or straight?" "Is it short or long?" "What color are your eyes?"

Option:
Have children make pictures of each other, looking at their subject while they create the portrait.

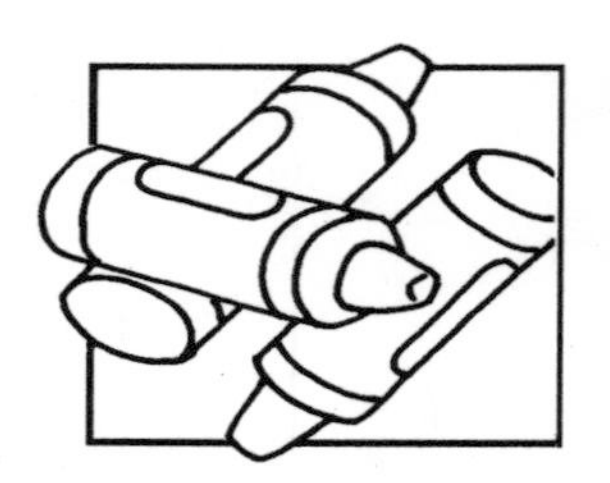

ME!
Art Activities

PEOPLE PRINTS

Children will be interested to see the designs they can make with their finger tips! Everybody in the world has a different fingerprint—just one more thing that makes each child feel special!

Materials:

Ink pads in various colors, paper, non-toxic markers

Directions:

1. Show children how to use the ink pads to make fingerprints on the paper.
2. Once they have made an assortment of prints, let the children use markers to turn their prints into different designs. Examples: a thumbprint can be a turtle's shell if you add a head and four short legs. A row of pinky prints can be the body of a caterpillar.

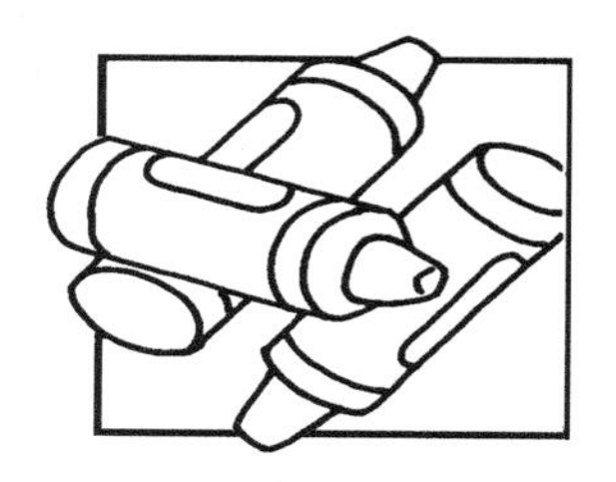

ME!
Art Activities

MAGIC EYES
Ida's magic eye reminds her that she's special. Read *A Magic Eye for Ida* by Kay Chorao (The Seabury Press, 1973) with your students before they make their own magic eyes.

Materials:
Eye patterns (p. 18), tagboard, hole punch, scissors, yarn, crayons, glitter, glue

Directions:
1. Duplicate the eye patterns onto tagboard and cut out.
2. Punch two holes at the top of each eye (for the yarn).
3. Have each child choose an eye to decorate using crayons, glue, and glitter.
4. When the eyes have dried, thread a length of yarn through the top of each and knot the yarn at the end. The children can slip the yarn loops over their heads to wear the eyes as necklaces. Or they can take the eyes home and hang them in their rooms.

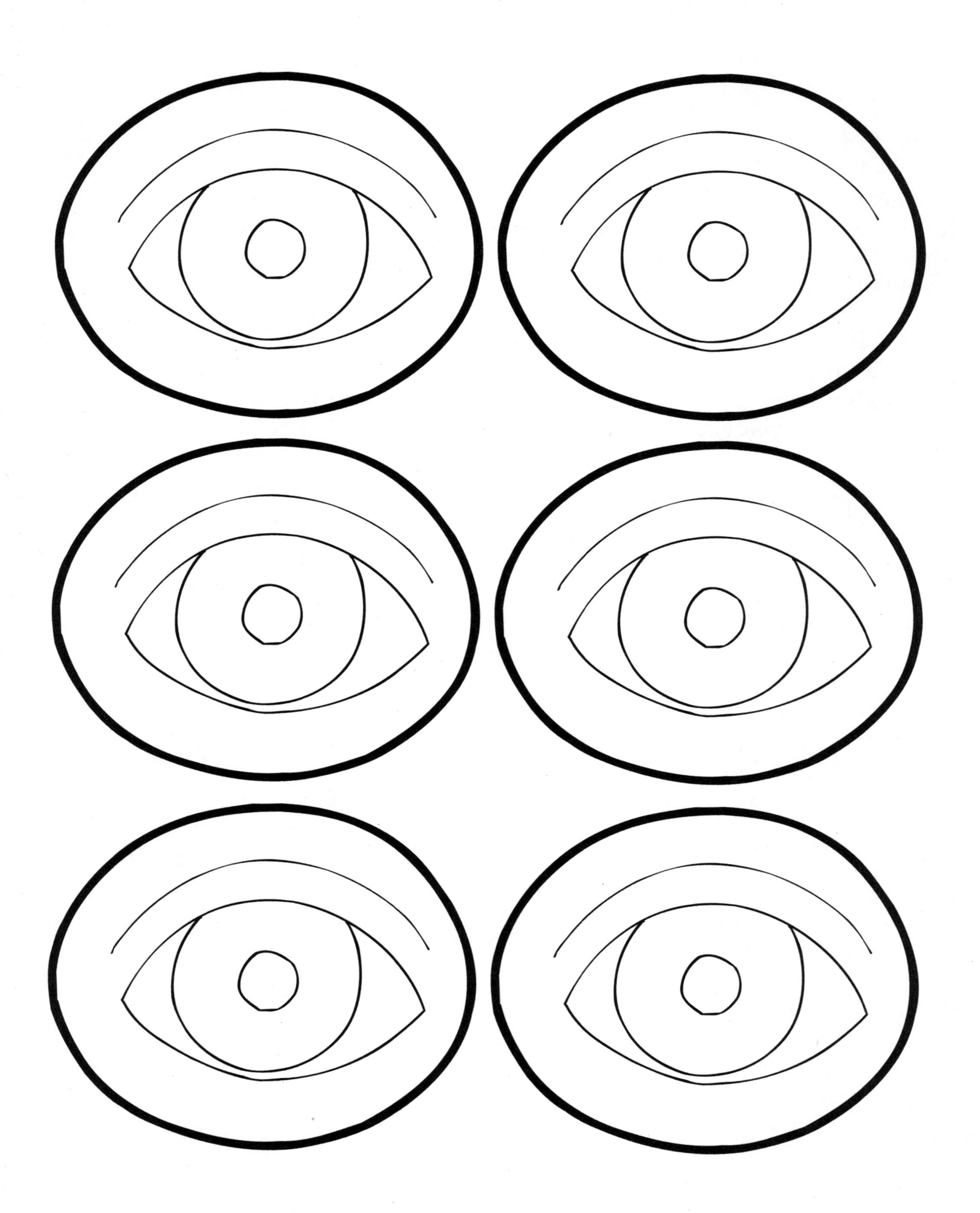

ME!

Storytime

FEATURED PICTURE BOOK

***The Runaway Bunny* by Margaret Wise Brown (Harper and Row, 1942).**

A little bunny tells his mother that he is planning to run away. But his mother says that she will run after him, because he is her own little bunny. Throughout this delightful book, the little bunny plans a variety of transformations, but his mother always comes up with a way to follow him. All children appreciate the message that no matter how you look, what you imagine, or what you become, you will still be you.

ART EXTENSION

Read this book with your children, showing them the pictures by Clement Hurd—black and white line drawings interspersed with brilliant colorful pages. Ask the children what types of materials they would use to make such vibrant pictures: paints, pastels, crayons, watercolors?

Materials:

One large sheet of white paper per child, black crayons or markers, assorted coloring materials (tempera paints and brushes, pastels, crayons, watercolors)

Directions:

1. Children fold their paper in half and then open it so that there is a crease down the center of the page.
2. Have children draw with black crayons or black markers on one side of the paper. They can choose their subject matter from *The Runaway Bunny*, or draw from their imagination. Ask them, "What would you change into?"
3. On the other side of the paper, let the children experiment with a colored form of media: paints, crayons, pastels. (They might want to try to draw the same shapes on each side of the paper.)
4. Post the completed half-and-half pictures on a "Runaway with Art" bulletin board.

ME!

Storytime

MORE PICTURE BOOKS

Chrysanthemum by Kevin Henkes (Greenwillow Books, 1991).
Chrysanthemum loves her name . . . until she begins school. The other girls have normal names, like Rita, Victoria, and Jo. But when their music teacher appreciates her name, the other girls wish they were named for flowers, too.

Hooray for Me! by Remy Charlip and Lillian Moore, paintings by Vera B. Williams (Parents' Magazine Press, 1975).
"What kind of me are you?" "I'm my cat's pillow, I'm a wriggler, I'm my shadow's body . . . ." Use this book as an inspiration at art time!

I Like Me! by Nancy Carlson (Puffin Books, 1988).
"I have a best friend. That best friend is me!" In this book, a happy pig tells all the reasons why she likes herself. After reading this story, ask the children to think of reasons that they like themselves!

I Want to Be by Thylias Moss, illustrated by Jerry Pinkney (Dial, 1993).
A young girl spends a summer day imagining what she'd like to be. She finally decides she wants to be "life doing, doing everything. That's all."

A Magic Eye for Ida by Kay Chorao (The Seabury Press, 1973).
Ida, a kitten who lives with her mother and her brother Fred, decides to run away because no one listens to her. She wanders until she sees an EYE. It is the eye of Madam Julia, a fortune teller, who reads Ida's paw and sees that she's special. Madam Julia gives Ida a special present to help her remember, even when nobody listens!

Mama, Do You Love Me? by Barbara M. Joose, illustrated by Barbara Lavallee (Chronicle Books, 1991).
An Inuit girl asks how much her mama loves her. "More than the raven loves his treasure," answers her mother. This reassuring tale is set in the Arctic, and is accompanied by a detailed glossary that explains Inuit words.

On Mother's Lap by Ann Herbert Scott, illustrated by Glo Coalson (Clarion Books, 1992).
Michael rocks alone on his mother's lap. Then he brings his doll, his boat, his reindeer blanket, and his dog. When the baby tries to join, Michael starts to feel crowded. But mother comforts him, and reminds him that there's always room on mother's lap.

Owen by Kevin Henkes (Greenwillow Books, 1993).
Owen has a blanket that he's very attached to. His neighbor, Mrs. Tweezers, suggests ways for Owen's parents to get rid of the blanket. Luckily, Owen's mother saves the day, and all are happy with her solution—including the nosy Mrs. Tweezers.

Yo! Yes? by Chris Raschka (Orchard, 1993).
When two boys meet on the street, one asks "What's up?" The other answers, "Not much," because he doesn't have any friends. The first boy has an idea, "Look!" he says, "Hmmm?" asks the other. "Me!" This budding friendship is told in very simple text with LOUD pictures!

ME!

Flannel Board

HOW LI'L RED OUTSMARTED THE WOLF!

A long time ago, in a town far away,
A **girl** went to visit her granny, one day.
Her **granny** was sick, she was stuck in her bed,
So off went the girl, whose name was Li'l Red.
Red carried a **basket** filled with good things to eat:
Strawberries, apples, and one or two treats
That her granny liked best, and Red liked them, too.
Then along came a **wolf** who knew just what he'd do.
He would steal all those treats, and perhaps a bit more—
So he ran to beat Red to her granny's front door,
And he tucked himself up in her granny's own **bed**,
And he snuggled on down to wait for Li'l Red.
When Red came to granny's, she had a surprise—
For there was the **wolf**, who had much bigger eyes
Than her granny's, and he had much bigger teeth, too.
But smart little Red said, "Wait one minute, you
Are the wolf, you're not granny, I know of your tricks!
You can't hurt me, wolf—because I'm almost six,
And I learned in my preschool the number to call
When someone bad comes. See, it's right on the wall,
Just over the **phone**, it says 'Call 911.'
I'm calling it, wolf, so you'd better run!
I knew it was you by your big scary eyes.
You didn't fool me with that granny disguise.
And where is my grandma?" asked smart Li'l Red.
"She's there, in the closet," the mean old wolf said,
And he slunk out the door, as Red set grandma free.
"I'm so glad you're here," granny said. "Let's have tea!
We will celebrate what a smart girl you are, Red."
But Red smiled and said, "Let's have **apples**, instead."

ME!

Discovery

FACE PAINTING

Many of your students may have had their face painted at a fair or for Halloween. In this self-awareness activity, they paint their own faces while looking in mirrors. You might want to take pictures of the process and results to keep in a classroom photo album.

Materials:

Non-toxic face paints (crayon-form paints are easiest to use), mirrors (hand mirrors or small ones that can be propped up on the table), damp tissues and paper towels for cleanup

Directions:

1. Provide a variety of face paints for children to use, and give each child a small hand mirror or set up a few large mirrors around the classroom.
2. Children paint their own face while looking in a mirror. Later, they may want to take turns painting each other's faces.
3. Take pictures of the children's unique new "looks" and post on a "We're Clowning Around" bulletin board. (This would be a good day to serve circus animal crackers at snack time.)

ME!

Discovery

HOORAY FOR HOLLYWOOD!

The Chinese Mann Theater in Hollywood boasts a concrete patio with the hand and footprints of the brightest stars of the silver screen. You can display the hand prints of your students—the stars of tomorrow!

Materials:

Plaster of Paris, disposable plastic plates (recycled microwave meal trays make wonderful forms), tempera paints, brushes, stick or pencil

Directions:

1. Mix plaster of Paris according to instructions on package.
2. Pour plaster into the individual plastic dishes.
3. When the plaster is firm enough to make an impression (about 10-15 minutes) have children press their hands gently into the plaster.
4. Scratch each child's name into his or her plaster block with a stick or a pencil.
5. Wait for prints to dry (about 45 minutes).
6. Provide tempera paints for children to use to decorate their prints.

Note:

Do not pour plaster of Paris mixture (even if diluted) down the drain. It will solidify in your pipes.

ME!

Discovery

SAND SKELETONS

All you need for this experiment is a sandbox. However, a paper skeleton or a chart of the bones in the human body may make the Sand Skeletons more meaningful for your students.

Materials:
Sandbox, lots of little hands

Directions:
1. Have children cover their hands with a pile of dry sand and then carefully lift their hands up.
2. The excess sand will fall away from their hands, leaving only thin lines of sand balanced over and outlining the bones in their hands.

Option:
Trays or tubs of cornmeal work well indoors. Also, try mixing powdered tempera, ground-up chalk, or glitter with the sand to make it more colorful.

ME!

Discovery

HOW MUCH DO I WEIGH?

The more children know about themselves and their bodies, the stronger their sense of identity will be. Remember that weighing more than someone else is not a bad thing. Weight and height are characteristics that make people unique, just like their hair color and the sound of their voice.

Materials:

Bathroom scale, balance scale, small blocks, stones, shells, corks, feathers, buttons, plastic animals (and other small objects)

Directions:

1. Weigh each child and let him or her see the number on the scale that represents how heavy he or she is.
2. Provide a balancing scale and a variety of objects for children to weigh.
3. If possible, help children find objects that are the same weight that they are for comparison. For example, a student might weigh as much as five hollow blocks or four buckets of sand, etc.

Extension:

Children can also look for objects that are approximately the same height as they are. (Ask, "How many unit blocks does it take to be as tall as you?" and "How tall was the paper person [p. 10] you made?") Or, have children measure themselves with soft tape measures, stressing that everyone grows at different speeds and that each child is the right size for him or her. The children can compare the width of their waists, the lengths of their arms, etc. Post a strip of paper on a wall or door frame, and mark each child's height.

ME!

Discovery

PHONE HOME

Materials:
One telephone pattern (p. 31) for each child, pages from old phone books, crayons, glue, scissors, unplugged or toy telephones

Directions:
1. Give each child a telephone pattern.
2. Help children write their home phone numbers in the box on the phone, and the emergency numbers next to the firefighter and police icons.
3. Let children decorate their phones with crayons and then cut out.
4. Provide pages from old telephone books for children to use as a background for their phone. Then they can glue the phone pattern onto a phone book page. Or they can cut apart phone book pages and make a collage on a larger sheet of paper, then glue their telephone pattern to that page.
5. Post finished phones on a "Phone Home" bulletin board.
6. Let children experiment with unplugged phones. They can pretend to call home, practice dialing emergency numbers, or just "give each other a ring."

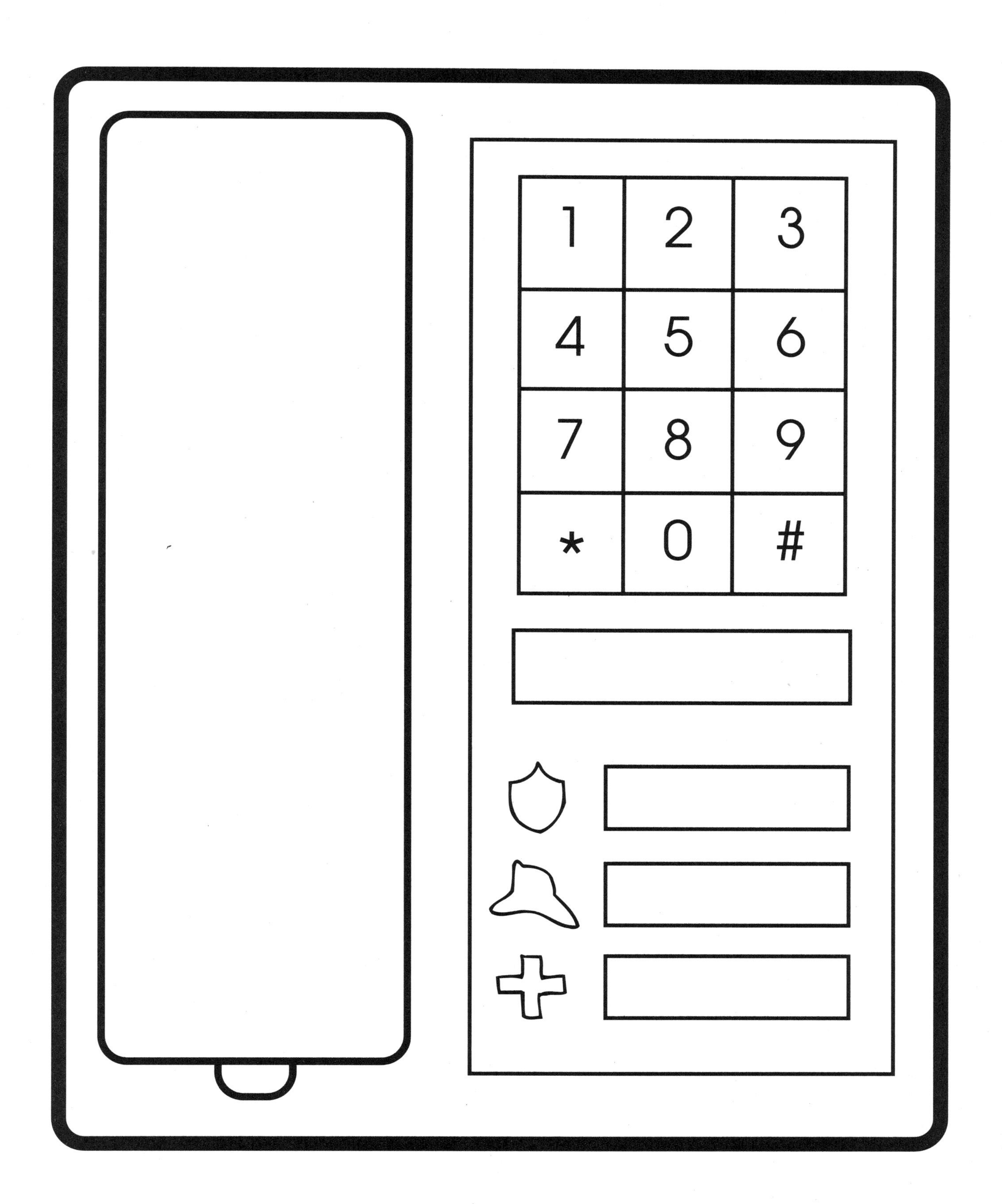
1
2
3
4
5
6
7
8
9
*
0
#

ME!

Class Project

ALL ABOUT US!

Use the walls of your classroom for this display.

Post paper people (p. 10) as if holding hands, either all together on one long wall or in small groups around the room. Have the children help decide where the portraits are placed. If your children are divided into small groups, you might want to post their artwork in the same configurations.

Create a background "Footprint Mural" for the paper portraits. Spread large sheets of butcher paper on a hard surface (linoleum or flat tiles). Pour different-colored finger paint into assorted aluminum tins. Show children how to carefully place one foot in a tin and then step onto the butcher paper. They can paint their feet different colors (using brushes) and make rainbow prints. Provide markers and crayons for children to use to decorate their prints (using the same skills they learned in the "People Prints" activity). Attach the murals to walls or bulletin boards, and pin or tack the paper people on top of the personalized backdrops.

Above and below each of the paper portraits, post an assortment of the results from the "Me!" activities:

- Real Me drawing of face
- Walk of Fame star (or use all the stars as a border along the top and bottom of your chalkboards)
- Unbirthday Cake (if not already on a "Birthday Wall")
- Telephone pattern
- Information sheet with height and weight
- Photo of painted face
- Child's name in large letters

While the children are working on the murals or helping you post their artwork, play Me! music from *Free to Be You and Me, Really Rosie,* or appropriate Broadway musicals, for example, "I've Got the Sun in the Morning and the Moon at Night" from *Annie Get Your Gun,* or "My Favorite Things" from *Sound of Music.*

Let each child visit the space in the room that is "All About Me!" This is a very welcoming display for a beginning-of-the-year potluck or open house.

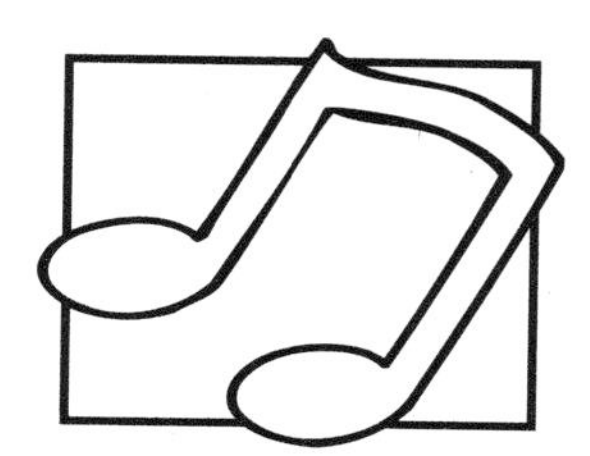

ME!
Songs

I've Got Two Hands
(to the tune of "Are You Sleeping?")

I've got two hands,
I've got two hands.
I can clap!
I can clap!
Clap your hands together.
Clap your hands together.
Clap, clap, clap!
Clap, clap, clap!

Do You Want to Be My Friend?
(to the tune of "London Bridge Is Falling Down")

Do you want to be my friend,
Be my friend,
Be my friend?
Do you want to be my friend,
And play with me?

Yes, I want to be your friend,
Be your friend,
Be your friend.
Yes, I want to be your friend,
And play with you.

Additional Songs:
"Hokey Pokey"
"Head, Shoulders, Knees, and Toes"
"We're All Together Again"

ME!

Mother Goose

Lavender's Blue

Lavender's blue, diddle, diddle,
Lavender's green;
When I am king, diddle, diddle,
You shall be queen.

Girls and Boys

Girls and boys come out to play,
The moon doth shine as bright as day.
Leave your supper and leave your sleep,
And come with your playfellows into the street.
Come with a whoop, come with a call,
Come with good will or not at all.

Little Jumping Joan

Here am I,
Little Jumping Joan;
And when nobody's with me
I'm all alone.

Jerry Hall

Jerry Hall,
He is so small
A rat could eat him,
Hat and all.

Little Tommy Tittlemouse

Little Tommy Tittlemouse
Lived in a little house;
He caught fishes
In other men's ditches.

Moses Supposes

Moses supposes his toeses are roses,
But Moses supposes erroneously;
For nobody's toeses are posies of roses,
As Moses supposes his toeses to be!

ME!

Mother Goose

I Sing
I sing, I sing,
From morn 'till night;
From cares I'm free.
My heart is light.

There Was a Little Girl
There was a little girl
Who had a little curl,
Right in the middle of her
forehead.
And when she was good
She was very, very good.
But when she was bad,
She was horrid.

Do You Love Me?
Do you love me,
Or do you not?
You told me once,
But I forgot.

Be If This Be I
Be if this be I,
As I do hope it be,
I have a little dog at home
And he knows me;
If it be I
He'll wag his little tail,
And if it be not I
He'll loudly bark and wail!

If You Love Me
If you love me as I love you,
No knife shall cut our love in two!

Little Miss
Little miss, pretty miss,
Blessings light upon you!
If I had half a crown a day,
I'd spend it all upon you.

As I Walked By Myself
As I walked by myself
And talked to myself,
Myself said unto me:
Look to thyself
Take care of thyself,
For nobody cares for thee.
I answered myself
And said to myself
In the self-same repartee:
Look to thyself
Or not look to thyself
The self-same thing will be.

I Would If I Could
I would if I could,
If I couldn't, how could I?
I couldn't without I could, could I?
Could you, without you could, could ye?
Could ye, could ye?
Could you, without you could, could ye?

ME!

Snacks

PIZZA FACES

Pizzas are even more fun to eat when they are individualized with a variety of silly faces!

Ingredients (per pizza):

1/2 English muffin, approx. 3 Tbs. tomato sauce (use squeeze bottles for easy handling), grated mozzarella and Parmesan cheese, sliced vegetables (olives, green peppers, mushrooms, etc.), baking pans, aluminum foil, permanent marker

Directions:

1. Let each child put together a pizza using the English muffin half, sauce, and cheese.
2. Children then can make "faces" on their pizzas with cut vegetables. For example, there might be olive eyes, a mushroom nose, and a wide green pepper smile.
3. Cover baking pans with aluminum foil and place children's pizzas on the foil. Write names directly onto the foil in permanent marker to make sure each child gets the correct pizza. (Aluminum foil saves on pan cleaning, too.)
4. Bake briefly until cheese melts (350 degrees for three to five minutes).

ME!

Snacks

ME SOUP

In a twist on the Stone Soup story, each child brings one item from home to be used in this tasty dish. The combination of foods makes a delicious soup, just as the mix of individual children makes your classroom a more exciting place.

Ingredients:
Variety of pre-cooked vegetables (onions, potatoes, carrots, celery, peppers, squash, peas, corn, etc.), pasta, chickpeas, kidney beans, cheese, broth, salt, pepper, oregano, paprika, and other spices

Note:
For a vegetarian soup, have children bring different types of pre-cooked pasta and vegetables and use vegetable broth. For a meat-based soup, ask for cans of chicken or beef bouillon to use as the base.

Directions:
If you start with pre-cooked vegetables, this is a very quick-cooking soup.
1. Add the vegetables to the broth and stir. Let the soup simmer.
2. If you're using chickpeas or kidney beans, add these next, followed by the pasta.
3. Season to taste with salt, pepper, oregano, paprika, and a variety of other spices. Provide grated cheese for a delicious topping.
4. As children eat their soup, read *Stone Soup* by Marcia Brown (Aladdin, 1986).

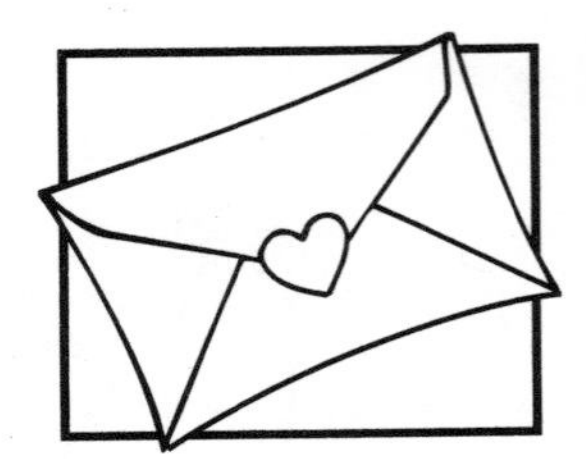

ME!

Letter Home

I've seen you where you never were,
And where you ne'er will be,
And yet you in that very same place,
May still be seen by me.
—Mother Goose

This month we are exploring individuality with an "All About Me!" unit. We will be making "Paper People" (large replicas done on butcher paper), creating our own version of Hollywood's "Walk of Fame," and celebrating our "Unbirthdays."

We will also be learning our phone numbers (and emergency numbers), and having fun with scales and tape measures!

We will become chefs this month, and create a wonderful pot of "Me Soup." I am asking all children to bring in one ingredient from home, and will send more detailed information about this later in the month.

This month we will be weighing ourselves, as well as other objects. We need:

- buttons
- shells
- corks

for this activity, and

- old phone books
- small hand mirrors

for other projects.

Thank you for your help!

October: Family

This chapter celebrates families with activities that recognize the variety of home situations that children live in today. Through art, music, science, stories, and dramatic play, you can encourage children to recognize and appreciate all of the people who are important to them: immediate family members, extended family members, stepparents and half sisters or brothers, care-givers, pets, and friends. In addition to the skills and concepts children master in this unit, they will build a sense of their class and teacher as another type of family.

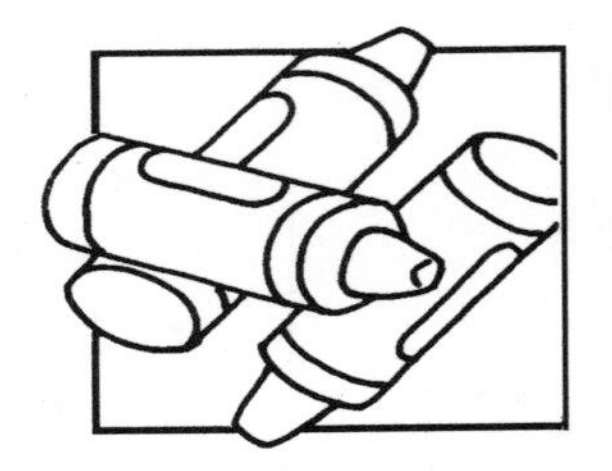

FAMILY

Art Activities

MY FAMILY

This is a fun and easy way for children to create a family portrait. Some children may want to include other relatives and friends as well.

Materials:
People-colored paper (see Resources), people patterns (p. 41), scissors, colored construction paper, non-toxic markers, felt, fabric scraps, ribbon or yarn, glue

Directions:
1. Use people patterns to cut out an assortment of people shapes (in people-colored paper). Some children will be able to use stencils made from people patterns to do this themselves.
2. Let children glue their own family configuration onto a piece of colored construction paper. (If desired, draw attention to different skin tones, emphasizing how unique your students are.)
3. Help children name and label the members of their family.
4. Provide assorted materials for children to use to decorate their family pictures: felt and fabric scraps for clothes, markers to draw on faces, and ribbon or yarn for hair.

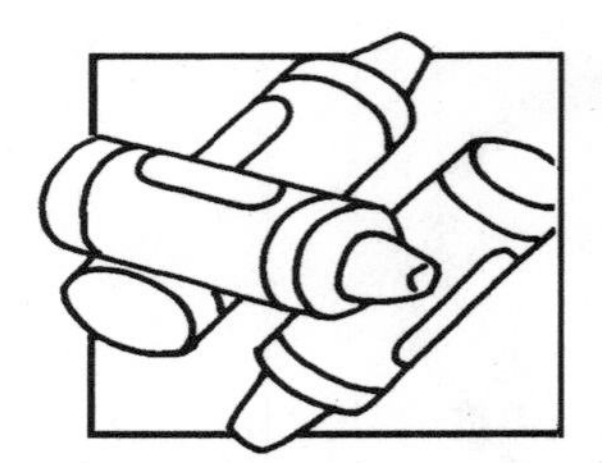

FAMILY
Art Activities

PAPER DOLL CHAINS

Ask the children to imagine their whole family holding hands: mother, father, uncles, aunts, grandparents, cousins, siblings, and themselves, all linked together!

Materials:
Paper doll pattern (p. 43), scissors, multicolored paper or people-colored paper, crayons, tape

Directions:
1. Show children how to cut out paper doll chains, or cut out the chains ahead of time. Help children tape ends together.
2. Children can color the faces and bodies to represent their family members.
3. Post paper doll chains on the bulletin board or around the classroom for decoration.

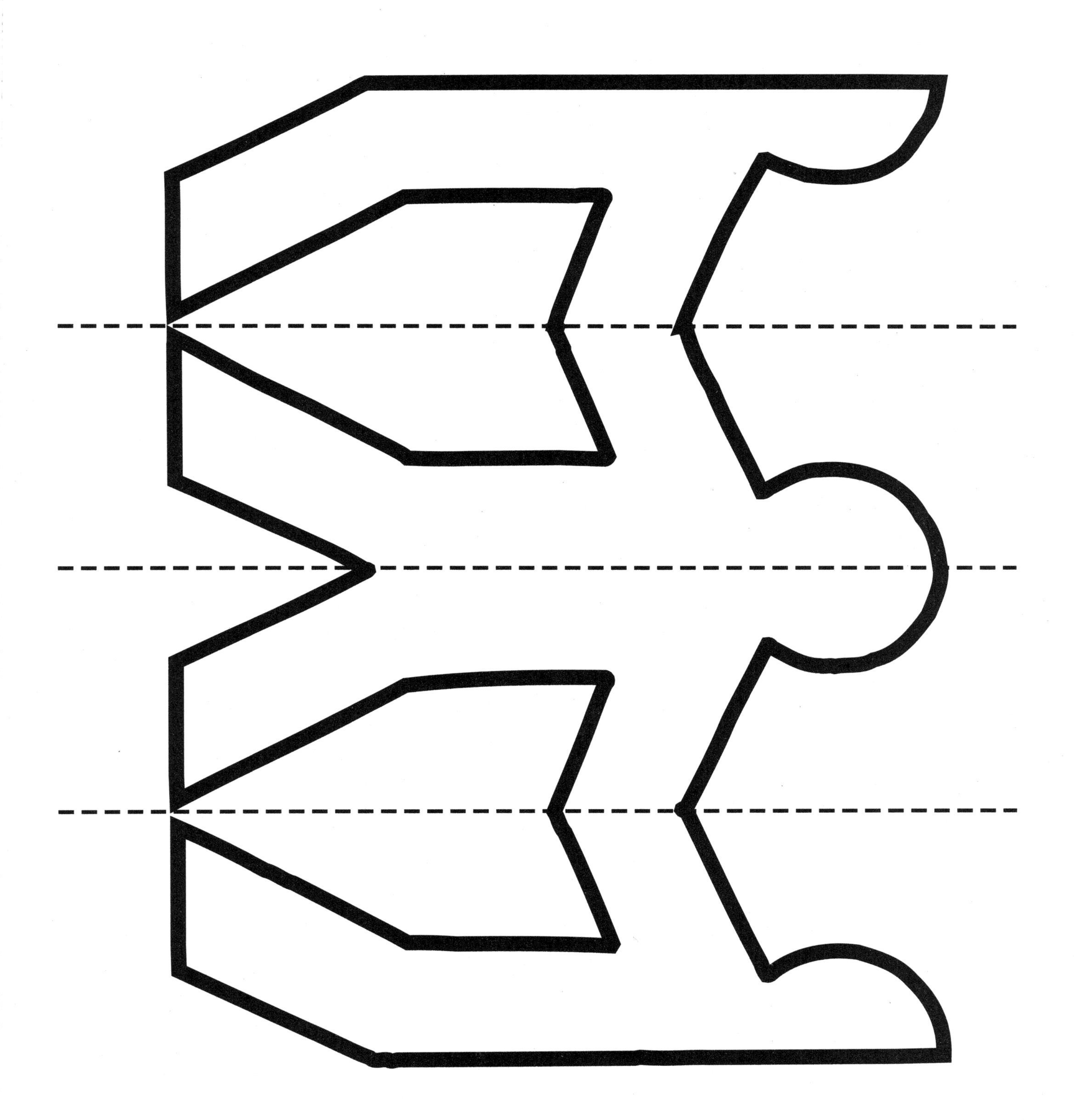

FAMILY
Art Activities

CLASSROOM FAMILY ALBUM

This project emphasizes the idea that classmates and teacher make up another type of family unit.

Materials:
Children's extra family photos (send a letter home requesting them), colored construction paper, hole punch, white paper, non-toxic markers or crayons (including those in people colors), scissors, glue, yarn or metal fasteners

Directions:
1. Have children bring photos from home of their immediate family members, pets, relatives, care-givers, etc.
2. Let children draw pictures of their families on white paper with markers or crayons and cut them out. Help children with ideas. For example, they could draw a picture of their siblings or pets in their bedroom or backyard, and they could draw a picture of some of the adults in their family (care-givers, parents, guardians, grandparents).
3. Give each child a piece of colored construction paper. Children can glue their photos and pictures onto the construction paper. (If you want, show children how to make borders for their pictures with markers, glued-on strips of paper in other colors, or crayons.)
4. Punch two holes in each piece of construction paper. Bind the pages together in a classroom family photo/picture album using yarn or metal fasteners.

Discussion Ideas:
Talk about the concept of a family reunion. If your students had one, who would be there?

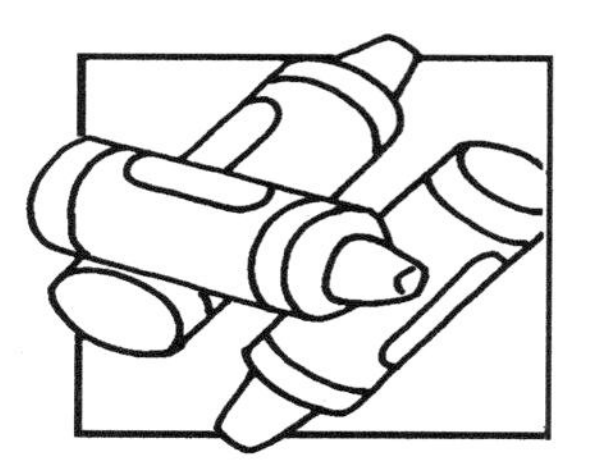

FAMILY

Art Activities

FAMILY TREE

A family tree reminds us how closely connected we are to the people in our family. This family tree activity also emphasizes basic shape concepts.

Materials:
Construction paper (green, white, blue, brown), people-colored paper, scissors, twigs or Popsicle sticks, leaves, glue, crayons, wiggly eyes (optional)

Directions:
1. Have children cut out a green construction paper circle or triangle for a tree top and a long construction paper rectangle for the trunk.
2. Have them glue both shapes to a large square of blue construction paper.
3. If possible, let children gather real twigs and leaves to glue to their tree shape. Or they can use Popsicle sticks for the limbs.
4. Children draw pictures of their family's faces on circles of people-colored paper (or on white paper with people-colored crayons). If available, let them glue on wiggly eyes. Encourage the children to include extended family members: grandparents, aunts, uncles, cousins, stepparents, half siblings, pets, etc.
5. Children glue their pictures next to the branches of their family tree. Help them write the name of each family member under the appropriate picture.

FAMILY

Storytime

FEATURED PICTURE BOOK

***Peter's Chair* by Ezra Jack Keats (Harper, 1967).**

Peter is upset when his parents paint his favorite blue chair pink so that his baby sister can sit in it. He runs outside with his baby pictures and his best friend Willie (the dog). When he comes back inside, he tries to sit in his old chair, only to discover that he has outgrown it!

ART EXTENSION

After reading *Peter's Chair*, bring the book to the art table and look at the pictures with the children. Have them guess the different materials Keats used to make his collages. Ask them what they would like to include in their own collages, and provide a variety of textured materials (the children might bring additional materials from home).

Sample Materials:

Wallpaper samples, fabric scraps (velvet, corduroy, flannel, felt, and cotton in a variety of prints and solids), paper scraps (glossy, sandpaper, construction paper, corrugated cardboard, newspaper)

Directions:

Provide scissors, glue (paste, glue sticks, or tape also work well), and sheets of construction paper for children to assemble collages.

1. Have children explore the different textures, colors, and patterns of the materials provided.
2. Encourage children to cut out interesting shapes from the materials.
3. Children can glue their cuttings onto the construction paper sheets to recreate the look of the art in *Peter's Chair*.
4. If they want to, children can follow Keats' style by selecting materials to suit objects in their pictures. For example, they might use wallpaper for walls in a room, fabric for curtains, and fuzzy materials for a pet.

FAMILY

Storytime

MORE PICTURE BOOKS

Arthur's Baby by Marc Brown (Little, 1987).
D.W. is very excited about the new baby, but Arthur's not so sure. Once Kate arrives, though, Arthur turns out to be a great big brother!

Ira Sleeps Over by Bernard Waber (Houghton Mifflin, 1972).
Ira is invited to sleep over at his friend's house, but first he must decide if teddy should come, too. His sister says one thing, and his parents say another. Ultimately, it's up to Ira.

Julius: The Baby of the World by Kevin Henkes (Greenwillow, 1990).
Lilly isn't pleased with the arrival of Julius. She draws family pictures that don't include him. But when her cousin Garland insults Julius, Lilly rushes to his defense, proclaiming, "JULIUS IS THE BABY OF THE WORLD!"

Love You Forever by Robert Munsch, illustrated by Sheila McGraw (Firefly, 1986).
A mother sings to her baby, "I'll love you forever. I'll like you for always. As long as I'm living my baby you'll be." She sings to him as he grows into a boy, a teenager, and a man. Then it's his turn to sing to his own baby.

Make Way for Ducklings by Robert McCloskey (Puffin, 1941).
This Caldecott Award winner tells the story of Mr. and Mrs. Mallard and their search for a home in which to raise their children. The Mallards befriend a police officer, who makes sure that the family stays safe.

Mama Zooms by Jane Cowen-Fletcher (Scholastic, 1993).
Mama has a "zooming machine." She zooms her son through puddles, down ramps, across a bridge, and all over town. Her wheelchair becomes an airplane, a buckboard wagon, a train, and a spaceship.

Much Bigger Than Martin by Steven Kellogg (Dial, 1976).
Henry is tired of being the little brother. He tries everything he can think of to grow bigger than Martin. Although only time will make him grow, he and Martin become better friends. (Watch for the kitty in each picture!)

My Mama Says There Aren't Any Zombies, Ghosts, Vampires, Creatures, Demons, Monsters, Fiends, Goblins, or Things by Judith Viorst, illustrated by Kay Chorao (Atheneum, 1973).
Nick's mother says there are no scary creatures. But he's not sure if he can believe her, because sometimes she makes mistakes. She says he can carry the bag with the eggs . . . but it turns out to be too heavy! Luckily, his mama is right about the most important things.

Sarah's Room by Doris Orgell, illustrated by Maurice Sendak (Harper, 1963).
"On Sarah's wall, green trees grow tall and morning glories bloom. Of all the rooms in all the world, the best is Sarah's room." But when younger sister Jenny plays there, she ruins the wallpaper, and is banished from the room. Jenny learns responsibility, and gets morning glory wallpaper of her own.

FAMILY

Storytime

Some Things Go Together by Charlotte Zolotow, illustrated by Karen Gundersheimer (Harper & Row, 1969).
Peace goes with a dove, a home goes with love, and a mother "goes with" her little boy.

Stanley and Rhoda by Rosemary Wells (Dial, 1978).
This book contains three tales: "Bunny Berries" (about a messy room), "Don't Touch It, Don't Look at It" (about a bee sting), and "Henry" (about outsmarting a baby sitter). *Don't Spill It Again, James* and *Morris's Disappearing Bag* are two more books about siblings by the same author.

The Stupids Step Out by Harry Allard, illustrated by James Marshall (Houghton Mifflin, 1974).
The Stupids are one wild family. They have a dog named Kitty (who drives), and a cat that Mother Stupid likes to wear for a hat. Boy, are they stupid! Children are sure to love the crazy antics of this funny family.

Tell Me a Mitzi by Lore Segal, illustrated by Harriet Pincus (Scholastic, 1970).
This is a book of stories: "Mitzi Takes a Taxi" (about an unsuccessful trip to grandma's), "Mitzi Sneezes" (about being sick), and "Mitzi and the President" (a parade story). *Tell Me a Trudy* is by the same author.

To Hilda for Helping by Margot Zemach (Farrar, 1977).
Hilda is very helpful. She sets the table every night without complaining. One day, her father makes her a medal that says "To Hilda for Helping." The medal doesn't bother sister Rose, but it makes sister Gladys mad!

Tucking Mommy In by Torag Loh, illustrated by Donna Rawlins (Orchard, 1987).
Mommy is so tired she "can't even think straight," so Sue tells the bedtime story instead. Sue and Jenny are very surprised when Mommy falls asleep in their room! They play the grownups and help Mommy into her nightclothes and into bed.

FAMILY
Flannel Board

RUBY SOCKS AND THE THREE CHAIRS

Once upon a time there lived a family of bears. There was a big **papa bear**, a medium-sized **mama bear**, and a little **child bear**. They lived in a house on the edge of the forest.

Their only problem was a little girl named Goldilocks who had come into their house, eaten their porridge, broken a chair, and slept in their beds.

One day, while the Bear family was on a walk, a little girl named **Ruby Socks** came by their house. She was called Ruby Socks because she always wore bright red socks.

Ruby Socks knocked on the door but there was no answer, so she opened the door and went inside. First, she went into the kitchen. On the table were three bowls of porridge: a **big bowl**, a **medium-sized bowl**, and a **small bowl**.

Ruby was a very smart girl. She knew that the porridge was someone else's breakfast, and she didn't eat any.

Next, Ruby went into the living room, where there were three chairs. The first was a **very big chair**, too big for Ruby Socks. The second was a **medium-sized chair**, but it was still too big for Ruby Socks. The third was a **small chair**. "Just right for me!" Ruby Socks said. She climbed on the chair and sat down carefully.

When the Bear family came home they looked around their house. Nothing was broken. Their porridge was still in the bowls. No one was sleeping in their beds. Mama Bear went into the living room and found Ruby Socks.

"My, my," Mama Bear said. "You are a very smart little girl to know which chair would be right for you."

Ruby Socks smiled. "I know the difference between big, medium, and small. I learned about sizes in preschool."

The Bear family was impressed, and they invited Ruby to have a bowl of porridge with them. (She had a small one.)

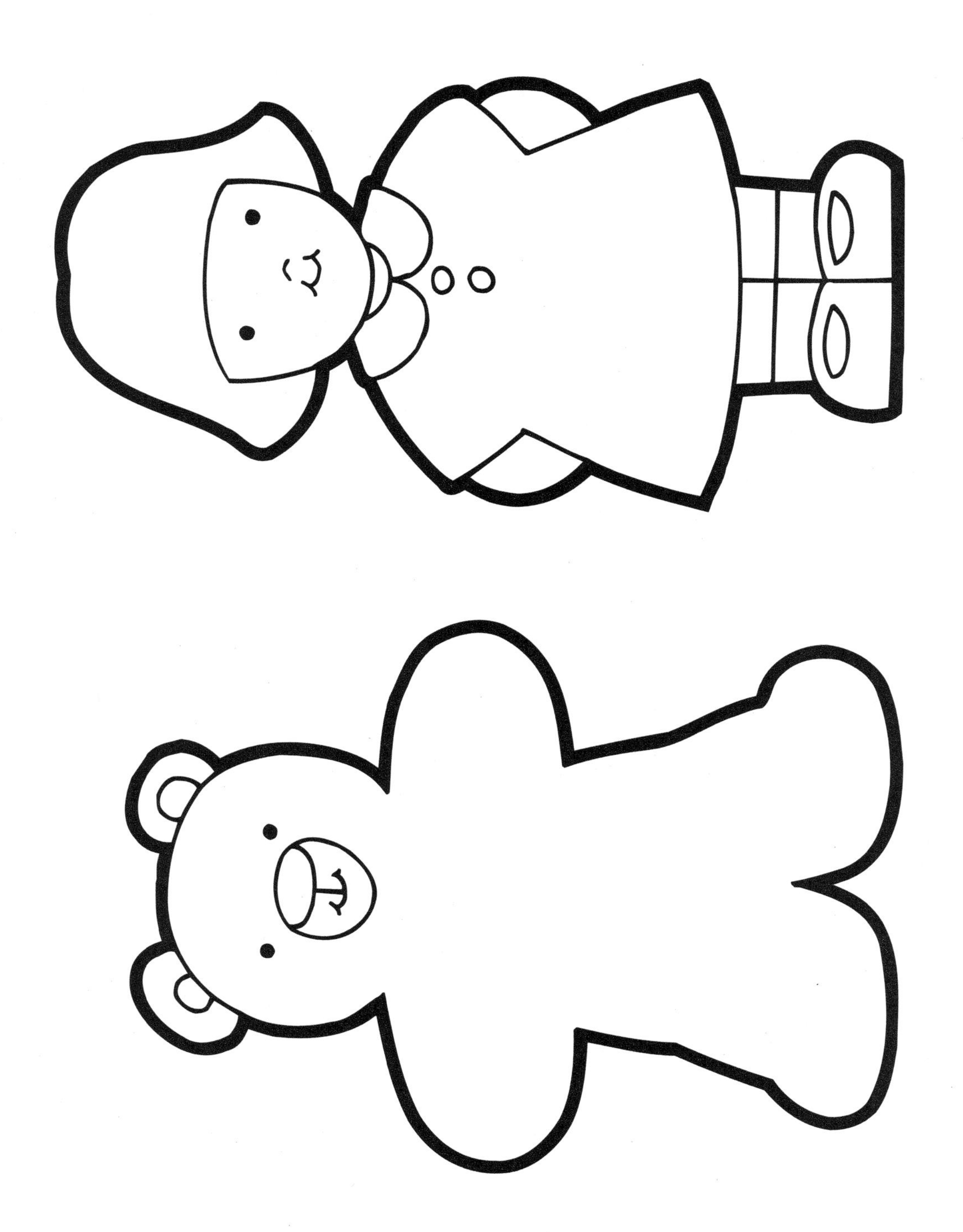

Papa
Mama
Baby

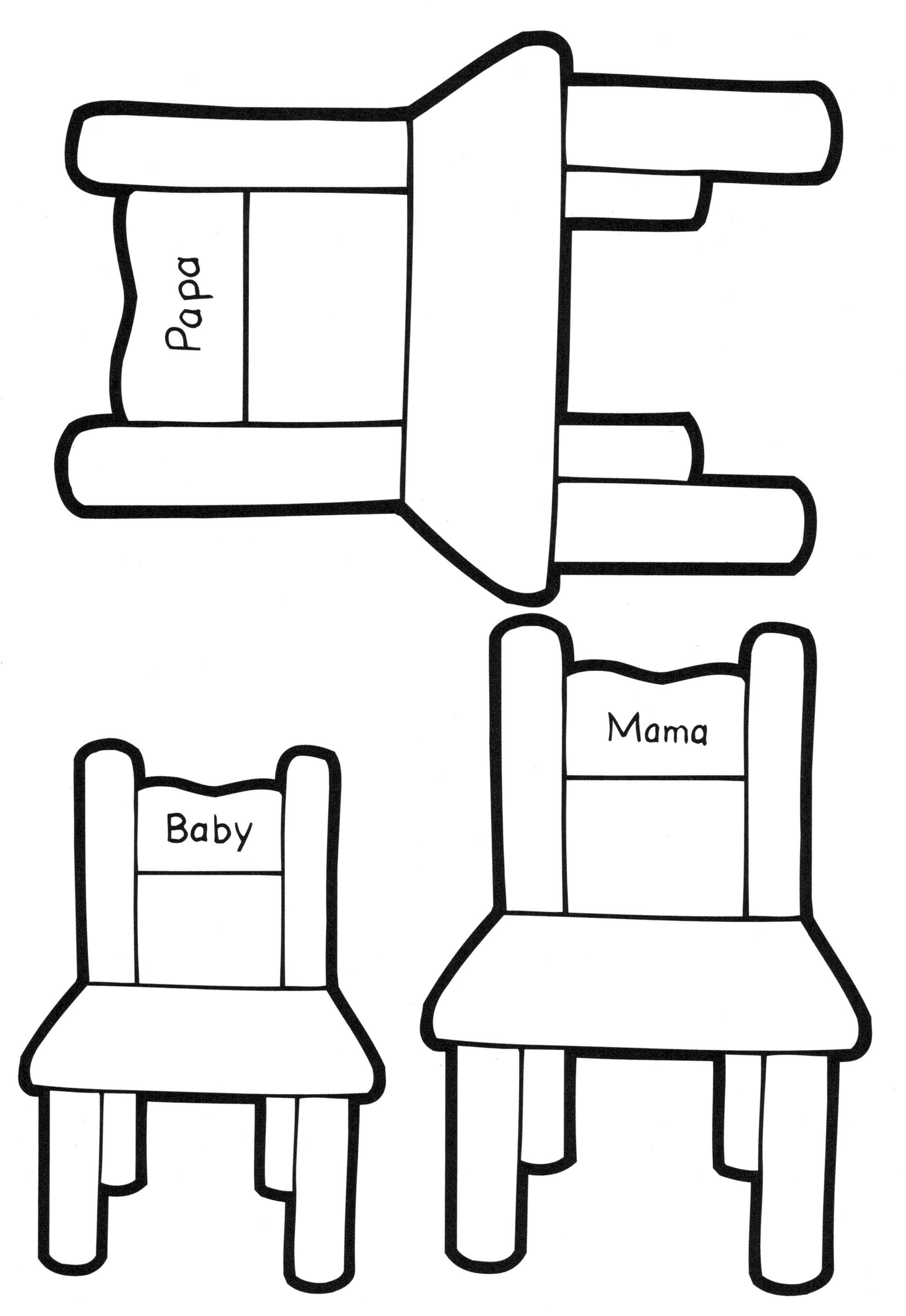
Papa
Mama
Baby

FAMILY

Discovery

CARING FOR BABY

Materials:
Toy baby dolls, doll clothes, bottles, water table, rubber dish-washing tubs, hand towels, plastic bowls and spoons

Directions:
1. Let children use toy dolls to learn how to wash, hold, rock, dress, and feed a baby.
2. If possible, have a parent bring a new baby in to demonstrate giving a bath, changing a diaper, feeding, or holding.

HELPING OUT

Today's busy families often depend on each person doing his or her share. (See *To Hilda for Helping* in the More Picture Books section.) Here are a few ways for children to get involved in helping out at school:

- Let children practice setting the table at snacktime.
- Encourage children to help each other pick up in the block area.
- Provide semi-sudsy water at the water table for washing toy dishes. Also set out dish towels or a real dish rack for drying.

Give children badges (p. 55) to color, cut out, and wear (pin on with safety pins), just like Hilda's badge.

Super Snack
Helper!
Super Snack
Helper!
Super Snack
Helper!
Wonderful
Washer!
Wonderful
Washer!
Wonderful
Washer!
Perfect at
Pick Up!
Perfect at
Pick Up!
Perfect at
Pick Up!

FAMILY

Discovery

PAPA'S POCKETS

Materials:
Different-sized keys, paper clips, coins (pennies, nickels, dimes, quarters—use foreign coins, too, if available), buttons, zip-lock bags, crayons, blank newsprint

Directions:
1. Put assorted materials in different zip-lock bags.
2. Ask children, "What's in Papa's pockets?"
3. Let children examine the contents of the bags.
4. Have children choose materials and make rubbings using crayons and newsprint.

MAMA'S PURSE

Materials: old purse, wallet, keys on a key chain, coin purse with coins, handkerchief, pocket calendar, sunglasses, etc.

Directions:
1. Fill an old purse with an assortment of typical purse items.
2. Have children sit in a circle on the floor with the purse in the center.
3. In turn, have children close their eyes and reach into the purse to remove one item.
4. Children attempt to guess what the item is by the feel of it.

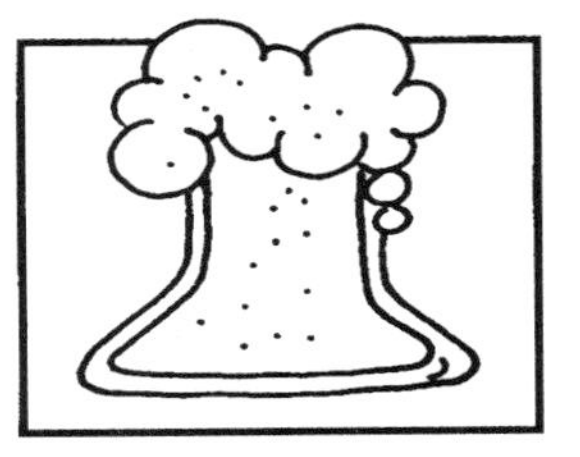

FAMILY

Discovery

FAMILY STORIES

Materials:
Pillows or mats, stuffed toys, blankets

Directions:
1. Have children gather in a circle on the floor. Let them get comfortable by cuddling with blankets on mats or pillows. Consider letting them bring favorite stuffed toys from home to hold (or tell stories about).
2. Begin by sharing a story about your own family.
3. Encourage children to tell stories about their families, about times they've spent together, favorite family stories, etc.
4. If children need prompting, choose a theme to talk about: pets, grandparents, camping trips, playgrounds, circuses, and so on. You might want to start by reading *Tell Me a Mitzi* or *Tell Me a Trudy*. Both family-oriented books have stories within stories.

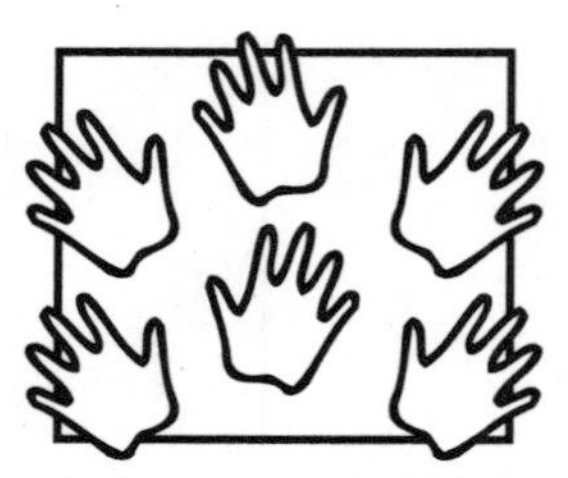

FAMILY
Class Project

FAMILY FOREST

Forests are filled with a variety of trees the way that your classroom is filled with a variety of children. One thing that makes the children special is the fact that they come from unique families. Emphasize this idea by making a cooperative "Family Forest" mural.

Have children collect leaves and make prints on butcher paper. Provide tempera paints in various colors. With large brushes, children can paint the leaves and then press the painted side to the butcher paper. If orange, yellow, and brown paints are used, a colorful autumn mural will result.

Once the painting has dried, post "Family Tree" pictures (p. 45) and "My Family" portraits (p. 40) either on the butcher paper or on a bulletin board nearby. Set the "Classroom Family Album" (p. 44) on a table in front of the mural. Place a blank notebook for a guest sign-in on the table, too. Paper doll chains (p. 42) can be a border for the forest, or post them along the base of bulletin boards so they're "standing" among the trees.

While children are creating, play different family songs, such as "We Are Family" by Sister Sledge and "Family Tree" by Bev Bos, Tom Hunter, and Michael Leemon from *Memories*.

FAMILY

Dramatic Play

BEAR FAMILY MASKS

The children can use these masks to pretend to be a bear family and act out the story of Goldilocks or Ruby Socks (p. 49). (Ruby Socks can wear a pair of bright red socks.)

Materials:
Paper plates, construction paper, glue or paste, non-toxic magic markers, Popsicle sticks, scissors

Directions:
1. Show children how to cut the following simple shapes from construction paper: (per mask) two circles, two squares, one triangle.
2. Have children glue the circles to the top of the paper plate for ears, the squares onto the plate for eyes, and the triangle in the center for a nose.
3. Children can draw a mouth on the plate with markers.
4. Show children how to glue Popsicle sticks to the bottom of the masks for handles.

HOME IS WHERE THE HEART IS

Most classrooms have the materials needed to set up a home in the dramatic play center. You can use doll beds to set up a bedroom, pots and pans for the kitchen area, and blocks to build room dividers. Let children help decide what is important for a classroom "home." They might want to bring things from their own homes, or create items from cardboard boxes and crayons such as a stove, bookshelf, or dog house.

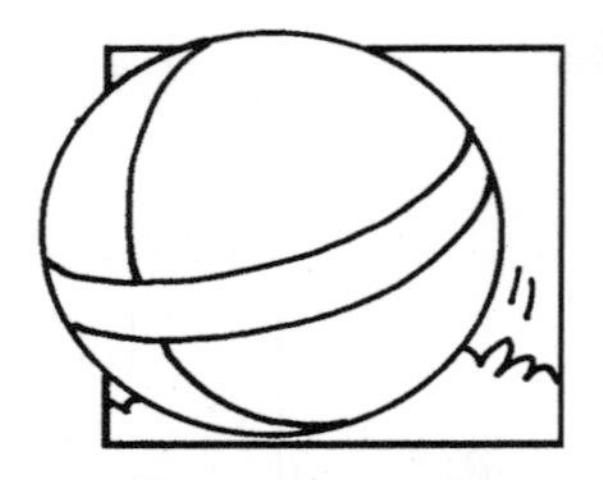

FAMILY

Games

FAMILY LOTTO

Materials:
People patterns (p. 61), scissors, glue, construction paper

Directions:
1. Photocopy the people patterns.
2. Create lotto cards by cutting apart the patterns and gluing them in different configurations on construction paper—four faces per card. For example, put together cards of babies, mothers, fathers, or grandparents. Keep family cards together or combine them to make multicultural families.
3. Let children play lotto by picking individual people patterns from a pile in the center and then matching them with those on their cards. The game is over when one child has filled his or her card.

FAMILY CONCENTRATION

Materials:
People patterns (p. 61), scissors, glue, construction paper

Directions:
1. Duplicate the patterns and cut them apart.
2. Have the children spread all the cards face down on a table and then turn two cards over at a time. If the cards match, the child holds onto them and takes another turn. If not, the child turns the cards face down again, and the next player tries.

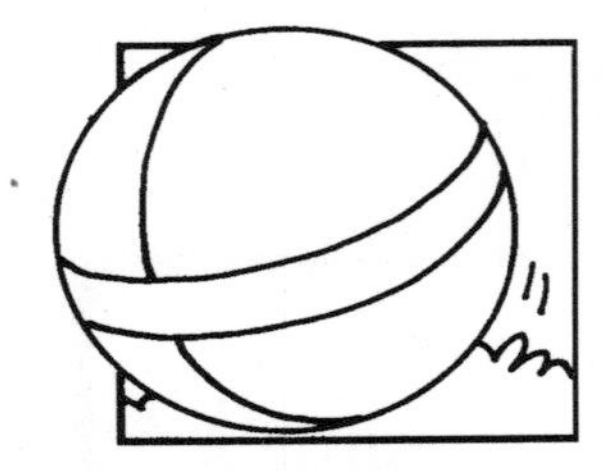

FAMILY

Games

MOTHER, MAY I?

In this old favorite, children line up at one end of the room (or outside along a wall or fence). One child plays the "mother," and the other children ask "mother" for permission to come forward. The hitch is that the child has to ask to walk a certain amount of steps and take those steps in a certain way. Examples:

- "Mother, may I take seven baby steps?"
- "Mother, may I take four backwards steps?"

The "mother" gets to decide whether or not the child in question can take the steps requested. The "mother" says, "Yes, you may," or "No, you may not." The child who reaches the "mother" first becomes the "mother" in the next round. (Boys may be the "father.") Children can also make up steps. What would an "uncle step" or a "sister step" be like?

FAMILY

Songs

I Have a Big Family
(to the tune of "I'm a Little Teapot")

I have a big family,
Yes, I do.
If you think about it,
You do, too.

My family is made of
Me and you,
And _____ (fill in name)
Is in my family, too.

Families Come in Many Forms
(to the tune of "Bingo")

Families come in many forms,
There're big ones and there're small ones.
Some are very big.
Some are very small.
Some are medium.
And, gosh, we love them all.

Do You Know My Good Friend?
(to the tune of "Do You Know the Muffin Man?")

Do you know my good friend ______,
My good friend ______,
My good friend ______?
Do you know my good friend ______,
Who has a mom named _________?
(Substitute "dad," "brother," "sister," etc.)

Other family tunes:
"Rock-a-bye-baby"
"Hush Little Baby"
"Brother and Sister" (from *Free to Be You and Me*)

FAMILY

Mother Goose

Tommy Trot, a Man of Law

Tommy Trot, a man of law,
Sold his bed and lay upon straw;
Sold his straw and slept on grass,
To buy his wife a looking-glass.

Bye, Baby Bunting

Bye, baby bunting,
Daddy's gone-a-hunting
To get a little rabbit's skin,
To wrap a baby bunting in.

Hush-a-Bye, Baby

Hush-a-bye, baby,
Daddy is near,
Mommy's a lady,
And that's very clear.

Dance to Your Daddy

Dance to your Daddy,
My little baby;
Dance to your Daddy
My little lamb.

You shall have a fishy
In a little dish;
You shall have a fishy
When the boat comes in.

Jack-a-Nory

I'll tell you a story
About Jack-a-Nory,
And now my story's begun.
I'll tell you another
Of Jack and his brother,
And now my story is done.

FAMILY

Mother Goose

Sleep, Baby, Sleep

Sleep, baby, sleep,
Thy father guards the sheep;
Thy mother shakes the dreamland tree
And from it fall sweet dreams for thee,
Sleep, baby, sleep.

Sleep, baby, sleep,
Our cottage vale is deep;
The little lamb is on the green,
With wooly fleece so soft and clean,
Sleep, baby, sleep.

Sleep, baby, sleep,
Down where the woodbines creep;
Be always like the lamb so mild,
A kind and sweet and gentle child,
Sleep, baby, sleep.

Traditional Lullaby

Sweetest little baby
Anybody knows.
Don't know what to call her,
But she's mighty like a rose.

When she lays asleep
In her little bed,
Makes me think the angels come
And whisper overhead.

When the night is falling,
When the shadows creep,
Then they come on tiptoe
To kiss her in her sleep.

Sweetest little baby
Anybody knows.
Don't know what to call her,
But she's mighty like a rose.

FAMILY

Snacks

BABY FOOD

This is a good snack activity for children who have a new baby in their family.

Ingredients:
Pureed fruit (ripe peaches work well) or applesauce

Directions:
1. Discuss why babies eat strained food.
2. Serve pureed fruit in small dishes with plastic spoons.
3. Encourage the children to notice that this food doesn't need much chewing (which is why babies can eat it), and it's yummy, too!

Option:
Ask if any children have a new sibling, and let them explain how this new member has changed their family. You might want to invite parents to bring their new babies in at snack time.

BEARS' BREAKFAST

When Goldilocks came to visit, she had to decide which kind of porridge was "just right" for her.

Ingredients:
Porridge (oatmeal, cream of wheat, cream of rice, wheatena, etc.), brown sugar, butter, milk, raisins

Directions:
1. Follow directions on a package of porridge or hot breakfast cereal.
2. Let the children choose the amount of porridge they would like, and then choose their own toppings.
3. They can keep their porridge hot, make it cold with milk, or blow on it to cool it until it's "just right."

Option:
Provide an assortment of different-sized bowls for children to choose from. Read or tell the story of "Goldilocks and the Three Bears."

FAMILY

Snacks

GINGERBREAD FAMILIES

This delicious snack is fun to cook, and encourages the children to think about the members of their own family.

Ingredients:

Your favorite gingerbread dough recipe or pre-made cookie dough (available in refrigerator sections of most grocery stores), rolling pins, large and small cookie cutters in people shapes

Directions:

1. Talk with the children about the members in their family. You may need to limit the family concept in this particular activity to "immediate" family; otherwise the children may want to make a cookie for every aunt, uncle, cousin, etc.
2. Roll out the cookie dough with the children.
3. Help the children cut out a cookie for each person in their family using different sizes and shapes of cookie cutters.

Option:

Provide icing and candies for decorating the finished cookies.

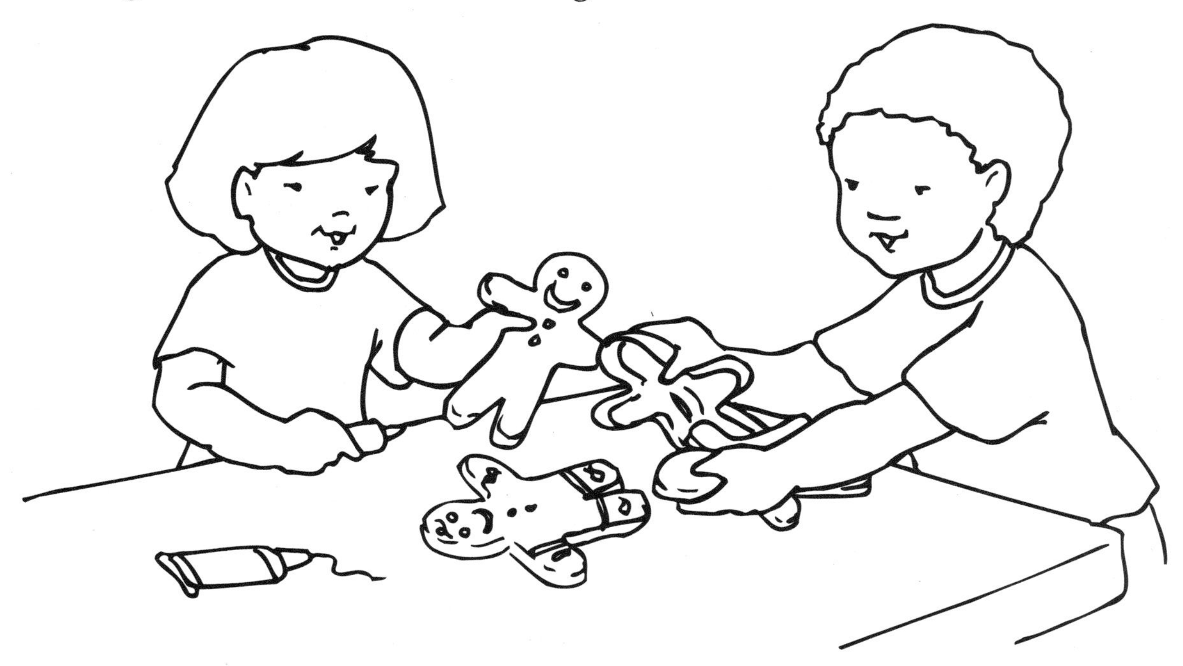

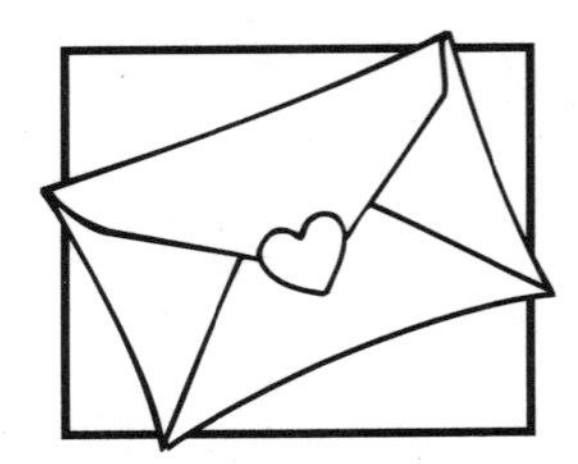

FAMILY

Letter Home

Molly, my sister, and I fell out,
And what do you think it was all about?
She loved coffee and I loved tea,
And that was the reason we couldn't agree.
—Mother Goose

This month we are celebrating the family in all of its forms. We will be eating porridge (like the Bear family) and practicing our size concepts. We will be making a classroom family album. Any extra pictures of your family would be appreciated for the album.

At story time we will read *To Hilda for Helping*, and we'll practice our helping skills throughout this unit (and all this year). Expect to see your child proudly displaying a helper's badge (just like Hilda's)!

Families with new babies are invited to come in for a feeding, bathing, or dressing demonstration. We will be tasting "baby food" (strained fruit) at snack time, and washing our baby dolls at the water tables.

This month we will be making rubbings and playing guessing games. We need:

- old keys and/or key chains
- buttons
- old purse, wallet, or coin purse
- pocket calendar
- sunglasses

Thank you for your help!

November: Food

Many of the first rhymes that children learn deal with food, from "Pat-a-cake, Pat-a-cake" to "Peas Porridge Hot" to "Do You Know the Muffin Man?" This chapter is devoted to food throughout the curriculum: food snacks (of course), food art, food discovery, food in books, and so on. You might want to start this unit with a round of "Who Stole the Cookie from the Cookie Jar?" (p. 86), or begin by reading *Bread and Jam for Frances* and serve the accompanying snack (p. 90)!

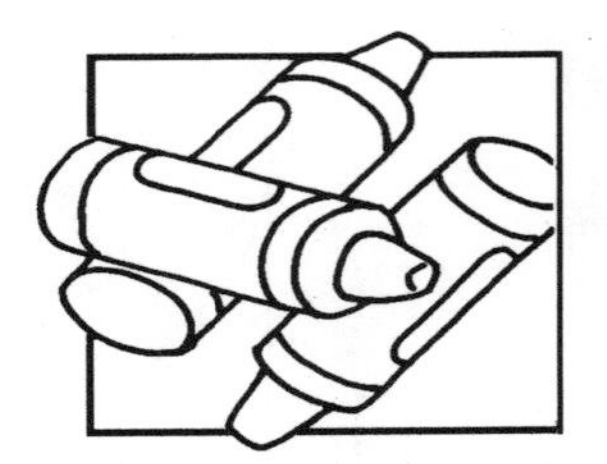

FOOD

Art Activities

SET THE TABLE!

This is a helpful skill for children to have at snack time and at home, too. It also builds basic shape recognition.

Materials:

Construction paper in assorted colors, place-setting patterns (p. 71), scissors, crayons, non-toxic markers

Directions:

1. Duplicate the place-setting patterns for children to follow when making their own utensils from construction paper.
2. Children can cut a circle for a plate, a large rectangle for a place mat, and a triangle for a folded napkin.
3. They can make their own silverware or use the silverware patterns as stencils to trace, color with crayons or non-toxic markers, and cut out.
4. Let children practice setting the table with their unique settings.
5. Use the completed projects in a home or restaurant dramatic play center.

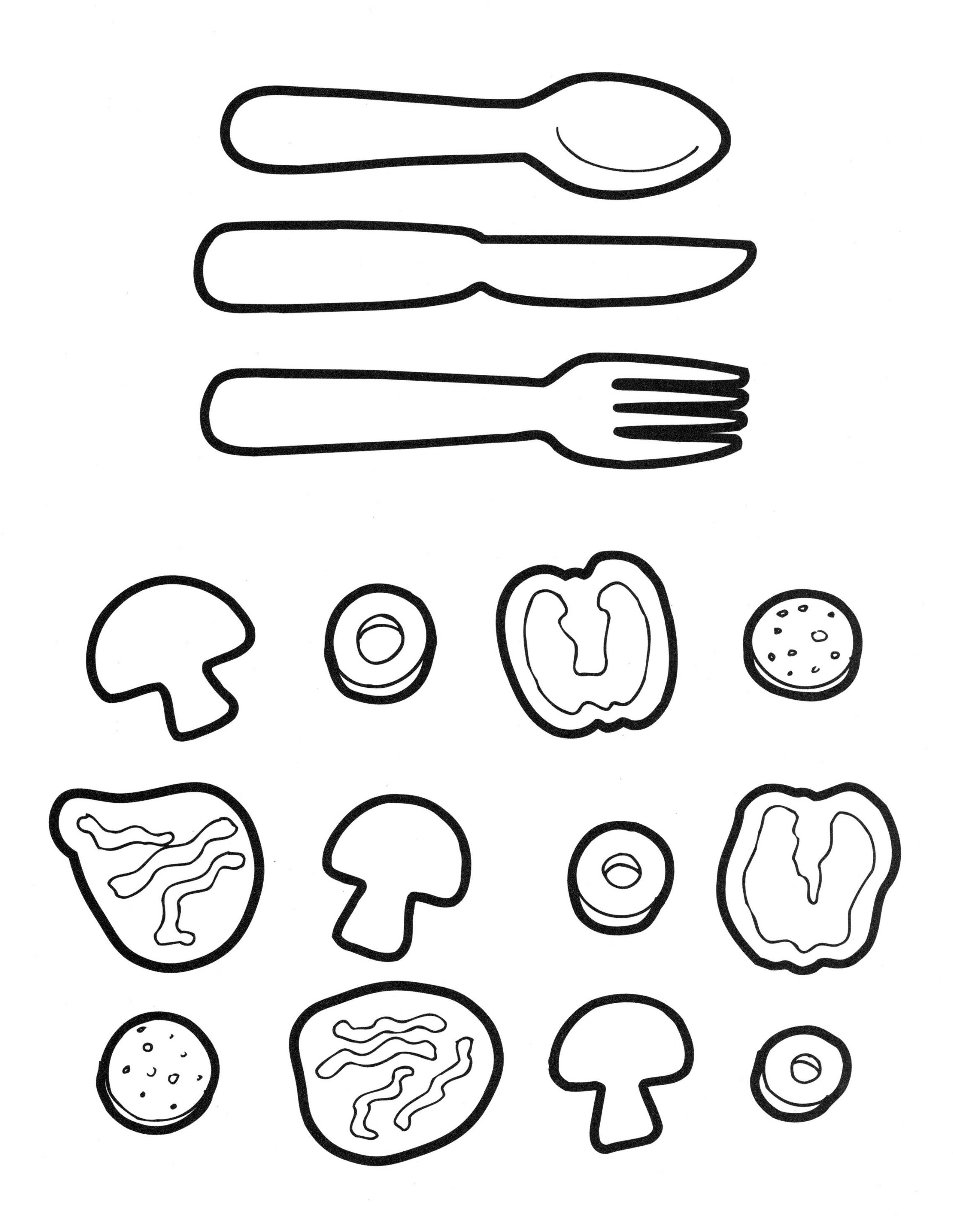

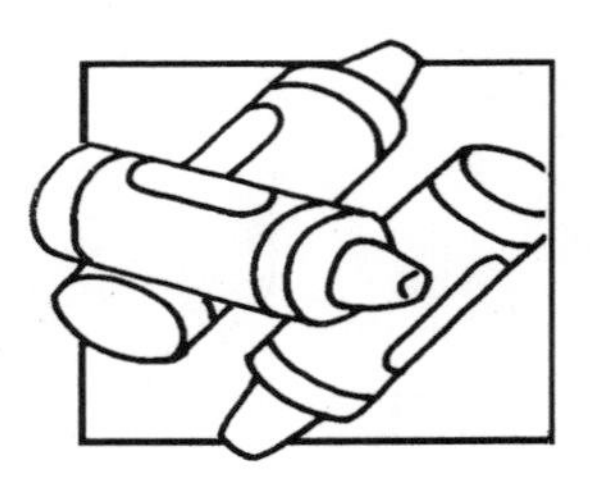

FOOD

Art Activities

SILLY SPAGHETTI

Children like the wiggly shape of spaghetti, and will have fun squeezing playdough into long, thin, spaghetti-like strings. Your children will feel just like Italian chefs!

Materials:
White and red playdough or baker's dough, garlic press

Directions:
1. Children can use the garlic press and white playdough to squeeze out "spaghetti," or roll strands of "spaghetti" with their hands (snake-style). They can also try making ravioli and tortellini, curly rotelli, and bow tie-shaped farfalle.
2. Red playdough balls work well for "meatballs."
3. Play meals may be served on paper place settings.

Option:
String can also be used for pasta. Use a variety of odds and ends for pasta toppings: button "meatballs," felt scrap "vegetables," and glitter "herbs."

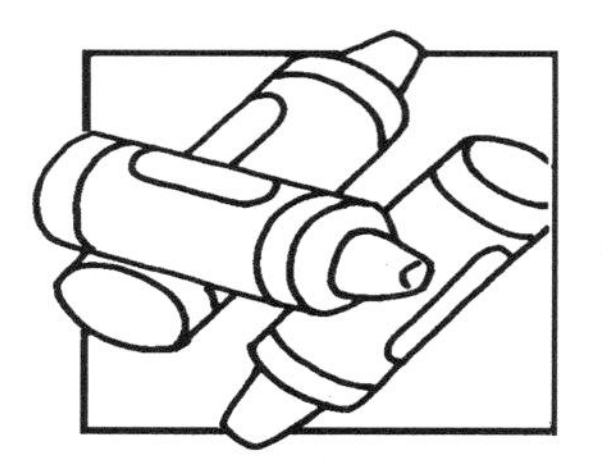

FOOD

Art Activities

PRETEND PIZZA

This activity simulates every child's dream—to build a pizza with all of their favorite toppings!

Materials:

Small paper plates, glue, red food coloring, small brushes, crayons, scissors, patterns for toppings (p. 71)

Directions:

1. Duplicate the toppings patterns. Children can either use the patterns as stencils to trace, or they can color the actual patterns with crayons and then cut them out.
2. Stir some food coloring into the glue until it's a dark red color. Have the children use brushes to spread this "sauce" on their paper plate "crusts."
3. They can then stick their toppings to their "pizzas," choosing only those they like to eat.
4. Post the completed pictures on a "Pretend Pizza" bulletin board.

Option:

Make a simple classroom graph of the toppings that the children like and don't like. Count up the results, and discuss class favorites. Ask the children to figure out the kinds of pizzas they would have to order for everyone to have what they want. For a special treat, put the children's plan into action and have a real pizza party!

FOOD

Art Activities

SUPER SANDWICHES

Here's an easy way for the children to be creative cooks—they can design their own recipes and instructions to build the perfect sandwich!

Materials:
Sandwich patterns (p. 75), scissors, crayons, non-toxic markers, glue, white paper

Directions:
1. Ask children to think about their favorite type of sandwich.
2. Pass out the sandwich patterns, and have children choose their bread and fillings.
3. The children can cut out the patterns and color them in.
4. Have parent volunteers or aides help children glue the sandwich icons on paper in the correct order, adding + and = symbols and proper words. Example: two pieces of bread + peanut butter + jelly + raisins = Peter's Perfect Peanut Butter Sandwich.
5. Bind the completed drawings in a classroom *Super Sandwich Recipes* book. Cut out the bread patterns for the front and back covers. (Parents might like duplicate copies of this project.)

Option:
As a special party snack or cooking activity, bring in real sandwich fixings so children can follow their own "rebus recipes."

Peanut Butter
Grape Jelly
Strawberry Jam
Tuna Fish
Raisins
Mustard
Cream Cheese
Mayonnaise

FOOD

Storytime

FEATURED PICTURE BOOK

The Very Hungry Caterpillar **by Eric Carle (Collins-World, 1969).**
The very hungry caterpillar eats his way through a variety of foods during the week before he spins his cocoon. On the first day, he eats one piece of fruit. On the second day, two, and so on. Children will enjoy seeing the holes made in the foods by the very hungry caterpillar as he munches on, and on, and on!

ART EXTENSION

Read this book with your class, showing them the holes in the food on each page. Have them count along with you as you follow the caterpillar on his filling journey. Ask your children what types of materials they think the author used to make the colorful pictures in this book.

Materials:
Tissue paper in assorted colors, slick "fingerpaint" paper, starch, brushes, scissors, hole punch

Directions:
1. Have your children cut different shapes from the tissue paper. They may want to make food, following the theme in the story, or choose any other theme they like.
2. Show children how to position the tissue paper onto the slick paper, and then brush the starch over both.
3. If children make their own "hungry caterpillar" pictures, let them use a hole punch to make caterpillar nibbles after their pictures have dried.

FOOD

Storytime

MORE PICTURE BOOKS

Blueberries for Sal by Robert McCloskey (Puffin, 1948).
In this Caldecott Honor Book, two mothers and two offspring go picking blueberries: little Sal and her mom and a bear and her cub. There is a funny mix-up on the hill amidst the berries, but everything works out in the end!

Bread and Jam for Frances by Russell Hoban, illustrated by Lillian Hoban (Harper, 1964).
Frances only wants to eat bread and jam—for breakfast, lunch, snack, and dinner! That is, until she feels left out when she sees what other members of her family are eating.

Cloudy with a Chance of Meatballs by Judi Barrett (Atheneum, 1978).
The townspeople of Chew and Swallow enjoy having their meals come down from the sky — orange juice rain, mashed potato snow, even hamburger storms. But when odd weather hits, it makes for some pretty ridiculous meals!

Growing Vegetable Soup by Lois Ehlert (Harcourt, 1987).
This colorful book takes children through the process of planting, cultivating, harvesting, and preparing vegetables for a delicious soup. Each page is filled with informative illustrations and labels.

If You Give a Mouse a Cookie by Laura Joffe Numeroff (HarperCollins, 1985).
A little boy befriends a mouse with a cookie offering. However, the mouse wants a glass of milk to go with the cookie, and the milk leads to a look in the mirror (for a milk mustache), which leads to a haircut, and so on in this silly tale! *If You Give a Moose a Muffin* is a sequel.

In the Night Kitchen by Maurice Sendak (Harper & Row, 1970).
"Did you ever hear of Mickey?" He dreams of the bakers in the night kitchen and embarks on an adventure that takes him "over the top of the milky way," and for a ride in a bread-dough plane.

Lunch by Denise Fleming (Henry Holt, 1992).
Mouse devours a huge and colorful lunch, including a white turnip, yellow corn, green peas, and tart blueberries. With each dish, Mouse becomes a bit more colorful himself—and by the end of the book, he has collected all of the colors in the rainbow!

Mrs. Pig's Bulk Buy by Mary Rayner (Atheneum, 1981).
Mrs. Pig's ten piglets insist on drenching every meal in catsup. Mrs. Pig retaliates by serving only catsup for breakfast, lunch, snack, and dinner. The piglets decide that they would prefer real food, and save catsup for a condiment. But their brief catsup diet has lasting consequences!

On Market Street by Arnold Lobel, illustrated by Anita Lobel (Greenwillow, 1981).
A child walks down Market Street to see what there is to buy. On each page, he finds something that begins with the next letter of the alphabet: apples, books, clocks, doughnuts, eggs. . . . Children will enjoy the whimsical pictures and learn by matching words with the ABCs.

The Tale of Peter Rabbit by Beatrix Potter (Warne, 1902).
Poor Peter Rabbit wanders into the neighbor's garden. He nibbles on a variety of vegetables before Mr. McGregor catches sight of him and begins the chase. Luckily, Peter escapes, but he learns his lesson!

FOOD

Flannel Board

I KNOW AN OLD LADY WHO SWALLOWED A PIE!

(to the tune of "I Know an Old Lady Who Swallowed a Fly")

I know an **old lady** who swallowed a **pie**,
She wanted to try to eat a whole pie.
Oh me, oh my!
I know an old lady who swallowed . . . **spaghetti**!
She'd had pie already, but not the spaghetti.
She swallowed spaghetti to go with the pie.
She wanted to try to eat a whole pie.
Oh me, oh my!
I know an old lady who swallowed some **rice**,
She thought rice was nice, and swallowed some rice.
She swallowed the rice to follow spaghetti,
She'd had pie already, but not the spaghetti.
She swallowed spaghetti to go with the pie,
She wanted to try to eat a whole pie.
Oh me, oh my!
I know an old lady who swallowed a **muffin**,
She stuffed it right in—that blueberry muffin.
She swallowed the muffin to go with the rice,
She thought rice was nice, and swallowed the rice.
She swallowed the rice to follow spaghetti,
She'd had pie already, but not the spaghetti.
She swallowed spaghetti to go with the pie,
She wanted to try to eat a whole pie.
Oh me, oh my!
I know an old lady who finished her dinner,
She felt like a **winner** for finishing dinner.
She'd eaten a muffin to go with her rice,
Rice is quite nice, she really liked rice!
She'd eaten her rice to go with spaghetti,
She'd had pie already, but not the spaghetti.
She'd eaten spaghetti to go with the pie,
She wanted to try to swallow a pie!
Oh me, oh my!

WINNER

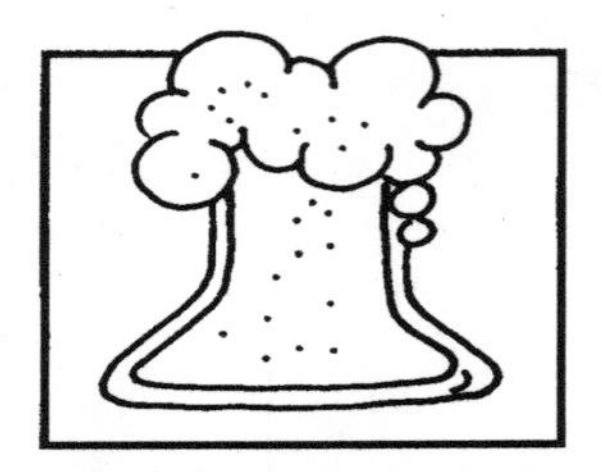

FOOD

Discovery

KITCHEN EQUIPMENT 1

Materials:
Garlic press, rolling pin, meat tenderizer, cookie cutters, plastic knives, clay or baker's dough

Directions:
1. Provide an assortment of kitchen utensils for children to experiment with.
2. Children can roll out clay with a rolling pin, cut it into shapes with cookie cutters, pound it with a meat tenderizer, squeeze it with a garlic press, etc.

KITCHEN EQUIPMENT 2

Materials:
Garlic press, rolling pin, meat tenderizer, whisk, cookie cutters, tempera paints in a variety of colors (in pie tins), easel paper

Directions:
1. Provide an assortment of kitchen utensils for children to paint with.
2. Show children how to use the different objects to make designs on their papers in a variety of colors.
3. Post finished artwork on a "We're Really Cooking" bulletin board.

FOOD

Discovery

WATER TABLE

Materials:
Measuring cups, measuring spoons, bowls or other containers, water

Directions:
1. Let children use the measuring cups and spoons to measure water at the water table.
2. Children can transfer water to other containers and then pour it back in the water table.

Option:
Provide containers of colored water (with food coloring) for children to measure and then mix together. Show them how to mix red and yellow for orange, red and blue for purple, and blue and yellow for green. Use the finished products from this project in the Class Project display as colorful, fanciful "drinks."

FIELD TRIPS

Visits to a farm, greenhouse, bakery, restaurant, or grocery store are appropriate for this unit. Take field trips with your class if you can, and encourage parents to draw special attention to food—growing, selling, preparing, serving, and eating it—as they do errands with their children or eat together.

FOOD

Class Project

FABULOUS FOOD

The results of the projects in this chapter are perfect for creating a table display. Let your students help you set the table. Use a large sheet of butcher paper for the tablecloth. Children can decorate this by hand printing with finger paints—but make sure the "cloth" is completely dry before you spread it on the table.

Have children use their paper table settings to set each place. Help them write their names on small cards for place cards. They can individualize the cards with drawings, too.

Let children decide which meal they wish to serve (pizza, pasta, or another paper favorite), and have them place the meals at their settings.

Create a decorative centerpiece together. Each child can make a flower for a fancy bouquet. To make the flowers, cut apart egg cartons and give each child one section. Let children decorate their section with tempera paints, glue, sequins, and glitter. Help children fasten a pipe cleaner stem to the bottom of the egg carton by taping or poking a hole through the bottom and fastening the end over. Collect the flowers, turn them upright, and place them in a vase at the center of the table.

Add colored water (see Discovery) in plastic glasses.

While children are creating this display, play "Coconut" by Harry Nilson.

Note:

If the table you're using isn't large enough to accommodate one place per child, have two to three children work together on a place setting (e.g., one child can make the place mat, another the main course, and a third the beverage).

FOOD

Dramatic Play

GROCERY STORE CENTER

Every child has been to the grocery store—what fun to set one up right in the classroom!

Materials:

Canvas shopping bags or mesh bags, paper bags, play cash registers, shopping carts or wagons, empty health and beauty aid boxes, cans, milk and egg cartons, and other grocery items

Option:

Provide children with play money. You can use bills cut from construction paper, plastic poker chips, or let children design and make their own money. For a math project, label the grocery items with prices, and then assign values to the money you make. Keep it simple—you might have all the items worth whole dollar amounts from 1 to 10, and provide different-colored bills worth 1, 5, and 10 dollars.

BAKERY

Mmm! Muffins, breads, cookies. . . . Children can pretend to make and share pastries and other baked goods.

Materials:

White playdough or baker's dough, rolling pins, cookie sheets, muffin tins, bread pans, spatulas, mixing bowls, baker's hats, pink bakery boxes, cookie cutters, hot pads, oven mitts, aprons

RESTAURANT/BISTRO

Young waiters and waitresses will enjoy serving meals to their friends at the "Classroom Cafe."

Materials:

Tablecloths, plastic silverware, paper plates and cups, order pads, water pitchers, carrying trays, plastic foods, "menus" covered in Contact paper, play pizza and spaghetti (see Art)

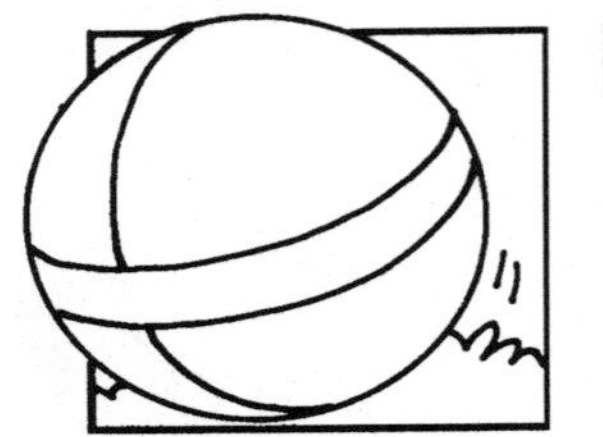

FOOD

Games

FOOD CONCENTRATION

Children will enjoy playing this classic game while building visual memory skills and their concentration span.

Materials:
Food patterns (p. 87), thick paper or tagboard, crayons, scissors

Directions:
1. Make two copies of each food pattern on thick paper or tagboard.
2. Let children decorate the foods with crayons.
3. Cut the patterns apart and place them face down on a flat surface.
4. Have children practice their memory skills by turning over the patterns two at a time, trying to match two pieces of food.

WHO STOLE THE COOKIE FROM THE COOKIE JAR?

This lively circle game reinforces rhythmic sense and name memorization.

Have your children gather in a circle on the floor, and teach them this rhyme. The first person to be named chooses the next person. You can play this in a round, one child naming the person at his or her side, and so on. Or you can play the game randomly, with each child naming whomever he or she wishes. Have children alternate slapping their hands on their thighs and then clapping them together as they say the chant.

Who stole the cookie from the cookie jar?
_____ stole the cookie from the cookie jar.
Who me?
Yes, you!
Couldn't be.
Then who?
______ stole the cookie from the cookie jar!
Who me . . .

MILK

FOOD

Mother Goose

Do You Know the Muffin Man?
Do you know the muffin man,
The muffin man,
The muffin man.
Oh, do you know the muffin man
Who lives on Drury Lane?

Yes, I know the muffin man,
The muffin man,
The muffin man.
Yes, I know the muffin man
Who lives on Drury Lane.

Pat-a-Cake, Pat-a-Cake
Pat-a-cake, pat-a-cake,
Baker's man,
Bake me a cake,
As fast as you can.
Roll it and knead it,
And mark it with a "B,"
And put it in the oven for baby and me.

Little Lad, Little Lad
Little lad, little lad, where was thou born?
Far off in Lancashire, under a thorn,
Where they sip buttermilk from a ram's horn,
And a pumpkin scooped, with a yellow rim,
Is the bonny bowl they breakfast in.

Little King Pippin
Little King Pippin, he built a fine hall,
Pie-crust and pastry-crust that was the wall;
The windows were made of black pudding and white,
And slated with pancakes, you never saw the like.

Jack Sprat
Jack Sprat could eat no fat,
His wife could eat no lean,
And so betwixt them both, you see,
They licked the platter clean!

FOOD

Mother Goose

Peter, Peter, Pumpkin Eater
Peter, Peter, pumpkin eater
Had a wife, but couldn't keep her;
He put her in a pumpkin shell
And there he kept her very well.

Peter, Peter, pumpkin eater,
Had another, and didn't love her;
Peter learned to read and spell,
And then he loved her very well.

Peter Piper
Peter Piper picked a peck of pickled
peppers;
A peck of pickled peppers Peter Piper
picked;
If Peter Piper picked a peck of pickled
peppers,
Where's the peck of pickled peppers
Peter Piper Picked?

Polly Put the Kettle On
Polly put the kettle on,
Polly put the kettle on,
Polly put the kettle on,
We'll all have tea.

Sukey take it off again,
Sukey take it off again,
Sukey take it off again,
They've all gone away.

An Apple Pie
An apple pie, when it looks nice,
Would make one long to have a slice;
But if the taste should prove so, too,
I fear one slice would scarcely do.
So to prevent my asking twice,
Pray, Mama, cut a good large slice.

Little Tommy Tucker
Little Tommy Tucker
Sang for his supper.
What shall he eat?
White bread and butter.
How shall he cut it without any knife?
How shall he marry without any wife?

Sippity Sup
Sippity sup, sippity sup,
Bread and milk from a china cup,
Bread and milk from a bright silver
spoon,
Made of a piece of the bright silver
moon!
Sippity sup, sippity sup,
Sippity, sippity sup!

Peas Porridge Hot
Peas porridge hot,
Peas porridge cold,
Peas porridge in the pot
Nine days old.

Some like it hot,
Some like it cold,
Some like it in the pot
Nine days old.

FOOD

Snacks

Almost any food will work for this theme. However, we have linked these snacks with books found in the storytime section. Read the books with your children and then serve these delicious snacks. Or read the books at snack time!

FRANCES' BREAD AND JAM

Frances loves bread and jam, for breakfast, lunch, and dinner. Your students are sure to enjoy this simple treat in Frances' honor. Read *Bread and Jam for Frances* by Russell Hoban (Harper, 1964) as the children spread jam on their own bread.

Ingredients:
Bread, jam (raspberry, strawberry, blueberry, gooseberry, grape, etc.), milk

Directions:
1. Provide an assortment of jams for children to spread on slices of bread.
2. Let children enjoy their snack with milk. Ask them if they would get tired of eating only bread and jam like Frances did.

PETER RABBIT'S SALAD

When Peter sneaks into Mr. McGregor's garden, he snacks on a variety of fresh vegetables. Read *The Tale of Peter Rabbit* by Beatrix Potter (Warne, 1902) while the children eat their salads.

Ingredients:
Lettuces, carrots, string beans, radishes, parsley

Directions:
1. Cut up the ingredients and mix them together in a big bowl.
2. Let children pretend to be little rabbits in Mr. McGregor's garden and nibble on this yummy vegetable salad.

FOOD

Snacks

STREGA NONA'S MAGIC SPAGHETTI

When Big Anthony makes too much spaghetti with the magic pot, he has to uncover the village . . . by eating all the extra pasta! Read *Strega Nona: An Old Tale* by Tomie de Paola (Prentice-Hall, 1975) before making this snack.

Ingredients:
Spaghetti, tomato sauce, Parmesan cheese, butter

Directions:
1. Prepare spaghetti according to directions on the package.
2. Serve spaghetti with sauce and cheese or pats of butter.
3. Children can imagine they are eating spaghetti from Strega Nona's magic pot—but make sure no one eats as much as Big Anthony!

Option:
If you make a sauce with meatballs, you can link this snack to *Cloudy with a Chance of Meatballs*.

YUMMERS!

James Marshall's *Yummers!* (Houghton, 1973) is filled with a variety of snack ideas, including:

- tuna fish sandwiches
- corn on the cob
- scones with butter and jam
- Eskimo pies
- pizza
- banana splits

Other literature links to snacks:
Green Eggs and Ham by Dr. Seuss (Random House, 1960). To make a snack based on this story, use green food coloring to dye eggs before cooking.
Growing Vegetable Soup by Lois Ehlert (Harcourt, 1987) describes the growth and preparation of fresh garden vegetables.

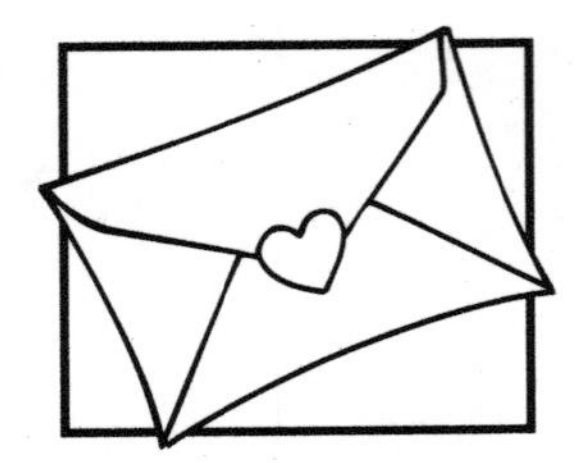

FOOD

Letter Home

Alas! Alas! for Miss Mackay!
Her knives and forks have run away;
And when the cups and spoons are going,
She's sure there is no way of knowing.
—Mother Goose

Food, glorious food is our focus this month: food in storybooks (like *Bread and Jam for Frances*), make-believe food ("Silly Spaghetti"), food for thought (in our dramatic play center), and exploring food!

We'd like to invite any chefs to come cook with us. On our menu is "Peter Rabbit's Salad" (made from all the good vegetables in Mr. McGregor's garden). Do you have a favorite dish you'd like to share with us?

We will be creating a grocery store in our dramatic play center. We are looking for many "food" items to stock our shelves. Please check and see if you have any of the following:

- empty cereal boxes (especially the small ones from multi-packs)
- plastic tubs with lids (margarine, cream cheese, etc.)
- egg cartons
- small milk cartons
- empty health/beauty product boxes (soap, toothpaste, bandages)

Thank you for your help!

December: Weather

Each section in this chapter has been split into four parts: Autumn, Winter, Spring, and Summer. The activities in these parts deal with the type of weather that is appropriate to that particular time of the year. However, most of these projects may be done in any month. Children will explore the colors associated with each season—golden browns in fall, sparkly winter white, flowery spring pastels, and bold summer brights. Introduce this unit by reading *I Am A Bunny* (always a favorite), by Ole Risom, illustrated by Richard Scarry (Golden Press, 1963), and making Holiday Postcards (p. 97) or Falling Leaves (p. 95).

WEATHER

Art Activities

WIND PAINTINGS

This activity will help children imagine that they are outside on a windy day. Have them imagine the wind blowing through their hair and making the falling leaves swirl about!

Materials:
Liquid watercolors or food coloring in autumn hues (orange, yellow, red, brown), water, plastic eyedroppers or paintbrushes, glossy paper, straws cut in half or hollow coffee stir-sticks, small dishes or ice cube trays

Directions:
1. Dilute watercolors or food coloring slightly with water and place an assortment of colors in small dishes or ice cube trays. (Ice cube trays work well to give a selection of colors to each child.)
2. Give each child a piece of paper, a plastic eyedropper, a clean straw half or stir-stick, and an assortment of autumn-colored watercolors.
3. Have children drop or brush dabs of the watercolors onto their paper with the eyedroppers or brushes.
4. The children can use their straw sections or stir-sticks to blow their colors into beautiful patterns. They can take a big breath and then pretend to be the wind!

Option:
Post the completed paintings on a classroom "Autumn Weather" bulletin board. You can further decorate the board with real leaves collected outdoors, or with cut-out paper leaves (pattern on p. 96).

WEATHER

Art Activities

FALLING LEAVES

These frames are a beautiful way to observe and preserve autumn leaves.

Materials:

Real leaves or leaf patterns (p. 96) and oak tag, craft knife, scissors, construction paper in a variety of autumn colors, white construction paper, clear Contact paper, glue or tape, markers

Directions:

1. If you are using the patterns instead of real leaves, photocopy them onto heavy oak tag and cut out to make enough stencils to go around.
2. Let the children use the stencils to trace leaves onto different colors of construction paper and cut out. Use these paper leaves, real leaves, or both.
3. Make a frame for each child from white construction paper. Use rectangles of paper and cut out a smaller rectangle from the center, leaving a border (approx. 2") all the way around.
4. Let the children decorate both sides of their frames with markers.
5. Place a piece of Contact paper along the back of each frame so that the open part is sticky. (Cut Contact paper ahead of time to the same size as the frames—two pieces of Contact paper per frame.)
6. Show the children how to place their leaves on the sticky Contact paper.
7. Place a second piece of Contact paper, sticky side down, on top of the open frame to seal the leaves in place.
8. Post the frames on a window so that the sun can shine through them.

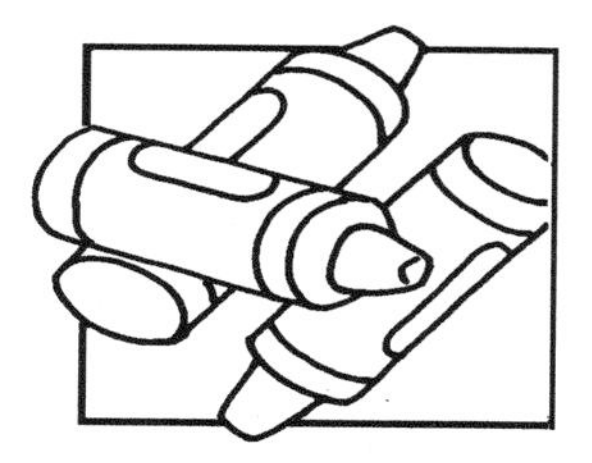

WEATHER

Art Activities

HOLIDAY POSTCARDS

Many people send cards to family and friends at this time of year. Here's a way for your students to make and "send" their own holiday greetings!

Materials:

Postcard-sized pieces of oak tag, glitter, glue, doilies, wrapping paper and ribbon scraps, crayons

Directions:

1. Give each child a "postcard" to decorate using a variety of art media. Children may want to make glitter snowmen by making circles of glue (one on top of the other) and then sprinkling on glitter to cover. Or they might cover the postcard with wrapping paper and ribbon scraps to look like a wrapped present. Cut-up doilies make good snowflakes, as does glitter sprinkled over a hand-drawn holiday scene.
2. When the postcards are dry, help children write a holiday message to a friend or loved one.

Option:

If the children write postcards to each other, set up a post office center and have the children use rubber stamps to hand cancel their postcards, then deliver them to each other!

WEATHER

Art Activities

SUNNY DAY MASKS

Let the children wear their sunny day masks on a cloudy, rainy, or snowy day to bring a bit of summer into the classroom! You might want to teach the children the song "You Are My Sunshine" to sing while making these masks.

Materials:
Large paper plates with the central circle cut out (one per child), construction paper cut in triangles (orange, yellow, and red), glue, hole punch, yarn, mirror

Directions:
1. Give each child a paper plate with the center cut out and an assortment of colored triangles to glue to the plate rim for sun rays.
2. Help children punch two holes in the plate (one on each side of where the face will be).
3. Tie a separate length of yarn through each hole. (The mask will be worn by tying the two pieces of yarn together in a bow at the back of the child's head.)
4. Help the children put on their masks, and then have them look in a mirror at their "shining" faces.

SUN CATCHERS

"Sunny Day Masks" can easily be made into "sun catchers."

Materials:
Sunny Day Masks, colored cellophane, tape or glue, hole punch, yarn

Directions:
1. Have the children glue or tape colored cellophane across the center hole in the plates.
2. Hang plates by punching a hole in the top and threading with yarn.

WEATHER

Storytime

FEATURED PICTURE BOOK

***The Rain Door* by Russell Hoban (Thomas Y. Crowell, 1986).**
On a hot summer Thursday, Harry looks out the window to see the rag-and-bone man going by with his horse and cart. The rag-and-bone man yells out nonsense sentences, such as, "Rainy numbers up" and "Any thunder up." Harry, who is intrigued by these weird statements, follows the rag-and-bone man through the magical "Rain Door" and discovers where thunder and lightning come from!

ART EXTENSION

Read this book with your children, showing them the colorful pictures by Quentin Blake. Ask the children to point out the different types of art media used by Blake (watercolors and markers), and see if they have ideas about how to create the images of the "Rain Door."

Materials:
Watercolors, water, keyhole patterns (p. 100), glue, paintbrushes, white paper

Directions:
1. Have children make designs on their papers, painting only with water.
2. Show the children how to add a drop of watercolor to the water designs to achieve the smudgy, spread-out "Blake" effect. This project works like invisible ink, the watercolor illuminating the "secret" water design.
3. If children would like, they can draw their own rain doors, or even their own magical rainy shapes (spirals, curlicues, circles, etc.). Otherwise, let children simply experiment.
4. Children who draw "rain doors" might like to glue on keyhole patterns.

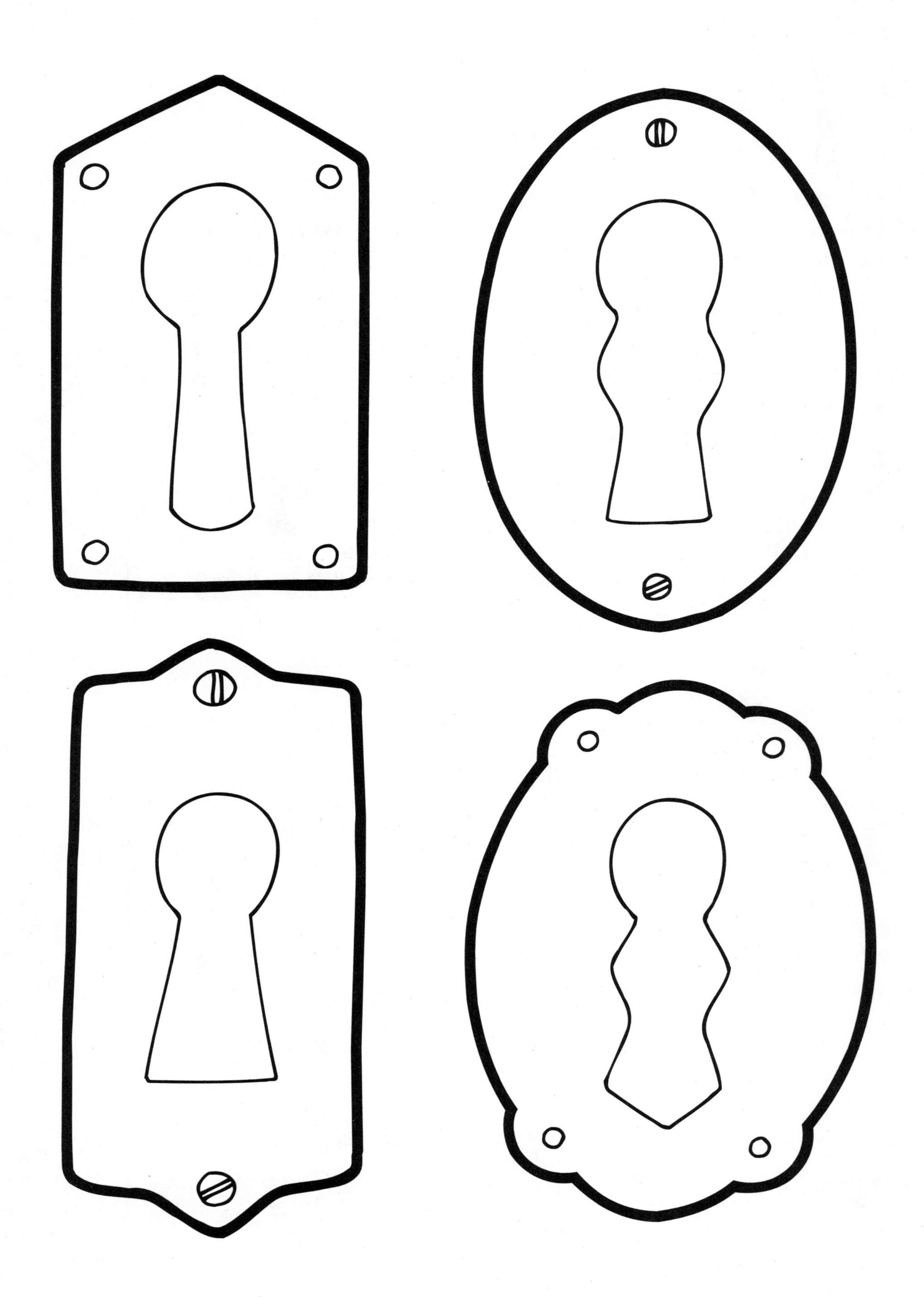

WEATHER

Storytime

MORE PICTURE BOOKS

Can't Sit Still by Karen E. Lotz, illustrated by Colleen Browning (Dutton, 1993).
A young girl experiences all four seasons in the city. She plays in the autumn leaves, makes animal tracks in the snow, climbs up to the roof in the springtime rain, and plays hopscotch on pavement warmed by the summer sun.

Frog and Toad All Year by Arnold Lobel (Harper, 1976).
Frog and Toad are good friends who spend time together all year long. This "I Can Read Book" has five short chapters, with stories appropriate for different kinds of weather: snow, rain, sun, wind, and a bonus holiday tale.

The Happy Day by Ruth Krauss, illustrated by Marc Simont (HarperTrophy, 1949).
Field mice, bears, snails, squirrels, and groundhogs sleep through the winter. The smell of the first spring flower wakes them up, and they dance and laugh with joy!

The House of Four Seasons by Roger Duvoisin (Lothrop, 1956).
Father, Mother, Billy, and Suzy drive out to the country to buy a house. They choose a fixer-upper, but before they can fix it they must pick a color to paint it. Along the way, the children learn about both colors and seasons.

I Am a Bunny by Ole Risom, illustrated by Richard Scarry (Golden Press, 1963).
Nicholas the bunny lives in a hollow tree and watches the weather change. In each season he has different favorite pastimes. In the spring he picks flowers. In the summer he watches the birds. The children may want to try out some of Nicholas's favorite activities.

The Snowy Day by Ezra Jack Keats (Puffin, 1962).
Peter wakes up to discover that it snowed during the night. He puts on his snowsuit and goes outside to explore. This Caldecott Award Book has been a favorite for years.

Spring Is Here by Taro Gomi (Chronicle Books, 1989).
This Graphic Prize winner is sure to be a hit with young children! The delightful color pages and simple text describe the changing seasons.

The Story of a Boy Named Will, Who Went Sledding Down the Hill by Daniil Kharms, translated by Jamey Gambrell, illustrated by Vladimir Radunsky (North-South, 1993).
"Willie went for a sled ride / And slid swiftly down the hillside. / Down the hill he slid his sled, / And hit a hunter as he sped." On the way to the bottom of the hill, Will also picks up a dog, a fox, a hare, and more!

The Stranger by Chris Van Allsburg (Houghton Mifflin, 1986).
In early fall, a stranger with amnesia comes into the lives of Farmer Baily and his wife. While he stays with them, the weather stays the same. The leaves on the trees at the Baily's farm don't change color and the pumpkins grow larger and larger. Then one day, the stranger remembers who he is—and his importance to nature and the world around him.

Summer Is . . . by Charlotte Zolotow, illustrated by Janet Archer (Abelard-Schuman, 1967).
"Summer is porches and cold lemonade." When summer's over, fall brings "squirrels on the rooftop." Winter means "pink skies early in the evening." And "spring is cats prowling and the green of new grass."

WEATHER

Flannel Board

HOPPER AND ANT

On a hot summer day when the weather was lazy
A **grasshopper** lay out on top of a **daisy**,
Drinking sweet nectar from a rose petal cup.
He slurped and he slurped as he drank it all up.
Then he heard a "Hey you, Mr. Hopper, hello!"
And he saw a small **ant** on the dirt down below.
"You should work hard today," the ant yelled from the ground—
Once summer has gone, the food won't be around!"
The grasshopper just shook his big, lazy head,
"I'd rather stay here in this warm flower bed.
I'll find food when I'm hungry—don't worry about me.
Now, go on your way, Ant, you just let me be."
So the ant trudged along, carrying **dandelion seeds**,
On her second and third trips she picked up two weeds.
She stored them away—because winter was coming
And as the ant worked she was singing and humming.
She knew she'd have plenty of good food to last
Once summer had become a thing of the past.
Then Ant thought of her friend and she stocked a bit more,
Some walnuts, and **acorns**, and small **apple cores**.
And when winter had come with fluffy, white snow,
The grasshopper called to the ant, "Oh, hello!
Mrs. Ant, I was hoping to find you, you see—
There is no more food—And I'm getting hungry.
Do you have any extra? Do you think you could spare . . ."
The ant said, "Sure, Mr. Hopper, I'll share.
But remember come summer when good times are here—
I'll expect you to help me and plan for next year!"
And off the two went, into Mrs. Ant's place
Where they snacked on a dandelion seed and a trace
Of the sweetest dried apple you ever could find,
Then they had their dessert—some nice cantaloupe rind,
And they crawled into bed, two quite satisfied friends,
And this is where Hopper and Ant's story ends.

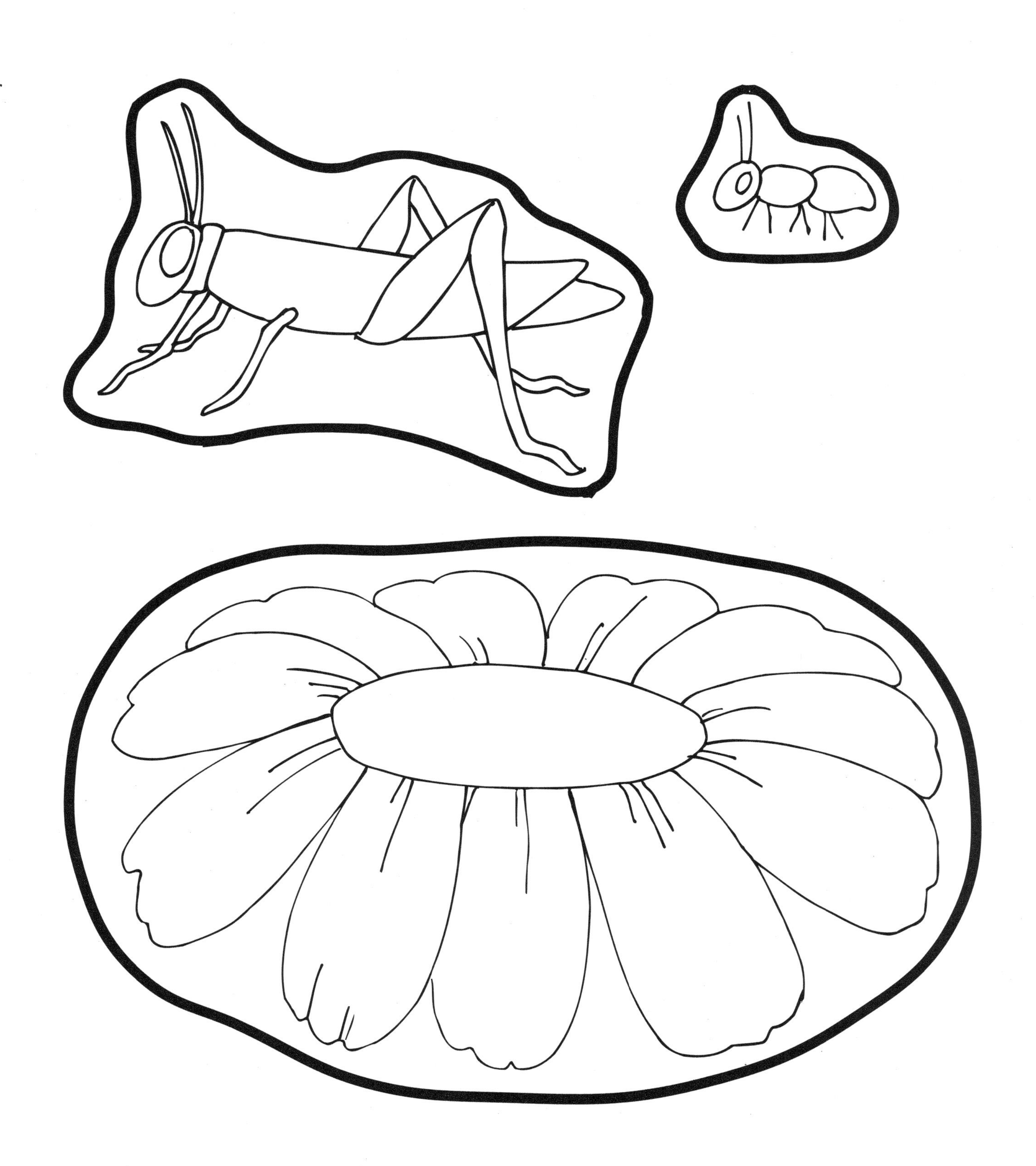

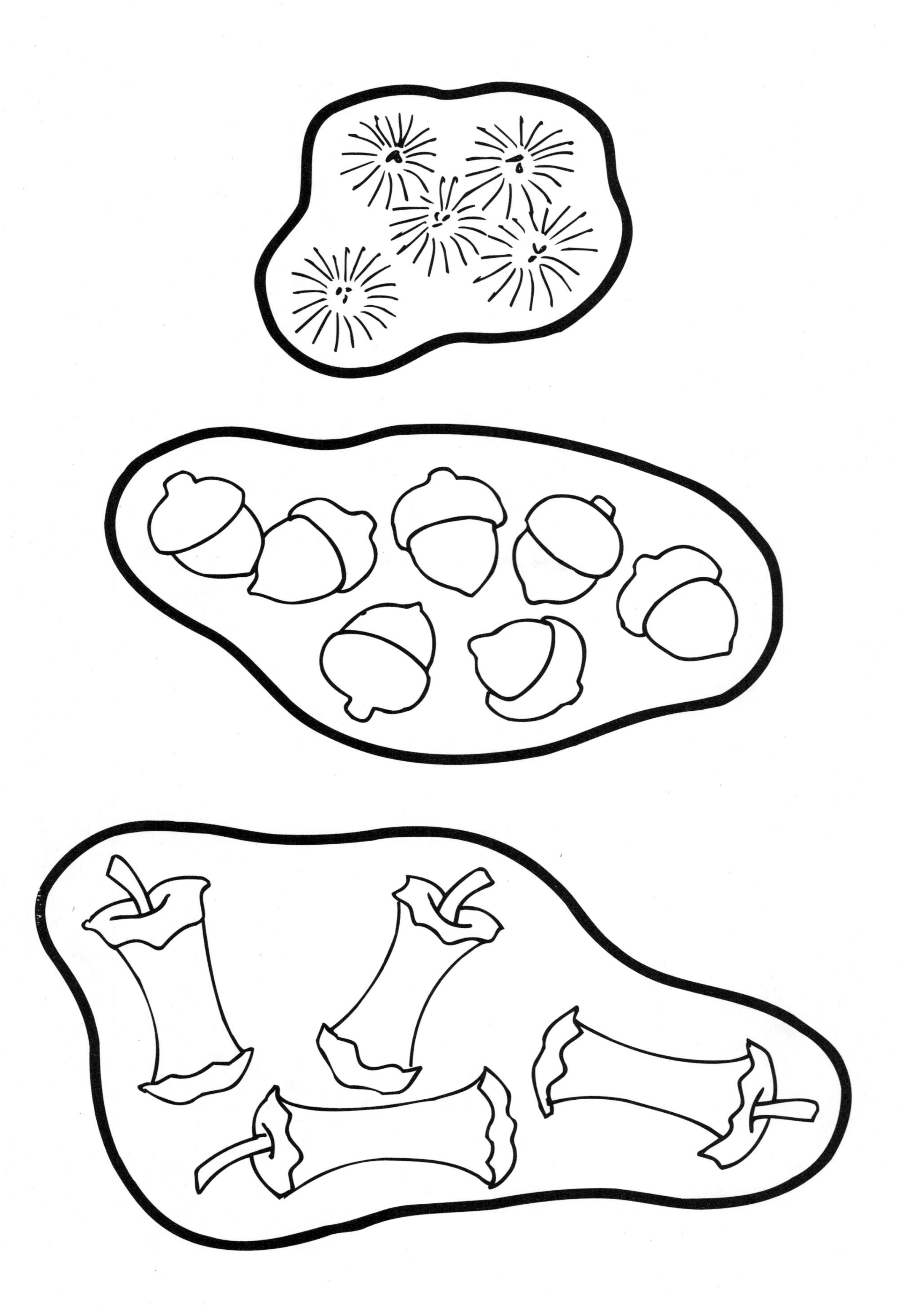

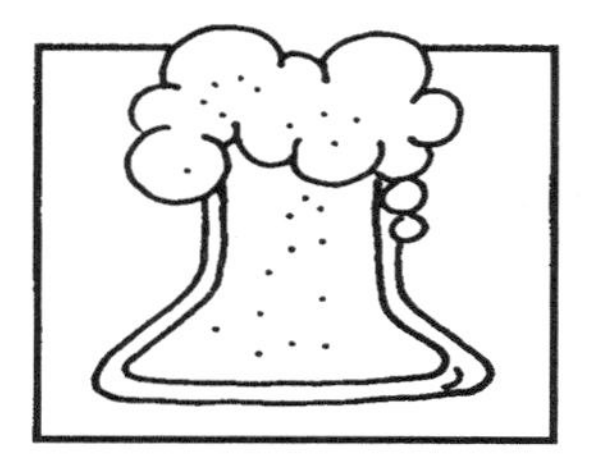

WEATHER

Discovery

AUTUMN OBSERVATION

Take your children outside to observe the leaves changing color. If possible, do this two or three times during the fall to see the transformation of the trees. If you do not live in an area where trees change color, show children pictures in a book like *How LEAVES Change* by Sylvia A. Johnson (Lerner Publications, 1986).

COLOR SORTING

1. Have children help you collect a big basket of leaves. If you do not live in an area where leaves change colors—or if you are doing this activity at a time of the year other than autumn—duplicate the leaf pattern (p. 96) onto different colors of construction paper, cut out, and proceed with the activity.
2. Spread a blanket on the floor or outside and pour out the leaves.
3. Let children sort the leaves into piles by color: red, orange, yellow, brown, or still green.
4. Once all of the leaves are sorted, choose the prettiest ones to bring inside to decorate an autumn bulletin board.

LEAF RUBBINGS

1. Have your students pick three or four leaves from your collection.
2. Show children how to place a piece of paper over the leaves and then rub (using the flat side of an unwrapped crayon or charcoal pencil) to make the leaves "magically" appear on their papers.
3. Children may want to use different-colored crayons to make their pictures more dramatic.

Option:

For an even more colorful effect, have children rub the paper-covered leaves with crayon, then paint over them with watercolors for "crayon resist."

WEATHER

Discovery

WINTER WONDERLAND

Take a field trip to a greenhouse where children can see how plants and flowers grow even when it's very cold outside.

WINTER WATER TABLES

Freeze colored ice cubes (made with food coloring) and place them in warm water at the water table. Have children observe the ice as it melts. If you make primary-colored ice cubes, children can choose which colors to melt together and then see what new colors result from their choices.

MAKING SNOWFLAKES

Materials:
Doilies, scissors, black construction paper, glue

Directions:
1. Explain to your students that no two snowflakes are ever alike.
2. Have children create their own unique snowflakes by folding doilies in half, and then in quarters.
3. Show children how to cut out slits (along the folded sides).
4. When children open their doilies, they will each have an original snowflake!
5. Snowflakes may be glued to black construction paper backgrounds and then posted on a "Snow Two Are Alike" bulletin board. (Children can also decorate the black construction paper background with glitter, sequins, or metallic crayons.)

WEATHER
Discovery

SPRING FLOWERS
Spring is the perfect time to prove the old rhyme "April showers bring May flowers." Take your children on a field trip to a garden in bloom (a botanical garden, or the garden of one of your children). Invite a gardener in to discuss what plants need to grow (sun, rain, soil, air, and lots of attention).

SUMMER SHADES
Take your students outside and have them observe their shadows. Ask them to jump and see if their shadows jump with them. Have them run and try to leave their shadows behind. Inside, try hanging a white sheet in your classroom with a bright light or empty slide projector behind it. If children stand (dance, move, jump) in front of the light, their shadows will be cast onto the sheet.

ME AND MY SHADOW TRACING

Materials:
Butcher paper, scissors, crayons

Directions:
1. Divide children into pairs.
2. Outdoors, partners take turns standing in front of a piece of butcher paper so that their shadow falls onto the paper while the other child traces around the shadow. Inside, tape butcher paper to a wall and shine a light on the paper to create the shadows.
3. When both partners have had their shadows traced, they can cut out their shadows to be posted around the classroom.

Option:
Shadows may be decorated to look like the children, or like "snow people," and hung up in the classroom.

WEATHER

Class Project

WEATHER WINDOW

Your classroom windows make the perfect backdrop for a four seasons weather display. Let children help you tape their falling leaf displays, snowflake hang-ups, and sun catchers near the windows (so that light can shine through). You can further decorate the windows by hanging crystal prisms from fishing line to cast rainbows around the room.

Children can make "stained glass" to add to the display by poking holes in sheets of black construction paper with a hole punch and then gluing different colored bits of tissue paper behind the holes. When the sun shines through these pictures, the colors are a marvel to look at!

Your little weather people can also make mobiles from the leaf patterns (p. 96). Have them cut out and color the leaves first. Then display them by dangling them on string from hangers.

Scented paper sachets filled with dried flowers, leaves, and spices will sweeten your classroom. Make the sachets from colorful origami paper, taped or stapled along three sides. Fill them with your choice of dried flower petals (roses, lilac, lavender), leaves (bay leaves, eucalyptus, pine), and spices (cloves, nutmeg, ginger). Then seal the fourth side with tape or staples. Post by punching a hole, threading with string, and hanging from the window ledge. The sachets can also be made in flower or heart shapes by cutting the paper into the desired shapes.

Play "weather" music as your children work on this display: "Raindrops Keep Falling on My Head," "You Are the Sunshine of My Life" by Stevie Wonder, "Summertime" by Ella Fitzgerald, "Summer Wind" by Frank Sinatra, or "Winter Wonderland" by Bing Crosby.

Option:

On cloudy days, use a flashlight or an overhead projector to shine light through your various sun catchers.

WEATHER

Games and Dramatic Play

SUMMER/WINTER

This is a twist on the classic "Hotter / Colder" hide-and-seek game.

Directions:

1. Hide something in your classroom (a rubber ball, a stuffed toy).
2. Have the children try to find the item by the clues you give. When they are far away from it, say, "Fall, it's getting colder." If they continue to look in the wrong direction, say, "Winter, it's snowing!" As they get closer, say, "Spring, it's getting warmer." And as they reach the item, say, "Summer!"
3. Once children understand the rules, they can play this game themselves.

Option:

Begin by just saying "hotter" or "colder" and then add seasonal clues.

WEATHER CENTER

Provide the following dress-up items for children to use to play act different seasonal scenes. Read books from the storytime list and have children dress in clothing appropriate to the setting in the book.

Fall Hats: football helmets, rain hats
Winter Hats: ski masks, wool caps (optional: gloves and scarves)
Spring Hats: Easter bonnets, baseball caps, sombreros
Summer Hats: straw hats, sun visors, bathing caps

Fall Shoes: galoshes, boots, soccer cleats
Winter Shoes: snowshoes, ski boots, fuzzy slippers
Spring Shoes: sneakers, ballet shoes, party shoes
Summer Shoes: sandals, flip-flops, fins (for swimming)

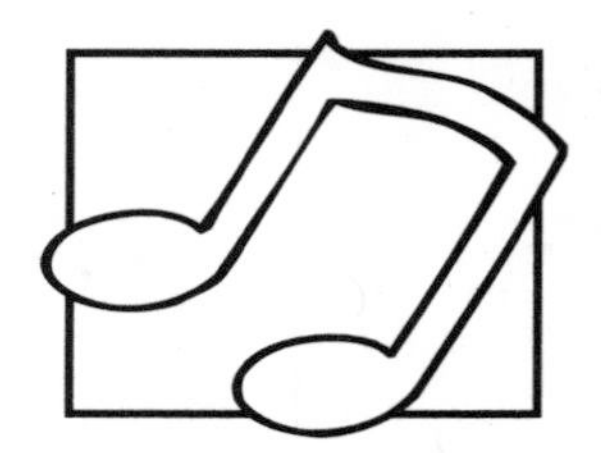

WEATHER

Songs

The Season Song
(to the tune of "The Farmer in the Dell")

In autumn it gets cool,
In autumn it gets cool,
In autumn leaves fall from the trees
And children go to school.

But winter's colder still.
Yes, winter's colder still.
In wintertime we bundle up
So we won't catch a chill.

Then springtime brings the rain,
Oh, springtime brings the rain.
The flowers all are happy
And they bloom along the lane.

The summer's hot and bright.
Yes, summer's hot and bright.
The sky is filled with kites and birds,
And summer's golden light.

Do You Wear a Coat?
(to the tune of "Do Your Ears Hang Low?")

Do you wear a coat
And a scarf around your throat—
When the snow is on the ground,
Or the wind blows you around?
When your teeth begin to chatter,
Do six sweaters help the matter,
Do you wear a coat?

When the Rain Is Falling Down
(to the tune of "London Bridge")

When the rain is falling down,
Falling down,
Falling down,
When the rain is falling down,
I wear rain clothes.

I put on my coat and hat,
Coat and hat,
Coat and hat.
I put on my coat and hat,
And galoshes!

Additional favorites:
"It's Raining, It's Pouring"
"Rain, Rain Go Away"
"You Are My Sunshine"
"Jingle Bells"
"Winter Wonderland"
"The Eensy, Weensy Spider"
"Singing in the Rain"
"Mr. Sun"
"If I Had a Red Umbrella"

WEATHER

Mother Goose

One Misty, Moisty Morning

One misty, moisty morning,
When cloudy was the weather,
I chanced to meet an old man
Clothed all in leather.
He began to compliment,
And I began to grin.
How do you do?
And how do you do?
And how do you do again?

Doctor Foster Went to Gloucester

Doctor Foster went to Gloucester
In a shower of rain;
He stepped in a puddle,
Right up to his middle,
And never went there again.

Blow, Wind, Blow!

Blow, wind, blow! And go, mill, go!
That the miller may grind his corn;
That the baker may take it,
And into rolls make it,
And send us some hot in the morn.

Cuckoo

Cuckoo, cherry tree,
Catch a bird, and give it to me;
Let the tree be high or low,
Let it hail, rain, or snow.

WEATHER

Snacks

AUTUMN APPLE CIDER

On a chilly day, have children assist you in making this warming drink.

Ingredients:
Peeled apple quarters (soak in water with a few drops of lemon juice), juicer, cinnamon sticks

Directions:
1. Let children help drop the pre-peeled, pre-cut apples into the juicer and turn the apples into juice. (Follow the directions on your juicer.)
2. When everyone has had a turn helping (and when you have enough juice for the class), pour the cider into a pot and heat it on the stove.
3. Serve the warm cider with sticks of cinnamon and let children drink the rewards of their labor.

Option:
Use store-bought apple cider and warm it.

SNOWY WITH A CHANCE OF BUTTER

The characters in *Cloudy with a Chance of Meatballs* by Judi Barrett (Atheneum, 1978) lived near mashed-potato mountains—your children will enjoy making their own potato cliffs and valleys.

Ingredients:
Mashed potatoes, butter pats, parsley, sour cream, chives

Directions:
1. Read this book before snack time, or at the snack table.
2. Serve each child a helping of mashed potatoes and provide plastic spoons for children to use to sculpt their potatoes into mountain shapes.
3. Let children use sour cream for snow, butter for a sunny horizon, and parsley and chives for trees and greenery on their mountains.
4. Once the children have sculpted the potatoes to their liking, they can dig in.

WEATHER

Snacks

SPRING SALAD CELEBRATION

This fresh-fruit salad is the perfect dish to serve at the start of spring, or any day you want a light and fruity snack.

Ingredients:
Cantaloupe, honeydew, watermelon, mint, melon ball maker

Directions:
1. Make melon balls from cantaloupe, honeydew, and any other melons available in your area.
2. Place the different types of melon balls in separate bowls along with a bowl of mint leaves.
3. Let children make their own salads by choosing the types of melon they want and spooning the balls into small paper bowls (with mint garnish for those who like mint).

QUICK COOLERS

These summertime snacks are a cool way to cool down!

Ingredients:
Fruit juice, ice cube trays (in various shapes if available), paper towels, small plastic pitchers

Directions:
1. Have children help you pour juice into ice cube trays.
2. Freeze the cubes overnight.
3. Serve these mini-pops outside wrapped in a paper towel or napkin.

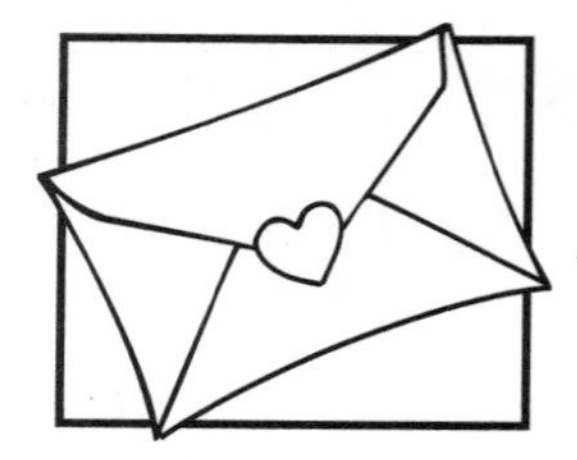

WEATHER

Letter Home

This little man lived all alone,
And he was a man of sorrow;
For if the weather was fair today,
He was sure it would rain tomorrow.
—Mother Goose

This month we are celebrating weather and seasons. We will be creating a window display filled with colorful "sun catchers," snowflakes, and falling leaves.

We will be learning about rainbows, shadows, and planting. If you are a gardener or a planting enthusiast and would like to share your garden or come in to discuss planting—we would love to listen! We would also appreciate dried flowers or spices from your garden to use in making sweet-scented paper sachets.

This month, the theme for our Dramatic Play corner is weather gear. We would like to borrow shoes and hats that are weather-related:

- snowshoes
- galoshes
- rain hats
- bathing caps
- sandals or flip-flops
- Easter bonnets . . .

All loans or donations are appreciated!

Thank you!

January: Homes

Home is where the heart is, and this chapter is dedicated to your children's hearts and homes. Begin this unit by reading *A House Is a House for Me* by Mary Ann Hoberman (Viking, 1978) and discussing the many different types of homes in the world. Ask your children to name the kinds of houses that they can think of. Help them if they get stuck by describing tepees, igloos, houseboats, trailers, and so on. You might also ask children to think of places where characters live in books they know: princes and princesses live in palaces or castles; the three little pigs lived in houses of straw, twigs, and bricks; and the witch in Hansel and Gretel lived in a gingerbread house!

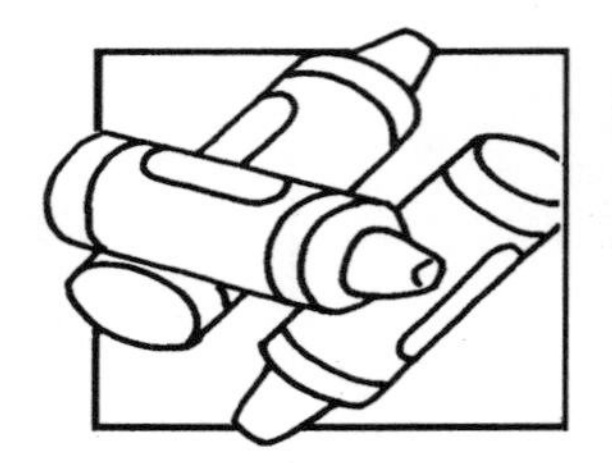

HOMES

Art Activities

MY HOUSE

Children can make a milk carton replica of their current house, or of a house they would like to live in someday.

Materials:

One milk carton per child (pint-sized milk cartons work well for single-family homes, while quart-sized cartons are good for children who live in apartment buildings), one mailbox pattern per child (from the city patterns, p. 119), construction paper in a variety of colors, crayons, decorations, scissors, glue, tempera paints, brushes

Directions:

1. Let children decorate their milk carton "homes" with construction paper, crayons, tempera paints, and various decorations.
2. Help the children write their street address on their mailbox pattern. They can glue the mailbox pattern onto a piece of construction paper and decorate the paper for a background to their house.
3. Encourage children to put together an entire neighborhood using their milk carton houses, as well as the dwellings they build in the "Box City" project (p. 117).

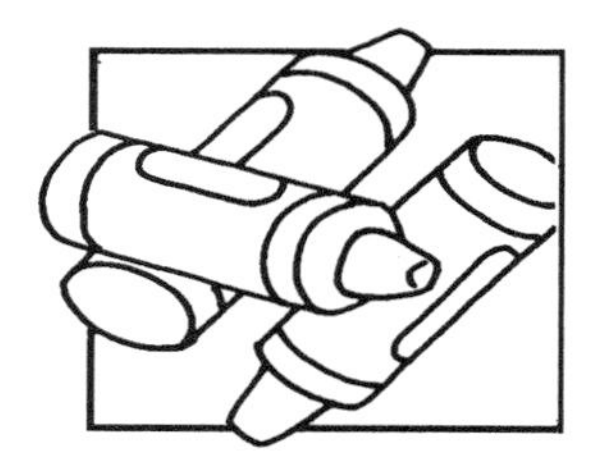

HOMES
Art Activities

BOX CITY
Your future architects and civil engineers will love building and developing this miniature city.

Materials:
City patterns (pp. 118-119), assorted empty containers (cereal boxes, tissue boxes, shoe boxes, coffee cans, plastic margarine tubs, etc.), Popsicle sticks, clay, glue, markers, crayons, decorations

Directions:
1. Provide assorted materials for children to use to make additional buildings to go with their houses:
   - Small square construction paper windows can be glued to cereal box apartment buildings.
   - Margarine tubs make perfect swimming pools for backyards. (Optional: Add water with a bit of blue food coloring.)
   - A shoe box can be decorated to look like a school.
   - Tissue boxes with oak tag circle wheels make trailers or motor homes.
2. Give children city patterns to decorate and glue to Popsicle sticks (with clay circle bases).
3. Children can build a whole city with their milk carton houses (p. 116), these box city buildings, and the city patterns.

Optional:
Spread a large sheet of butcher paper or a large sheet of cardboard on the floor. The children can draw in streets and use the paper as a base for their city.

BANK
Library
Post Office
Restaurant
Grocery Store
Laundry

MAIL

HOMES
Art Activities

PEEK-A-BOO TENT
For many, tents provide portable shelter from the elements. They also make a great hiding place!

Materials:
Tent and outdoor patterns (p. 121), construction paper in a variety of colors, scissors, tape, crayons or non-toxic markers

Directions:
1. Give each child a tent pattern, and have all the children cut along the center line.
2. Have children tape the outside edges (but not the bottom or the flaps) of the tent onto a piece of construction paper.
3. Provide drawing materials for children to use to draw a person or people on the construction paper "inside" the tent. (When the flaps are open, the people can be seen.)
4. Children can decorate the rest of the page to represent the "great outdoors" using the patterns or creating from their imaginations.

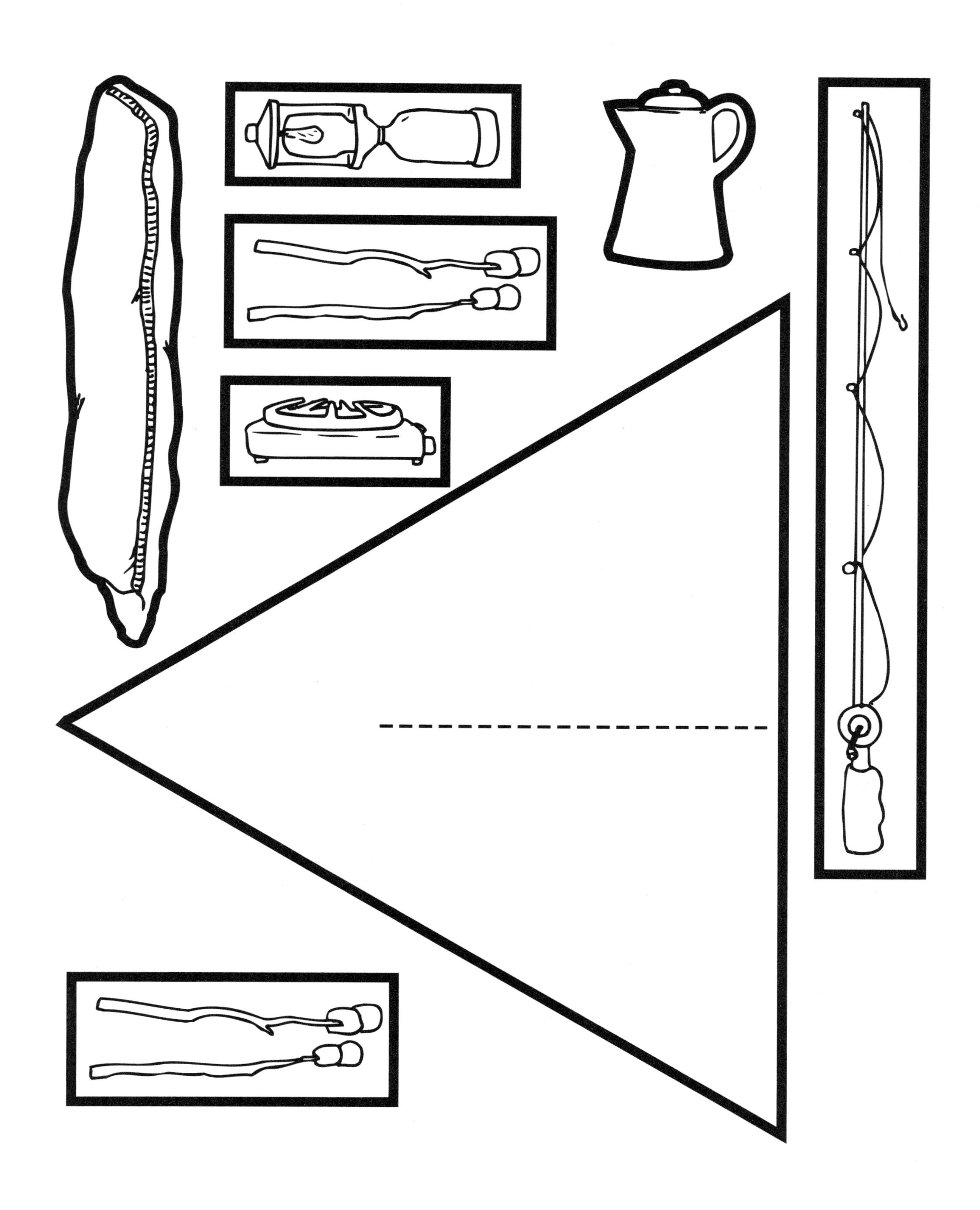

HOMES
Art Activities

CEREAL BOX CASTLES

If our homes are our castles, then children will certainly enjoy designing their fantasy castle-homes!

Materials:

Oatmeal boxes, coffee cans, or other cylindrical containers (one per child); castle patterns (p. 123); aluminum foil; colored cellophane; construction paper; wrapping paper; glue; markers; scissors; Popsicle sticks

Directions:

1. Let children decorate their can or box using the various castle coverings (aluminum foil, colored cellophane glued over construction paper, wrapping paper, etc.).
2. Give each child a copy of the castle patterns to decorate, cut out, and glue to their castles.
3. Create a special "Castle Corner" on a table near the picture books. Provide an assortment of castle-theme books for children to look at.

HOMES

Storytime

FEATURED PICTURE BOOK

***Harold and the Purple Crayon* by Crockett Johnson (HarperTrophy, 1955).**

Harold is a very creative young boy who has a wonderful purple crayon. With it, he is able to make a moon (for his walk in the moonlight), a long straight path (so he doesn't get lost), and a forest (where he thought a forest ought to be). After a long and exhausting journey, Harold decides it is time to get back to his home and his own bed . . . and with the help of his big purple crayon, he has no trouble at all!

ART EXTENSION

After reading this book to your students, ask them to imagine what they would create if they had a magic purple crayon. They may want to close their eyes as you read through portions of the book a second time, so that they can create the pictures in their heads.

Materials:

Purple crayons (one per child), large sheets of white paper

Directions:

1. Give each child a purple crayon and a sheet of paper.
2. If children want to, they can follow Harold's story and create a forest, an ocean, a picnic, a city, and their own home. Or, children can use their crayons to create anything they wish!
3. Post these "Magic Crayon" pictures on a bulletin board—and ask the children to describe their drawings for the rest of the class. You might want to title the pictures using each child's name. Example: "Sarah and the Purple Crayon."

HOMES

Storytime

MORE PICTURE BOOKS

Always Room for One More by Leclaire G. Alger, illustrated by Nonny Hogrogian (Holt, 1965).
A kind farmer and his wife have plenty of room in their house for visitors—there's "always room for one more." Then too many visitors stop by, and the house falls down!

Ben's Dream by Chris Van Allsburg (Houghton Mifflin, 1982).
Ben tries to study for his history test on the landmarks of the world, but instead he falls asleep. In his dream, his house rides on a sea of rain, taking him past many famous places—all seen from his own front porch!

Hillel Builds a House by Soshana Lepon, illustrated by Marilynn Barr (Kar-Ben Copies, 1993).
Hillel is a little boy who loves to build houses. He creates cardboard houses, pillow houses, a tree house, a secret house under the basement steps, and more. Then, for the Jewish holiday called Sukkot, Hillel builds the best house of all!

A House for Hermit Crab by Eric Carle (Picture Book Studio, 1987).
Poor Hermit Crab keeps growing too big for his shell houses. When he finally finds a shell that's big enough, it's rather empty. He decorates it to protect it from sea anemones, coral, urchins, and other ocean dwellers.

A House Is a House for Me by Mary Ann Hoberman (Penguin, 1987).
This book shows houses for various animals and objects. A chicken's house is a coop, a hand's house is a glove, an ant's house is a hill, and a potato's house is a pot!

How We Live by Anita Harper, illustrated by Christine Roche (Harper, 1977).
There are many different types of places where people live, including boats, trailers, houses, apartments, and rooms. *How We Live* describes the different ways people live, for example, with friends or alone.

The Little House by Virginia Lee Burton (Houghton Mifflin, 1942).
People begin building around the Little House, and one day she finds herself living in the middle of a city. Luckily, a relative of the original owner finds the Little House and brings her back to the country.

The Old House by Hans Christian Andersen, adapted by Anthea Bell, illustrated by Jean Claverie (North-South, 1984).
A little boy makes friends with an elderly man who lives in an old, magical house across a busy city street. The boy sends the man a gift of a tin soldier. The toy reappears many years later, on the spot where the house used to be.

When the Moon Shines Brightly on the House by Ilona Bodden, illustrated by Hans Poppel (Houghton Mifflin, 1991).
At night, when the house is quiet and everyone sleeps, the moon shines overhead. A mouse comes out of its hole and the moon lights the way for the mouse to travel from room to room, having fun.

The Wind in the Willows: Home Sweet Home by Val Biro (Simon & Schuster, 1987).
Mole and Walter Rat return to Mole's abandoned home. Although the home is cold and dusty, Walter Rat soon helps make it a warm, comfortable home again, and Mole is happy.

HOMES

Flannel Board

HOW THE THREE LITTLE PIGS FRIGHTENED THE WOLF!

This is the **house** that **pig** built,
Of straw and bits of hay.
This is the house that pig built,
But **wolf** blew it away.
So piggy ran to his good friend,
Named **piglet number two**.
They settled in this piggy's **house**
Of twigs, and sticks, and glue.
But wolf came by and huffed and puffed.
The house of twigs fell down.
And piggies one and two ran out,
And scrambled 'cross the town
To their good friend, named **piggy three**,
Whose **house** was built of bricks.
They knew no wolf could blow it down,
But wolf had other tricks.
He slid right down the chimney flue,
He hoped to dine on pigs.
Instead he landed in the **stew**,
Hot from a fire of twigs.
The wolf jumped up and hopped about,
And left those pigs alone.
They never heard of wolf again,
Not even on the phone.
And now the friends live in one home
The house of piggy three,
And since the bricks keep wolves away,
The pigs live happily.

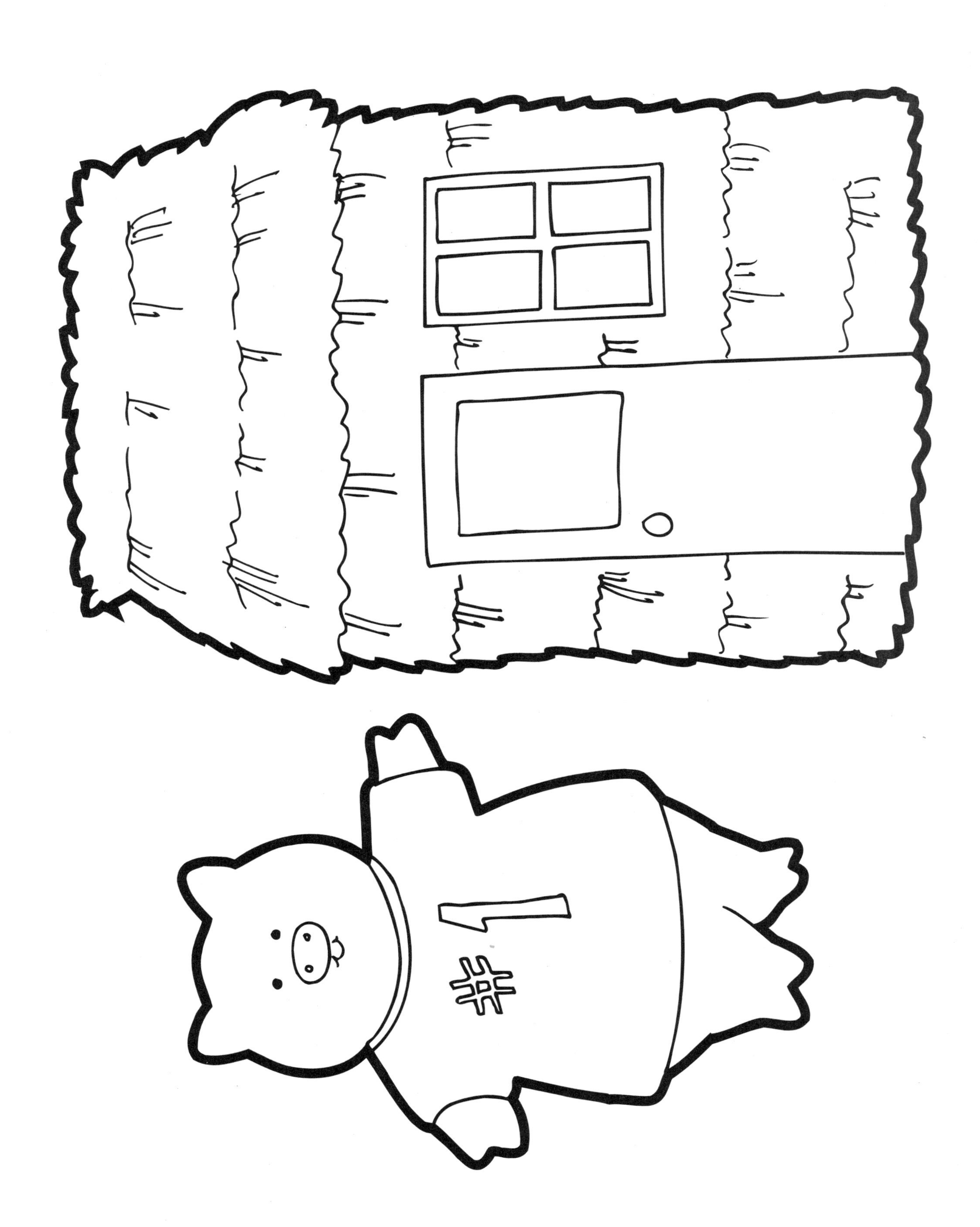
#1

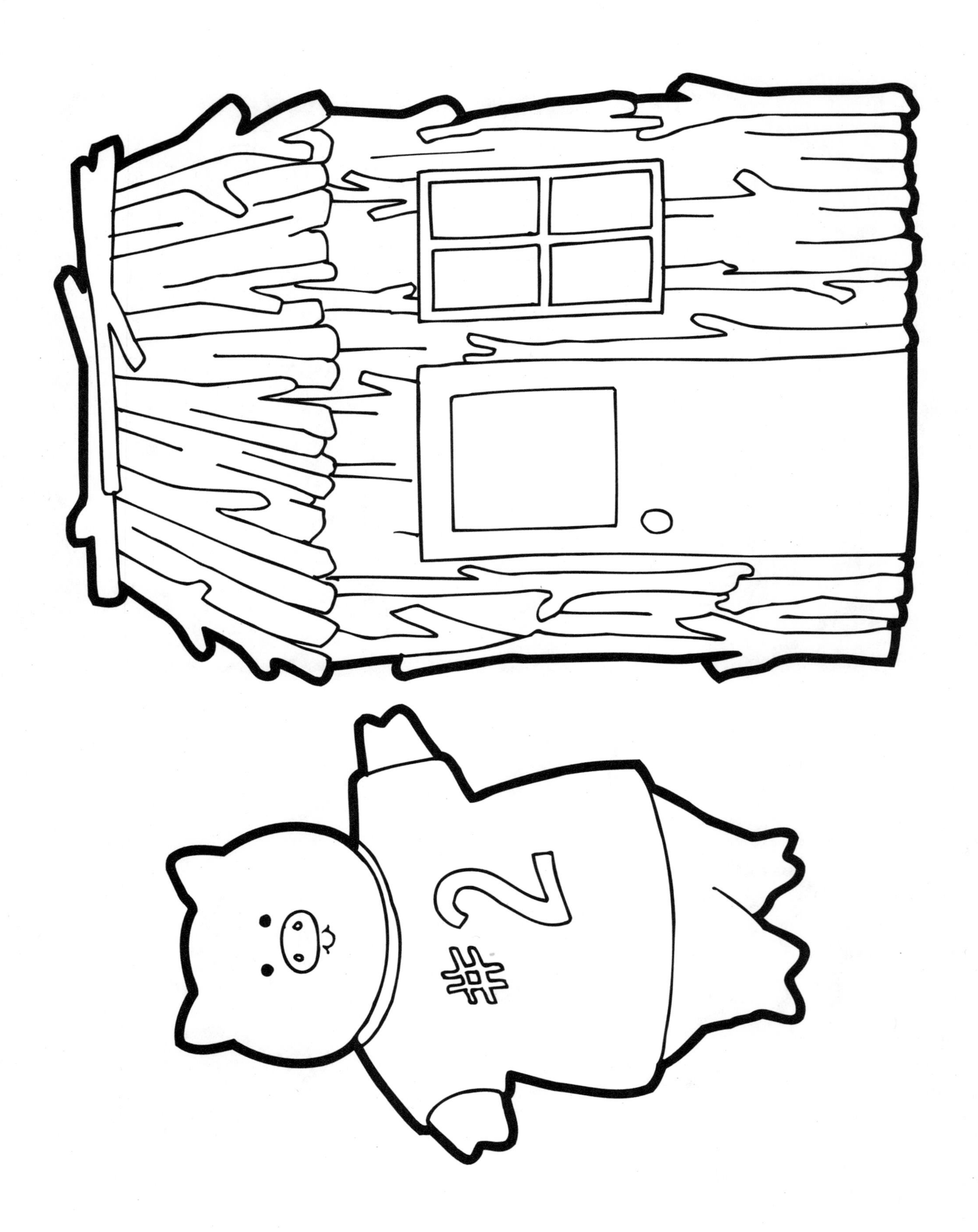
#2

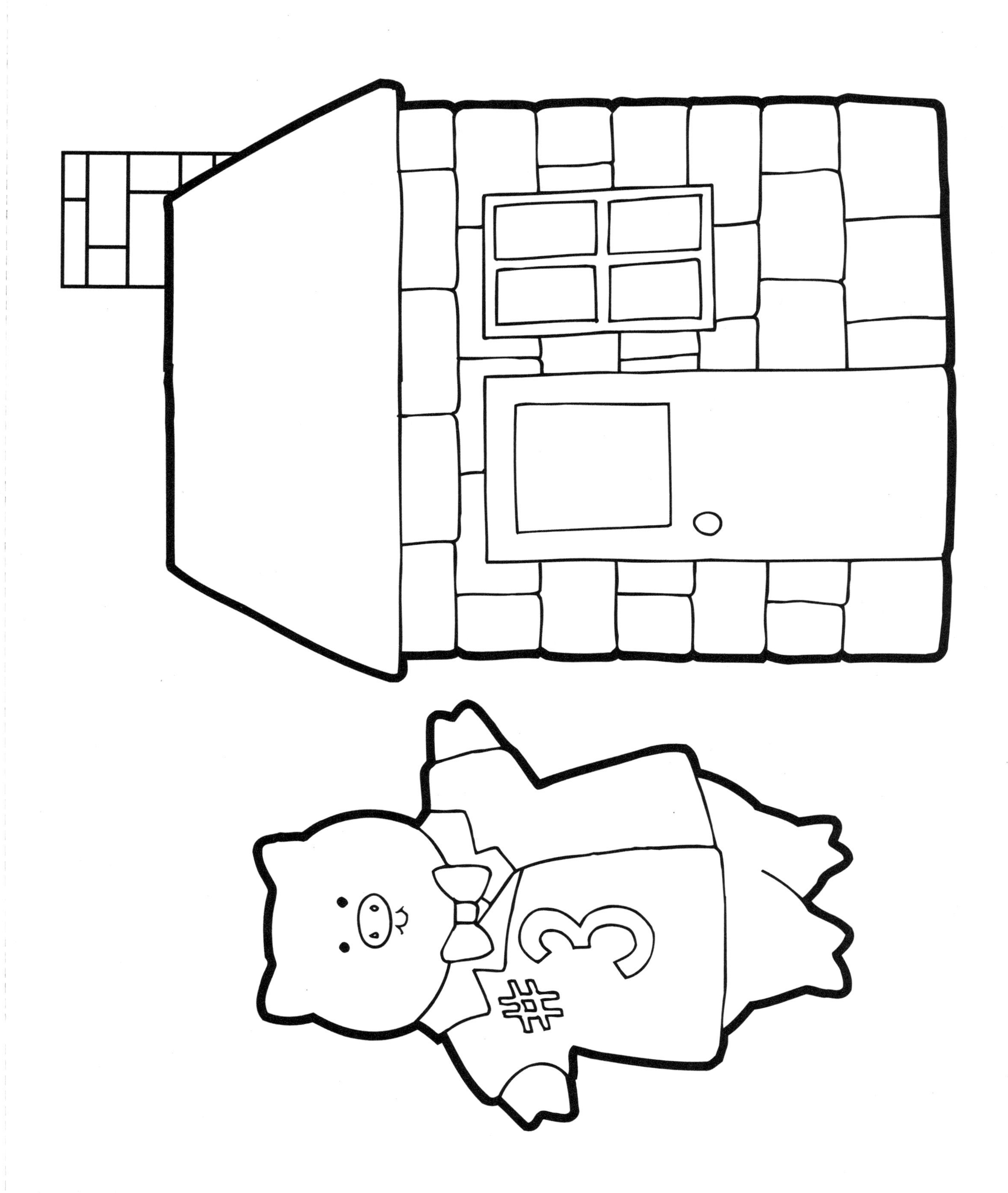
#3

HOMES

Discovery

WATER TABLE HOUSEBOATS

Materials:
Small plastic boats, water (dyed blue with food coloring), plastic figures and animals

Directions:
1. Set up the water table with blue water.
2. Provide floating boats and small "passengers" (plastic dinosaurs and "counting bears" are always a big hit).
3. Let children float the houseboats in the water table. You might want to suggest that children imagine that they live on the houseboats. Ask them what they think would be good about living on a boat, and what problems they might have. (How would you get food? Where would you go to school? Could you keep a pet? What kind?)

Option:
Float ice cubes in the water (for icebergs or glaciers) for the children to steer their boats around.

HOMES

Discovery

FIELD TRIP 1

Take children on a field trip to a construction site, or invite a builder or a construction worker into the classroom to discuss the tools of the trade (hammers, nails, saws) as well as the safety precautions (hard hats, alarms, gloves, etc.).

FIELD TRIP 2

Visit a local hardware store to look at tools (hammers, nails, screwdrivers, and so on). When you return to the classroom, set up a woodworking area where children can build by gluing scraps of wood together and painting the finished product. Try adding food coloring or liquid watercolors to the glue for more colorful creations.

FIELD TRIP 3

If there is an unusual house in your city, such as an old Victorian, a very modern house, or a landmark house built by a famous architect, try to plan a classroom visit. Prepare the children for the experience by reading books about that type of house, or by looking at pictures.

HOMES

Discovery

WOODWORKING PRACTICE

If the children in your class haven't tried woodworking before, prepare with a simple variation.

Materials:

Styrofoam, roofing nails, small hammers, soft wood

Directions:

1. Bring large pieces of Styrofoam (left over from packing boxes) into the classroom.
2. Let the children hammer roofing nails (which are less sharp than regular nails and have larger heads) into the soft Styrofoam.
3. Once the children get the hang of this, they can graduate to working with soft woods.

Note:

All carpentry activities must be closely supervised.

HOMES

Discovery

MAP IT OUT!

Materials:
Local map, butcher paper, non-toxic markers

Directions:
1. Show children a map of your city or town.
2. Help the children find your school and a few local landmarks that they will recognize (parks, the City Hall, a community swimming pool, etc.).
3. Spread a sheet of butcher paper on a flat surface, and have the children work together to make a "map" of their school, including the front door, their room, the playground, etc. You might also want them to make a map of the interior of your classroom on a smaller sheet of paper that can be shown to classroom visitors who want to know where everything is.

Option:
Have the children use their new map-making skills to plan out the mini-city (see the Class Project) before they build it.

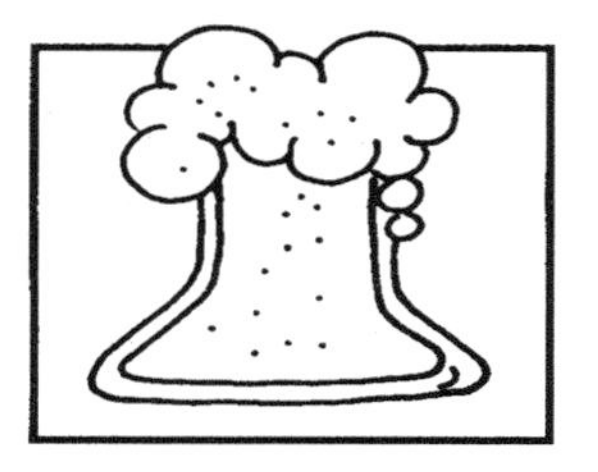

HOMES

Discovery

ARCHITECT ALERT

Materials:
Unit blocks (and lots of them!)

Directions:
1. Let your children be creative in the block corner, building houses that they have seen in picture books or in their own imaginations.
2. Ask each child to describe his or her house, naming the style (is it a Tom Sweet original? a Purple Pisa by Paula?).
3. Have the children take each other on "tours" of their houses, pointing out the type of backyards and swimming pools that will be developed in the later stages of construction.

Option:
Post photos and drawings of local landmarks (or famous buildings) around the block area for inspiration.

HOMES

Dramatic Play

TEPEE

Set up a tepee, available through teacher supply catalogs. Talk about the materials Native Americans used to build them, and why there's an opening at the top. Encourage the children to act out daily work that might take place in a tepee.

TENT

Invite a parent to set up a tent in the classroom or outside. Children can pretend to go camping—especially if you provide a few camping accessories: backpacks, sleeping bags, water canteens. (Be sure to limit the number of children inside the tent at one time.) Read *Hester in the Wild* by Sandra Boynton (Harper, 1979) while sitting inside the tent.

IGLOO

Have the children help you build the foundation for an igloo in the block corner. Use a white sheet for the top for a "snowy" look. The children can pretend to be Eskimos and go ice fishing—use the fish patterns (p. 248) to set up an ice hole! Any stray teddy bears can be friendly polar neighbors.

HOMES

Class Project

HOME SWEET HOME

The end result of this cooperative project may last in your dramatic play corner for some time—and children will be proud to play in something that they made themselves!

Materials:
Refrigerator box, wrapping paper (for wallpaper), tempera paints and brushes, cardboard, paper flowers, small boxes (for chimney, window boxes, mailbox, etc.), scissors, craft knife, old magazines, glue, construction paper

Have your children decide what type of house they want to build. Suggestions:

- For a castle, stand the refrigerator box upright and cut a rounded door in the front that can fold down like a drawbridge. Children can paint stones on the sides.
- For a single-level house, lay the box on its side. Cut out windows and a door so that they can open and close.
- For a trailer, follow the directions for the single-level house, but provide additional pieces of cardboard for children to use to make wheels.

Children may want to cover their house with bricks (red construction paper, or red tempera-covered paper divided by white lines). They may want to make pictures to hang on the walls by cutting out magazine pictures that they like (or using outdated calendars) and creating frames for their "art" from construction paper.

A skylight cut from the top of the box and covered with clear cellophane will add extra light to the interior.

Let children move in any extra furniture from the dramatic play corner: mini washer/dryer, sink, small chair, etc.

Use shoe boxes as planters for paper flowers in the front yard.

Have an "Open House" when the project is completed and invite parents and guardians to join in the fun.

Play "Our House" (by Madness) during the construction.

HOMES

Games

WHO'S IN THE TENT?

Directions:
1. Let children help you build a tent or a fort by draping a blanket over a table or over two chairs (or use a real tent or tepee if either is available).
2. Have children sit in a circle and close their eyes.
3. Tap one child to hide in the fort.
4. Have children open their eyes and try to guess who's in the fort either by asking questions which you answer with "Yes" or "No" (20 questions-style), or by the clues you give them.

MATCHING GAME: WHO LIVES IN THIS HOUSE?

Materials:
Patterns (p. 139), crayons or markers, scissors

Directions:
1. Duplicate the patterns, color (or have children color them), cut out, and laminate.
2. Have children spread out the cards face up to learn the pictures and the vocabulary. The object of the game is to match the person or animal with the appropriate house. As they master the game, the children can spread out the cards face down (concentration-style).

FIDO

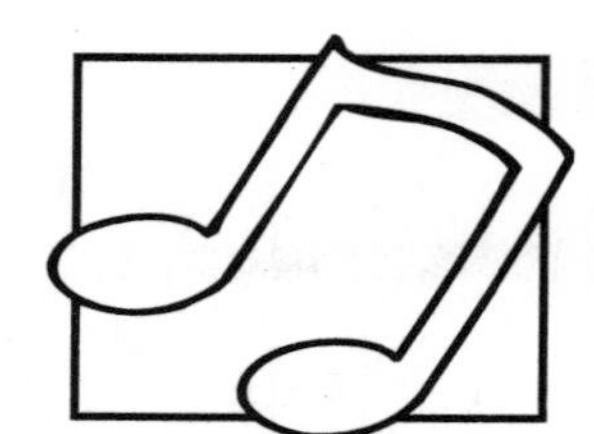

HOMES

Songs

Pig Song
(to the tune of "Home, Home on the Range")

Oh give me a home,
With TV and a phone,
And nice carpeting on all the floors,
With walls made of straw,
That the wolf cannot claw,
Oh, no piglet could want any more.

What's that I hear now?
Huff and puff and my walls all fall down.
I don't give a fig,
My friend's house is of twigs,
So I'll visit him in his home town.

We'll stay in our home
Made of twigs, but we'll phone,
Just to see if the wolf is around.
I hear him outside,
Huff and puffing, oh, my.
Now our twig house is spread on the ground.

Let's run to our friend,
I know his brick house will not bend.
That wolf, he can huff,
And that wolf, he can puff,
But his days as a pest will soon end.

(chorus)

Home, home made of bricks,
Not as flimsy as straw or as sticks.
Now we're three little pigs
In our comfortable digs
'Cause we stopped that mean wolf and his tricks!

HOMES

Mother Goose

To Market, To Market

To market, to market
To buy a fat pig
Home again, home again
Jiggity jig.

There Was an Old Woman

There was an old woman who lived in a shoe.
She had so many children;
She didn't know what to do.
So she gave them some broth,
And baked them some bread.
Then she read them a story,
And tucked them in bed.

This Is the House That Jack Built

This is the cheese that lay in the house that Jack built.
This is the rat who ate the cheese that lay in the house that Jack built.
This is the cat who chased the rat . . .
This is the dog who frightened the cat . . .
This is the cow with the crumpled horn who "moo'd" at the dog . . .
This is the maiden all forlorn who milked the cow . . .
This is the man, all tattered and torn, who kissed the maiden . . .
This is the priest, all shaven and shorn, who married the man, all tattered and torn, who kissed the maiden all forlorn who milked the cow with the crumpled horn who "moo'd" at the dog who frightened the cat who chased the rat who ate the cheese that lay in the house that Jack built!

HOMES

Snacks

TORTILLA TEPEE

These tortilla tepees are a new version of nachos. (You can tell your students that these are "nacho ordinary nachos." Translation: not your ordinary nachos.)

Ingredients:

Small corn tortillas cut into triangle wedges (like pieces of pizza), grated cheese, chopped tomatoes, aluminum foil, cookie tin, permanent marker

Directions:

1. Let children decorate triangle-shaped tortilla "tepees" with grated cheese and chopped tomatoes.
2. Place "tepees" onto aluminum foil-covered cookie sheets and write each child's name next to his or her tepee (to make sure children receive their own).
3. Bake for two to three minutes at 350 degrees (until cheese melts).
4. Let cool slightly before serving to avoid burned tongues.

ICE CREAM IGLOO

Ice cream igloos are simple to make and fun to eat!

Ingredients:

Vanilla ice cream, ice cream scoop, coconut shavings

Directions:

1. Give each child an igloo-shaped scoop of ice cream (simply a round scoop made with an ice cream scooper).
2. Let children decorate their igloos with falling snow (coconut shavings) before eating.

Option:

Provide toothpicks for carving "ice block" patterns into the outside (show pictures of igloos).

HOMES

Snacks

HOUSE BREAD

Decorating bread slices to look like houses really makes them taste "home-made!"

Ingredients:
Sliced bread, jack cheese cut into small squares, orange Cheddar cheese cut into rectangles, sliced olives, sliced cucumbers, strips of green pepper

Directions:
1. Let children decorate a slice of bread with jack cheese windows and Cheddar cheese doors.
2. They can add olive doorknobs, a cucumber-thatched roof, etc., before eating.

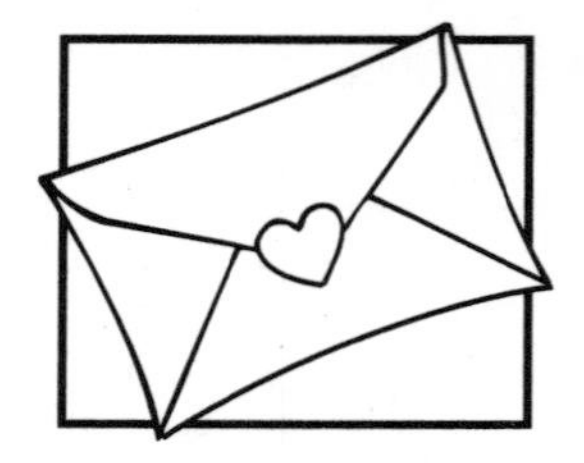

HOMES

Letter Home

This little piggy went to market.
This little piggy stayed home.
This little piggy had bean soup.
This little piggy had none.
And this little piggy cried,
"Wee, wee, wee, wee,"
All the way home.
—Mother Goose

Home is where the heart is, and homes are what we're learning about this month. We will explore the different dwellings of people all over the world, as well as the homes of some storybook characters.

We are interested in learning about tents. Campers are invited to demonstrate tent assembly. We would also like to take a field trip to see the inside of a motor home or trailer.

Bring in a photo of your home to share with the class. Or come tell us about any construction or remodeling.

This month we are building a city within our classroom. We need empty:

- milk cartons (big and small)
- cereal boxes
- tissue boxes
- plastic margarine tubs
- oatmeal and coffee canisters

Thanks for your help!

February: Dragons

Puff the Magic Dragon lived by the sea, but dragons can live anywhere there are active imaginations! Introduce this unit by whipping up some "Magic Cherry Frappes" (p. 169) for the children to drink while listening to *Whinnie the Lovesick Dragon* by Mercer Mayer (Macmillan, 1986). The songs in this unit are easy to learn, so you could start a circle time session with a round or two of "I'm a Dragon" (p. 167; to the tune of "Alouette"). And, of course, don't forget to play "Puff" for your children, either on the guitar or on a record or tape (your children will have fun "frolicking" to this tune—even if there isn't any "Autumn mist!").

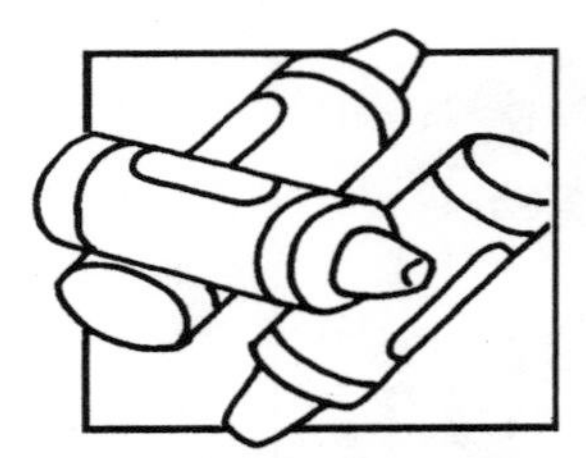

DRAGONS

Art Activities

WHINNIE THE LOVESICK DRAGON'S VALENTINES

Read *Whinnie the Lovesick Dragon* by Mercer Mayer (Macmillan, 1986) to your class, and discuss other ways (besides magic) that Whinnie might have shown Alfred that she liked him.

Materials:
Red construction paper, heart patterns (p. 147), tagboard, doilies, scissors, glitter, glue, dragon patterns (p. 147)

Directions:
1. Make heart stencils from tagboard using the patterns.
2. Have the children fold sheets of red construction paper in half.
3. Show them how to place a folded tagboard heart on the paper crease and cut out to make Valentines.
4. Let the children cut out as many heart shapes as they'd like.
5. Provide doilies, glitter, glue, and dragon patterns for the children to use to make Valentines for their friends and families, or for hanging up in the classroom.

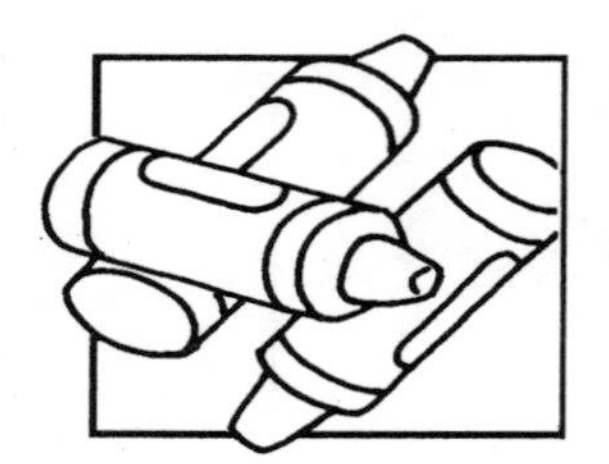

DRAGONS

Art Activities

MR. DRAGON'S SCALED WINGS

Sing "Mr. Dragon" (p. 167) with your children, and have them imagine what the dragon might look like.

Materials:

Butcher paper, tempera paints (blue, green, black, purple), paintbrushes, scissors, hole punch, yarn

Directions:

1. Cut simple wing shapes from butcher paper or large easel paper as shown. (You'll need one per child.)
2. Punch two holes on each side of the wings (four total) for yarn to be threaded through when the children have finished decorating.
3. Have the children paint colorful scales on one side of the wings. They can do this by just pressing the brush to the paper. (See the illustration.)
4. Let the wings dry thoroughly, then thread one length of yarn through each set of holes (as shown).
5. The children can slip their arms through the tied strings and wear their dragon wings for dramatic play.

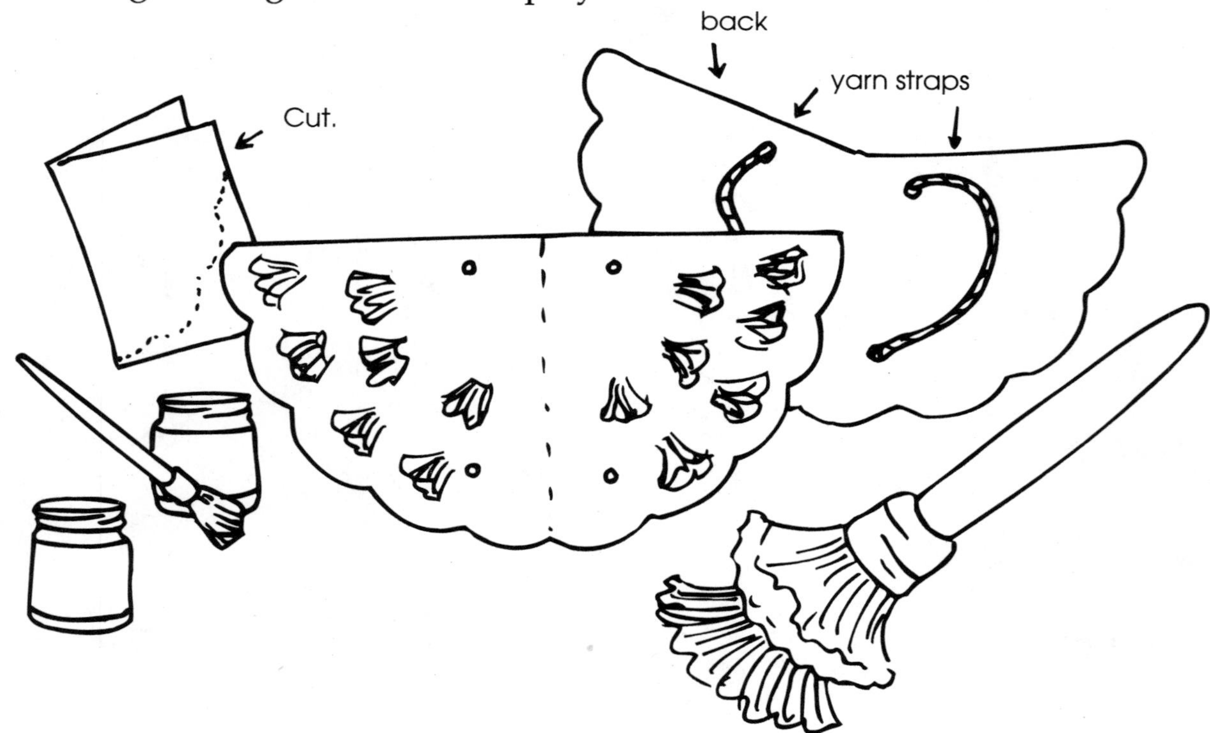

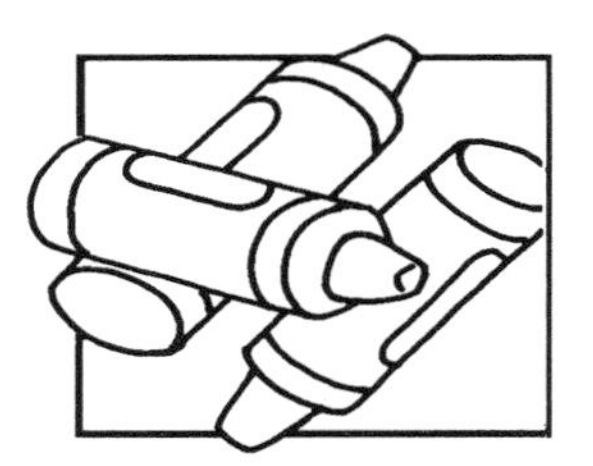

DRAGONS

Art Activities

CHINESE DRAGON PAINTED BODY

The result of this activity will be used in the Dragons Class Project (p. 163) as the dragon's "body." Or hang the finished sheet in your classroom as a colorful backdrop.

Materials:
Large solid-colored sheet, colored glue (this can be made by mixing white glue with food coloring or liquid watercolors), glitter, newspaper, shiny-fabric scraps, tinsel, foil, sequins

Directions:
1. Place newspaper over the work area (the floor would be fine).
2. Spread the sheet on top of the newspaper.
3. Give the children colored glue and glitter to use to decorate the sheet. Show them how to make designs with the glue and then sprinkle the glue with glitter. The children can use squeeze bottles, or apply glue with brushes. Use small shaker cans for the glitter.
4. Let the sheet dry and then shake the excess glitter onto the newspaper to be recycled for another project.
5. Children can also glue on shiny fabric, tinsel, tinfoil, and sequins to make the dragon body sparkle!

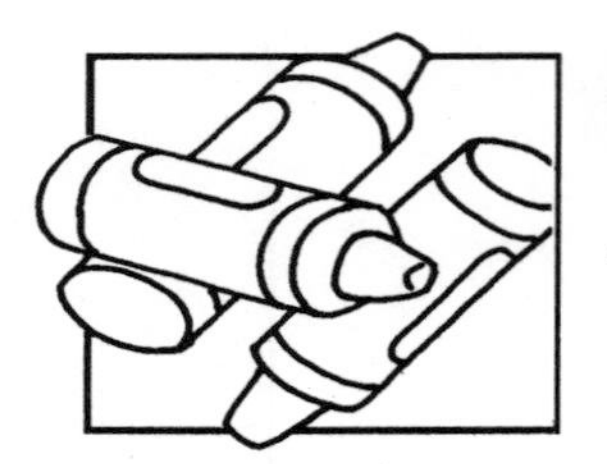

DRAGONS

Art Activities

DRAGON HATS

Let the children wear these hats while playing "Dragon Tag" (p. 164) or while they're wearing wings.

Materials:

Long (18") and short (12") strips of green construction paper, purple construction paper triangles, tape, glue sticks, scissors, stapler

Directions:

1. Help the children make headbands from the long green construction paper strips. Wrap a strip around a child's head and mark where the strip should be cut and taped to fit the child comfortably.
2. Let the children decorate the short paper strips by gluing on purple construction paper triangles. To make the triangles stand upright, they should tape a triangle to each side of the band and then staple the top together in the middle. Or make a fold and tape along the crease. (See the illustration.)
3. Show the children how to fasten the shorter green strip across the top of the band.

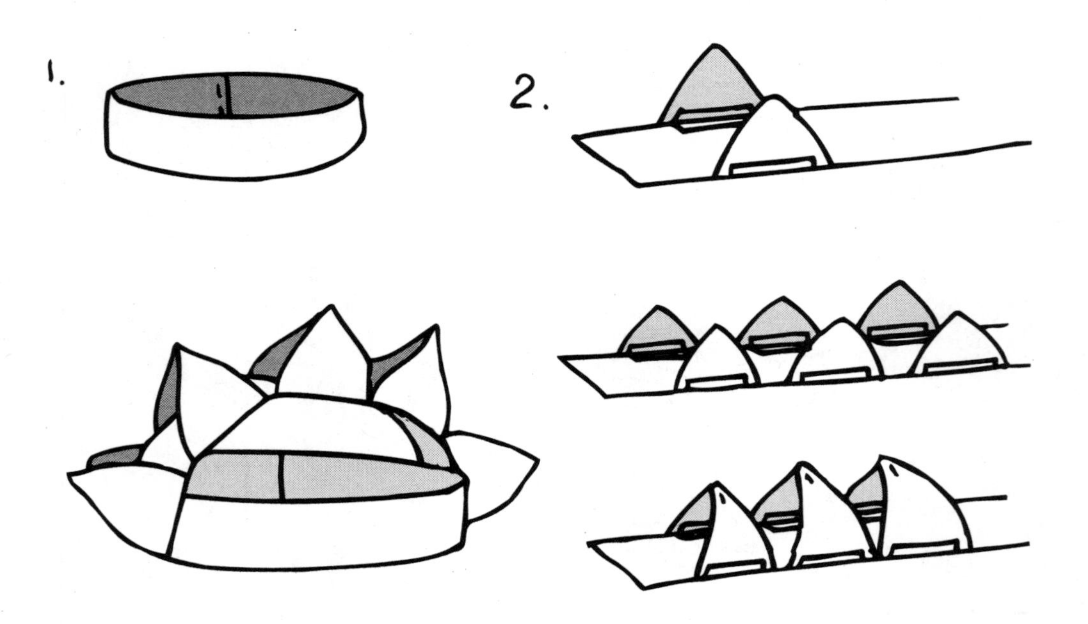

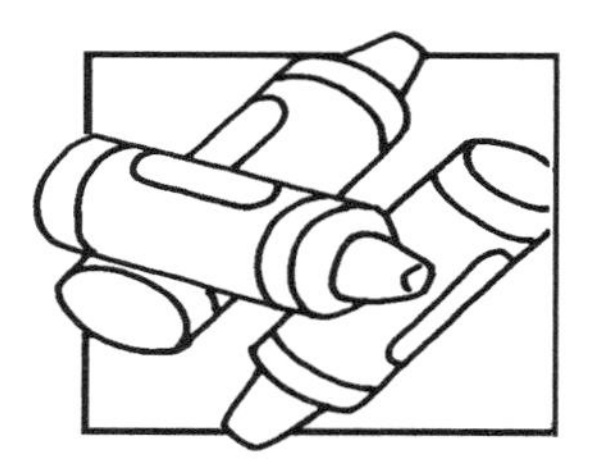

DRAGONS
Art Activities

CHINESE DRAGON MASKS
Read *Everyone Knows What a Dragon Looks Like* by Jay Williams, illustrated by Mercer Mayer (Four Winds Press, 1976) before doing this project.

Materials:
Paper bag (one per child, with a rectangular slit cut out for the eyes and slits up the sides for the arms), tempera paint, paintbrushes, colored cellophane, glue, glitter, streamers, ribbons, scissors

Directions:
1. Have your children picture what they think a dragon looks like. Let them know that there is no wrong answer—all the children can have their own ideas and everyone can be right!
2. Give each child a bag to decorate in the fashion of his or her imaginary dragon. The children can use paintbrushes to make scales, or glue on shiny cellophane. Streamers or ribbons glued to the back can be a tail, or to the front for bursts of flame (in red or orange).
3. When the bags are finished, let the children put them on and do a dragon dance to "Puff the Magic Dragon."

DRAGONS

Storytime

FEATURED PICTURE BOOK

***Max's Dragon Shirt* by Rosemary Wells (Dial Books, 1991).**
Max and Ruby, brother and sister bunnies, venture to the mall to buy Max some new pants. Max would rather spend their five dollars on a dragon shirt. At the mall, Ruby and Max become separated, and Max finds himself in the boys' department—where dragon shirts are on prominent display. When Ruby catches up with her little brother, he is happily (and messily) eating ice cream with two policemen and a teenager. The pistachio-ice-cream-covered Max gets his shirt after all.

ART EXTENSION

Read this book with your children, pointing out Max's dragon shirt when it appears in the pictures.

Materials:
White or colored T-shirts (one per child), fabric paints (in individual squeeze "pens"), smocks, dragon patterns (p. 153), tagboard, newspaper or thin cardboard, scissors

Directions:
1. Duplicate the dragon patterns onto tagboard and cut out to make stencils. Give each child a T-shirt, a dragon stencil, and a smock to wear.
2. Have children place flat sections of newspaper or cardboard inside their T-shirts so that the paint won't go through the shirts.
3. Show the children how to trace the stencil onto their T-shirt with the fabric paints. (Some children may want to draw their own dragons.)
4. Let the children use different colored fabric paints to color in their dragons or to add background designs.
5. The children may wear their shirts while (carefully) eating ice cream!

Option:
Trace a dragon outline onto each shirt with a permanent marker. The children can use fabric paints or fabric crayons to color it in.

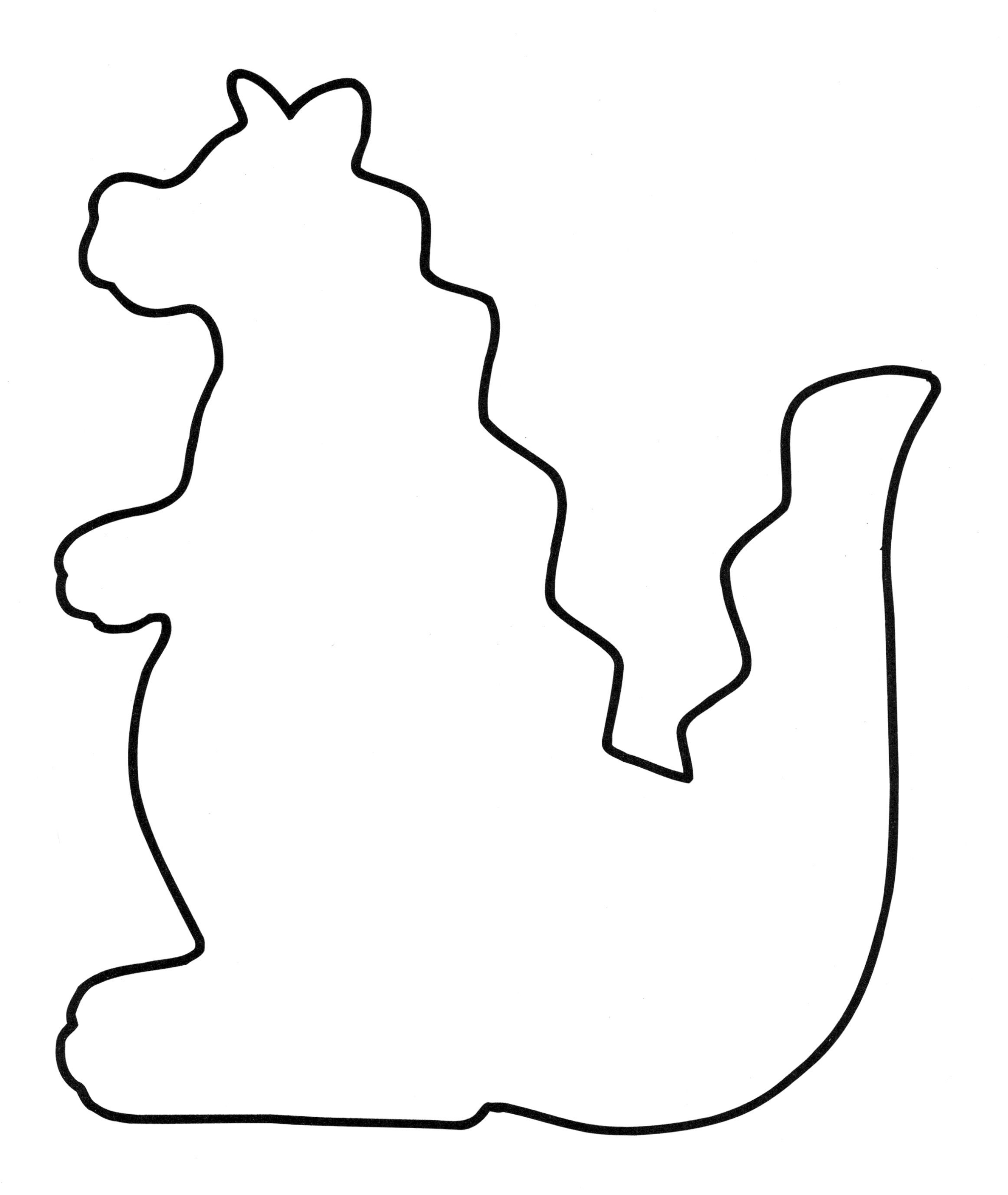

DRAGONS

Storytime

MORE PICTURE BOOKS

Custard the Dragon by Ogden Nash, illustrated by Linell (Little, 1959).
Belinda lives with her cat, her dog, her mouse, and a "realio trulio little pet dragon." Poor Custard isn't as brave as most dragons. The other animals tease him until he defeats a pirate and saves the day.

Eric Carle's Dragons, Dragons compiled by Laura Whipple (Philomel, 1991).
This is a book of poems about mystical creatures (including, of course, dragons). Eric Carle's classic art accompanies poems from sources such as the Book of Job, Rainer Maria Rilke, and a Chinese Mother Goose rhyme (illustrated by an amazing fold-out dragon).

Everyone Knows What a Dragon Looks Like by Jay Williams (Four Winds Press, 1976).
Almost all the characters thinks they know what a dragon looks like: the Emperor, the Wisest Wise Man, the Chief Workman, and the Captain of the Army. But only Han, the poor gate sweeper, knows the truth. (Everyone might know Mercer Mayer's style—but he outdoes himself in this book!)

I'm Going on a Dragon Hunt by Maurice Jones, illustrated by Charlotte Firmin (Four Winds Press, 1987).
In this version of a classic camp game, the addition of a dragon adds to the fun, as do the pictures. Your children might try to make up hand/body motions to go with the text.

Klippity Klop by Ed Emberley (Little, 1974).
Prince Krispin and his horse, Dumpling, go for a ride ("klippity klop"). They come to a bridge and ride over it ("klump, klumpity, klumpity, klump"). But when they come to a cave with an angry dragon inside, they return home very quickly—making all the same noises in the reverse order!

The Knight and the Dragon by Tomie de Paola (G.P. Putnam's Sons, 1980).
"Once upon a time, there was a knight in a castle who had never fought a dragon. And in a cave not too far away was a dragon who had never fought a knight." Their ultimate meeting is not too successful. However, the solution to their troubles is completely unexpected!

One Dragon to Another by Ned Delaney (Houghton Mifflin, 1976).
A little caterpillar falls in love with a dragon. She thinks that she will grow up to be just like him. Instead, she turns into a butterfly. But she decides that she is simply a flying dragon, while he is a smoking dragon!

Princess Smartypants by Babette Cole (G.P. Putnam's Sons, 1986).
Princess Smartypants thinks she's something else—and she is! This is not your average fairy tale (with a helpless princess rescued by a pompous prince). In this story, Ms. Smartypants outsmarts all of her suitors.

Terrible Troll by Mercer Mayer (Dial, 1968).
A little boy wishes he lived a thousand years ago when he would have been a knight's assistant—vanquishing dragons and rescuing princesses. However, when he dreams up a terrible troll to fight, he decides that he's happy living in the present!

Whinnie the Lovesick Dragon by Mercer Mayer, illustrated by Diane Dawson Hearn (Macmillan, 1986).
Whinnie, a dragon, is in love with a prince named Alfred—not a very likely match. With the help of a wizard, Whinnie turns herself into a princess, only to discover that Alfred is actually a dragon (in knight disguise) himself!

DRAGONS
Flannel Board

MARY HAD A DRAGON PAL

Mary had a **dragon pal**.
His scales were green and blue.
And everywhere that Mary went,
The dragon followed, too.

The dragon went to **school** with her,
And frightened all the kids.
Mary's preschool **teacher** even
Ran away and hid!

"He's friendly," said young Mary—
"He is sweet and never pouts."
But nobody believed her,
And they just would not come out.

"Now, look," said Mary gently,
"He will take you all on rides.
I promise he won't fly too high—
You really shouldn't hide."

"You'll hurt his feelings, yes you will—
And dragons hate to cry."
That made the **children** all come out,
And take rides in the sky.

The teacher even came out, too,
And shook the dragon's wing.
The dragon smiled—as best he could—
Then he began to sing:

"You shouldn't judge a person,
Or a dragon colored blue—
Different just means special.
Being special makes you YOU."

SCHOOL

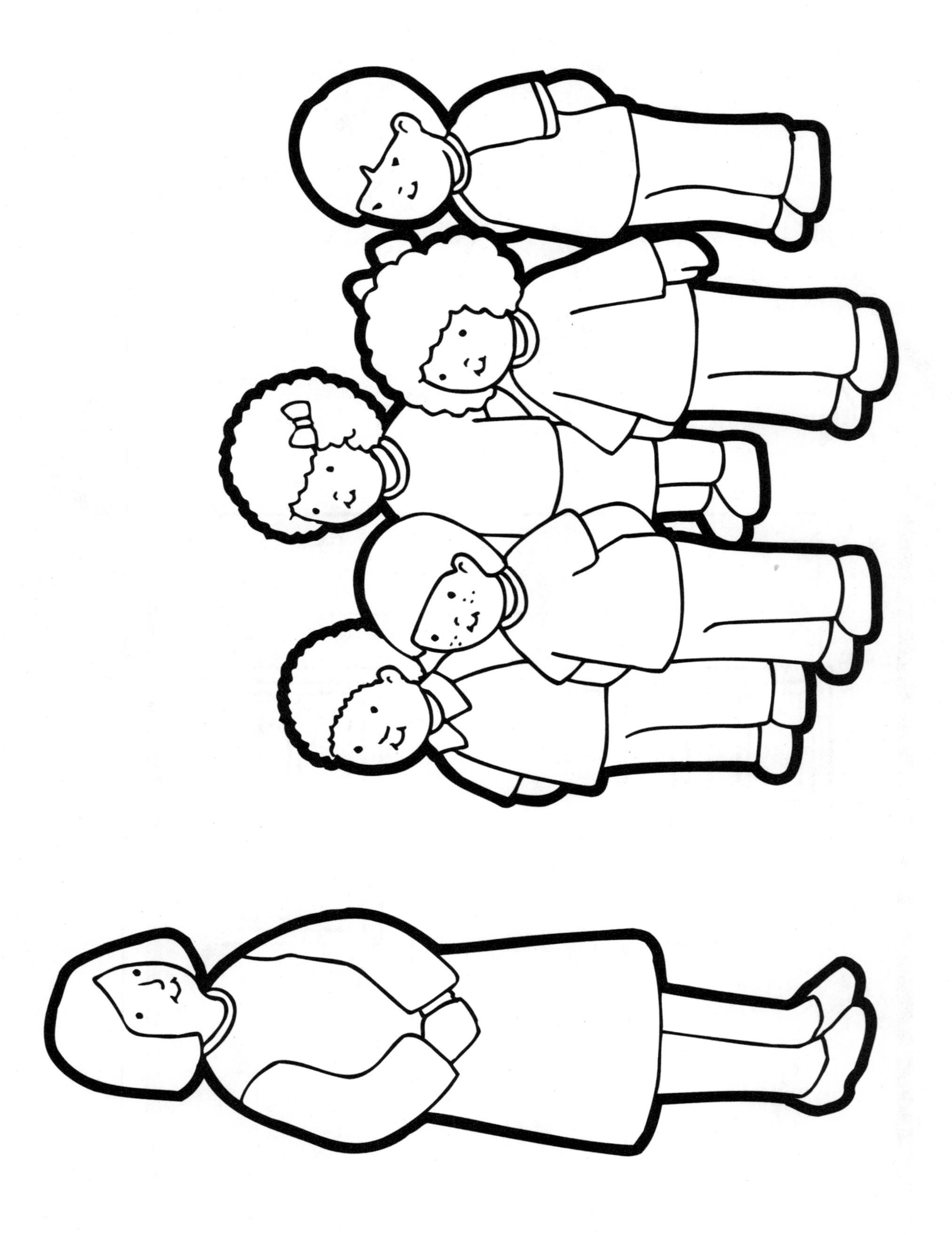

DRAGONS
Discovery

BE A CASTLE BUILDER
This activity is based on the book *The Castle Builder* by Dennis Nolan (Macmillan, 1987). In the story, Christopher, a young boy, builds "the best castle ever" on the beach. He makes a giant castle, complete with a dragon (in his imagination)—and it lasts until the tide comes in!

Materials:
Sand table or sandbox, small toy figures, pails, water, shovels, castle molds or other empty containers

Directions:
1. Read *The Castle Builder* to your students.
2. Have the children imagine building a castle like the one made by Sir Christopher, Builder of Castles and Tamer of Dragons.
3. Let the children build sand castles in a sandbox or at the sand table. Encourage them to use sandbox utensils to build and shape their castles. Note: It is easier to build castles out of damp sand than dry sand.
4. Provide an assortment of small figures for the children to use to decorate their castles. Plastic dragons would be perfect for this project!
5. When the castles are finished, the children can wash them away using a pail of water—or leave them standing. Or they can use the water to make a protective moat around their castle!

Option:
For a magical touch, sprinkle glitter on the completed castles.

DRAGONS

Discovery

CAVE CREATURES

According to the tales, dragons live in caves. Ask if any of your children have ever been inside a cave. If any have, let them share their experiences with the class. Otherwise, read a story in which a dragon lives in a cave, for example, *One Dragon to Another* by Ned Delaney (Houghton Mifflin, 1976).

Materials:
Large sheet, 2 to 4 chairs, beanbags, flashlights, pillows

Directions:
1. Let your children help you create a "cave" by stretching the sheet over the chairs and anchoring with beanbags. (You can use the decorated sheet [p. 149] if it's not currently part of a Chinese dragon.)
2. The children can furnish their cave with pillows.
3. Have the children enter the cave. Before you join them, turn out the classroom lights.
4. Sit in the cave with the children and read to them from *One Dragon to Another* using a flashlight for illumination!

DRAGONS

Discovery

WRITING IN DRAGON SMOKE

Ask your students the following questions: If a dragon were to write a letter, what would it look like? Would the edges be scorched with flames? What if a dragon could write in smoke or fire?

Materials:

Fingerpaints (red, orange, yellow, and gray), glossy paper

Directions:

1. Have the children imagine that they are dragons. They might want to roar or flap their "wings" to get in the mood.
2. Now, tell them that they need to send an important letter to a friend—and have them picture what the letter will look like. Or they can make a picture and call it a "Dragon Drawing."
3. Provide tins of fingerpaints and glossy paper for the children to use to write in dragon smoke (gray paint) or fire (red, orange, or yellow paint). They can experiment with the different colors to get the right look.
4. Post the finished pictures on a "Writing in Dragon Smoke" bulletin board.

DRAGONS

Discovery

DRAGON CAVE

Read these cave books with the children: *The Boy Who Lived in a Cave* by Estelle Friedman (Putnam's, 1960), *The Cave of the Lost Fraggle* by Michael Tettelbaum (Holt, 1985), and Tomi Ungerer's *The Mellops Go Spelunking* (Harper, 1963). Nonfiction cave books include: *Going Underground* by Anabel Dean (Dillon Press, 1984) and *Caverns* by Geraldine Sherman (Julian Messner, 1980).

Materials:
Egg cartons, tempera paint (black, green, brown), paintbrushes, dragon patterns (p. 147), shiny rocks (see directions below), aluminum foil, colored cellophane, crayons, scissors, glue

Directions:
1. Give each child a six-sectioned egg carton, or a 12-sectioned carton cut in half.
2. Have the children paint the inside of the cartons black, and the outside green and brown to look like a hill or mountain.
3. Provide aluminum foil, colored cellophane, and shiny rocks for children to glue inside the egg carton sections to represent stalactites (deposits which hang from cave ceilings) and stalagmites (which are slowly built up from cave floors).
4. Give each child a dragon pattern to color, cut out, and position inside their dragon cave.

SHINY ROCKS

Materials:
Small rocks, zip-lock bag, glitter, glue

Directions:
1. Put some glitter in a zip-lock plastic bag.
2. Dip small rocks in glue and then place them in the bag with the glitter.
3. Seal the bag and shake.
4. Remove the rocks and let them dry before the children use them to glue into their dragon "caves."

DRAGONS

Class Project

DRAGONS ON PARADE

In this movement activity, the children actually form a dragon! Have them line up and get under the decorated sheet. The child at the front of the line puts on the large dragon head (see below) and leads the parade.

To make the head, the children will work with the same media they've used in other projects. And they will use skills they've mastered in projects throughout this unit: gluing glitter ("Whinnie's Valentines"), making paintbrush scales ("Dragon Wings"), folding and gluing paper triangles ("Dragon Hats"), cutting cellophane ("Dragon Masks"), and experimenting with fingerpaint ("Writing in Dragon Smoke").

LARGE DRAGON HEAD

Materials:

Cardboard box (large enough to fit over a child's head and shoulders with lots of extra space for comfort and breathing), colored glue, glitter, tempera paint, paintbrushes, fabric, feathers, crepe paper, colored cellophane, streamers, construction paper, craft knife or scissors

Directions:

1. Cut out a rectangular slit in the box at eye level.
2. Have the children decorate the box with the paint, glue, glitter, and other collage materials.
3. The children can attach large construction paper eyes (above the rectangular eye hole), and long strips of crepe paper or cellophane or party streamers.
4. Let the children take turns wearing the dragon head and leading a group of children in a train behind, under the sheet. Other children can act as musicians, clapping hands, shaking rattles, ringing bells, and blowing whistles.

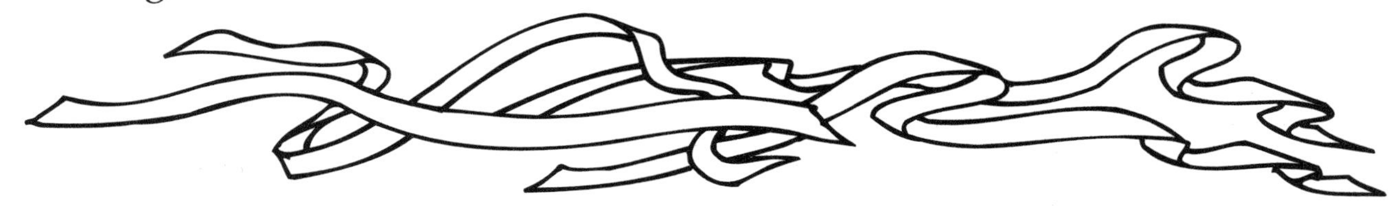

DRAGONS

Dramatic Play

DRAGON TAG

Have the children practice their dragon "roars" before beginning this game. (This a very good way to get out aggression!)

Materials:
Green streamers

Directions:
1. Divide your class into two groups of 10 to 15 children each.
2. Pick one child from each group to be that group's leader.
3. Have the two leaders stand facing each other. They are the dragons' heads. (They may want to wear their paper bag masks—p. 151.)
4. Have the rest of the children in each group line up behind their leader.
5. Turn the line of children in each group into a dragon chain by having each child hold onto the person in front (either with hands on the waist or touching the shoulders).
6. Tuck a two-foot length of a green streamer into the waistband of the last child in each dragon chain—the streamer serves as a tail.
7. Tell the children that the goal of the game is for each leader to try to steal the other chain's tail! However, when a leader moves, the whole chain must move, too—which adds to the difficulty, and fun, of the game.

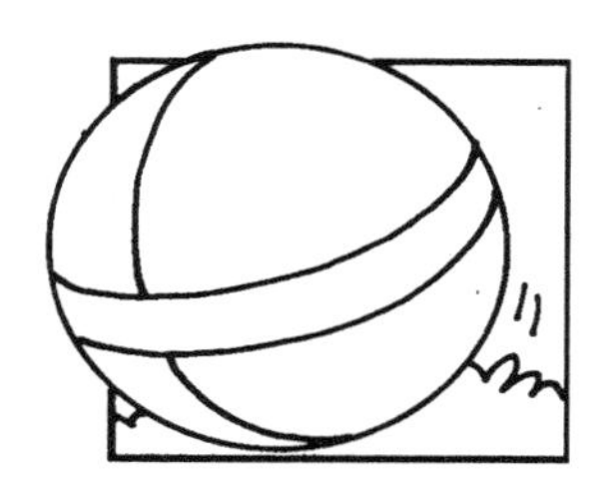

DRAGONS

Games

DRAGON PUZZLE

Materials:
One dragon puzzle pattern per child (p. 166), crayons, scissors, oak tag or tagboard, envelopes (one per child)

Directions:
1. Copy the dragon puzzle onto oak tag or tagboard.
2. Let each child color in a puzzle.
3. Laminate the colored puzzles and cut along the lines.
4. Give the children their puzzles (in pieces) in an envelope. (You might want to write their name on the envelope.)
5. Have the children try to put their puzzles back together. Assist them as needed.

DRAGONS

Songs

I'm a Dragon
(to the tune of "Alouette")

I'm a dragon,
Yes, I am a dragon.
I'm a dragon—
Look at all my scales.

I have scales of green and blue,
On my chest and my tail, too.
Green and blue,
Green and blue,
My tail, too,
My tail, too.
Ohhhhh,

I'm a dragon,
Yes, I am a dragon.
I'm a dragon—
Look at all my scales!

Mr. Dragon
(to the tune of "Home on the Range")

I live in a cave,
I can see ocean waves,
I have wings and a long, pointy tail.
I breath smoke and flames,
Mr. Dragon's my name—
And I'm covered with green and blue scales!

Dragons like to fly,
We can soar above clouds, way up high.
When you go outside,
Just look up in the sky—
And you might see a dragon fly by!

DRAGONS

Snacks

KNIGHT AND PRINCESS COOKIES

What do dragons eat? Some dragons, like Whinnie, slurp up Magic Cherry Frappes (see recipe on p. 169). But your little dragons might like munching on these cookies!

Ingredients:
Princess and knight patterns (p. 123), sugar cookie dough, flour, thin cardboard or oak tag, rolling pins, cookie sheets, plastic knives (with smooth surfaces), sprinkles or frosting, waxed paper, aluminum foil, permanent marker, scissors

Directions:
1. Prepare cookie dough according to your favorite recipe—or buy pre-made dough (found in the refrigerator section of most grocery stores).
2. Make princess and knight stencils by copying the patterns onto cardboard or oak tag and cutting out. (Make enough for your students to share.)
3. Show the children how to roll out the cookie dough onto waxed paper (lightly dusted with flour). Then have them place a princess or knight pattern on top of the dough and trace the shape with a knife. Help the children lift their cookies onto aluminum foil-covered cookie sheets.
4. Write the children's names next to their cookies with permanent marker on the foil.
5. Let the children decorate their cookies with frosting and / or sprinkles before they gobble them up!

Option:
Make the cookies ahead of time (or have a parent volunteer make them) and just let the children decorate the cookies before they eat them. Children might want to use some extra tinfoil to wrap their knight in "shining armor." (It serves as good protection against hungry dragons!)

DRAGONS

Snacks

MAGIC CHERRY FRAPPE

This drink may turn your children to dragons—and your dragons to children—so be careful! Read the book *Whinnie the Lovesick Dragon* by Mercer Mayer (Macmillan, 1986) before serving this snack.

Ingredients:
Vanilla ice cream, milk, pitted canned or pitted fresh cherries, blender, whipped cream

Directions:
1. Blend 1/2 cup ice cream, 1/4 cup pitted cherries, and 1/3 cup milk for every two "frappes."
2. Serve these treats in paper cups topped with whipped cream.
3. Ask the children to think about what type of magic they'd like the "frappe" to perform on them! Once they've finished eating, find out if the magic worked!

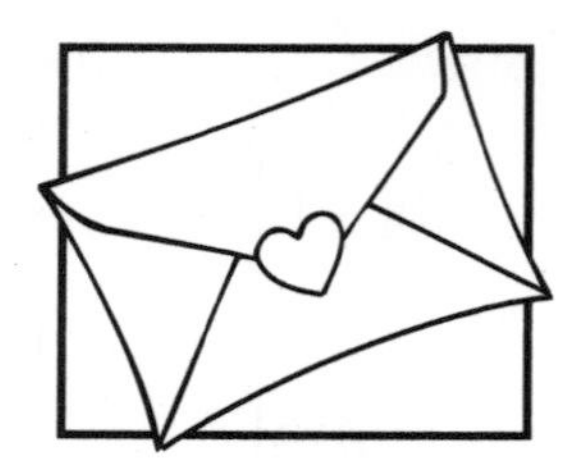

DRAGONS

Letter Home

As the sun came up, a ball of red,
I followed my friend wherever he led.
He thought his fast horses would leave me behind
But I rode a dragon as swift as the wind!
—Chinese Mother Goose

This month we are celebrating dragons in all their fiery glory! At snack time we will sample Magic Cherry Frappes—concoctions invented by the wizard in Mercer Mayer's book: *Whinnie the Lovesick Dragon.*

We are going to make dragon wings from butcher paper and tempera paint and write in gray dragon smoke fingerpaint. We will even become dragons for a game of "Dragon Tag!"

You are welcome to help us celebrate the Chinese New Year by participating in our dragon parade. Or cook with us—we will be making Knight and Princess Cookies to munch!

This month each child will need:

- an egg carton (for a dragon cave)
- a plain T-shirt (white or colored, but not patterned) to use in our art activity tie-in to the book *Max's Dragon Shirt.*

Thank you for your help!

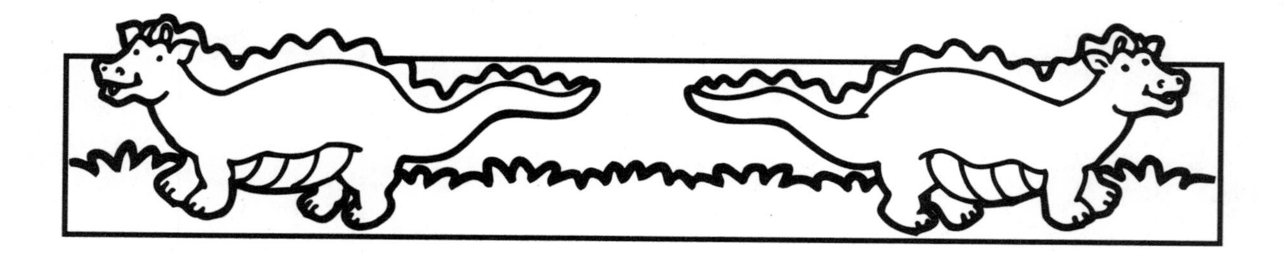

March: Animals

In this chapter, children do more than learn facts about animals—they create their own animals from colorful clay, observe and draw live animals, and become animals for the Paper Bag Parade! They will read many of their favorite stories starring a whole variety of animals, including *How the Rooster Saved the Day*; *Have You Seen My Cat?*; *Moo, Baa, La La La*, and more. Introduce the unit by singing the classic "Old MacDonald Had a Farm." Then teach the children the new version, "Old MacDonald's Funny Farm," on page 182.

ANIMALS

Art Activities

CLAY CREATURES

Many animals can be made from simple shapes. Show the children how to make the basics, and let them go from there.

Materials:
Modeling materials (clay, baker's dough, playdough, or Crayola dough), forks, sponges, toothpicks

Directions:
1. Have the children roll a ball of clay or dough between their hands for a head. They can roll long, snake-like strands for legs and tails. A molded oval or rectangle works for most bodies, and little triangles can be ears.
2. Show the children how to use the different tools to add texture to their creatures. They can use fork tines to draw fur lines, press damp sponges into the clay for scales, and use toothpicks to draw whiskers or stripes.

Option:
Crayola dough comes in bright colors, which gives children an opportunity to make a wild assortment of animals—blue giraffes, green monkeys, and purple bunnies. Clay or baker's dough can be painted with tempera once it's dry.

Display Options:
Let the children make individual habitats in shoe boxes using construction paper, grass, sand, leaves, and twigs.

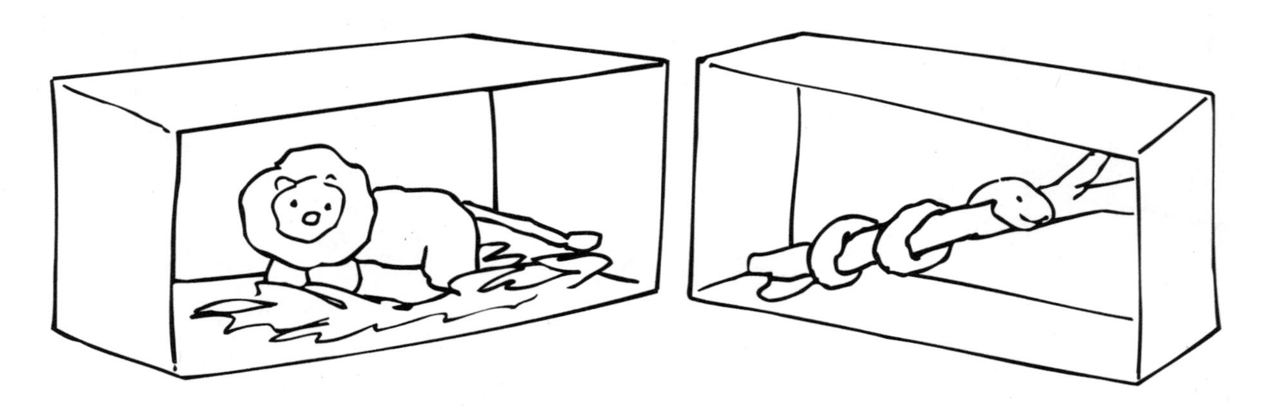

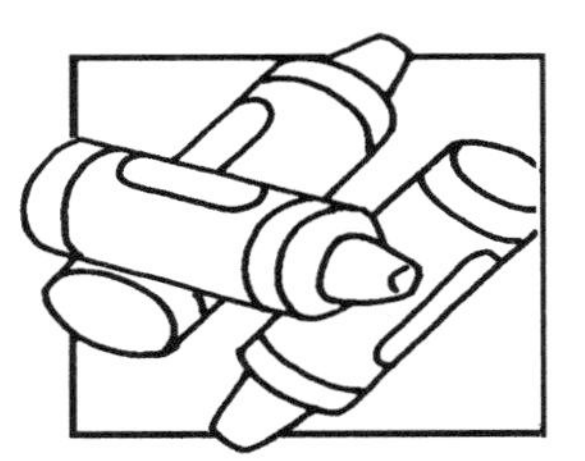

ANIMALS
Art Activities

CAROUSEL ANIMALS

Materials:
Carousel animal patterns (pp. 174-175), construction paper, scissors, tape, coffee filters, crayons, markers, glitter, glue, liquid watercolors, plastic eyedroppers

Directions:
1. Give each child a set of carousel animal patterns to color and cut out.
2. Have the children glue the patterns in any order on a piece of flat, colored construction paper.
3. Show the children how to roll the paper so that the ends meet and tape the edges so that the carousel stands up on one end. (See the illustration.)
4. Give each child a coffee filter, and show the children how to use the eyedroppers to drip liquid watercolors onto the filters.
5. When the filters are dry, have the children glue them to the top of the carousels for a canopy.

Option 1:
Let the children use tape to attach colorful curling ribbons to hang down the sides of the coffee filters for a festive look.

Option 2:
Have the children tape a straw to the back of each cut-out animal to represent carousel poles.

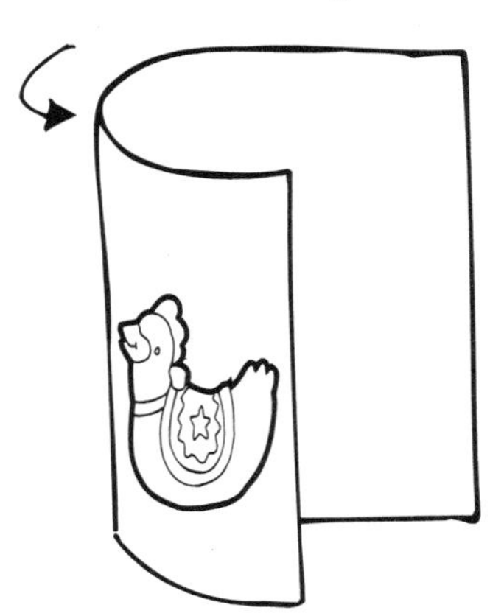

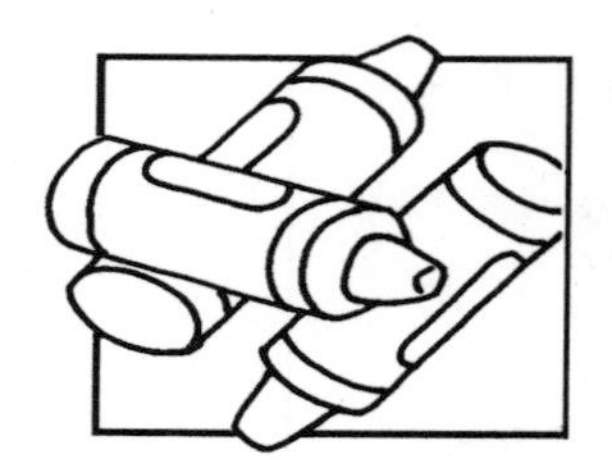

ANIMALS
Art Activities

FUNNY FARM!

Materials:
Popsicle sticks, flannel board patterns (pp. 183-185), barn patterns (p. 177), crayons or markers, empty shoe boxes (or other small boxes), empty canisters (oatmeal boxes, coffee cans, paper towel rolls, frozen-juice cans), scissors

Directions:
1. Duplicate a copy of the flannel board animal patterns for each child to color and cut out.
2. Give each child a barn pattern and box to decorate like a barn. The round canisters may be decorated as silos.
3. Let the children glue together Popsicle sticks for fences or animal pens.
4. The children can use their finished farms to recreate the original Old MacDonald song or the new version of it (p. 182).

Option 1:
Duplicate the animal patterns onto tagboard or cardboard and fold the edges to make the patterns stand up. Or tape children's finished paper animals onto cardboard for added stiffness.

Option 2:
Children can make a two-dimensional farm scene by coloring patterns and gluing them onto a background.

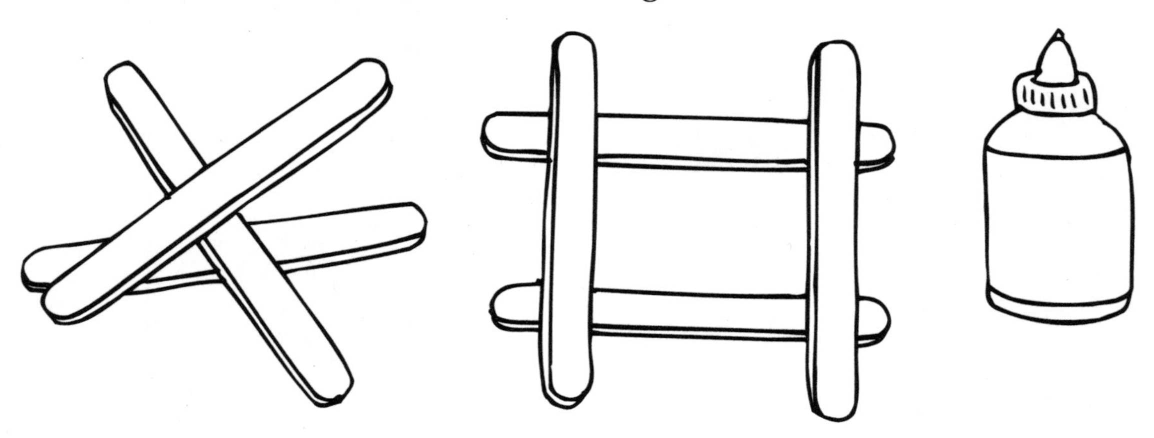

ANIMALS

Art Activities

PAPER BAG PARADE

Materials:
Large paper grocery bags with a rectangle cut out of the center for the face (one per child), tempera paints, brushes, scissors

Directions:
1. Have each child choose an animal to be in the parade. Help any children who are stuck for ideas. The children might pick an animal whose name begins with the same letter as their own name, for example, Catherine Cat, Tanya Tiger, Gregory Goldfish.
2. Give each child a paper grocery bag to decorate in the fashion of the chosen animal. (A tiger might have orange and black stripes and whiskers, a goldfish might have painted fins and bulging eyes.) Help children attach additions such as wings and tails.
3. Once the bags have dried, let the children slip them on to wear in the Paper Bag Parade. Have the children make the noises of their chosen animal on cue. You might ask all of the jungle animals to make noise at once, or all of the birds. Animals who don't make any sounds (fish, turtles, butterflies) could be allowed to create one.

Option:
Let the children use face paints to complete the costumes.

ANIMALS

Storytime

FEATURED PICTURE BOOK

***The First Song Ever Sung* by Laura Krauss Melmed, illustrated by Ed Young (Lothrop, 1993).**

A little boy wants to know what the first song ever sung was. He asks his relatives and he asks the animals. However, each time he repeats his question he receives a different answer. His father says it was a "man's song." His brother says it was a "proud song." The birds say it was a "wing song." Ultimately, the boy must decide for himself.

ART EXTENSION

Read this book with your children, pointing out the animals that hide in the designs in some of the pictures. Also have your children note the comparisons made between the world of humans and the world of nature: a spider web and a grandmother weaving.

Materials:

Construction paper in a variety of colors, crayons, watercolors, paintbrushes

Directions:

1. Have the children study the pictures in *The First Song Ever Sung*.
2. Then have them use crayons to draw pictures on construction paper. They can copy the theme of the book (animals and people), or draw simple shapes or designs. Encourage them to try to cover a lot of their page with the crayon picture.
3. Once they have finished, show the children how to use watercolors to paint over their crayon pictures. The result is a crayon-resist painting, and the pictures will resemble the ones in *The First Song Ever Sung*.
4. Post the dry pictures on an "Amazing Artists" bulletin board.

ANIMALS

Storytime

MORE PICTURE BOOKS

Along Came Toto by Anni Axworthy (Candlewick Press, 1993).
Percy, a dog, lived in a house all his own—that is, until Toto the kitten came along. Percy is none too pleased with the new arrival, until Toto helps him chase a bad dream away.

Animals Should Definitely Not Wear Clothing by Judi Barrett, illustrated by Ron Barrett (Atheneum, 1970).
The pictures in this book show what would happen if animals wore clothing: a porcupine in a dress would be disastrous, a camel wouldn't know how to wear a hat, and a snake would slide right out of its pants!

The Cat in the Hat by Dr. Seuss (Random House, 1957).
The Mess Fairy (see *Fritz and the Mess Fairy*, below) could take a lesson from Dr. Seuss' creative kitty, because the Cat in the Hat always picks up his playthings. (Sequel: *The Cat in the Hat Comes Back*.)

Crocodile Beat by Gail Jorgensen, illustrated by Patricia Mullins (Bradbury, 1989).
The brave lion king protects his friends from a mean and hungry crocodile in this colorful, magical book. Have children make the animal noises as they come up in the story.

Fritz and the Mess Fairy by Rosemary Wells (Dial, 1991).
Fritz is one messy badger, until his science experiment goes awry and he meets his match: the Mess Fairy. After a disastrous night of cleaning up after the fairy, Fritz decides to change his ways. Or to try, at least!

George and Martha Rise and Shine by James Marshall (Houghton Mifflin, 1976).
George and Martha are two hippos who are best friends, and their stories are sure to delight your students. (*George and Martha* and *George and Martha Encore* are in the same series.)

The Good-Night Kiss by Jim Aylesworth, illustrated by Walter Lyon Krudop (Atheneum, 1993).
"On the night of the good-night kiss" a string of animals observe each other, leading the reader from a frog in a lily pond to a snow-white moth at a window where a mother is kissing her child good night.

Have You Seen My Cat? by Eric Carle (Picture Book Studio, 1987).
A young boy searches for his missing cat. On his way, he meets a lion, a tiger, a cheetah, a puma, and many other "cats" that are not his. Finally, he finds his own cat . . . who has her own surprise for the boy.

Hey! Get Off Our Train! by John Burningham (Crown, 1989).
A little boy and his toy dog take a train trip through the night. On their journey, they rescue a variety of endangered species: an elephant, a seal, a crane, a tiger, and a polar bear. Each animal explains why it is in danger.

How the Rooster Saved the Day by Arnold Lobel, illustrated by Anita Lobel (Greenwillow, 1977).
A rooster is kidnapped, and unable to wake up the sun. Luckily, the brave and clever rooster is able to escape—and save the day!

ANIMALS

Storytime

Is Your Mama a Llama? by Deborah Guarino, illustrated by Steven Kellogg (Scholastic, 1989).
Lloyd asks all of his animal friends, "Is your mama a llama?" They answer with riddles describing their species. When he asks Llyn, she tells him of course, her mama's a llama. And he, of all llamas, should know that!

Max and Ruby's First Greek Myth: Pandora's Box by Rosemary Wells (Dial, 1993).
Ruby reads Max a story about Pandora. Of course, in Ruby's tale, Pandora is a little curious bunny (just like Max). Still, at the end of the tale, Max has some trouble figuring out the moral. (In the same series: *Max's Toys—A Counting Book, Max's New Suit, Max's Ride,* and *Max's First Word.*)

May I Bring a Friend? by Beatrice Schenk de Regniers (Atheneum, 1964).
When the King and Queen invite the narrator to bring a friend to tea, the young boy invites a giraffe, then a hippo, and then many monkeys! Children are sure to love the rhymes, as well as the idea of tea time at the zoo!

Moo, Baa, La La La by Sandra Boynton (Little Simon, 1982).
"A cow says moo. A sheep says baa. Three singing pigs say LA LA LA!" The author has also written *But Not the Hippopotamus, The Going to Bed Book,* and *Opposites* (all board books).

One Gaping Wide-Mouthed Hopping Frog by Leslie Tryon (Atheneum, 1993).
This counting book (to ten and back) is told in silly rhymes and delightful pictures. (Also by the author: *Albert's Alphabet* and *Albert's Play.*)

One Was Johnny by Maurice Sendak (HarperTrophy, 1962).
"One was Johnny who lived by himself." That is, until a troop of animals make themselves comfortable in his tiny home. Read this counting book and then play the song from "Really Rosie."

Six-Dinner Sid by Inga Moore (Simon & Schuster, 1991).
Six-Dinner Sid is a black cat who has six homes, six names, and six meals a night—until his many owners get together and cut him down to one dinner a day.

Would You Rather . . . by John Burningham (HarperCollins, 1978).
This book poses questions that children will enjoy answering. "Would you rather an elephant drank your bath water, an eagle stole your dinner, a pig tried on your clothes, or a hippo slept in your bed?"

ANIMALS

Flannel Board

OLD MACDONALD'S FUNNY FARM

Old MacDonald had a farm,
You've heard this song before.
But when Mac left his animals,
They snuck right in the door.
The **cows** took baths,
The **calves** baked cakes,
Taking baths, baking cakes,
What a mess those cows did make!
Old MacDonald's animals
Were silly as can be!

When MacDonald drove back home
The farm was such a mess.
The animals were in his house,
The **pig** had on a dress!
The pig wore clothes,
The **cats** wore hats,
Wearing clothes, wearing hats,
What a sight for poor Old Mac!
Old MacDonald's animals
Were funny as can be!

Old MacDonald said, "Oh, well,
I guess you all can stay.
It seems you like the house so much,
So why don't we all play."
The **horse** played horn,
And the **sheep** danced jigs,
Playing horn, dancing jigs,
Don't forget the cows and pigs!
Old MacDonald and his pals
Are happy as can be!

ANIMALS

Discovery

DRAWING FROM LIFE

Representational drawing builds observation skills. Children may notice new things about the classroom pet that have gone unobserved for the entire year.

Materials:
Classroom pet (silkworm, bunny, fish, guinea pig, bird, turtle, ant farm), magnifying glasses, white drawing paper, pencils or black pens

Note:
If your class doesn't have a pet, arrange for a student to bring one from home.

Directions:
1. Place the pet's cage or bowl in the middle of a table and have the children observe the animal. Pets can even be observed close up by using magnifying glasses. Note: If the children have trouble observing, help them by asking questions about the animal being studied. Have the children look at the shape of the ears, at the beak, fins, tail, fur, scales, legs, and so on.
2. Provide drawing paper and pens or pencils for children to use to make simple line drawings of the pet.

Option:
Have children add color to their finished drawings with pastels or colored pencils.

ANIMALS

Discovery

READ AND COMPARE

Materials: factual books on real animals, picture books about the same animals (see "More Picture Books," pp. 180-181).

Directions:

1. Read the children a picture book that has animals as the main characters. Often the animals talk and wear clothing like people.
2. Read to the children from a factual book about the real animals of the same species.
3. Have the children think about the differences in the two books. Ask the following questions: In the first book, did the characters have to be that type of animal? Could the characters have been any animal, or even people? How was the second book different? Did the animals in the two books look different or act different? Did they talk or make sounds?

ANIMALS

Discovery

ANIMAL SURVEY

Have a few children at a time be "interviewers" while the others work on different projects. Later, let the children switch.

Materials:

Survey pattern (p. 189), clipboards (or heavy cardboard and tape), crayons

Directions:

1. Give each child a crayon and a survey sheet attached to a clipboard or taped to a piece of cardboard (so they can write as they move around the room).
2. Help each child arrive at a "yes" or "no" question for his or her survey, e.g., "Do you have a pet?" or "Do you like cats?"
3. Write each child's question in the box at the top of the survey sheet.
4. Show the children how to make marks in the answer columns.
5. Have the children approach their classmates, ask their question, and then mark the appropriate column. Ahead of time, you might want to designate a certain number of children each survey taker should interview.
6. Help the children tally their results to find out statistics about their friends. For example, they may learn that everyone likes rabbits, or only three people own birds.
7. Compile the finished survey sheets in an "Animal Survey Book" for your class.

Name ____________________

ANIMAL SURVEY

Question ?

Yes	No

ANIMALS

Class Project

ANIMAL FAIR

Set up an animal fair on the tables in your classroom using the completed projects from this animal unit: carousel animals, clay creatures in their habitats, and funny farms. Post the "Drawing from Life" pictures on a bulletin board as a background display.

Have the children line up for a parade wearing their paper bag costumes. You might want to have the parade for parents or for other classrooms. Give each child a ribbon for participating, noting something special about the child's animal costume: Sarah's Silly Snake, Catherine's Colorful Chameleon, Tanya's Toothy Tyrannosaurus.

Play animal charades, with each child acting out an animal for the rest of the class. You can have the children pick an animal picture (from the animal family cards on pp. 192-193) to act out. Or let the children choose for themselves. Hint: Have the child act out an animal's behavior first. If the rest of the class can't guess it, let the child add that animal's sounds.

Set up a game corner in the classroom where children can play "Pin the Tail on the What?" (p. 191), and "Animal Families" (p. 191).

Place an assortment of animal books in the book corner for children to "read" or look at the pictures.

A fair is a perfect time for face painting. Designate one area as the face painting section, and provide a supply of paints and mirrors for children to use to turn themselves (and each other) into all sorts of animals!

Play "Would You Like to Swing on a Star" or "At the Zoo" (Simon and Garfunkle).

ANIMALS
Games

ANIMAL FAMILIES

Materials:
Animal family cards (pp. 192-193), scissors

Directions:
1. Duplicate the animal family cards, laminate, and cut them out.
2. Have the children lay out all the cards face up and try to match the baby animals with the adults.
3. Once the children have matched all of the cards and are familiar with the pictures, they can play "Animal Concentration." Have them turn the cards face down and take turns flipping two cards over at a time, trying to make matches.

PIN THE TAIL ON THE WHAT?

Materials:
Animal patterns (pp. 194-195), crayons, ribbons, tape, stickers, scissors, construction paper, glue

Directions:
1. Enlarge the animal patterns and cut out.
2. Cut the animals on the lines and put the heads in one pile, middles in another, and ends in a third.
3. Give each child a piece of construction paper to use as a base. Let the children create imaginary animals by choosing a head, middle, and end from each pile and gluing them together.
4. Let the children color in their creatures.
5. Use the crazy creatures to play the game as you'd play "Pin the Tail on the Donkey." (You can use ribbons with a piece of tape for the tail, or stickers.)

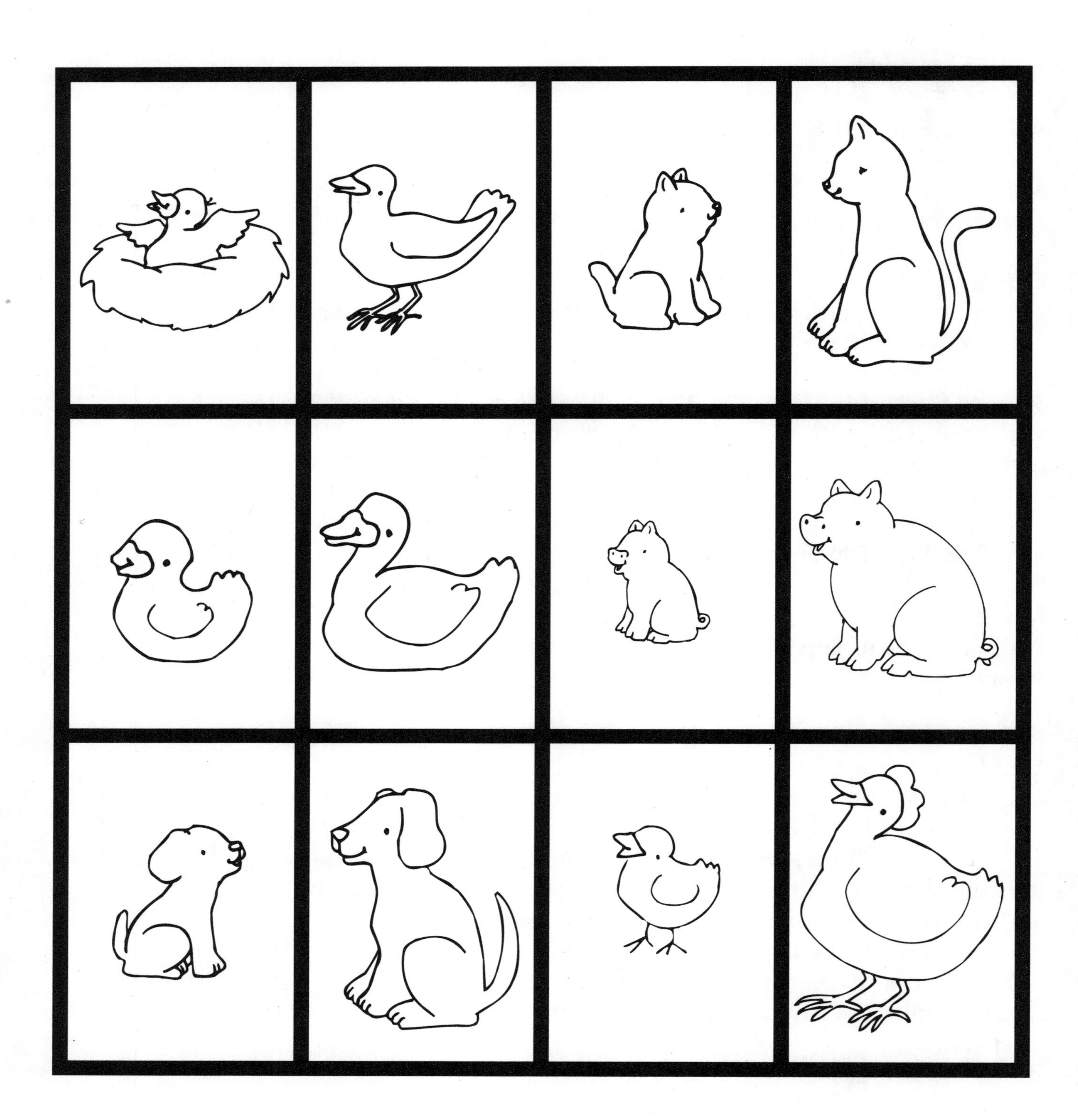

ANIMALS

Songs

Kangaroos
(to the tune of "Jingle Bells")

Kangaroos, elephants, manatees, and whales,
Angelfish and llamas, ostriches and snails.
They have one thing in common,
Now guess it if you can.
They all share planet Earth with an animal called man.

So let's all lend a hand,
And keep this planet safe,
We want to share our land
With each animal and race.

Now take a look around
And hold each other's hand.
Isn't that a pretty sound?
Peace rings across the land!

(chorus)

ANIMALS
Mother Goose

There Were Two Blackbirds
There were two blackbirds
Sitting on a hill;
One named Jack,
The other named Jill.
Fly away, Jack! Fly away, Jill!
Come again, Jack! Come again, Jill!

Bell Horses
Bell horses, bell horses,
What time of day?
One o'clock, two o'clock,
Off and away!

Goosey, Goosey Gander
Goosey, goosey gander,
Whither dost thou wander?
Upstairs, downstairs,
In my lady's chamber.

Hickory, Dickory, Dock!
Hickory, dickory, dock!
The mouse ran up the clock.
The clock struck one,
The mouse ran down,
Hickory, dickory, dock!

Ride a Cock-Horse
Ride a cock-horse to Banbury Cross,
To see a fine lady upon a white horse.
Rings on her fingers and bells on her toes,
She shall have music wherever she goes.

Leg Over Leg
Leg over leg,
As the dog went to Dover;
When he came to a stile,
Hop, he went over.

ANIMALS

Mother Goose

Pussy Cat

Pussy cat, pussy cat, where have you been?
I've been to London to visit the queen.
Pussy cat, pussy cat, what did you there?
I frightened a little mouse under her chair.

Hickety, Pickety

Hickety, pickety, my black hen,
She lays eggs for gentlemen;
Gentlemen come every day
To see what my black hen doth lay.
Sometimes nine and sometimes ten,
Hickety, pickety, my black hen.

I Love Little Pussy

I love little pussy,
Her coat is so warm,
And if I don't hurt her,
She'll do me no harm.
So I'll not pull her tail,
Nor drive her away,
But pussy and I
Very gently will play.

Of All the Gay Birds That E'er I Did See

Of all the gay birds that e'er I did see,
The owl is the fairest by far to me:
For all the day long she sits in a tree,
And when the night comes away flies she.

The Cock Doth Crow

The cock doth crow
To let you know:
If you be wise
'Tis time to rise.

A Wise Old Owl

A wise old owl lived in an oak;
The more he saw the less he spoke;
The less he spoke the more he heard.
Why can't we all be like that wise old bird?

ANIMALS

Snacks

ANIMALS ON PARADE

Animal crackers are always a hit—and this snack makes eating them extra fun!

Ingredients:
Animal crackers, waxed paper, peanut butter, jelly

Directions:
1. Let the children line up their animal crackers on waxed paper.
2. Provide small containers of jelly and peanut butter and rounded plastic knives for children to use to make mini PB & J cracker sandwiches.
3. Children can create either open-faced or closed sandwiches.

SIX-DINNER SID'S SUPER SUPPER!

Six-Dinner Sid, the cat in Inga Moore's book of the same name (Simon & Schuster, 1991), eats six meals a night: chicken, fish, liver, etc. In his honor, set up a six-choice buffet-style table for children to choose from.

Ingredients:
Buffet dishes could include: fruit salad, mini-muffins, yogurt or cottage cheese, celery and carrot sticks, crackers with cheese, raisins

Directions:
1. Place the buffet dishes on a long, low table with small paper plates at one end.
2. Let children choose which snacks they would like from the six offered.
3. Once they've chosen, have them take their plates back to their seats to eat.

Note:
You might want to limit quantities if your children aren't used to "buffet snacks."

ANIMALS

Letter Home

Wouldn't it be funny?
Wouldn't it now . . .
If the dog said, "Moo-oo,"
And the cow said, "Bow-wow"?
If the cat sang and whistled,
And the bird said, "Mia-ow"?
Wouldn't it be funny?
Wouldn't it now?
- -Mother Goose

This month we are celebrating animals. We will be reading about The Cat in the Hat, who makes a mess but always cleans up his playthings. And we will be eating a buffet in honor of Six-Dinner Sid (a cat in Inga Moore's storybook of the same name).

In art, we will be creating an assortment of creatures to display in a "Natural Habitat" exhibit, which you will be invited to visit. We would like to invite bird watchers, veterinarians, and zoologists to come and speak, as well as anyone with a friendly pet he or she would like to share.

We need:

- shoe boxes
- empty canisters (coffee and oatmeal)

Thank you for your help!

April: Earth

This unit celebrates the earth—with a special focus on recycling activities. Many young children are fascinated by recycling and by the trucks that come to pick up trash. Build on this fascination by starting a recycling program in your classroom (and in your school)! Introduce children to earth awareness by reading *Mother Earth* by Nancy Luenn, illustrated by Neil Waldman (Atheneum, 1992), and follow up with the suggested art activity (p. 206). Then explore deserts, mountains, meadows, and rain forests through the activities in this chapter. And don't forget Earth Day, April 22nd.

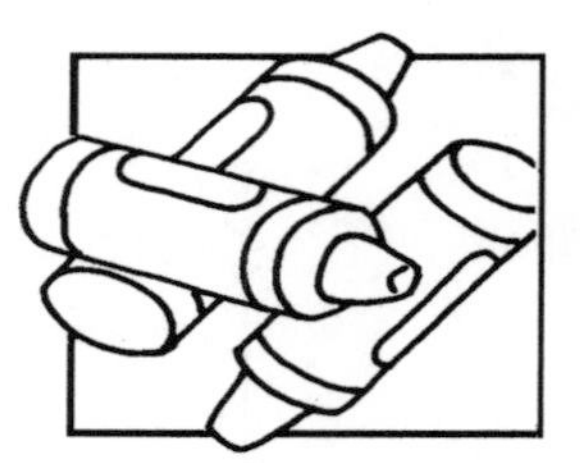

EARTH

Art Activities

DESERT DUNES

Sand painting is an ancient Native American art form that produces dramatic, textured pictures. Using a variety of colored sands lends extra beauty to the finished products.

Materials:

Sand, paper in neutral colors (white, tan, brown, or black), powdered tempera in a variety of colors, see-through plastic cups, glue in squeeze bottles (or small containers of glue and brushes), newspaper

Directions:

1. Mix cups of sand with different colors of powdered tempera to make colored sand. (Or use pre-bought colored sand products, available at art supply stores.)
2. Display the sand in see-through plastic cups so that children can see the different colors available for them to use.
3. Have children make designs on their papers with glue. Squeeze bottles will produce thin lines; brushes will make thicker lines.
4. Show the children how to sprinkle the sand onto the paper, and then shake off the excess over newspaper spread on the table.
5. Post the completed pictures on a "Desert Dunes" bulletin board.

Option:

Give each child a sheet of desert animal patterns (p. 203) to color, cut out, and glue to the desert scenes.

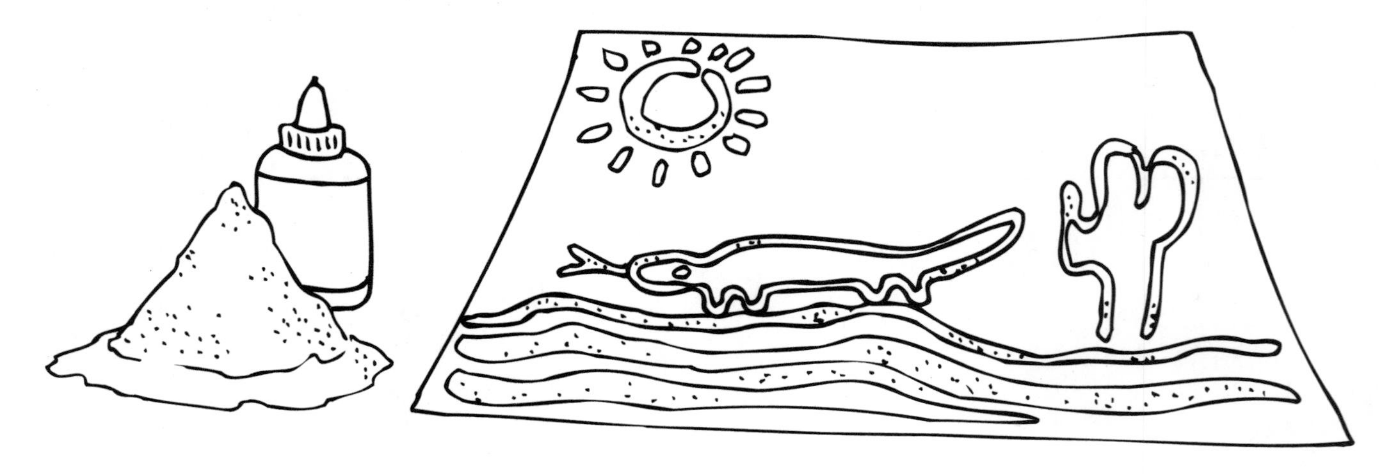

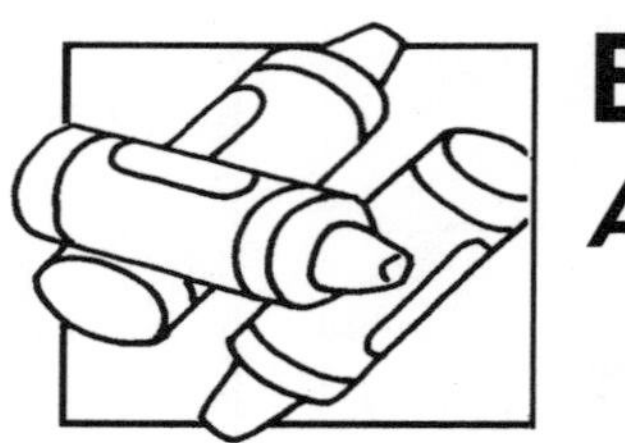

EARTH

Art Activities

MAKING MOUNTAINS

Children will feel very powerful as they make their own mountains! Provide a variety of small plastic animals (rams, deer, mountain lions) for children to play with among their finished mountain ranges.

Materials:

Cone-shaped paper cups (or cones made from construction paper rolled and stapled along the side), tempera paint (brown, white, green), brushes, glitter (silver or white), pebbles, shiny rocks, tiny leaves, glue, poster board squares

Directions:

1. Give each child two or three paper cups to glue onto poster board to create a mountain range.
2. Let the children paint their cone mountains with tempera paint.
3. The children can glue pebbles, shiny rocks (see p. 162), and small leaves to their mountains. For snow, they can dot glue along the tops of the mountains and then sprinkle on glitter. Or they can dribble white tempera paint across the tops of the mountains (using small containers to hold the paint).

Option:

Children can add icy lakes by gluing small circles of tinfoil in between the cone-shaped mountains. Squiggles of blue yarn or ribbon can become rivers that wind up and over the mountains.

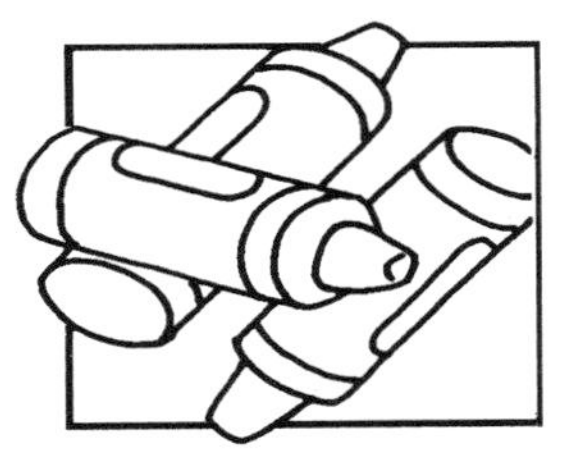

EARTH
Art Activities

CREATING A CANOPY

The top of the rain forest is called the canopy. Create a canopy replica with your children using recycled manila folders.

Materials:
Large cardboard box, old manila folders, leaf patterns (p. 96), tempera paint (different shades of green and brown), brushes, crayons, scissors, glue

Directions:
1. Read a rain forest book to your children, such as *The Great Kapok Tree* by Lynn Cherry (Harcourt Brace, 1990).
2. Explain that rain forests have different levels. The top layer is called the "canopy," followed by the middle layer and the bottom layer. The bottom layer, called the "understory," is made up of shrubs and herbs.
3. Turn the box on one side (with the opening facing out) and help the children make a rain forest canopy by gluing the manila folders to the top, spines pointed up. (See the illustration.)
4. Give each child a leaf pattern to color with crayon or tempera paint and cut out. When all of the leaves have been decorated, the children can glue them to the folders.
5. The finished "canopy" can be displayed on a table. Use the box to shelve books about the earth and the environment.

Option:
Children can paint tree trunks on the sides of the box using brown tempera paint.

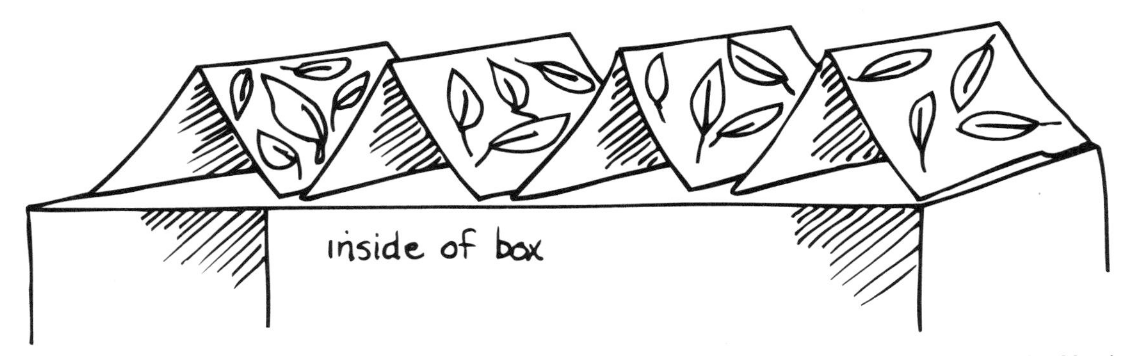

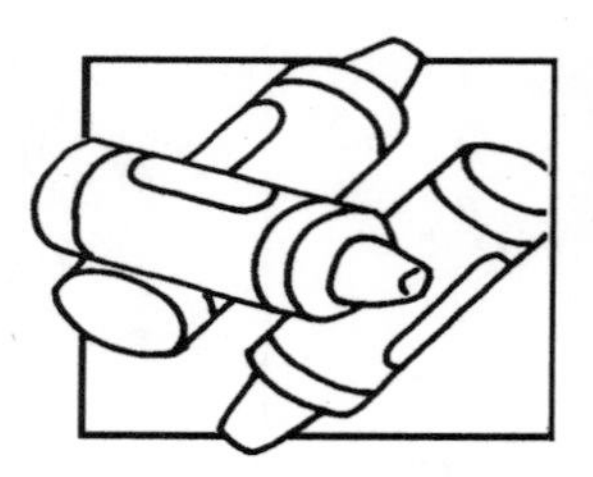

EARTH

Art Activities

MOTHER EARTH MURAL

Sing "We've Got the Whole Earth in Our Hands" (p. 227) before embarking on this project. Soon you'll have the whole earth in your classroom!

Materials:

Large round piece of poster board, leaves, pebbles, dried grass, glue, animal patterns (pp. 192-193), ocean patterns (p. 239), people patterns (p. 41), crayons, tempera paint (blue and green), brushes, scissors, white paper, marker

Directions:

1. Read *Mother Earth* by Nancy Luenn, illustrated by Neil Waldman (Atheneum, 1992) to your class.
2. Discuss the imagery in the book, including the concept that the natural world is an extension of the living body of Mother Earth ("trees and plants her living hair," and fish and ocean creatures "her dreams").
3. Let the children use a variety of art media to create a mural on poster board representing the images in the book. If possible, let them collect fallen leaves, pebbles, and dried grass to glue to the board. Or they can color and cut out various patterns to glue, as well. Provide a variety of colored tempera paint for the background.
4. Ask the children to describe the different parts of the poster to you, and transcribe their words. Write down the quotes on small pieces of white paper to pin up next to the finished poster.

Option:

If you have a globe in your classroom, use it to discuss the shape of the earth. Have the children notice that the globe is round, like the earth.

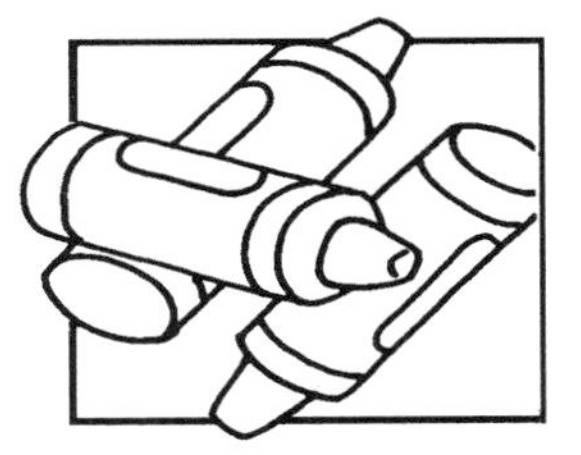

EARTH

Art Activities

OVER IN THE MEADOW

Read *Over in the Meadow* by John Langstaff, illustrated by Feodor Rojankovsky (Harcourt Brace Jovanovich, 1957). Then let the children create their own meadows.

Materials:
Construction paper, meadow patterns (1 per child; p. 208), scissors, glue, crayons, dried grass

Directions:
1. Give each child a piece of paper for a meadow and a page of meadow patterns to color and cut out.
2. Let the children create a meadow using dried grass and crayons. They can glue their meadow patterns onto the paper in the configuration of the story, or in any order they wish.
3. Post the finished patterns on an "Over in Our Meadow" bulletin board. Ask the children to name their meadows, and write the names on pieces of paper to pin next to the pictures.

EARTH

Storytime

FEATURED PICTURE BOOK

On the Day You Were Born **by Debra Frasier (Harcourt, 1991).**
This story describes a series of amazing events that took place on the eve of the reader's birth and then on the actual day of the birth. It says that the animals, earth, sun, and moon all prepared themselves for the marvelous arrival. This book will make children feel connected to their world in a powerful way, part of the family of animals and people, and related to the entire universe.

ART EXTENSION

Read this book with your students, showing them the colorful pictures. Let the children try to find the human figure who dances through most of the pages. Ask the students what kinds of materials they would use to make these types of pictures. Encourage creative responses!

Materials:
Stencil patterns (p. 210), tagboard, craft knife, white paper, tempera paints, paintbrushes, writing paper, pen

Directions:
1. Make stencils by copying the patterns onto tagboard and cutting out the objects. Children can use either the cut-out object or the tagboard outline.
2. Show children how to place a stencil on their paper and then paint over it. The result will be a solid figure (if they use the tagboard outline) or an outlined figure (if they use the cut-out object).
3. Let children continue to paint using a variety of stencils and colors of paint.
4. If children want, let them describe their picture to you, and transcribe their words on a separate piece of paper.
5. Post the pictures and descriptions on a "Super Stencil" bulletin board.

EARTH

Storytime

MORE PICTURE BOOKS

Burnie's Hill illustrated by Erik Blegvad (William Collins Sons, 1977).
This Mother Goose rhyme is beautifully illustrated, from the field of golden flowers that look like coins to the sun high up in the sky.

Coyote Dreams by Susan Nunes, illustrated by Ronald Himler (Atheneum, 1988).
When coyotes howl at the moonlight, they bring a whole desert world, and the normal world of people disappears. "Lizards, bats, and mountain cats . . . rocks, caves, and silver hills, moonlight on a buzzard's wings. These are what coyotes bring." The verse may well replace counting sheep when trying to sleep!

Dinosaurs and All That Rubbish by Michael Foreman (Thomas Y. Crowell, 1972).
While a factory owner is off visiting a distant star, dinosaurs wake up on earth to find that it is completely covered in rubbish. They clean the place up, and when the factory owner returns, he doesn't recognize the planet; it's so much cleaner and prettier.

The First Forest by John Gile, illustrated by Tom Heflin (1989).
The Tree Maker made the first trees ever. He helped the trees learn how to grow, and let them choose what type of tree they wanted to be. This story tells one version of why some trees lose their leaves in the fall.

The Great Kapok Tree by Lynne Cherry (Harcourt, 1990).
A man begins to chop down a great kapok tree in the middle of the rain forest. But soon he grows tired and goes to sleep at the base of the tree. While he sleeps, the many rain forest animals who live in the tree come and whisper to the man many reasons why he should not cut down the kapok tree.

Little Fox Goes to the End of the World by Ann Tompert, illustrated by John Wallner (Crown, 1976).
When Little Fox gets tired catching butterflies, she tells her mother that some day she will travel to the end of the world. Then she describes her future trip, traveling through a forest, over snow-covered mountains, across a hot desert, through treacherous rivers, and by an island of one-eyed cats!

The Little Island by Golden MacDonald, illustrated by Leonard Weisgard (Doubleday, 1946).
Life changes on the little island as the seasons go by. Animals come in the spring to have their babies. The summer brings other visitors, including a black kitten on a boat. Autumn and winter bring cold and snow. The little island is glad to be "a part of the world and a world of its own all surrounded by the bright blue sea." Caldecott Medal winner for 1947.

Over in the Meadow by John Langstaff, illustrated by Feodor Rojankovsky (Harcourt Brace Jovanovich, 1957).
There are many kinds of animals living in the meadow, from turtles to robins to beavers. The song and sheet music are included in the back of this Parents' Choice Honors book.

A River Ran Wild by Lynne Cherry (Harcourt, 1992).
This book follows the Nash-a-way River through six centuries, beginning when its waters were clear enough to merit the Native American name that means "River with the Pebbled Bottom." But as settlers arrive, and then factories and pollution, the river is no longer clean and clear. Luckily, environmentalists take notice and work to make the river healthy again.

EARTH

Flannel Board

WHAT'S UP, PUSSYCAT?

Pussycat, Pussycat, where have you been?
There's ice on your whiskers , and snow on your chin!

I've been out hiking up **mountains** and hills—
But the cold, icy snowflakes soon gave me the chills!

Pussycat, Pussycat, where did you go,
When you wanted to leave all the cold, icy snow?

I changed directions and went to the **sea**,
Where the hot summer sun made me purr happily.

Pussycat, Pussycat, how was your trip?
After the beach did you go on a **ship**?

I took a boat to a land far away,
Where a **volcano** shoots out hot lava all day!

Pussycat, Pussycat, what did you see
When you left the volcano and came home to me?

I went by **deserts** all covered with sand,
I went by **meadows** of grass-covered land,
I went by **forests** of tall, mighty trees,
I went by **islands** surrounded by seas.
I went by **cities** with buildings so high
That some of them seemed to go up to the sky.
I went by oceans, and played in the foam—
And when I'd seen it all, then I found my way **home**.

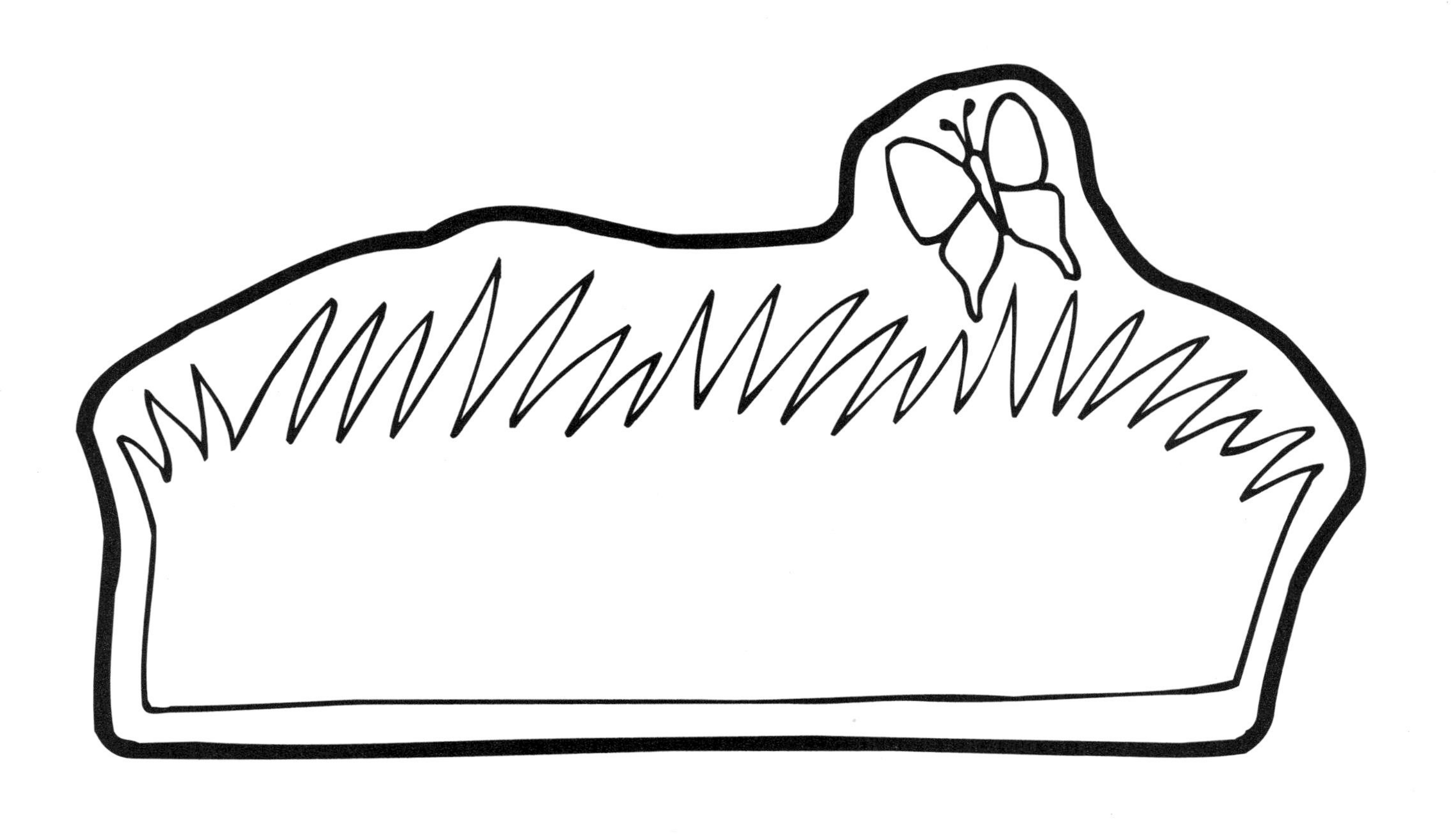

EARTH

Discovery

SHAKE IT UP!

Materials:
Large sheet, table, small table blocks, small doll house figures or plastic animals

Directions:
1. Spread the sheet on a table.
2. Have the children build a city using the blocks and figures.
3. When the city has been built—or after a designated period of time—call out "Earthquake!" Everyone holds onto the sheet and shakes it gently so that the buildings fall down.
4. Let the children rebuild for a little while, and then have another "Earthquake!"

Note:
In some states, law requires schools to have earthquake drills. This is a great activity to prepare students for the drills.

TIDAL WAVE!

Materials:
Water table, small plastic boats

Directions:
1. Have the children play with the boats at the water table.
2. Tell them, "News flash! A tidal wave is coming!"
3. Have the children dock their boats and then tip the water table up and gently set it back down to create a slow "wave."
4. Let the children watch the water until it becomes calm and safe enough for their boats to be brought out again.

EARTH

Discovery

PLAYGROUND SCAVENGER HUNT

The object of this hunt is to observe and become aware of natural beauty. Remind your children that living things should stay in their environment and continue to grow.

Materials:
Oak tag, Contact paper, scavenger patterns (p. 219), crayons, glue, scissors

Directions:
1. Decide which scavenger patterns work for your playground.
2. Duplicate these patterns and give them to the children to color with crayons.
3. Glue four or five patterns onto sheets of oak tag and laminate or cover with Contact paper. Make enough oak tag sheets so that each group of four children will have one.
4. Divide the children into groups of four and give each group a scavenger hunt sheet. Tell the children to go into the playground (or nearby park) and look for each item on the sheet. They only need to spot the items, not collect them.

Option 1:
Make different configurations of the patterns and use the sheets to play Bingo.

Option 2:
Give each child a scavenger pattern page. Have the children color or check off only the patterns representing items that they find in the playground.

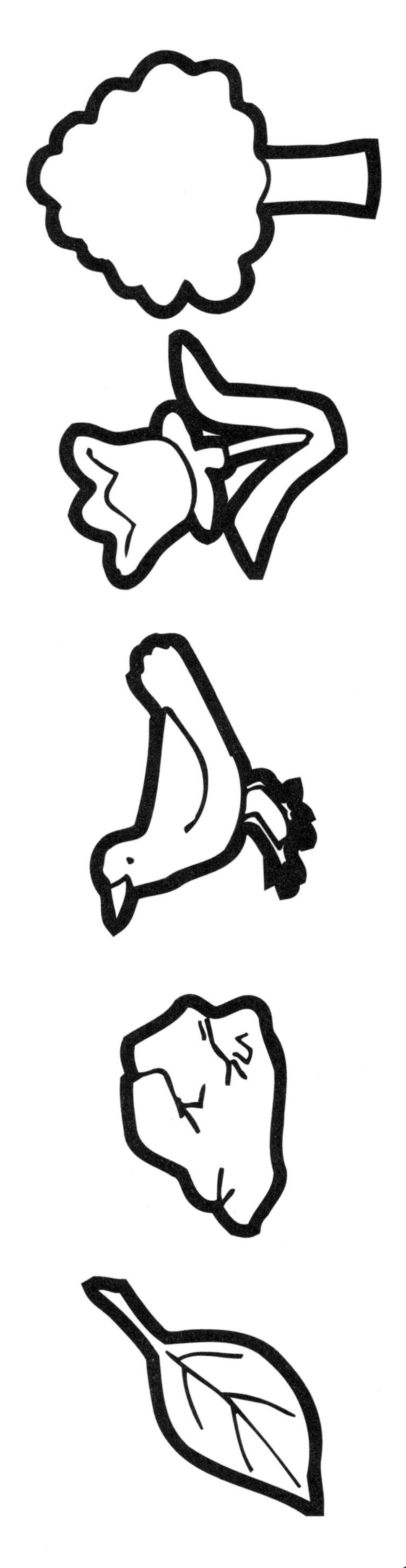

1
2
3
4
5
6
7
8
9
10

EARTH
Discovery

RECYCLING BINS

Introduce this project by reading a book about recycling to your students. Then ask if any of the children recycle at home, and let them tell the class about what their families do.

Materials:
Three cardboard boxes, Contact paper, recycling patterns (p. 221), crayons, scissors, glue

Directions:
1. Give each child a set of recycling patterns to color and cut out.
2. Label the boxes "glass and plastics," "cans," and "paper." Let the children work together to glue the patterns onto the cardboard boxes.
3. Discuss what types of items are okay to put in each box—get the guidelines from your city's recycling center. Make a collage of the types of items that are okay to go in each box.
4. Cover the boxes with Contact paper after decorating.
5. If your school's recyclables are picked up, let the children watch the recycling truck retrieve them. Otherwise, arrange for the recycled items to be taken to a recycling center.

Option:
Begin a school-wide recycling awareness program. Have your students display their recycling boxes for other classes to see.

Note:
In your classroom, you may just produce paper waste to be recycled. Find out which kinds of paper will be collected, and make a "touch and feel" collage of the things that do and don't go in the recycling box.

Recycling Book:
Recycle! A Handbook for Kids by Gail Gibbons (Little, 1992).
This factual book follows and explains the recycling process from start to finish. The book deals with five different types of garbage that can be recycled: aluminum cans, glass, paper, plastic, and polystyrene.

MILK

SOUP

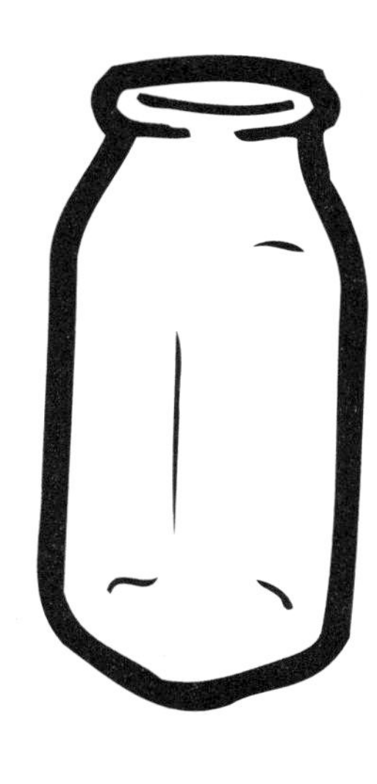

Juice

EARTH

Discovery

THIS ISLAND IS MY LAND

Have the children imagine visiting an island in the middle of the ocean. Ask them what they would like to have with them, and what they think they would need to survive.

Materials:
Paper plates, clay or baker's dough, leaves, sticks, branches, tempera paint, brushes, plastic animals and figures

Directions:
1. Give each child a paper plate with a large piece of clay or baker's dough.
2. Have the children form the clay into the shape of their island. Remind the children that they can build valleys, cliffs, and so on.
3. After the islands have dried, provide materials for the children to use to decorate and paint their islands.
4. Children can use plastic animals and figures to populate their islands.

EARTH

Class Project

THE WHOLE WORLD IN OUR CLASS

This month, the children in your class have learned about many terrains, climates, and environments. Using their acquired knowledge and the creative skills they practiced in the "Art" and "Discovery" projects, the children can assemble a large topographical map of a real or imagined world.

Choose a large table or floor area for the workspace. Add a large piece of cardboard, poster board, or foam core for the base. Discuss with your class the different projects they've created in this unit, including, "Making Mountains," "This Island Is My Land," and "Desert Dunes." Then help the children plan and map out where they'd like the different areas to be on their map: the mountains, deserts, oceans, rivers, and meadows.

The children can place existing works on the base (such as the paper cone mountains and paper plate islands) or build new ones for this project. They can also use tempera paint to connect the areas as in the "Mother Earth Mural."

Some ideas:

- Colored sand glued to the board for deserts
- Blue yarn or ribbon (or blue gel toothpaste) squiggles for rivers
- Paper cone cups glued upside down for mountains
- Paper towel tubes with crumpled green construction paper glued to the top for trees
- Milk carton houses (see "Homes," p. 116) for cities
- Blue tempera paint ocean waves with glitter foam (see "Ocean," p. 232)
- Dried grass glued on for meadows

Provide plenty of small boxes, empty containers, glue, construction paper, and decorations for children to experiment with while building their topographical map. During its creation, play "earth" music, such as *A Month in the Brazilian Rainforest* (Rykodisc, 1990) or "Rocky Mountain High" by John Denver.

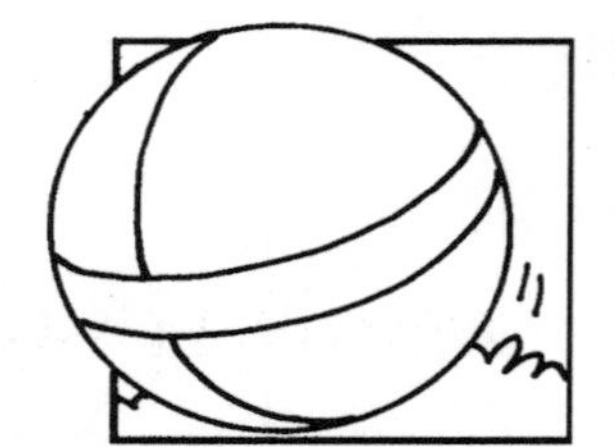

EARTH

Games

AROUND THE WORLD

Play this game with your class after doing the "What's Up, Pussycat?" flannel board (p. 212).

Directions:

1. Designate different areas in your yard as different environments. For example, the sandbox could be a desert, a big tree could be a forest, the water table could be the ocean, a grassy area could be a meadow, and so on.
2. Remind your class of the pussycat who traveled around the world. Tell the children that they will all be traveling pussycats for this game.
3. Have children go through a type of obstacle course, telling them to run to the "desert," hop to the "forest," skip to the "ocean," and then come back to you. Set up different routes for the children to "travel."

ECO-LAND

This board game teaches about the earth's different environments as well as a variety of natural occurrences.

Materials:

Game board (p. 225), pussycat markers (p. 226), dice

Directions:

1. Enlarge the game board, duplicate, and laminate it.
2. Have the children roll the dice and move forward on the game board. Play this game with the children at first, reading the instruction squares on the board out loud when a child lands on one.
3. After the children are used to the pictures on the board, they will be able to play the game themselves.
4. Duplicate enough game boards for each child to have one to color and take home to play.

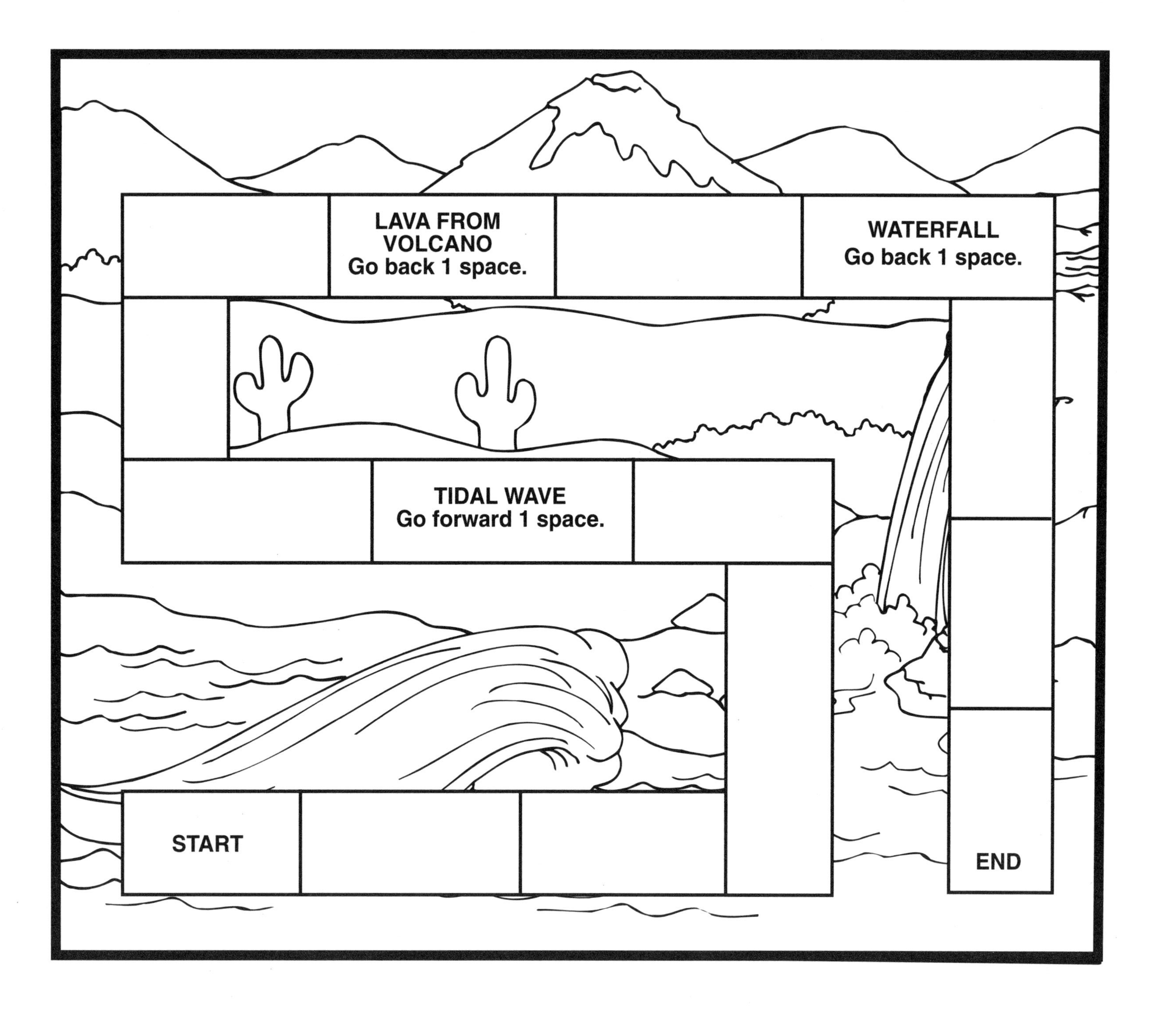
START
TIDAL WAVE
Go forward 1 space.
LAVA FROM
VOLCANO
Go back 1 space.
WATERFALL
Go back 1 space.
END

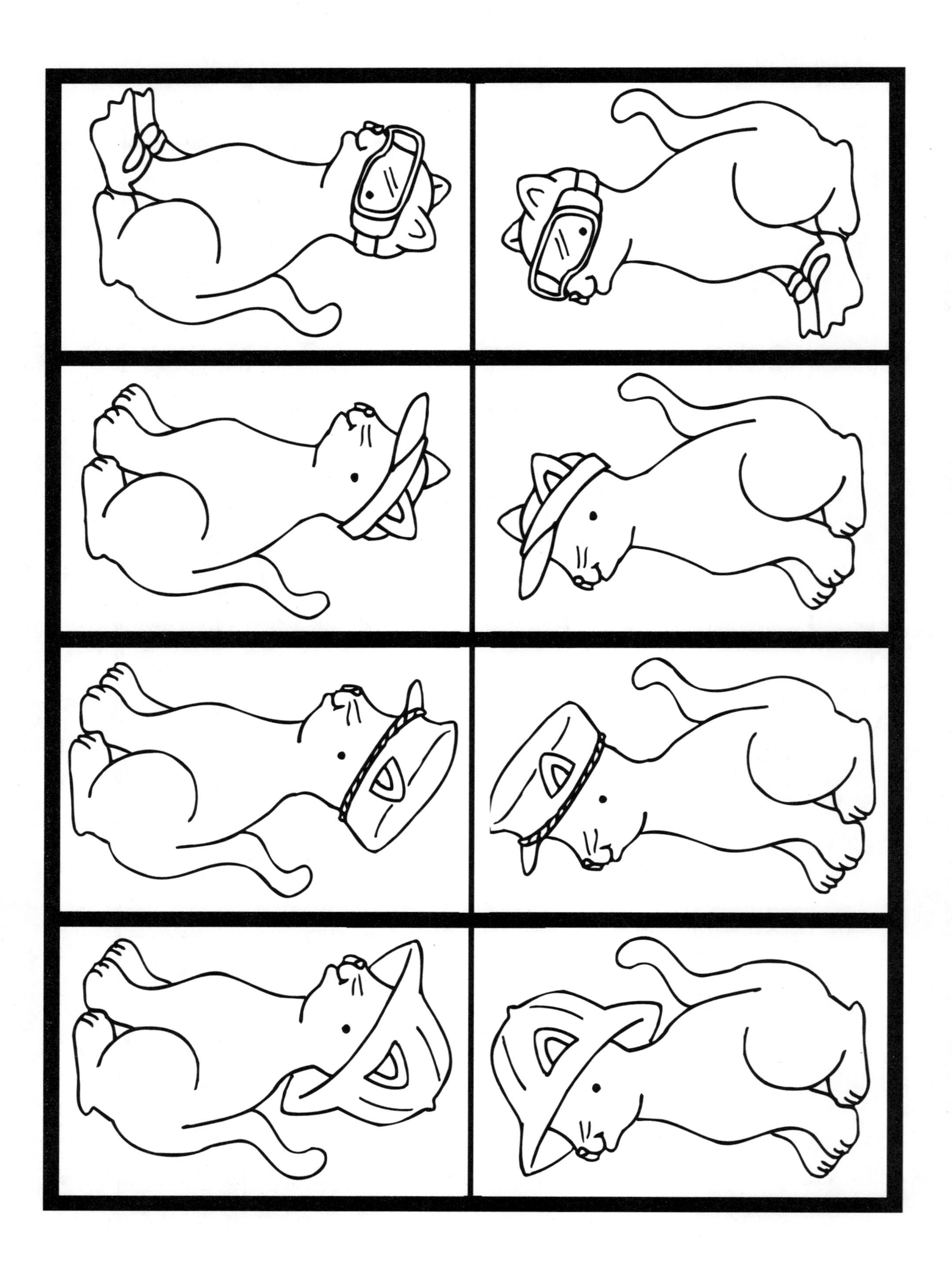

EARTH
Songs

Boom, Boom, Went the Mighty Volcano!
(to the tune of "Boom, Boom, Ain't It Great to be Crazy")

Boom, boom, went the mighty volcano!
Boom, boom, and the lava came down—
Orange and yellow and fiery hot—
Boom, boom, went the mighty volcano!

The South Pole's Cold
(to the tune of "The Ants Go Marching One By One")

The South Pole is the coldest spot on earth,
  On earth,
The South Pole is the coldest spot on earth,
  On earth.
The South Pole is the coldest spot,
Even in summer it won't get hot,
The South Pole's never hot,
  No, it's not,
It's just cold, cold, cold, cold.

We've Got the Whole Earth in Our Hands
(to the tune of "He's Got the Whole World in His Hands")

We've got the deserts and the jungles in our hands.
We've got the forests and the meadows in our hands.
We've got the oceans and the rivers in our hands.
We've got the whole earth in our hands.

Continue using the names of children in your class, for example:
We've got Catherine and Geoffrey in our hands,
We've got Meghan and Scobie in our hands,
We've got Lisa and Greg in our hands,
We've got the whole earth in our hands!

Traditional Songs
"This Land Is Your Land"
"Home on the Range"
"America the Beautiful"
"She'll Be Coming 'Round the Mountain"
"The Bear Went Over the Mountain"
"Over the River and Through the Woods"

EARTH

Mother Goose

This Is the Key of the Kingdom
This is the key of the kingdom;
In that kingdom there is a city;
In that city there is a town;
In that town there is a street;
In that street there is a lane;
In that lane there is a house;
In that house there is a bed;
On that bed there is a basket;
In that basket there are some flowers.

Flowers in the basket,
Basket in the bed,
Bed in the chamber,
Chamber in the house,
House in the weedy yard,
Yard in the winding lane,
Lane in the broad street,
Street in the high town,
Town in the city,
City in the kingdom.
This is the key of the kingdom.

What's in There
What's in there?
Gold and money.
Where's my share?
The mousie's run away with it.
Where's the mousie?
In her housie.
Where's her housie?
In the wood.
Where's the wood?
The fire burned it.
Where's the fire?
The water quenched it.
Where's the water?
The brown bull drank it.
Where's the brown bull?
Behind Burnie's hill.
Where's Burnie's hill?
All dressed in snow.
Where's the snow?
The sun melted it.
Where's the sun?
High, high up in the air.

A Curious Boy
There was a little boy
And a curious boy was he,
He sailed across the ocean
The country for to see.

There he found
The Earth's ground
Was as hard,
That a yard
Was as long,
That a song
Was as merry,
That a cherry
Was as red,
That lead
Was as weighty,
That four-score
Was as eighty,
That a door
Was as wooden,
As in England.

So he stood in his shoes,
And he wondered,
He wondered.
He stood in his shoes
AND HE WONDERED.

EARTH

Snacks

CARROT SALAD

Read the *Carrot Seed* by Ruth Krauss, illustrated by Crockett Johnson (HarperCollins, 1945) with your class. Then serve this carrot salad.

Ingredients:
Carrots, raisins, mayonnaise dressing

Directions:
1. Grate the carrots.
2. Mix the raisins with the grated carrots and toss with the dressing.
3. Serve the carrot salad in small bowls, and let the children take their snack outside to eat.

VEGETABLE FOREST

Let children create their own forests after reading *The First Forest* by John Gile, illustrated by Tom Heflin (1989).

Ingredients:
Asparagus spears, broccoli and cauliflower florets, sprouts, mushrooms, a variety of dressings (blue cheese, ranch, Italian, French)

Directions:
1. Provide a variety of vegetables for children to use to create forests. Sprouts can be grass, mushrooms can be bare trees, and asparagus and cauliflower can be leafy trees.
2. After children arrange their vegetables, they can dip them in their choice of dressing before eating.

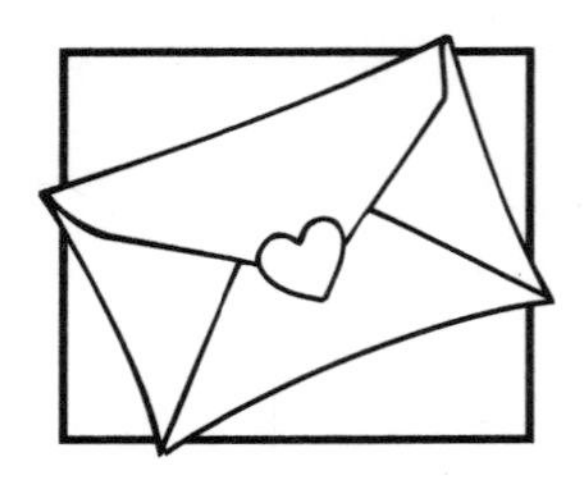

EARTH

Letter Home

The deer he loves the high wood,
The hare she loves the hill;
The knight he loves his bright sword,
The lady loves her will.
—Mother Goose

This month we are celebrating Earth Day, and learning about different environments and natural occurrences. We will be going on a nature scavenger hunt, making mountains, and creating colorful desert dunes.

We will be playing a board game called "Eco-land," and the children will each bring a copy home to play with you. The markers are pussycats, who travel through the desert, across meadows, and over the ocean!

We are building recycling boxes, and children will be learning how and what to recycle. We are asking parents to continue this project at home. Include your child in the sorting of items and, if possible, let him or her watch the trucks come—or visit a recycling center.

For our rain forest activity, we need:

- manila folders

For our earth map, we need:

- paper towel tubes
- empty, small boxes

Thanks for your help!

May: Oceans

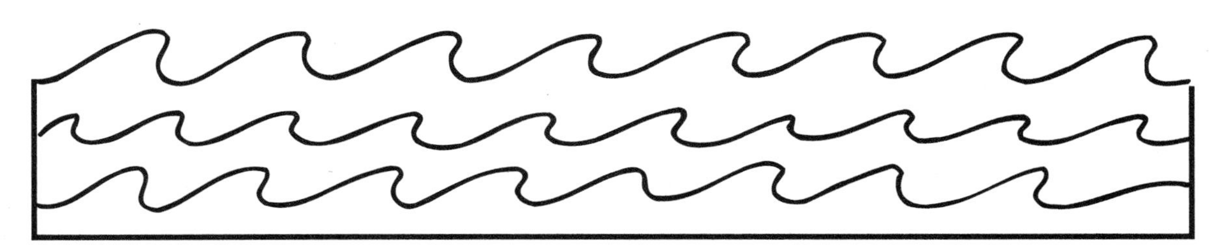

Oceans are brimming with swimming creatures, from schools of colorful fish to eight-legged octopuses, from swift-swimming seahorses to take-their-time tortoises. This chapter on oceans is brimming, too—brimming with ideas that will take your students on a magical trip to the deep, blue sea. It doesn't matter if you live in a land-locked state, these activities will make it seem as if the ocean is only a sea gull's cry away! Begin this unit by reading Leo Lionni's *Swimmy* (Pantheon, 1963) and making underwater art (p. 240) in the style of the book.

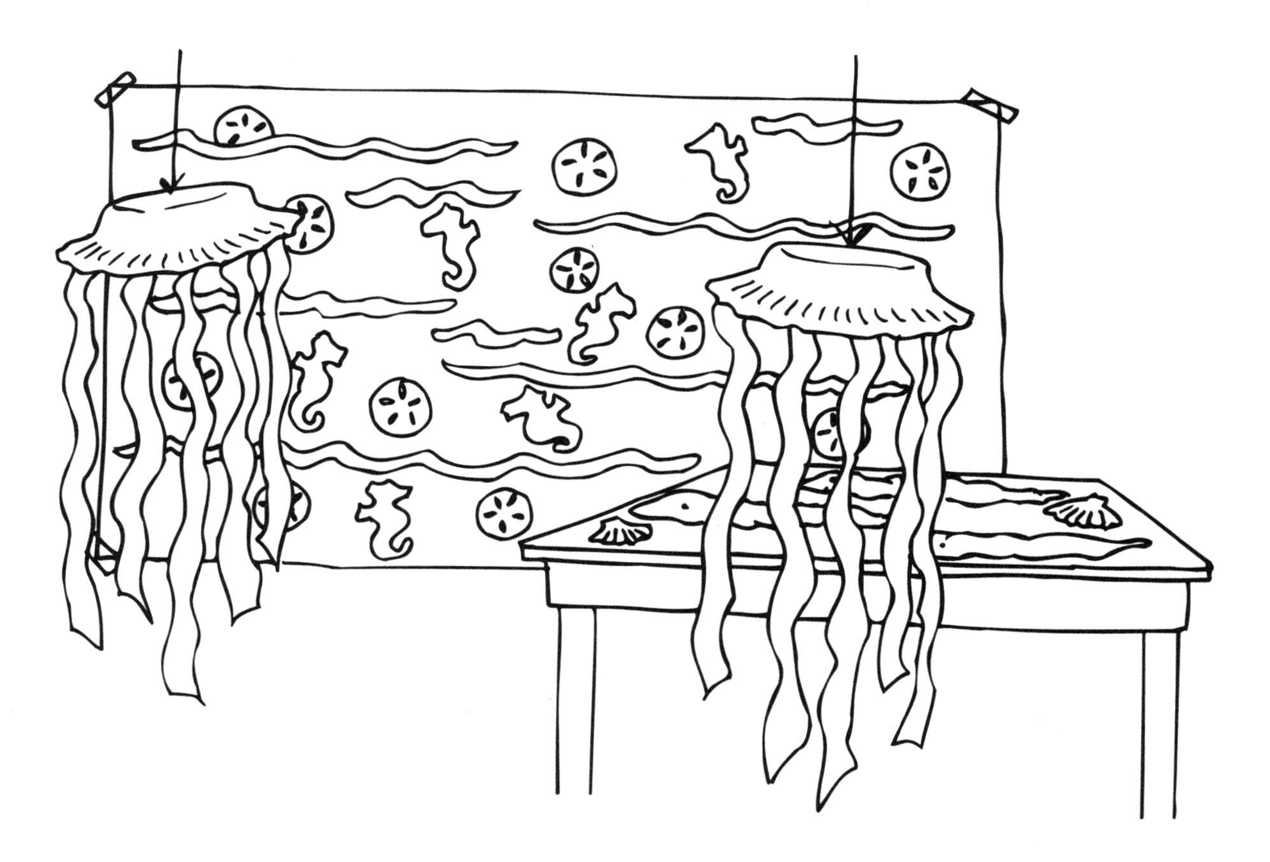

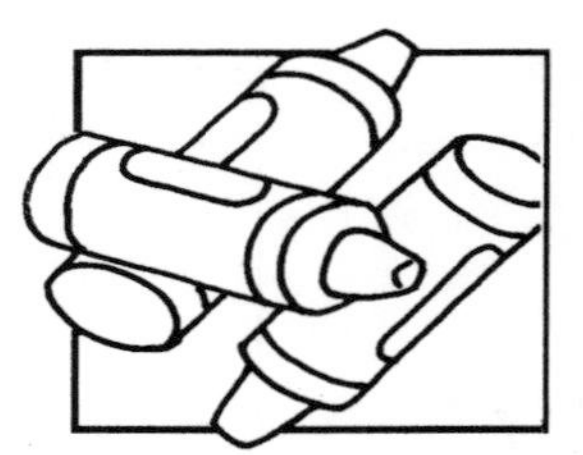

OCEANS

Art Activities

AQUARIUM ART

Post the finished projects on an "Aquarium Art" bulletin board, and decorate the borders with "Seaweed Chains" (p. 237).

Materials:
One large paper fish shape per child (cut from easel, newsprint, or butcher paper), tempera paint in an assortment of colors, paintbrushes, glitter, glue

Directions:
1. Give each child a fish shape to paint with tempera paints.
2. Children can make their fish sparkly by shaking glitter onto the wet paint. Or they can wait for the pictures to dry and dab glue where they want the glitter to stay.

OCEAN WAVES

This activity lets children paint their own representations of the ocean, either from remembrances of a visit to the beach, or from pictures they've seen in books.

Materials:
Tempera paint in a variety of blue and green shades (lighten with white paint and darken with black), brushes, paper, easels, silver or iridescent glitter, glue, tissue paper strips, scissors

Directions:
1. Set up easels, paper, and paints.
2. Children can start by painting W-shaped waves.
3. Once the pictures have dried, let children place their pictures on a flat surface. Provide glitter and glue for them to use for foam. They can also glue on tissue paper strips for seaweed.

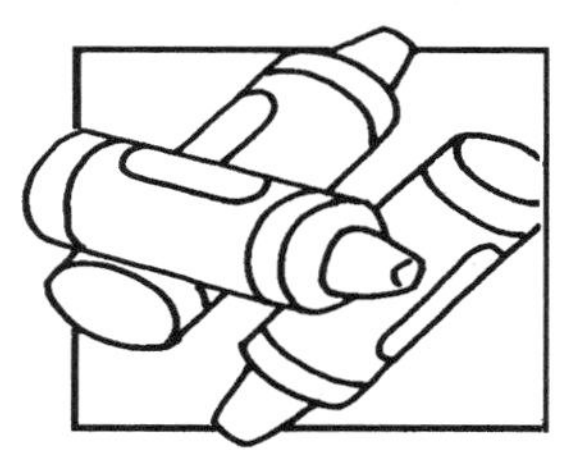

OCEANS

Art Activities

OCTOPUS HANDS

This is a great project for counting practice!

Materials:
Different-colored finger paints (in pie tins), glossy paper, glue, scissors, glitter, sequins, tissue or construction paper, wiggly eyes (optional)

Directions:
1. Show children how to place their hands in the tins of paint, and then rub their palms together to thoroughly coat. (This is fun to do, and feels good, too!)
2. Have children make "octopuses" by overlapping their palms, hands face down, spreading their fingers, and printing onto the paper. Or, they can print one hand on the paper, and then make a second handprint on top of the first. (These octopuses may have a few extra legs.)
3. Children can make different octopuses in a variety of colors.
4. For glittery octopuses, let the children drizzle glue on the octopus prints and then sprinkle on glitter or sequins. They can shake excess glitter and sequins onto a separate piece of paper to use in another activity.
5. After the pictures dry, let children glue on wiggly eyes if they like. Small circles of tissue paper or construction paper can also be glued on for octopus eyes.

OCEANS

Art Activities

PAPER PLATE JELLYFISH MOBILES

After these mobiles are dry, hang a colorful "school" of jellyfish from the ceiling or a bulletin board to brighten up the classroom.

Materials:

Multicolored strips of tissue paper cut with "wavy" edges or cut with shearing scissors (streamers also work well), large and small paper plates (one per child), glue (or glue stick or paste), glitter, yarn or string, tape

Directions:

1. Let each child choose a large or small paper plate.
2. Show children how to glue the tissue paper strips (or streamers) to the undersides and rims of their paper plates, so that the strips hang down toward the ground.
3. Children can decorate the tops or rims of the plates with glue and glitter.
4. Loop a length of string or yarn (long enough to hang from a bulletin board or the ceiling), and tape it onto the center top of each plate.

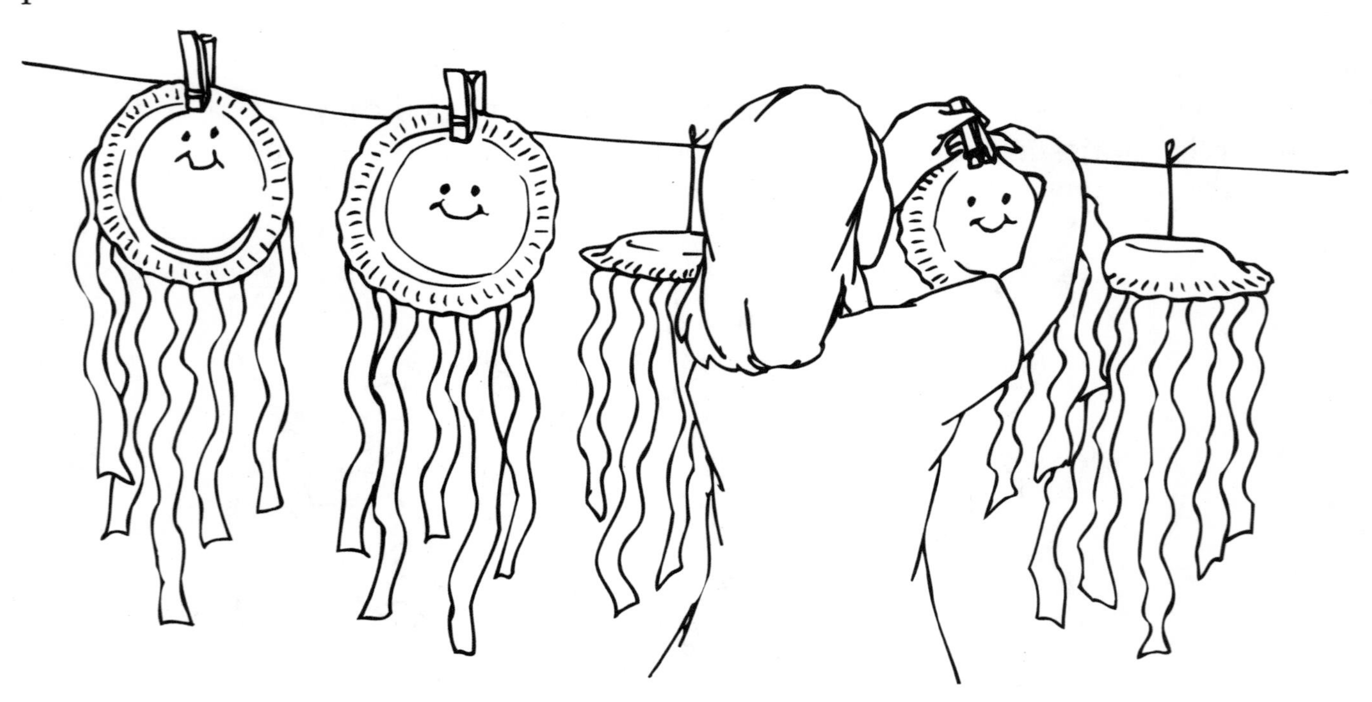

OCEANS
Art Activities

PLAYDOUGH EELS

Materials:
Playdough, colored baker's dough, or other modeling material

Directions:
Let children experiment with different colors of playdough, clay, etc., to make eels. They can roll out long eels, short eels, fat eels, or any that they desire.

SAND DOLLAR MONEY
Children can pretend that they are mermaids and mermen and that their sand dollars are underwater currency.

Materials:
Sand dollar patterns in various sizes (p. 236), metallic crayons (silver, gold, copper), oak tag (or thick paper), real sand dollar (if available), scissors, white paper

Directions:
1. Duplicate the sand dollar patterns onto oak tag to make stencils.
2. Have children use sand dollar stencils to draw their own sand dollars.
3. Show the class a real sand dollar or a picture of one.
4. Children can cut out their "dollars" and decorate with crayons.

OCEANS

Art Activities

SEASHELL TRACING

Have a day at the beach . . . right in your classroom!

Materials:
Seashells, pebbles, starfish, sand dollars (all are available in teacher supply stores, scientific shops, or through catalogs), non-toxic markers, paper

Directions:
1. Provide an assortment of ocean materials for children to trace onto paper using non-toxic markers. They can use the materials to make other designs—two shells together to make a butterfly shape, a pebble next to a fin-shaped shell to make a fish, etc.
2. Ask children to tell you about their drawings and transcribe their words onto their pictures (or onto a separate piece of paper).
3. The results of this project can be bound into a classroom seashore book and shared with parents.

"SEAWEED" CHAINS AND NECKLACES

The finished chains can be used to decorate bulletin boards or to help create an underwater dramatic play corner.

Materials:
Shell patterns (p. 236), thin construction paper strips (in different shades of blue, green, and turquoise), tape or stapler, glue, crayons, scissors

Directions:
1. Give children shell patterns to color and cut out.
2. Demonstrate how to make paper chains by looping small circles of paper strips together and taping or stapling the edges together.
3. Encourage children to personalize their chains before making them by gluing the cut-out, colored shells onto the sides of the paper strips.

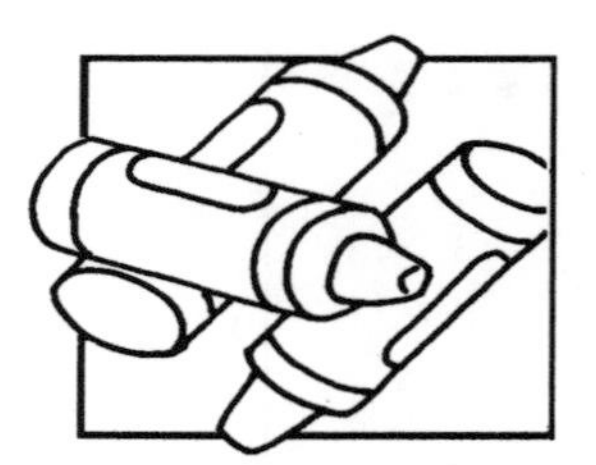

OCEANS

Art Activities

SPONGE PRINT PICTURES

Sponge printing is an easy hands-on activity that small hands can do well.

Materials:

Ocean patterns (p. 239), sponges, scissors, paper, tempera paint in an assortment of oceanic colors in shallow dishes or pie tins (try thinning the paint a little, so that it's "spongier")

Directions:

1. Use the patterns to cut out an assortment of sponge shapes.
2. Let children choose different sponges to print pictures.
3. When the pictures dry, post them on an "underwater" bulletin board.

The sponges can be used in other underwater art activities or at the water table.

TOILET PAPER TUBE SUBMARINE

Here's a way to transform toilet paper tubes into creative toys!

Materials:

Toilet paper tubes or paper towel tube sections (one per child), glue, pipe cleaners, construction paper, hole reinforcers, tempera paint, brushes

Directions:

1. Show children toy submarines or submarine pictures.
2. Let children turn their toilet paper tubes into submarines with paint, hole reinforcers for porthole windows, and pipe cleaners for periscopes. They can use these submarines in the dramatic play corner.

OCEANS

Storytime

FEATURED PICTURE BOOK

***Swimmy* by Leo Lionni (Pantheon, 1968).**

Swimmy is a fast little fish who voyages throughout the sea, looking at the different sights: jellyfish, lobsters, sea anemones, and forests of seaweed. One day, he finds a group of little fish very much like himself, and together they work out a way to see the wonders of the ocean.

ART EXTENSION

Show your children the pictures in *Swimmy*. Ask them what types of materials they think the author used to make the pictures. There are many correct answers: paint, stamps, prints, watercolors, doilies, and so on. (Even incorrect answers may be incorporated into an art extension.)

Provide materials for children to use to recreate the types of pictures in *Swimmy* (not necessarily the subject matter, but the "look" of the art).

Sample Materials:

Glossy paper, watercolors, thinned tempera paints, brushes, stencils, different kinds of leaves (eucalyptus, pine, ferns, bamboo), doilies, rubber stamps, markers, and other decorative materials

Directions:

Let children experiment with the different art materials. They can study the pages of *Swimmy* to find examples of art techniques that they'd like to duplicate.

1. Show them how to spread paint on one side of a piece of paper, fold and press it, and then open it for an "underwater look."
2. Doilies can be painted and then used for printing, or painted over and then removed to leave a reverse print behind.
3. Children can paint leaves and then press them onto the papers.
4. After a background has been created, let children use rubber stamps, stickers, and markers to add different creatures to their papers.
5. Bind the finished pictures in a classroom book.

OCEANS

Storytime

MORE PICTURE BOOKS

Boats by Anne Rockwell (Dutton, 1982).
Simple text and playful cartoon pictures make this informative book about boats an enjoyable read.

Come Away from the Water, Shirley by John Burningham (Crowell, 1977).
While Shirley's parents sit comfortably in their beach chairs, reading the paper and knitting, Shirley rows a boat out to a big ship, battles pirates, walks the plank, and ends up discovering a buried treasure in the sand. At least, she does all of those things in her imagination.

Emile by Tomi Ungerer (Dell, 1960).
Emile is an octopus who saves Captain Samofar from being eaten by a shark. In return for saving his life, the captain invites Emile to live with him. Emile has many adventures.

Fish Is Fish by Leo Lionni (Knopf, 1970).
A tadpole and a minnow are inseparable friends until the tadpole turns into a frog and climbs out of the lake. After a long time, the frog returns and shares his adventures with his fish friend. As the frog describes the many animals that live on land, the fish imagines what they look like.

The Great White Man-Eating Shark: A Cautionary Tale by Jonathan Allen (Dial, 1989).
Norvin is a boy who looks like a shark. In fact, he looks so much like a shark that he scares other people away from the ocean so that he can swim in the cool water all by himself. Luckily, Norvin learns a lesson from a real shark in this funny tale.

The Maggie B. by Irene Haas (Atheneum, 1975).
Margaret Barnstable wishes on a star that she had a ship named after her to sail for a day (with someone nice for company). Her wish comes true when she wakes up the next day on the ship with her baby brother James. Beautiful watercolor illustrations accompany the delightful text.

Otto Is Different by Franz Brandenberg (Greenwillow, 1985).
Otto the octopus, with his eight legs, doesn't always like being different from his friends. But he does find his many legs rewarding when he's doing his homework, practicing the piano, and sweeping up, all at the same time.

The Owl and the Pussy-cat by Edward Lear, illustrated by Gwen Fulton (Atheneum, 1977).
The crisp and colorful illustrations in this version of "The Owl and the Pussy-cat" are perfectly suited to Edward Lear's sparkling verse. This is a great book to read on a dreamy, cloudy morning. Give children paper and crayons and let them create their own pictures for the silly text.

Sea Sums by Samuel French Morse (Little, 1970).
This is a poetic counting book-by-the-sea. The objects are counted from one to ten—with a page in the middle to count them all in a row—and then back from ten to one again. Sweet, simple illustrations are the perfect complement to the gently rolling text.

The Seashore Book by Charlotte Zolotow (HarperCollins, 1992).
A little boy who lives in the mountains asks his mother what the seashore is like. His mother describes an entire day at the sea, making the scenes come alive in the little boy's imagination. The scenes will come alive for young readers as well through the beautiful paintings by Wendell Minor.

OCEANS

Flannel Board

FINDERELLA

This is the retold tale of "Cinderella." It takes place under the water, and the main character is a fish! (Hence the name, "Finderella.") Her "Fairy Codmother" helps her get to the ball, but the lesson she learns there isn't just your average fish story!

Once upon a time there was a tiny fish named **Finderella**. She lived with her two lazy **sisters**. One was very crabby. The other was an out-of-shape jellyfish.

Poor Finderella did all of the work for her sisters. She hardly ever had a moment to herself. Then one day, Finderella and her sisters received an **invitation** to the ball at the nearby underwater palace.

Finderella helped her sisters get ready for the ball. She polished her crabby sister's shell and hung pearls from her other sister's tentacles.

When it was time to go to the ball, her sisters were all ready. But poor Finderella had no time to get ready, so her sisters went without her.

Suddenly, the water began to sparkle and shimmer and POOF! Finderella's **Fairy Codmother** appeared before her!

With one flick of her magic tail, the Fairy Codmother turned Finderella's drab brown scales to shiny silver ones.

The **"new" Finderella** was ready to go to the ball, but her Codmother warned her to be back home by 12 o'clock, because that is when she would turn into herself again.

Finderella was the most dazzling fish at the ball! She even danced with the **prince** himself! He was a whale of a guy!

Finderella and the prince had so much fun dancing that they didn't even notice when the clock struck midnight. Suddenly, Finderella's pretty silver scales turned back into her normal brown ones.

Finderella was embarrassed. She began to swim home.

The prince stopped her. "I think that you're fun to be with, no matter how fancy you're dressed or what you look like!" he said.

That made Finderella very happy, and she and the prince became good friends.

INVITATION

OCEANS

Discovery

AQUARIUM

Materials:
Fish, fish food, aquarium "toys" (castles, rocks, etc.), magnifying glasses, crayons, paper, books on taking care of an aquarium, for example, *You and Your Aquarium* by Dick Mills (Knopf, 1986).

Directions:
1. Have children look at the fish and observe (with magnifying glasses).
2. Provide crayons and paper for the children to draw or write about what they see.
3. For in-depth observation, move one fish to its own private glass bowl.
4. Discuss how fish breathe, and ask children for their theories. Do they think people can breathe underwater?
5. Talk about the different kinds of animals that live in the ocean, and the fact that some breathe air like people do (dolphins, whales), while others filter the oxygen out of the water through gills. (A fish gulps a mouthful of water, which is forced through the gills. Oxygen is extracted from the water while carbon dioxide is passed out of the gills.)
6. Get children involved in setting up the tank, feeding the fish, and cleaning the tank.

Field Trip:
Take your class to a local aquarium to see the different underwater creatures that have been discussed in the classroom. Most children are especially interested in sharks and octopuses. Try and take this trip in the middle of your project, so that you can continue to explore the information learned on the trip when you return to the classroom. *My Visit to the Aquarium* by Aliki (HarperCollins, 1993) is a good preparation book.

OCEANS

Discovery

FISHING FOR FUN!

Materials:
Fish patterns (p. 248), paper clips, four small magnets, four 18" lengths of string, four yardsticks, tub, non-toxic markers, scissors

Directions:
1. Have children color and cut out the fish patterns.
2. Place a paper clip on each fish before putting it into the tub.
3. Tie a piece of string to the end of each stick.
4. Tie a small magnet to the end of each length of string.
5. Let children "go fishing" with their "magnet poles."

JAPANESE FLYING FISH WINDSOCKS

Materials:
Two kite patterns (p. 249) per child, hole punch, string, crayons, stapler

Directions:
1. Let children decorate the kite patterns with crayons and cut out.
2. Help them staple their patterns together, leaving the mouth open.
3. Have children punch two holes at each side of the mouth and tie string through for easy hanging.
4. On a crisp, windy day, let the children bring their flying fish kites outside to fly in the breeze or hang from trees.

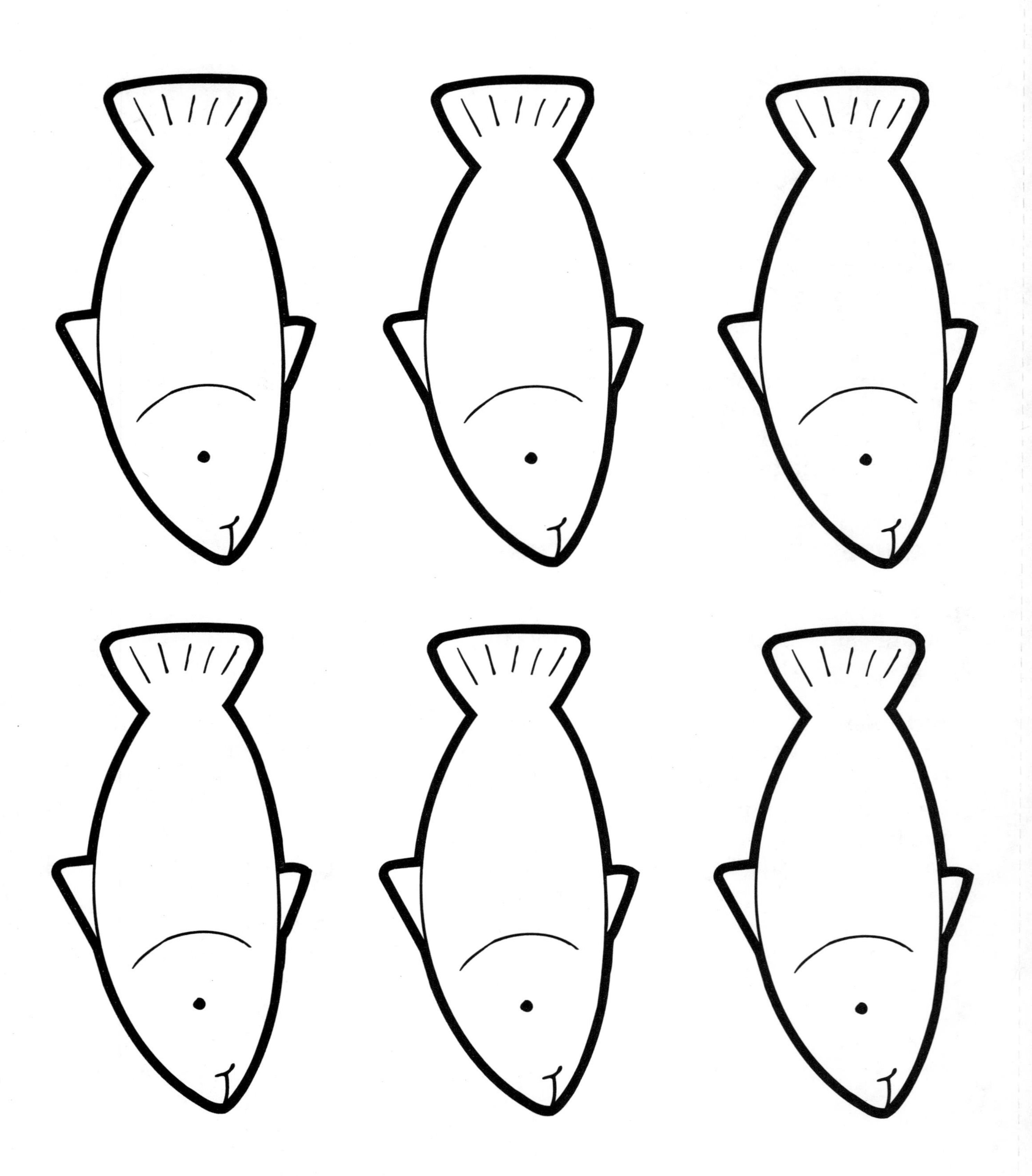

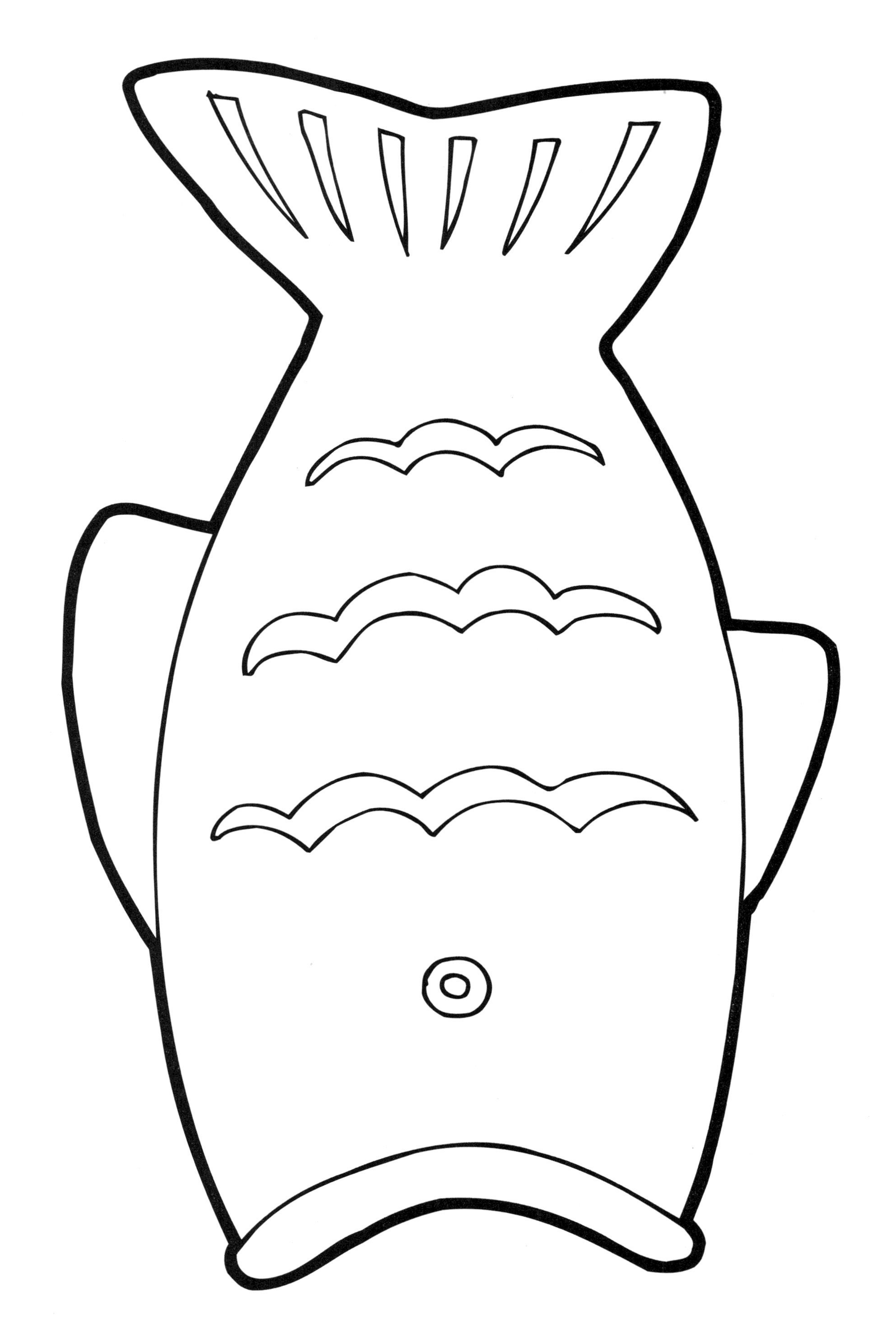

OCEANS

Discovery

SAND TABLE I: AT THE BEACH

Materials:
Sand table, sand, water, seashells, floating boats, plastic animals

Directions:
1. Build up a sand bank at one end of the sand table.
2. Pour in water and add plastic animals, seashells, and floating boats to make a beach scene.
3. For a more realistic ocean effect, prop up one end of the sand table by placing a few flat blocks under two legs. Place the water at the low end and the sand at the high end.
4. Encourage the children to make several scenes.

SAND TABLE II: SIFTING FOR SEASHELLS

Materials:
Sand table, sand, seashells (or small plastic animals, shiny pebbles), plastic sifters

Directions:
1. Fill the sand table with dry sand.
2. Bury seashells (or other small objects) in the sand.
3. Let children use the plastic sifters (or their hands) to uncover the buried "treasures."

OCEANS
Discovery

SEASHELLS

Materials:
Seashells (curly, not flat)

Directions:
1. Let students hold real seashells up to their ears to listen to the "ocean."
2. Discuss what they hear and ask for reasons why it sounds like waves are trapped in the shell. (Reason: The sound is actually a combination of sounds coming from outside the shell. Because of the shell's shape and the smoothness of its inside, the sound from outside the shell echoes and re-echoes as the air inside the hollow shell vibrates. This causes the roaring sound that we associate with waves. One of the sounds that echoes is the sound of blood rushing through your ear!)

SWIMMING

Materials:
Wading pool, water, sun, water toys

Directions:
1. On Beach Day, have children bring their swimsuits and beach towels.
2. Fill a small wading pool and let children practice swimming. They can also float water toys in the pool.
3. If it's cold where you live, have Beach Day indoors! Let children dance to Beach Boys music, and have them sit on their towels during storytime. Take them on an imaginary trip to the beach by reading *The Seashore Book* by Charlotte Zolotow (HarperCollins, 1992).

Option:
Sprinklers are also a big hit on hot days.

OCEANS

Discovery

WATER TABLE

Materials:
A variety of small objects (corks, measuring cups, funnels, tubes, rocks, utensils, tub toys, magnifying glass)

Directions:
Children will be interested in experimenting with objects that sink and float. Place a label on the water table (on oak tag covered with Contact paper) that says, "Will it SINK or FLOAT?"

WHALE WATCHING

Materials:
Book on whale watching (see list below), tape of whale "songs" (such as *Voyaging with the Whales* by Nature Recordings or *Songs and Sounds of Orcinus Orca* by Total Records), paper, crayons

Directions:
1. Read a whale-watching book to the children, pointing out the different types of whales that exist.
2. Play a tape of whale "songs" and ask children what they think the whales are doing. (Are they singing to each other? Gossiping? Telling stories?)
3. Have children draw pictures of what they imagine it looks like when whales "sing" to each other.
4. Post pictures on a "Whale of a Tale" bulletin board.

Field Trip:
If you live on the coast, consider taking children whale watching. Even if whales do not cooperate and appear, children will probably get to see sea lions, sea gulls, and, of course, the sea. Whale books: *Whales* by The Cousteau Society (Simon & Schuster, 1992), *Going on a Whale Watch* by B. McMillan (Scholastic, 1992), *The World's Whales* by Kenneth Brower (Friends of the Earth, 1979), or *Wake of the Whale* by S. Minasian (Smithsonian, 1984).

OCEANS

Class Project

OCTOPUS'S GARDEN MURAL

Your class can use the skills they've learned this month to create a decorative mural. The finished product will make a good underwater background for your dramatic play corner—or put it on display with other art activities the children have produced this month.

On a large sheet of butcher paper, children can paint ocean waves with various shades of tempera paint, using glitter and sequins for the surf.

Provide an assortment of sponge stamps and sand dollar stencils for further decoration. Seaweed chains can be glued, taped, or stapled directly onto the mural, and jellyfish mobiles can hang in front of it.

Let children position their playdough eels on a table covered with blue construction paper. Additional mural add-ons: colorful paper fish, hermit crabs, shells, seahorses, etc. (See patterns on p. 239. You can make stencils, or show children the patterns to give them ideas.)

Play the Beatles' "Octopus's Garden" to get in the mood, and serve goldfish crackers for a yummy snack.

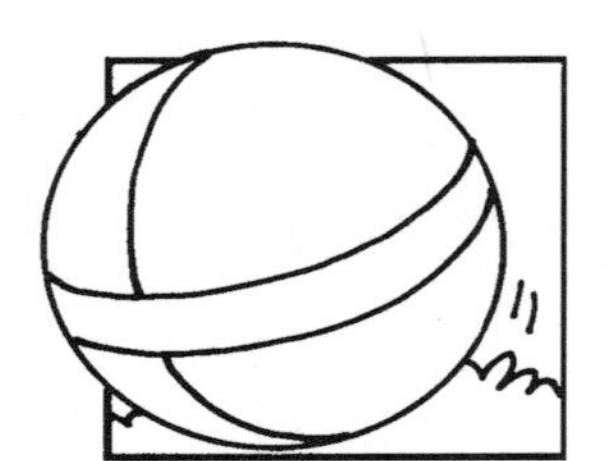

OCEANS

Games

GO FISH

Materials:
Card patterns (pp. 255-256), scissors, non-toxic markers, oak tag or heavy paper, Contact paper

Directions:
1. Photocopy the pattern pages onto oak tag or heavy paper to make a deck. In this card game, the children play for two, three, or four of a kind.
2. Let the children color the cards with non-toxic markers.
3. Laminate the cards by covering the sheets on both sides with Contact paper.
4. Cut the cards apart.
5. Have the children play Go Fish in pairs with the cards. Children can play by asking for seashells or seahorses. If the other child doesn't have any, he or she says, "Go fish." Children can play by colors, too, if cards are programmed first with different colors.

SHARKS AND MINNOWS

All of the children except one are minnows. They line up along one side of the yard. The remaining child is the "shark," and he or she stands in the middle of the yard. When the "shark" says, "Minnows, swim!" all of the "minnows" try to reach the other side of the yard without being tagged. Those tagged become additional "sharks." Play continues until everyone has been tagged. The last remaining "minnow" is the "shark" for the next round. (The game can also be played indoors on a rug or in a multipurpose room.)

FISH, FISH, SHARK!

This is played the same way as "Duck, Duck, Goose," but with different names. Instead of the mushpond in the middle, call it the "tide pool."

OCEANS

Songs

I Went Swimming in the Ocean
(to the tune of "I've Been Working on the Railroad")

I went swimming in the ocean,
On a summer day.
I went swimming in the ocean,
And I kicked, and splashed, and played.

After lunch we looked for seashells,
I found three or four.
You can hold one up to your ear,
And hear the ocean roar.

Hear the ocean roar,
Hear the ocean roar,
You can hear the ocean
Roar, roar, roar.
Hear the ocean roar,
Hear the ocean roar,
Hear the ocean roar, roar, roar.

Underneath the Fisherman's Boat
(to the tune of "Pop! Goes the Weasel")

Underneath the fisherman's boat,
Down in the deep blue water,
The fishes swim in groups called schools,
Parents, sons, and daughters.

Fishes come in many shapes,
There're big ones and there're small ones.
Sharks are big and minnows small,
And eels are great big long ones.

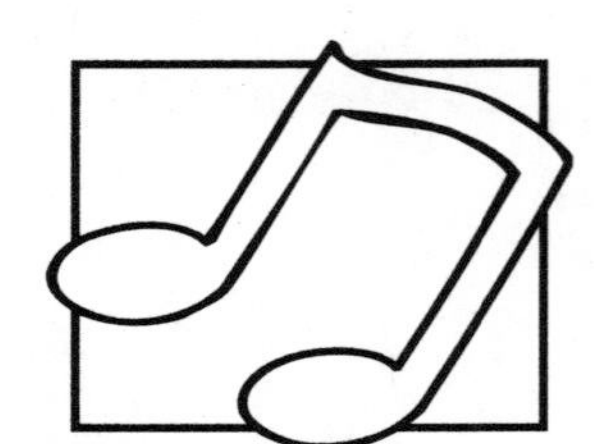

OCEANS

Songs

Underneath the Deep Blue Sea
(to the tune of "London Bridge Is Falling Down")

Underneath the deep blue sea,
Deep blue sea,
Deep blue sea,
Underneath the deep blue sea,
Live the fishes.

Fishes swim in groups called schools,
Groups called schools,
Groups called schools.
Fishes swim in groups called schools,
In the ocean.

In the Water
(to the tune of "Oh, Susannah")

The octopuses swim along,
The crabs crawl on the sand,
The sea gulls cry out their sea song,
And fly above the land.

In the water,
The dolphins jump and play,
And the children all build sand castles
The ocean sweeps away.

Other Seaside Songs to Sing:
"Down by the Bay" by Raffi
"Baby Beluga" by Raffi
"Slippery Fish" by Charlotte Diamond
"The Yellow Submarine" by the Beatles
"My Bonnie Lies Over the Ocean" (substitute name of each child for "Bonnie")
"Cockles and Mussels"
"Row, Row, Row Your Boat"

OCEANS

Mother Goose

The Man in the Wilderness

The man in the wilderness asked of me,
How many strawberries grew in the sea.
I answered him, as I thought good,
As many as fishies grow in the wood.

One, Two, Three . . .

One, two, three, four, five.
Once I caught a fish alive.
Six, seven, eight, nine, ten.
Then I threw it back again.
Why did you let it go?
Because it bit my finger so.
Which finger did it bite?
The little pinkie on the right!

If All the Seas

If all the seas were one sea,
What a great sea that would be!
If all the trees were one tree,
What a great tree that would be!
And if all the axes were one axe,
What a great axe that would be!
And if all the men were one man,
What a great man that would be!
And if that great man took the great axe,
And cut down the great tree,
And let it fall into the great sea,
What a splish-splash that would be!

OCEANS

Mother Goose

I Saw a Ship

I saw a ship a-sailing,
A-sailing on the sea,
And oh but it was laden
With pretty things for me.

There were comfits in the cabin,
And sweetmeats in the hold;
The sails were made of silk,
And the masts were made of gold.

The four-and-twenty sailors,
That stood between the decks,
Were four-and-twenty white mice
With chains about their necks.

The captain was a duck
With a jacket on his back,
And when the ship began to move
The captain said, "Quack! Quack!"

I Saw Three Ships Come Sailing By

I saw three ships come sailing by,
On New Year's Day in the morning.

And what do you think was in them then,
Was in them then, was in them then?
And what do you think was in them then,
On New Year's Day in the morning?

Three pretty girls were in them then,
Were in them then, were in them then;
Three pretty girls were in them then,
On New Year's Day in the morning.

And one could whistle, and one could sing,
And one could play the violin—
Such joy there was at my wedding,
On New Year's Day in the morning!

OCEANS

Snacks

SUBMARINE SANDWICHES

Discuss the name of these sandwiches, and ask children if they can guess where the name came from. You may get more interesting answers than "because they look like submarines." (Encourage creative responses!)

Ingredients:

Hot dog buns (one per child), lettuce, tomato slices, bell pepper strips, pickles, cheese slices, mustard, mayonnaise, sliced olives, carrot or celery strips, plastic knives with rounded edges, knife (for the teacher)

Directions:

1. Let the children put their own sandwiches together according to their tastes.
2. The children may add periscopes to their subs (strips of carrots or celery stuck to the top with mayonnaise), or portholes (olives stuck on with mustard), if they wish.
3. Slice the children's sandwiches in half for easier eating.

OCEANS

Snacks

FRUIT BOATS

Cut, cut, cut your fruit,
Apples, peaches, plums,
Cantaloupe, oranges, kiwis, and grapes,
Yummy, yum, yum, yum!

Ingredients:
A "boat" for each child (half an apple, small cantaloupe, or peach), seasonal fruit cut into small pieces (pears, nectarines, plums, bananas, kiwis, grapes), raisins, shredded coconut, chopped nuts, plastic spoons

Directions:
1. Have the children fill their fruit "boats" with cut-up pieces of fruit.
2. They may want to add "passenger" raisins, or decorate their boats with coconut or nuts.
3. Provide plastic spoons or, if you're using mostly "dry" fruits (apples, grapes, bananas), children can use their fingers. If it's a sunny day, let the children take their fruit boats outside for snack.

OCEANS

Snacks

OH, MY GOSH! IT'S AN OCTOPUS!

This is a fun, easy snack that children can make themselves.

Ingredients:

Round crackers (large or small rice crackers work well), cream cheese spread, julienned carrot or cucumber sticks, sliced olives, sprouts (optional), rounded plastic knives

Directions:

1. Let children use the plastic knives to spread their crackers with cream cheese.
2. Let the children "attach" the very thin carrot or cucumber "legs" to their crackers. (The "legs" will stick to the cream cheese.) Remind them that octopuses have eight legs.
3. If they want, children can use the olive slices for the octopus's eyes.
4. Children can place sprouts on a plate to represent seaweed, and then position their octopus in the sprouts.
5. This snack is finger food, so let the children dig in!

OCEANS

Letter Home

Little drops of water,
Little grains of sand,
Make the mighty ocean,
And the pleasant land.
—Mother Goose

This month we are learning about oceans. We will be making waves with underwater mural scenes, learning about whales, eating submarine sandwiches, and singing songs about the deep blue sea!

Open call for: fishing experts, sailors, and SCUBA divers. Please come to our class and talk about your experiences. We are planning on doing some fishing ourselves . . . at our water tables. Come tell us about the one that got away! We are interested in learning about the many materials used by seafarers: fishing poles, lures, nets, fins, air tanks, life preservers, and masks. We'd also like to know about boats: kayaks, canoes, tugboats, submarines, paddle boats, sailboats, etc.

This month, we need:

- life preservers (for our dramatic play corner)
- shell or sand dollar collections (for discovery)
- toilet paper or paper towel tubes (we're making submarines!)

Thank you for your help!

June: Sky

This chapter celebrates many aspects of the sky, from clouds and rainbows to stars and planets to birds and nests. Begin this unit by reading *It Looked Like Spilt Milk* by Charles G. Shaw (Harper, 1947). If it's a cloudy day, you can go outside with your students and try to find shapes and designs in the clouds above. Then have the children make their own shaving cream clouds (p. 279)—messy, but lots of fun! If it's a clear day, your class might go outside and try to spot birds in the trees or flying overhead.

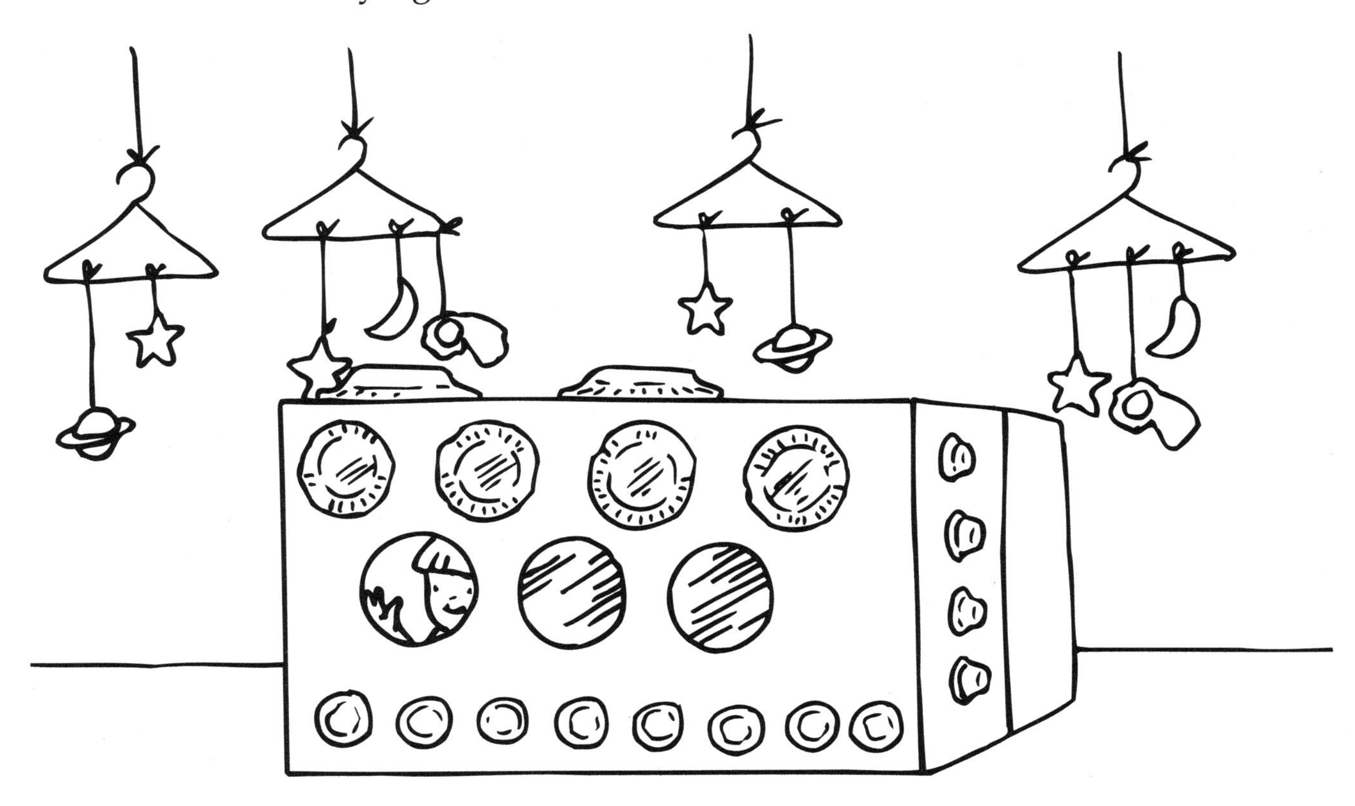

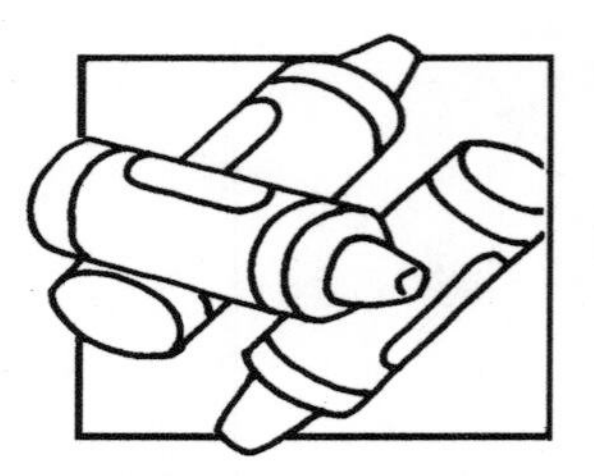

SKY
Art Activities

BUTTERFLY WINGS

After making these wings, let the children put them on and pretend to be butterflies. This would be a good time to reread Eric Carle's *The Very Hungry Caterpillar* (Collins-World, 1969).

Materials:

Easel paper, tempera paints, brushes, stapler, thick yarn, scissors

Directions:

1. Cut out a set of "butterfly wings" from easel paper for each child. Fold the paper in half and cut out a simple wing shape. Open.
2. Fasten two lengths of yarn to each set as shown—one on each side of the wings—for children to slip their arms through to wear.
3. Let children decorate their wings with tempera paints in an assortment of spring colors (pink, lavender, light blue, pale green, light yellow).
4. After the wings dry, children can wear them to flutter around the classroom or outside.

Option:

Make simple bug headbands to wear with the wings by stapling two strips of construction paper together, measuring for fit around each child's head, and then stapling the ends together. Children can add pipe cleaner antennae with staples or tape. Show them how to bend their antennae around their fingers to curl them.

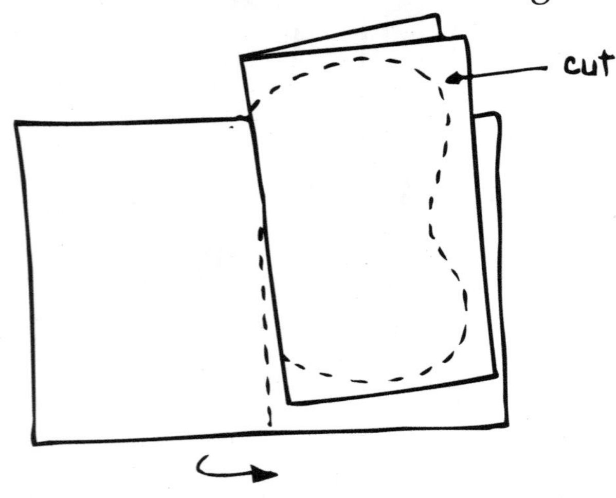

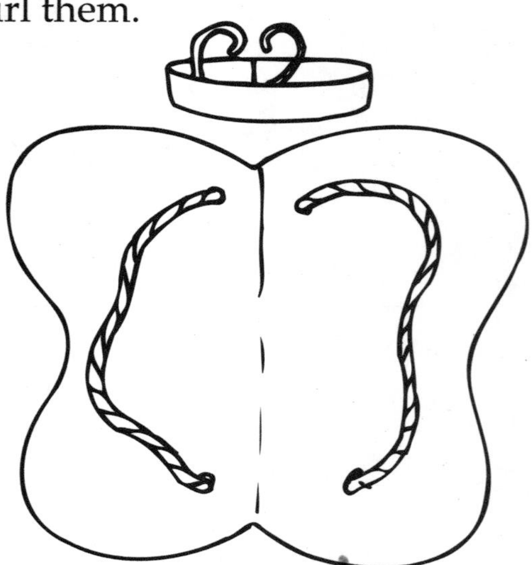

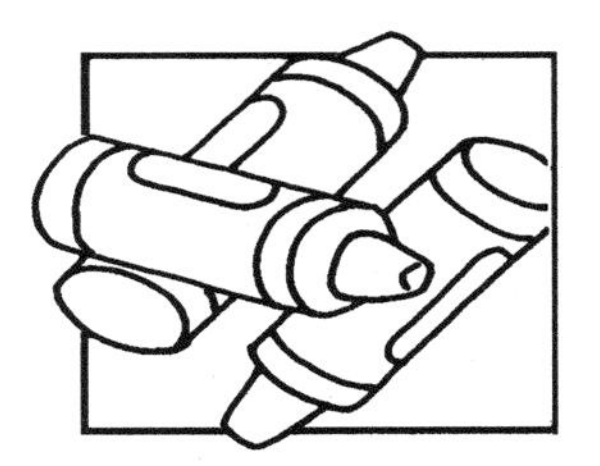

SKY
Art Activities

CELESTIAL MOBILES

You can create a classroom solar system with these colorful mobiles, and bring a touch of the sky indoors.

Materials:
Mobile patterns (p. 268), tagboard, crayons, glue, glitter, hole punch, yarn, hangers, scissors, string

Directions:
1. Duplicate the planetary patterns onto tagboard and cut them out.
2. Punch a hole in the top of each pattern.
3. Give each child a set of patterns to color and decorate with glue and glitter.
4. Tie a length of string onto each pattern and attach the patterns to the hangers, making a mobile for each child.
5. Hang the celestial mobiles in the classroom, from the ceiling or from a clothesline strung across the classroom.

Option:
Cover the body of each hanger with colored construction paper to make it more attractive. (See the illustration.)

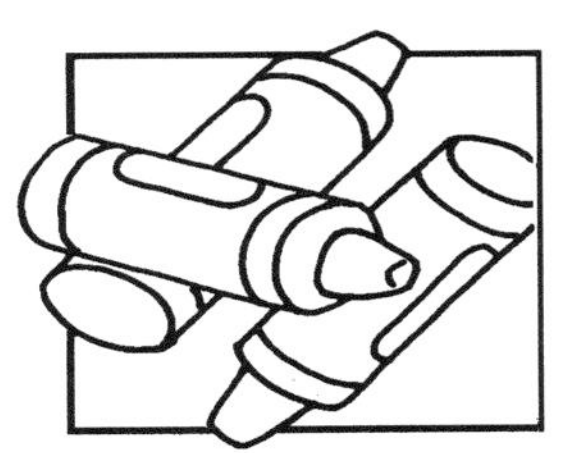

SKY
Art Activities

FOR THE BIRDS

Read a few bird books, such as *Birds*, created by Gallimard Jeunesse, Claude Delafosse, and Rene Mettler (A First Discovery Book, Scholastic, 1990) to show children a variety of birds: peacocks, flamingos, owls, woodpeckers, and ostriches. Then let the children create their own birds!

Materials:
Egg and bird patterns (pp. 270-271), colorful feathers, glue, glitter, construction paper, crayons, yarn, scissors

Directions:
1. Give each child a page of bird and egg patterns.
2. Let the children choose which patterns they want to use. They can cut out their desired patterns and glue them onto colored construction paper.
3. Have the children decorate the eggs with crayons, glitter, and glue, and the birds with feathers.
4. If they want, the children can glue a piece of yarn (or draw a line with a crayon) to attach each bird to its appropriate egg.
5. Post the completed pictures on a "For the Birds" bulletin board, with additional eggs cut out of colored construction paper and glued on for a border.

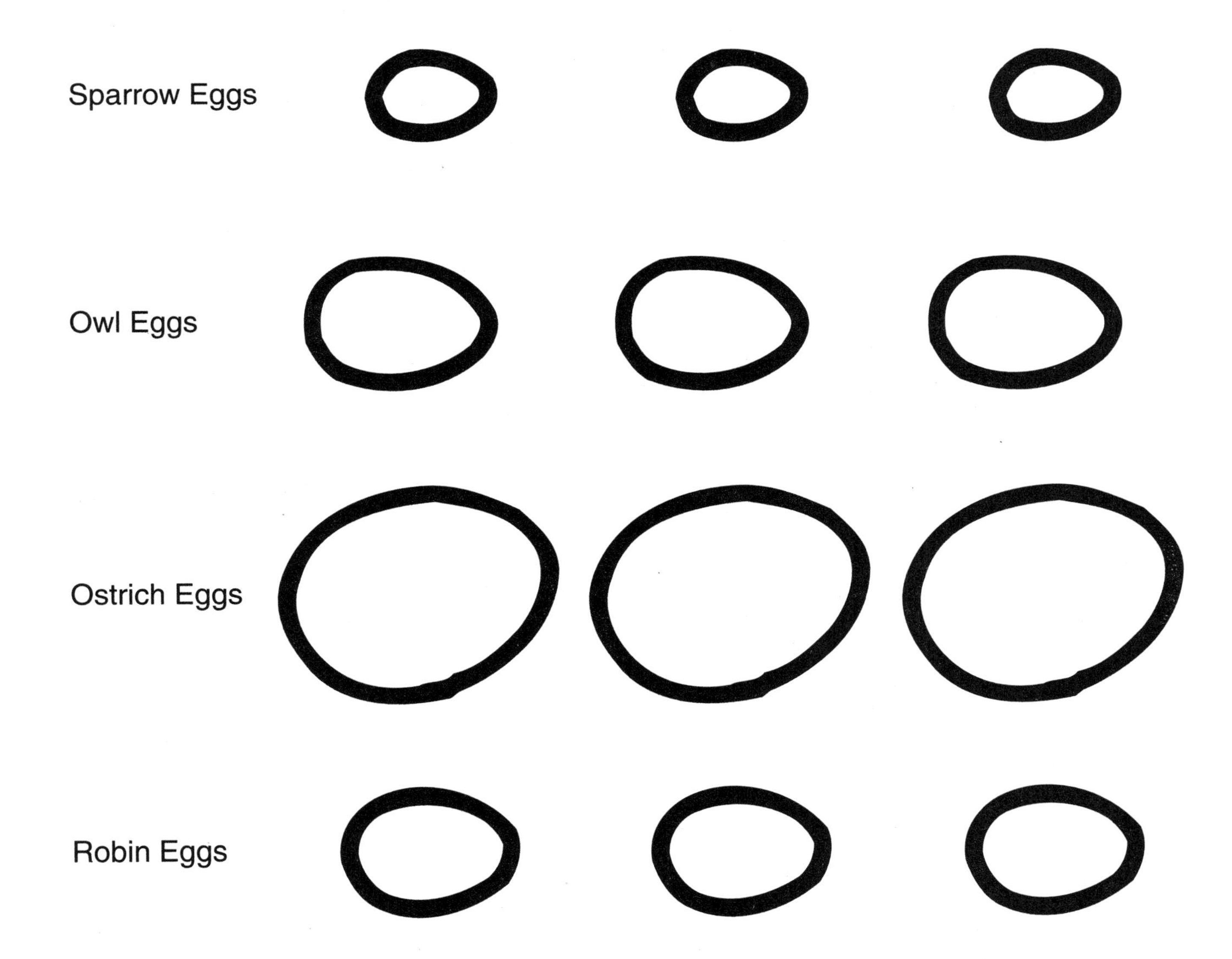
Sparrow Eggs
Owl Eggs
Ostrich Eggs
Robin Eggs

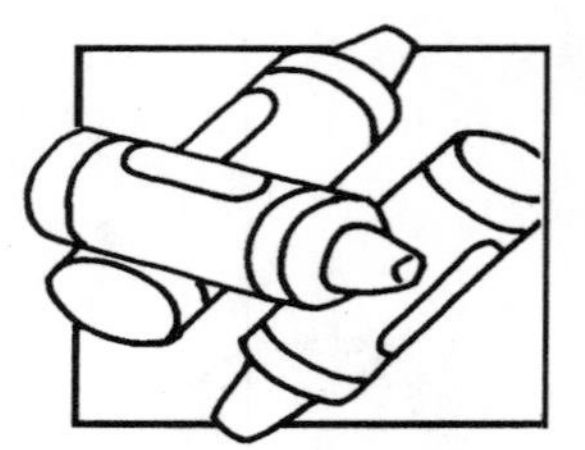

SKY
Art Activities

EGG PAINTING

Materials:
Hard-boiled eggs, egg dyes (available at Easter, or use watercolors), brushes, cardboard egg cartons

Directions:
1. Give each child a single egg carton section to hold an egg in place.
2. Show the children how to paint eggs, either using brushes and watercolors or using Easter egg dyes.
3. When the eggs have dried, display them in nests. (See below.)

NESTS

Materials:
Shredded newsprint or shredded crepe paper, small paper bowls (one per child), markers, crayons, glitter, sequins, glue

Directions:
1. Let the children decorate the small paper bowls with markers, crayons, glitter, and sequins.
2. Have children arrange the newsprint or crepe paper pieces in the paper bowls and glue in place.
3. Children can display their painted eggs in the nests.
4. Arrange the nests on a table display in front of a window. If available, place stuffed toy birds near the nests.

SKY

Storytime

FEATURED PICTURE BOOK

***It Looked Like Spilt Milk* by Charles G. Shaw (Harper, 1947).**
With its blue background and fluffy white cloud illustrations, this book mimics a crisp, springtime sky. Each page shows a different shape a cloud can make.

ART EXTENSION

Choose a day when the sky is filled with puffy white clouds to take the children outside for some cloud watching. Ask the children to try to find different shapes in the clouds. Then read *It Looked Like Spilt Milk.*

Materials:
Blue construction paper, white tempera paint in squeeze bottles

Directions:
1. Show the children how to use a paint-filled squeeze bottle to make cloud shapes.
2. Let the children use the paint to make simple cloud shapes on the blue construction paper.
3. After the pictures have dried, post them on a "Cloudy Day" bulletin board, and have the children try to find different shapes in the cloud pictures.

Option:
Have children cut out shapes from white construction paper to glue onto a blue background.

SKY

Storytime

MORE PICTURE BOOKS

Caretakers of Wonder by Cooper Edens (Green Tiger Press, 1980).
This story tells about the friends who put stars in the sky, fly the clouds (like kites), and make sure that the sun gets down safely. Each illustration, framed in gold, invites children to become one of these wonderful caretakers.

Dawn by Uri Shulevitz (Farrar, Straus and Giroux, 1974).
As you turn the pages of this book, the children will be able to witness the sky changing colors and night turning into day. Children will be mesmerized by the breathtaking watercolor pictures of a new day dawning.

Dougal Looks for Birds by Martha Bennett Stiles, illustrated by Iris Schweitzer (Four Winds Press, 1972).
When Dougal and his parents go bird watching, Dougal spots all sorts of birds that no one else can see—they're called "beginner's birds!"

How the Sun Was Brought Back to the Sky by Mirra Ginsburg, illustrated by Jose Aruego and Ariane Dewey (Macmillan, 1975).
When the sun doesn't appear for three days, a group of little chicks get worried. They enlist their animal friends to help them find the sun. The animals work together to bring the sun back to the sky.

Nora's Stars by Satomi Ichikawa (Philomel, 1989).
Nora and her dog Kiki go to visit Grandmother's house. In Nora's room, a toy box spills out toys that want to play with Nora. The toys take Nora outside to look at the stars, and they even go up into the sky to bring back stars for her. When the sky begins to cry, Nora gives the stars back.

Squawk to the Moon, Little Goose by Edna Mitchell Preston, illustrated by Barbara Cooney (Viking, 1974).
When Mrs. Goose goes to visit a friend, one of her little goslings decides to take a dip in the pond. At first, the gosling is fooled by the reflection of the moon in the pond, but is then able to use her knowledge to fool the fox.

NONFICTION BOOKS

Bird by David Burnie (Knopf, 1988).
This book shows feathers, down, eggs, and nests in great detail.

Bird Egg Feather Nest by Maryjo Koch (Stewart, Tabori & Chang, 1992).
This beautifully illustrated book will intrigue your children. Let them turn the pages and look at the pictures, or choose different types of birds, eggs, feathers, and nests to study in depth.

Birds by Maurice Burton (Orbis, 1985).
Color photographs show all kinds of birds in great detail: ostriches, penguins, pelicans, orioles, sparrows, and many more.

Feathers by Dorothy Hinshaw Patent, photographs by William Munoz (Dutton, 1992).
Show the children the color photographs of birds and feathers, and use the text to gather information that you feel will interest your class.

A First Look at Bird Nests by Millicent E. Selsam and Joyce Hunt, illustrated by Harriett Springer (Walker, 1984).
This is a factual book on specific birds and their nests. Use it to gather information for your students, and show them selected pictures.

SKY

Flannel Board

CHICKEN LITTLE

Once upon a time, on a nice sunny day,
Chicken Little decided to go out and play.
As she played in the dirt that was dusty and red,
Something small and quite hard went "kerplunk" on her head.
She'd been playing beneath her favorite **oak tree**,
"Oh, my gosh," the chick cried, "something fell and hit me!"
So she ran to her friend's house, all the way calling,
"Oh, Ms. **Henny Penny**, I think the sky's falling!
We must tell the king, we must tell him today!"
And off the two went, but they stopped on the way,
At their friend **Ducky Lucky**'s, who lived by a lake—
When they told her, she said, "It must be a mistake!"
"But I felt it," the chick said, "I was hit on the head."
"Then let's go and ask Lucy," her friend Ducky said.
When they reached **Goosey Lucy**, she made them be quiet,
And said, "Wait a minute, let's not cause a riot.
Now, why do you think that the sky's falling down?
We must be quite sure before we go to town."
"Well, something hit me, while I played in the yard,
Something small, very small, hit my head very hard,"
Chicken Little said, anxious to be on her way.
But Goosey said, "Wait, I know just where you play.
You were under the oak tree, now isn't that true?"
Chicken Little just nodded, then out of the blue,
She realized what old Goosey Lucy was saying,
Chick thought about where she'd been standing, while playing.
She'd been under the oak tree that very same morn,
She'd been hit on the head by a little **acorn**!
Chicken Little invited her friends for some pie—
To celebrate NOT being hit with the sky!

SKY

Discovery

COLOR ME A RAINBOW

Materials:
Construction paper in rainbow colors, white construction paper, scissors, glue or glue sticks

Directions:
1. Have your children try to spot a rainbow after it rains—or take them outside when the sprinklers are on and try and find the rainbow in the sprinkles. Or hang a prism in your classroom and find the time when the sun creates rainbows on your walls.
2. Discuss the colors that make up a rainbow: red, orange, yellow, green, blue, purple.
3. Cut out strips of construction paper in rainbow colors.
4. Have children make rainbows by gluing the strips onto a piece of white background paper in rainbow order.
5. After the glue dries, children may want to cut out a rainbow or other shape from their rainbow-striped pictures.

Option:
Post the rainbow-striped papers or rainbow cutouts on a "Pot of Gold" bulletin board. Make a construction paper pot of gold (black paper pot with gold glitter on top) and place it in the center of the bulletin board.

SKY

Discovery

CRAZY CLOUDS

Shaving cream has an extremely interesting texture for children to work with, creating "crazy clouds" and other shapes.

Materials:
Paper plates (one per child), shaving cream, Popsicle sticks, plastic spoons, newspaper (spread on table)

Directions:
1. Spray a small mound of shaving cream onto each child's plate.
2. Have the children use their hands to mold the shaving cream into cloud shapes. The shaving cream will hold the shapes for a while.
3. Children can try using Popsicle sticks, spoons, or other tools to shape their shaving cream clouds.
4. Ask the children to look at their clouds and describe what they've made, or if they see any familiar shapes within the cloud forms (like in *It Looked Like Spilt Milk*).

Option:
Go outside and look at the clouds before doing this project. Have the children try to find different shapes in the real clouds before making their own "crazy" ones.

MOON FACES

People often think they see a face in the moon. Now children can make their own moon faces!

Materials:
Face paints (blue, yellow, white, silver), mirrors

Directions:
1. Let the children create a variety of sky pictures on their faces. Simple suggestions: clouds, sun, or moon.
2. Provide standing mirrors for the children to look into while painting. Some children may want to paint each other's faces. Or have parent volunteers on hand to help out.

SKY

Discovery

CREATING CONSTELLATIONS

Introduce this activity by showing the children pictures of constellations in a book, for example, *The Earth and Sky*, created by Gallimard Jeunesse and Jean-Pierre Verdet (A First Discovery Book, Scholastic, 1989).

Materials:
Star stickers (or silver and gold crayons), blue or black construction paper

Directions:
1. Tell the children that people have been finding "pictures" in the stars for thousands of years.
2. Let the children create their own constellations using star stickers or silver and gold crayons on blue or black construction paper.
3. Post the finished pictures on a "Starry, Starry Night" bulletin board.
4. Have the children try to find designs among the stars in their made-up Milky Ways.

Option:
Help the children name their constellations, and write the names on star patterns (p. 268) to attach to their pictures. For example, if a child sees a tiger in her picture, she might want to call it "Tanya's Terrific Tiger!"

Note:
If possible, ask that parents take their children outside at night to look at the stars sometime during this unit. Then, hold a discussion with your children about what they saw in the sky.

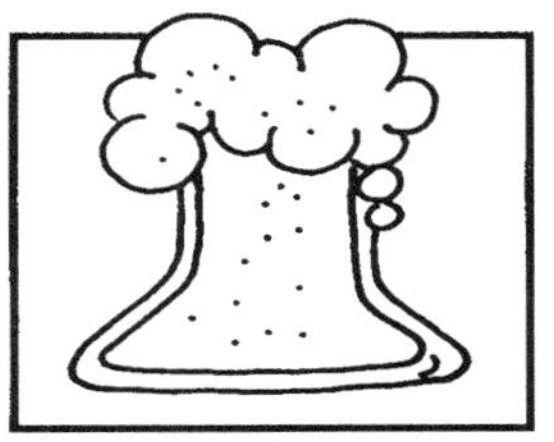

SKY

Discovery

PLANET PLACING

This project allows children to create their own magical night skies.

Materials:

Planet patterns (p. 282), blue and black construction paper, a variety of crayons including silver and gold, glitter, glue, celestial stickers (see Resources), scissors

Directions:

1. Duplicate and cut out enough planet patterns for every child to have one set.
2. Give each child a piece of blue or black construction paper to decorate with glitter, glue, silver and gold crayons, and stickers.
3. Have the children glue their planet patterns to their page. They may want to color the planets in, using one color for Mercury, another for Venus, a third for Earth, and so on.
4. Post the finished pictures on a "Perfect Planets" bulletin board.

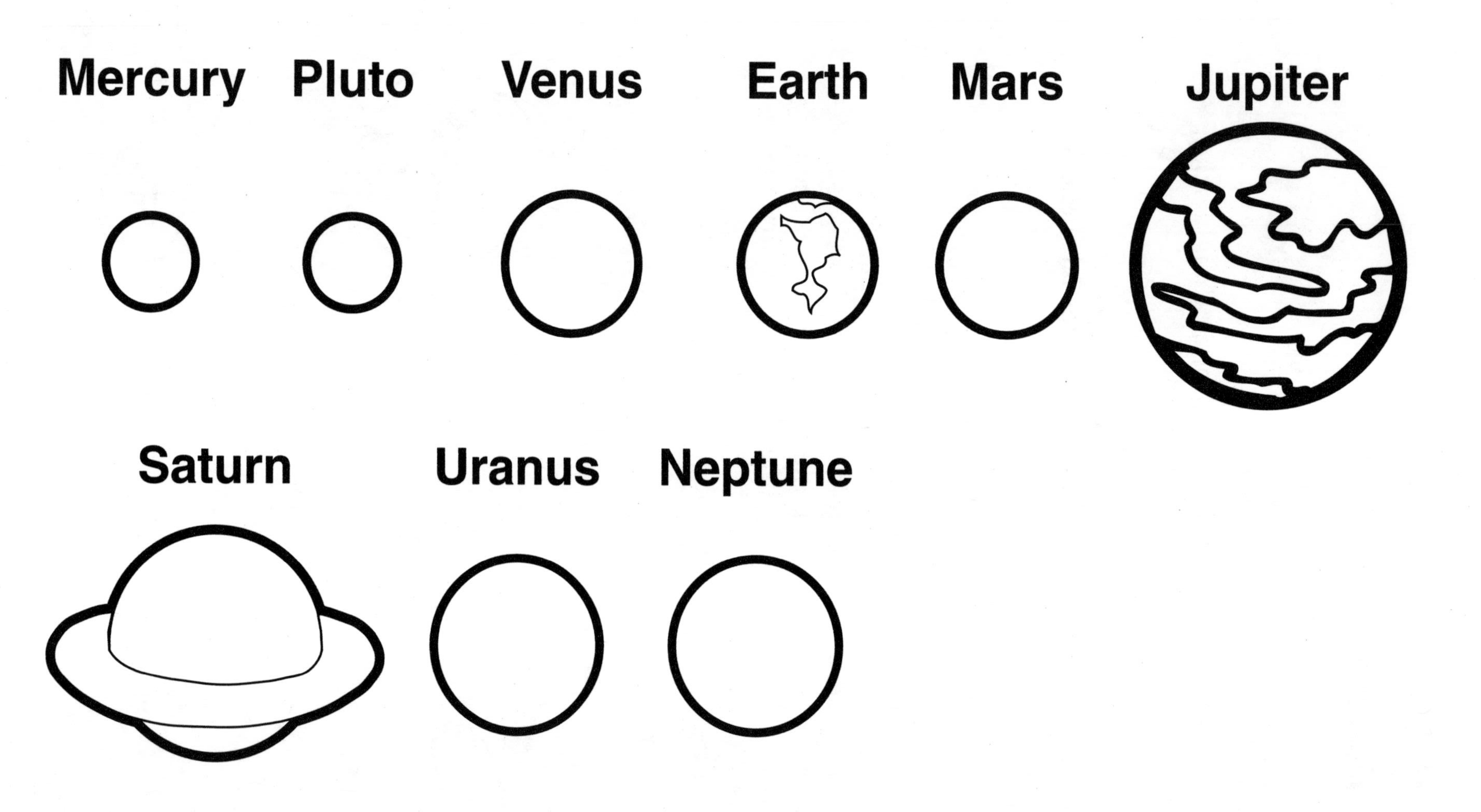
Mercury
Pluto
Venus
Earth
Mars
Jupiter
Saturn
Uranus
Neptune

SKY

Discovery

STAR SCULPTURES

This sparkly dough will lend a celestial air to any objects the children make with it. The glitter looks like stars in a night sky.

Materials:

Black or blue playdough, silver glitter, kitchen utensils (cookie cutters, garlic press, rolling pin), zip-lock bag

Directions:

1. Add glitter to the playdough and mix it with your hands until it is glittery.
2. Give each child a ball of the playdough to work with. The children can use various utensils to shape or mold their playdough into sculptures.
3. When the children are done playing, store the dough in a plastic bag until the next time you want to use it.

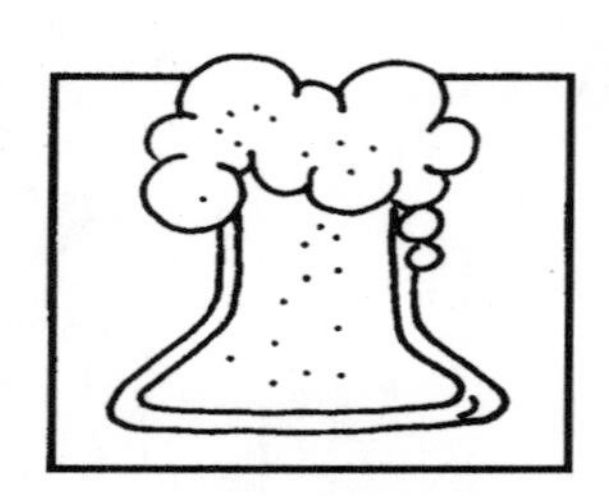

SKY

Discovery

BIRD WATCHING

Take your class bird watching, either in the playground, a park, or in your classroom. Read *Dougal Looks for Birds* by Martha Bennett Stiles, illustrated by Iris Schweitzer (Four Winds, 1972), to the children before doing this project. Refer to *Crinkleroot's Guide to Knowing the Birds* by Jim Arnosky (Bradbury, 1992) for more bird watching information.

Directions:

Do one or all of the following activities:

• Invite a bird specialist or a member of a local ornithology group to talk to the children.

• Play a game in which you describe a bird and have the children guess what kind it is. Play this after you have looked through a few picture books. Some bird choices include woodpeckers (make loud noises, are famous cartoon characters), owls (sleep at night, say "whooo"), flamingos (pink, stand on one foot), ostriches (largest bird in the world—up to 300 lbs.), hummingbirds (smallest bird in the world, moves wings fast), and peacocks (colorful feathers that spread in fan shape).

• Some birds are easy to act out. Have the children stand on one foot with their other leg up to become cranes. Or they can become pelicans by opening their "beaks" wide enough to scoop up fish (they can hold their arms in front of their faces to make pelican beaks). Show pictures of the different birds as you describe them. Bird books include *Feathers* by Dorothy Hinshaw Patent, photographs by William Munoz (Dutton, 1992), and *Birds* by Maurice Burton (Orbis, 1985).

• If any children have birds for pets, ask parents if they are available to bring in for observation.

• Egg comparisons are also interesting. Get a book on eggs, such as *Bird Egg Feather Nest* by Maryjo Koch (Stewart, Taori & Chang, 1992), and then bring in similarly sized objects. (An ostrich egg can weigh up to 3.3 lbs., or as much as 4,500 robins' eggs.) Eggs also vary in colors and designs.

SKY

Class Project

UNUSUAL UFO

Since nobody knows what the inside of a UFO looks like, children will have fun letting their imaginations run wild.

Materials:
Large box and assorted small boxes and containers, paper plates, tinfoil, non-toxic watercolors (gold and silver), tempera paint, paintbrushes, glue, pipe cleaners, scissors, egg cartons, craft knife

Directions:
1. Provide a large appliance box (from a washer, dryer, or refrigerator) for children to paint on the outside and decorate on the inside. Cut out porthole-shaped windows using a craft knife.
2. Cover paper plates with tinfoil, or let children paint the plates with gold and silver non-toxic watercolors. These disks can be glued to the outside of the "ship" or along a control panel.
3. Make sure that there are plenty of margarine tubs, lids, and assorted boxes for children to paint and glue to the UFO.
4. Pipe cleaners make good antennae (for radioing back to the home planet), and painted egg cartons, cut in half, make good control panels.
5. Steering wheels can also be plates covered with tinfoil.

To play with the creation:

- Place the UFO in the center of the room.
- Hang the Celestial Mobiles from clotheslines strung across the room. Children can look out the windows to see the stars and planets outside.
- Provide an assortment of colored face paints for children to use to turn themselves into wacky aliens.
- Children may want to create an interplanetary telephone using egg cartons or empty boxes so that they can "phone home."

To set the mood:
Play Elton John's "Rocket Man," David Bowie's "Major Tom," or music from *2001* ("Sprach Zarathustra" by Richard Strauss).

SKY

Mother Goose

There Was an Old Woman
There was an old woman tossed up in a basket
Nineteen times as high as the moon;
Where she was going I couldn't but ask it,
For in her hand she carried a broom.

"Old woman, old woman, old woman," cried I,
"Where are you going to up so high?"
"To brush the cobwebs off the sky!"
"Shall I go with thee?" "Ay, by-and-by."

The Man in the Moon
The man in the moon,
Came tumbling down,
And asked his way to Norwich;
He went by the south,
And burnt his mouth
With supping cold pease-porridge.

There Was a Maid on Scrabble Hill
There was a maid on Scrabble Hill,
And if not gone, she lives there still.
She grew so tall she reached the sky,
And on the moon hung clothes to dry.

Twinkle, Twinkle, Little Star
Twinkle, twinkle, little star,
How I wonder what you are!
Up above the world so high,
Like a diamond in the sky.

When the blazing sun is gone,
When he nothing shines upon,
Then you show your little light,
Twinkle, twinkle, all the night.

SKY

Mother Goose

There Was an Old Woman Who Rode on a Broom

There was an old woman who rode on a broom,
With a high gee ho, gee humble;
And she took her old cat behind for a groom,
With a bimble, bamble, bumble.

They travelled along till they came to the sky,
With a high gee ho, gee humble;
But the journey so long made them very hungry,
With a bimble, bamble, bumble.

Says Tom cat, "I can find nothing here to eat."
With a high gee ho, gee humble;
"So let's go back again, I entreat,"
With a bimble, bamble, bumble.

Old Mother Goose

Old Mother Goose
When she wanted to wander,
Would ride through the air
On a very fine gander.

A Star

Higher than a house,
Higher than a tree.
Oh, whatever can that be?

What's the News?

What's the news of the day,
Good neighbor, I pray?
They say the balloon
Has gone up to the moon.

SKY

Snacks

STAR-SPANGLED PASTA

Sing "Twinkle, Twinkle, Little Star" before you serve this snack.

Ingredients:
Star-shaped pasta, Parmesan cheese, butter

Directions:
1. Make the pasta according to the directions on the package.
2. Let the children sprinkle Parmesan cheese or add butter on top if they'd like.

Option:
Serve chicken soup with stars.

APPLE STARS

Once you've served this snack, you'll never cut apples the same way again!

Ingredients:
Whole apples (washed)

Directions:
1. Lay each apple on its side and cut it in slices down the middle (not from top to bottom; see illustration). Each round apple slice cut from the center will have a star shape where the seeds were.
2. Serve the apple slices to the children, making sure that every child gets one with a star.

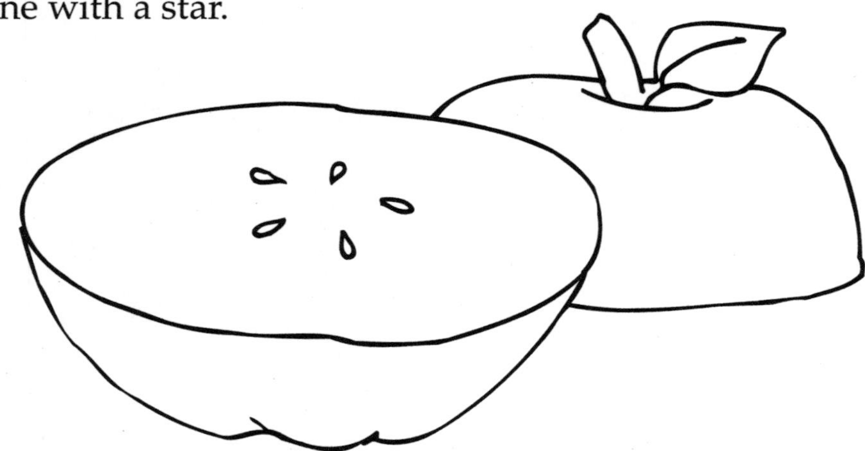

SKY

Snacks

RAINBOW TOAST

This colorful snack tastes as good as it looks.

Ingredients:
Pre-sliced white bread, milk, sugar, food coloring, clean paintbrushes (new or sterilized), cookie sheets, aluminum foil, permanent marker

Directions:
1. Mix milk with sugar to sweeten (approximately one teaspoon sugar per cup of milk).
2. Pour the milk mixture into several small dishes, and add a different food coloring to each one.
3. Let the children color pieces of white bread with the milk mixtures, "painting" with new or sterilized paintbrushes.
4. Place the decorated bread on foil-covered cookie sheets, labeling the nearby foil with each child's name.
5. Toast the bread lightly in an oven to dry and warm it. Serve while still warm and crunchy.

BIRD'S NEST

Do your children think vegetables are "for the birds"? Here's a snack idea that will have them chirping for more!

Ingredients:
Alfalfa sprouts, radishes, cherry tomatoes, small paper bowls or cups, olives

Directions:
1. Let children create a bird's nest by lining a small paper bowl or cup with alfalfa sprouts.
2. Have them add radish, cherry tomato, or olive "eggs," then eat!

Option:
Let the children observe real birds' nests they or you find to see how birds weave a variety of found sticks and string into their nest. You could provide grated carrot or other vegetables to weave into the sprouts.

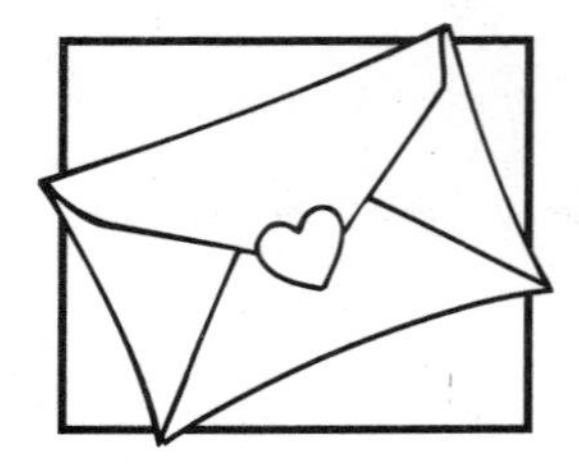

SKY

Letter Home

Hey, diddle, diddle,
The cat and the fiddle,
The cow jumped over the moon.
The little dog laughed,
To see such a sight,
And the dish ran away
With the spoon.
—Mother Goose

This month we are honoring the sky by studying birds, clouds, rainbows, spaceships, and UFOs. We will be learning about the planets, creating "Celestial Mobiles," and dying eggs.

If possible, take your child outside to look at the stars. We will be discussing the constellations in class, and making star sculptures from glittery playdough.

We will be learning about the different kinds of bird eggs, nests, feathers, and sounds. We would like to invite any ornithologists and bird watchers to come to our classroom and discuss birds and share bird stories.

For our spaceship and UFO activities, we need:

- egg cartons (for control panels)
- old stereo headsets (to radio the control tower)
- lids from margarine tubs and juice jars (for buttons and dials)
- metal hangers (for mobiles)

Thanks for your help!

July: Transportation

Planes, trains, and automobiles fascinate most children. But your students may not be as familiar with the other modes of transportation that are used around the world and in space travel. Introduce this unit by reading *On the Go* by Ann Morris, photographs by Ken Heyman (Lothrop, 1990). While you read this book, have the children imagine that they are riding on the back of a camel, or blasting off on a rocket ship to the moon! Then let them create their own "Totally Tubular Rocket" (p. 294).

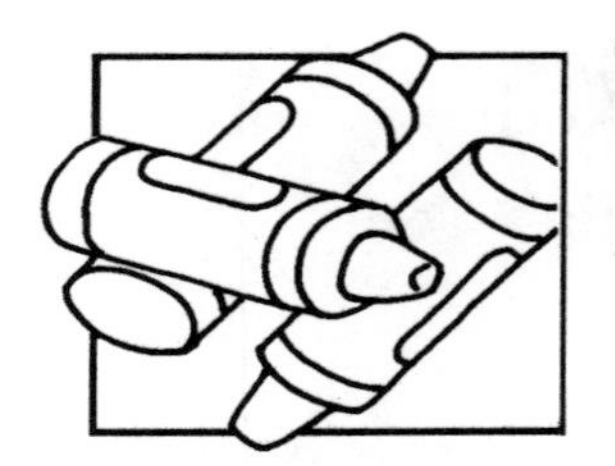

TRANSPORTATION

Art Activities

AIRPLANE ART

Have your children imagine that they are in an airplane, high above the ground. Read *Going on an Airplane* by Fred Rogers, photographs by Jim Judkis (G. P. Putnam's Sons, 1989), or *Your First Airplane Trip* by Pat and Joel Ross, illustrated by Lynn Wheeling (Lothrop, 1981).

Materials:
Window pattern (p. 293), cotton balls, glue, stickers (stars, suns, moons, clouds, rainbows; see Resources), crayons

Directions:
1. If any children have flown on an airplane, have them describe their experience to the rest of the class. Ask them what they remember seeing from the window. If no children have flown, invite a child from another classroom to describe his or her flying experience.
2. Have the children use the various materials to create a picture outside their "airplane window." Their pictures can be realistic (with mountains below, clouds, a sun) or fanciful (with rocket ships, other planets). They can make a night sky with lots of stars or a day sky with a big, yellow sun.
3. Post the completed pictures in a row along one wall and use them for part of your Airplane Class Project (see p. 312).

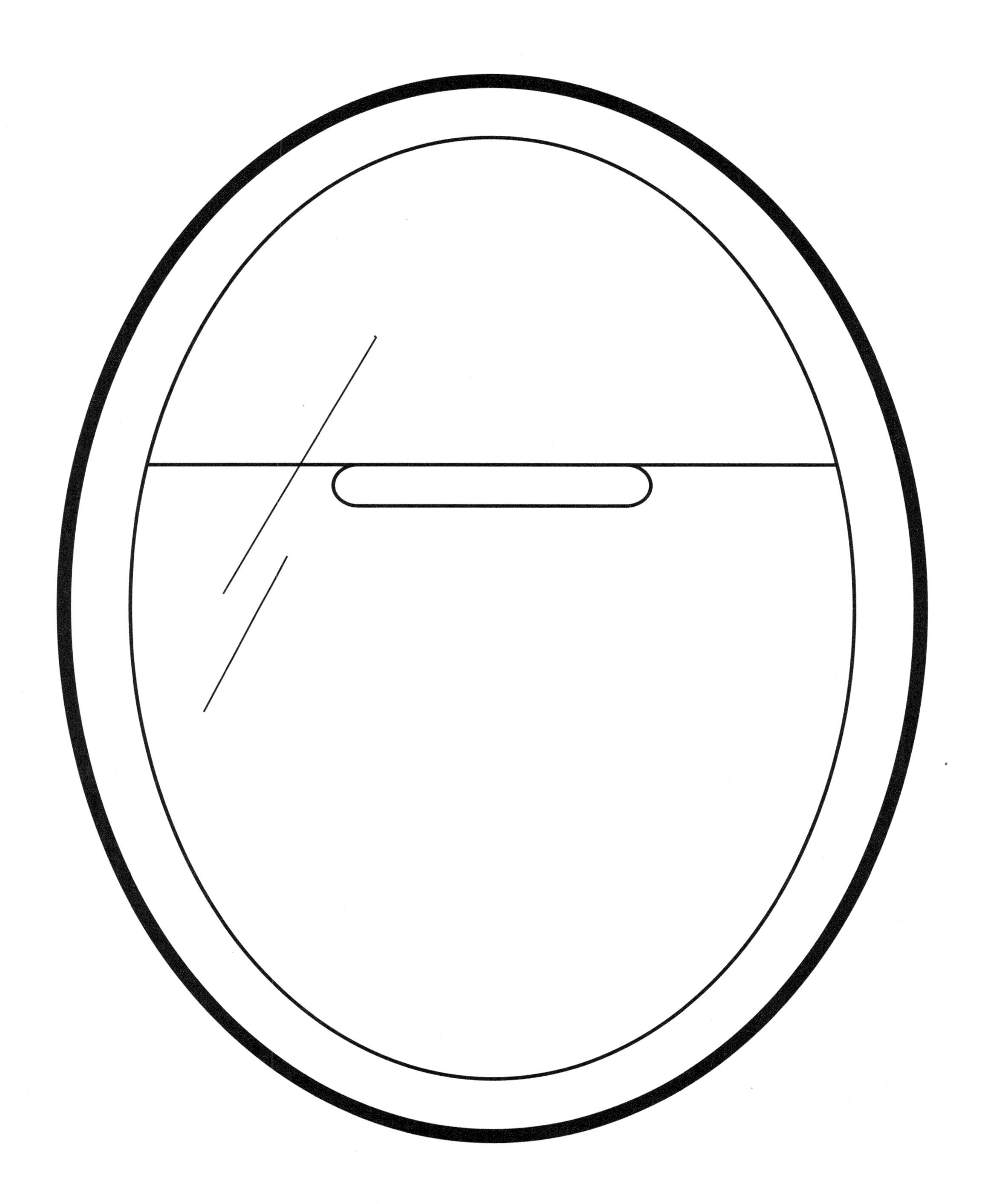

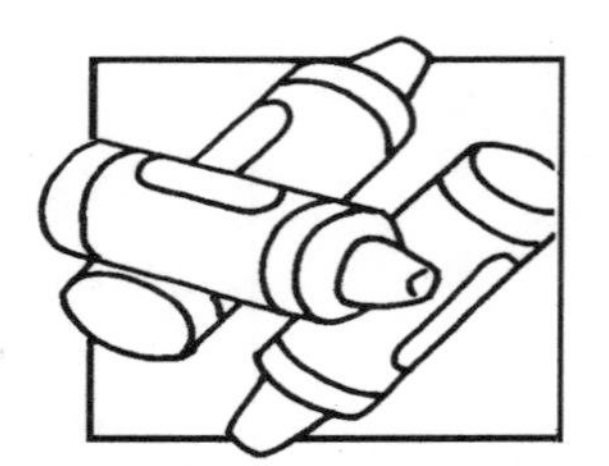

TRANSPORTATION
Art Activities

TOTALLY TUBULAR ROCKET
Your children will think these toilet paper tube rocket ships are awesome!

Materials:
Toilet paper tubes (one per child), aluminum foil, hole reinforcers, shredded crepe paper (orange, yellow, red), glue, scissors, small construction paper squares, large sheet of blue construction paper, glue

Directions:
1. Have the children cover their toilet paper tubes with aluminum foil.
2. They can use the hole reinforcers for porthole windows and shredded crepe paper for fire (glued to the base of the toilet paper tube).
3. Show the children how to make cone shapes from small squares of construction paper by rolling the edges toward each other and gluing along the seam.
4. The children can glue the cones to the top of the rockets.
5. After the rockets dry, display them on a table covered with blue construction paper. Label the display "We Are Out of this World!"

Option:
Let the children decorate the blue construction paper background using stick-on stars or gold and silver crayons. Or let them use planet patterns (see "Sky," p. 282) to cut out and glue onto the blue paper.

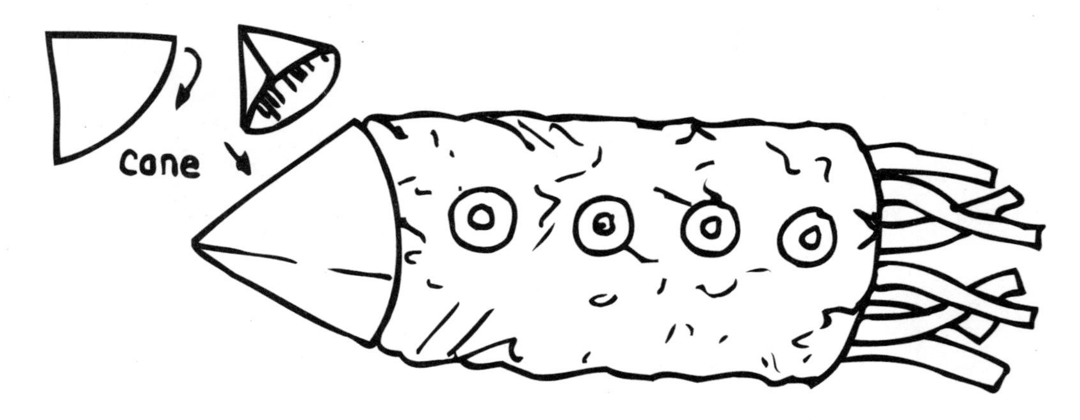

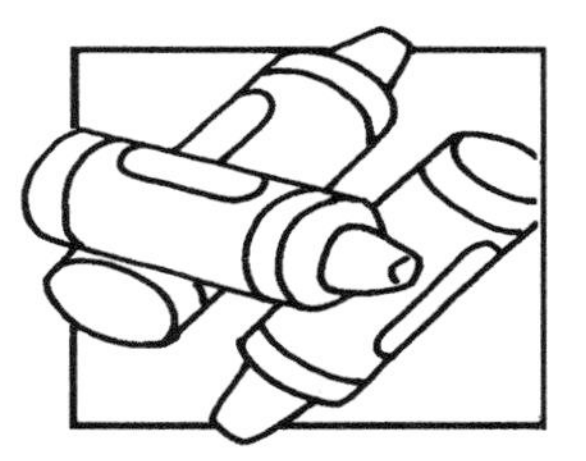

TRANSPORTATION

Art Activities

TERRIFIC TRACKS

Have your children observe the different tracks in the world around them: bird prints, cat prints, truck tracks, bike treads, car tire tracks, and so on. Explain to your students that their feet are a great means of transportation, and then let them make their own tracks!

Materials:
Butcher paper, a variety of colored tempera paint in pie pans, tape, soapy water in plastic tubs, paper towels

Directions:
1. Tape a long sheet of butcher paper to the floor.
2. Have children take off their shoes and socks.
3. Let children take turns dipping their feet in the paint (just to coat the soles) and then walk across the butcher paper. (Have soapy water in plastic tubs and paper towels at the other end for quick and easy washing and drying.)
4. Post the completed "Terrific Tracks" mural on a wall or bulletin board.

Option 1:
Provide glitter and glue for children to use to decorate their footprints. If you have old shoes in your dress-up area, you might let children use the soles to print with.

Option 2:
Give each child a copy of the Track patterns (p. 296), and let them try to guess what creature or vehicle made the tracks pictured.

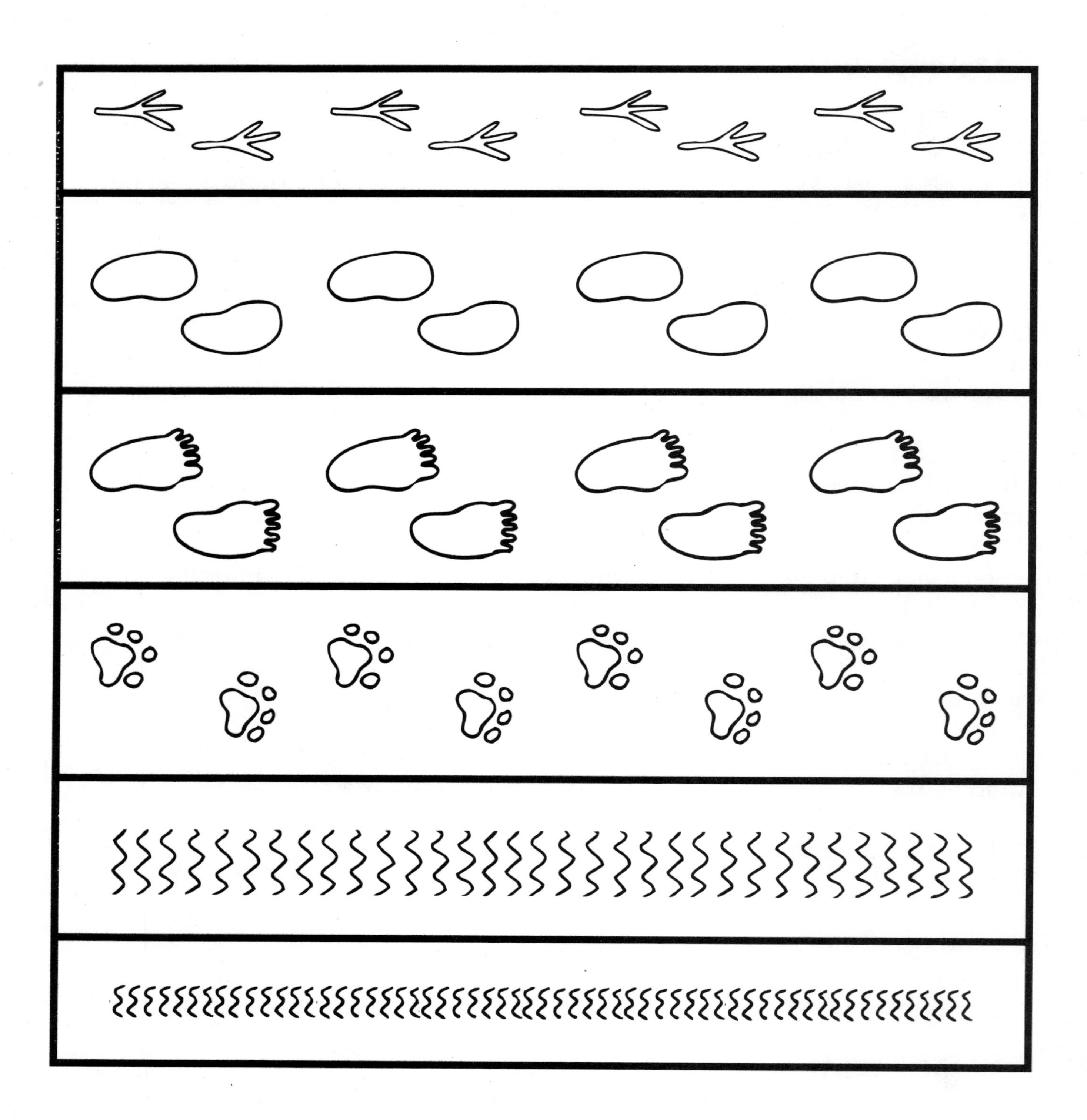

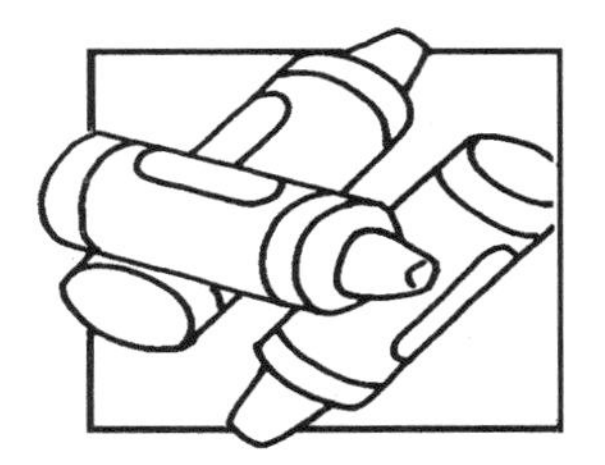

TRANSPORTATION

Art Activities

DOING THE CAN-CAN

Children can create treads from their own imaginary vehicles using recycled cans!

Materials:

Juice cans or aluminum cans (one per child), glue, an assortment of textured materials (Styrofoam packing peanuts, corks, sponges, sandpaper squares, cotton balls, buttons, beads, etc.), masking tape or packing tape, tempera paint in a variety of colors, paintbrushes, paper, pen

Directions:

1. Cover open edges of the cans with masking tape or packing tape, making sure that the edges are completely smooth.
2. Give each child a can to cover with textured materials. The children can glue on cut pieces of sponges and corks, whole packing peanuts, squares of sandpaper, cotton balls, and so on.
3. After the cans dry, let children roll them in tempera paint (or use brushes to paint the cans), and then roll the cans onto paper to make prints.
4. Ask children to imagine the type of vehicle that made the treads. (A Martian spaceship?) Write the names of their creations on separate pieces of paper and post on a bulletin board with the pictures.

TRANSPORTATION

Storytime

FEATURED PICTURE BOOK

Christina Katerina and the Great Bear Train **by Patricia Lee Gauch, illustrated by Elise Primavera (G. P. Putnam's Sons, 1990).**
Christina Katerina isn't too excited about the prospect of being an older sister. While everyone is busy preparing for the new baby, Christina takes her bears on an adventure through the neighborhood. The stuffed bears ride in a shoe box train, and everyone enjoys the excursion . . . until it begins to rain!

ART EXTENSION

Invite your students to bring in their stuffed teddy bears on the day you plan this activity. Read this book with your students (and their bear friends), and then let the children share the names of their bears. Ask if any of your students have ridden on a real train, and let them share their experiences.

Materials:
Shoe boxes (one per child), train patterns (p. 299), construction paper, wrapping paper, hole punch, yarn, scissors, crayons, glue

Directions:
1. Punch a hole in both short ends of each shoe box.
2. Give each child a shoe box to decorate with the train patterns, construction paper, wrapping paper, and crayons.
3. Thread yarn through the holes to link the boxes together. Tie a knot in the yarn at the last box, and leave enough yarn free at the first box to serve as a handle. You may want to make a few trains of three to four cars each depending on the number of students in your class.
4. Encourage the students to take turns playing the engineer who pulls the train along, or the conductor who calls out the names of the different places in your classroom, for example, "All aboard! Next stop is the Book Nook!"

ENGINE
99
TICKET

TRANSPORTATION

Storytime

MORE PICTURE BOOKS

The Caboose Who Got Loose by Bill Peet (Houghton Mifflin, 1971).
Katy Caboose doesn't like being last. She wishes she were almost anything but a caboose. When the train chugs its way up a steep hill, Katy's bolt breaks and she is free! This tale is told entirely in rhyme.

Christina Katerina and the Great Bear Train by Patricia Lee Gauch, illustrated by Elise Primavera (G. P. Putnam's Sons, 1990).
Christina Katerina takes her teddy bears (in their shoe box train) on a journey. She takes in the different sights with her bear companions, and always keeps her head—even when some of the bears get worried that they are lost. This is a very good "new baby" book.

Daisy's Taxi by Ruth Young, illustrated by Marcia Sewall (Orchard, 1991).
Daisy's taxi transports people and objects of various shapes and sizes. But it isn't a normal taxi. Daisy's taxi is a boat that she rows from the mainland to the island, out and back, every day!

I Go with My Family to Grandma's by Riki Levinson, illustrated by Diane Goode (E. P. Dutton, 1986).
Five cousins and their families meet up at grandma's house. The families come from the five boroughs of New York City, and each arrives by a different means of transportation: bicycle, trolley, train, car, boat.

Jenny's Journey by Sheila White Samton (Viking, 1991).
Jenny takes an imaginary journey to visit her friend Maria, who has moved away. Jenny travels across the sea, around islands, and through a storm to visit her pal.

Left Behind by Carol Carrick, illustrated by Donald Carrick (Clarion, 1988).
Christopher is very excited about the class field trip to the aquarium—but he is even more excited about the chance to ride a subway. When he becomes separated from his class, Christopher must figure out a way to let his teacher know where he is.

Mr. Grumpy's Motor Car by John Burningham (Thomas Y. Crowell, 1973).
Mr. Grumpy goes for an adventurous ride in his convertible with a group of children and animals. (*Mr. Grumpy's Outing* is in the same series.)

Mrs. Armitage on Wheels by Quentin Blake (Alfred A. Knopf, 1987).
Mrs. Armitage decides that the bell on her bike really isn't loud enough, so she buys three horns. When she gets dirty fixing her bike chain, she decides to add a bucket of water, then a toolbox, a snack basket, a dog chair, and on and on. Children will love the silly ending!

Rabbit Express by Michael Gay (William Morrow, 1982).
Rabbit receives a pair of skates for his birthday. But he has trouble finding a place to use them. He goes to the city, where he meets a flute-playing cat, and together they embark on a skating adventure.

This Is the Way We Go to School: A Book About Children Around the World by Edith Baer, illustrated by Steve Bjorkman (Scholastic, 1990).
Some children walk slowly to school, others jog, and others roller skate! Some children in San Francisco take cable cars to school, others in Venice ride the vaporetto! After reading this book, discuss the different ways your children go to school—and the ways they'd like to!

TRANSPORTATION

Storytime

NONFICTION BOOKS

The Elevator Escalator Book: A Transportation Fact Book by Bob Barner (Doubleday, 1990).
Children have many questions about daily means of transportation, such as, "What happens to the stairs at the top of an up escalator?" Use this book to gather answers—it is not a "read-aloud."

Going on an Airplane by Fred Rogers, photographs by Jim Judkis (G. P. Putnam's Sons, 1989).
This book describes an entire trip in photographs—from packing to arriving at the final destination.

On the Go by Ann Morris, photographs by Ken Heyman (Lothrop, 1990).
There are many different means of transportation around the world, including camels, oxen, buses, trolleys, and monorails. While you read this book, have the children imagine that they are riding on the back of a camel, or blasting off on a rocket ship to the moon!

Things That Go by Anne Rockwell (Dutton, 1986).
This book is divided into sections, including things that go on the road, on the water, in the air, and more. You can show the children different pages, depending on what area you are concentrating.

Your First Airplane Trip by Pat and Joel Ross, illustrated by Lynn Wheeling (Lothrop, 1981).
The text in this book may be a bit too long to read to children. Select passages that you think will interest your students, for example, about the jetway, the cockpit, or the seat belts.

TRANSPORTATION

Flannel Board

THE LITTLE CABOOSE THAT DID

Once upon a time, in a famous **train yard**,
A **papa caboose** was working too hard
To help his young **son** get over his fear
Of being too little to bring up the rear.

"A caboose is important," the papa train said.
"You aren't too little, it's just in your head."
But the little caboose just started to cry.
He went off and hid, he would not even try.

His **mama** said, "Look at your **brother**, my dear.
He's proud of caboosing, and he shows no fear.
If you want to be something, you just have to try.
That's all that we're asking, so please do not cry."

His brother said, "Think of the **book** that we read,
About that young engine, and what he said.
He said to himself, 'I can, yes, I can.'"
But the little caboose skipped a track and ran.

Then he thought to himself, "You know, maybe they're right.
I haven't tried it, and I'm sick of the fright."
So he hitched himself up to the very last car.
And he made it, he did it, he became a **star!**

He never was frightened, not ever again,
He was proud of caboosing, and ending the train.
He said to his family, "I'm sorry I hid."
And from then on they called him "The caboose that did!"

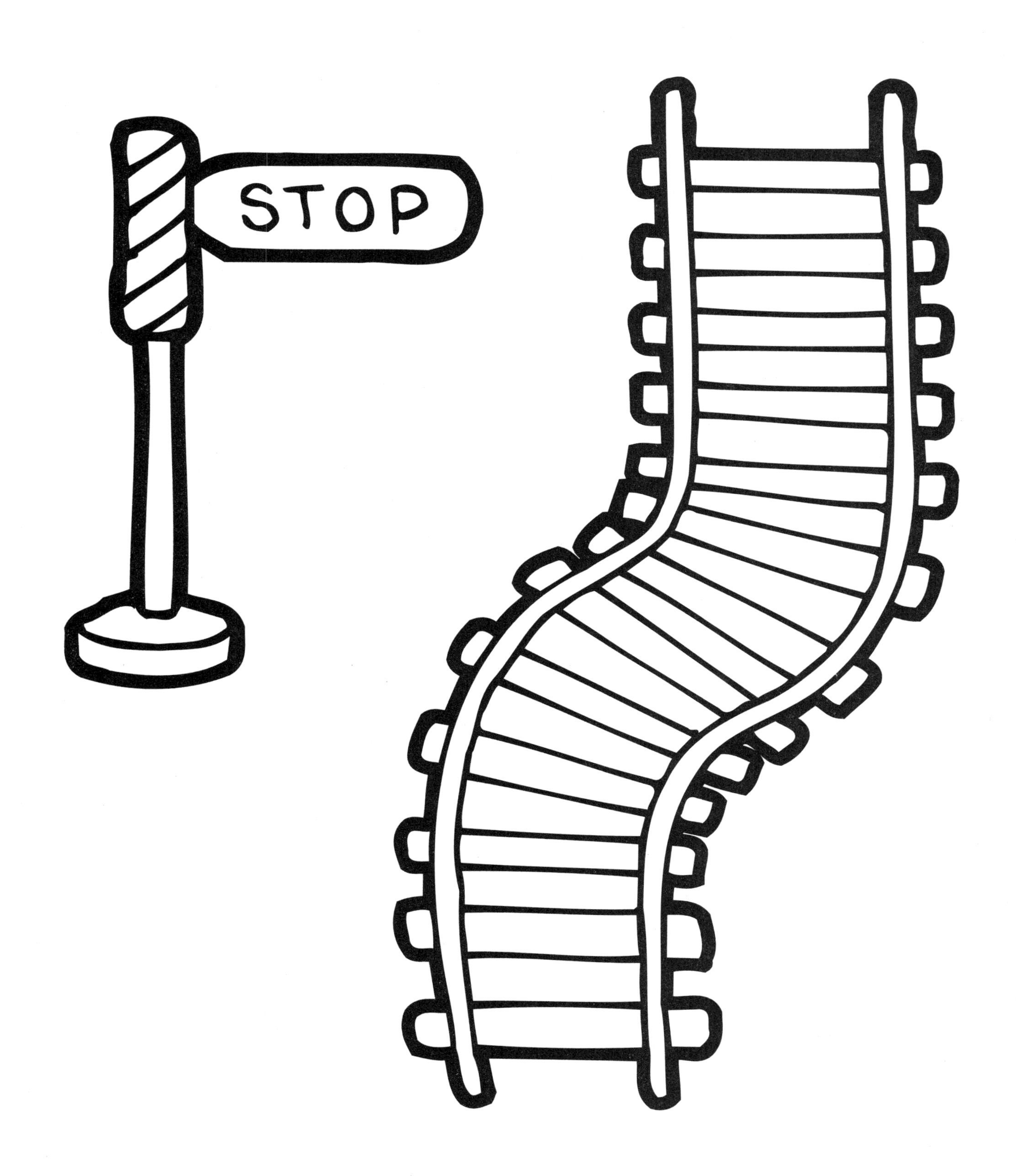
STOP

TRANSPORTATION

Discovery

TRUCK TRACKS

Materials:
Toy trucks and cars, mud or wet sand

Directions:
1. Let your children help create a setting to make tire tracks. Wet dirt (not too gloppy) or wet sand works well. Encourage your children to try out different types of environments to see which hold the best tracks.
2. Provide a variety of toy trucks, cars, trains, and other wheeled vehicles for children to use to make tracks.
3. Have the children observe the different treads of their tracks. You might have them play a game—one child uses a specific toy to make a track and another has to guess which toy was used.

TRANSPORTATION

Discovery

REAL TRACKS

Materials:
Real tires (truck, bicycle, car), wet sand or mud

Directions:
1. Let children roll the tires on a muddy or wet sand surface.
2. Have the children observe the different treads made by the different tires.
3. Ask the children why they think that some tires are thicker than others and some tires have more traction. Have children imagine that they are walking down a steep hill. Ask them if they would rather be wearing flat-soled sandals, or sneakers with extra grips on the bottom.

Option:
Let children paint the tires with tempera paint and thick brushes. Have them work together to roll the tires on butcher paper. Encourage children to observe the different tread marks made by the painted tires.

TRANSPORTATION

Discovery

FIRE ENGINE FIELD TRIP

Children are fascinated by fire engines. If possible, plan a field trip to a fire station where children can observe the trucks up close and even explore them. Otherwise, invite a firefighter into your classroom to discuss the experience of riding in a fire engine. Talk about the ladders and hoses, and the reason fire trucks are often painted in bright colors.

GREAT GARBAGE FIELD TRIP

On trash day, let your children observe the sanitation engineers at work. They will most definitely be enthralled by the large truck as it swallows the garbage. If possible, let them watch the recycling truck on its route, as well.

PICK-UP TRUCK

If any student's family owns a pick-up truck or camper, see if it can be driven into the school parking lot for "show and tell." Pick a non-busy time for your school and rope off an area where no other traffic is allowed. Campers are filled with interesting things to see, and pick-up trucks (which are high off the ground) will interest children who have only ridden in cars or on bikes.

BUS STOP

Plan a bus trip . . . anywhere! Children will enjoy watching the world from up above the rest of the traffic. If you are planning to visit a fire station, take a bus there. Or take a bus ride to a local park.

TRANSPORTATION

Discovery

TRANSPORTATION PARADE

Materials:
Roller skates, bikes and trikes, skateboards, other modes of transportation

Directions:
1. Invite your students to bring their favorite personal mode of transportation to school.
2. Have children assemble in groups by their transportation choices: a group of roller skaters (or in-line skaters), a group of trikers and bikers, a group of skateboarders, and so on. Some students may want to hop, skip, gallop, or walk.
3. Let your students put on a transportation parade in the schoolyard. Ask other classes to watch or participate.

Option:
Let children decorate their various devices before the parade. They can attach paper streamers to the backs of skateboards, lace skates with colorful glitter shoelaces, and tie bows to handlebars. Walkers, hoppers, and skippers may want to paint their faces or wear colorful clothes.

TRANSPORTATION

Discovery

FROM HERE TO THERE

Materials:
Toy vehicles (cars, trains, trucks, airplanes, helicopters, bicycles), blocks, toy people and animals

Directions:
1. Help your students set up a play town using their blocks and toy people and animals. They might even use the materials they created in "Box City" (see "Homes," p. 117) or the terrain map (see "Earth," p. 223).
2. Once the village is finished, let the children use the various transportation devices to maneuver the toy people around the city.
3. Ask the children questions, such as, "What would be the best way to get from this part of the city to the library?" Or "How should I get over that mountain to visit my family?" Encourage creative responses. You might ask the children what the shortest way would be, using the fewest types of transportation. Then let them figure out what the longest route would be, using all of the different modes of transportation available to them.

TRANSPORTATION

Class Project

AMAZING AIRPLANE

To create a classroom airplane, line up chairs along a bulletin board. Post the finished "Airplane Art" windows at child level, so that each seat has a corresponding window. Items to have on hand:

- seat belts (can be scarves or scraps of fabric)
- magazines to "read" during flight
- plastic cups for "beverages" (if you set up the plane near your housekeeping area, children acting as flight attendants can go to and from the kitchen to get play food and drink for the passengers)
- hats with brims for the pilots
- small cart or wagon for the "food" and "drinks"
- life vests, headsets, playing cards
- emergency procedure cards (duplicate the emergency procedure card pattern on p. 313 onto tagboard, and cover with Contact paper)

Have your children make a front window and control panel for the pilots. Spread two large sheets of butcher paper on a flat surface for children to decorate. Designate one sheet as a night sky and the other as a day sky. Let children use the skills they have mastered in "Airplane Art" and "Creating Constellations" (see "Sky") to decorate the pictures. Post the finished skies on a moveable divider and place it at the front of the "plane" for the pilots. The children can decide whether they want to use the day or night sky picture.

For control panels, let children paint egg cartons cut in half and metal caps from juice bottles and glue them to a heavy piece of poster board. Place the control panel on a table in front of the plane's windshield. A paper plate covered with tinfoil can work for a steering wheel, and old headphones from stereos make good radio headsets.

During this activity, play "Major Tom" by David Bowie or "Rocket Man" by Elton John.

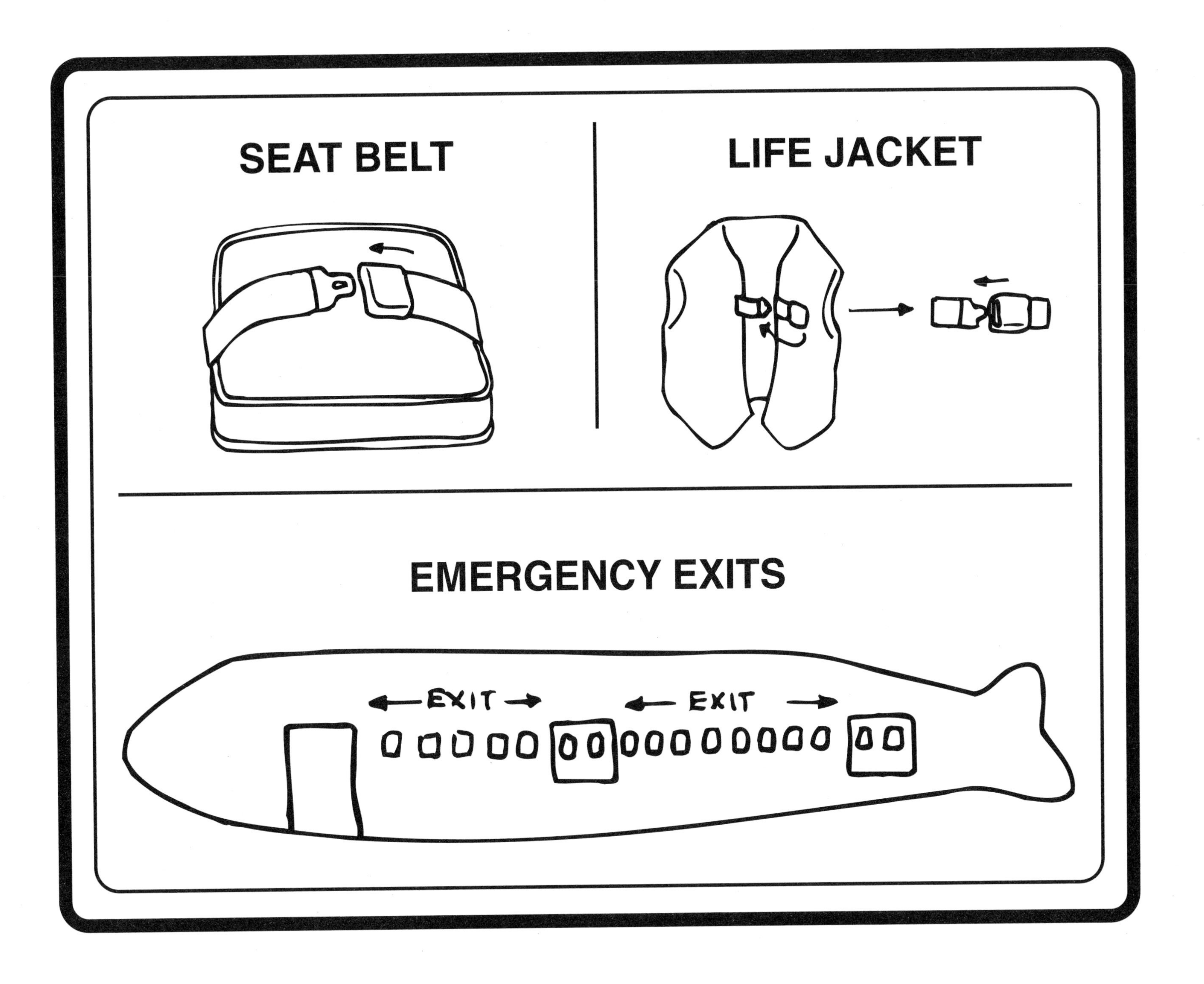

SEAT BELT
LIFE JACKET
EMERGENCY EXITS
EXIT
EXIT

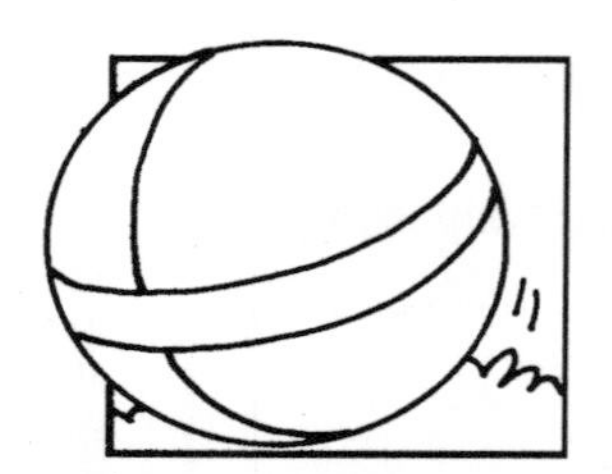

TRANSPORTATION

Games

RED LIGHT, GREEN LIGHT

One child is the stoplight and the rest of the children are cars, buses, bikes, and trolleys. When the stoplight says, "Green," he or she turns to face away from the vehicles and they get to "drive." When the stoplight says, "Red," he or she turns to face the vehicles and they have to stop (and freeze in position). The first vehicle to reach and tag the stoplight becomes the stoplight for the next game. Vehicles who do not stop at the red light are out.

THE GRAND OLD DUKE OF YORK

This motion game is played to the Mother Goose rhyme of the same name. Children begin the game by squatting on the floor. As they stand they can march in place.

Oh, the grand old Duke of York,
(Begin to stand.)
He had ten thousand men,
(Stand slowly, almost upright.)
He marched them up to the top of the hill,
(Stand fully upright with raised hands.)
And he marched them down again.
(Return to squatting position.)
And when they were up they were up.
(Stand up with raised hands.)
And when they were down they were down.
(Squat again.)
And when they were only halfway up
They were neither up nor down!
(Bend over from waist.)

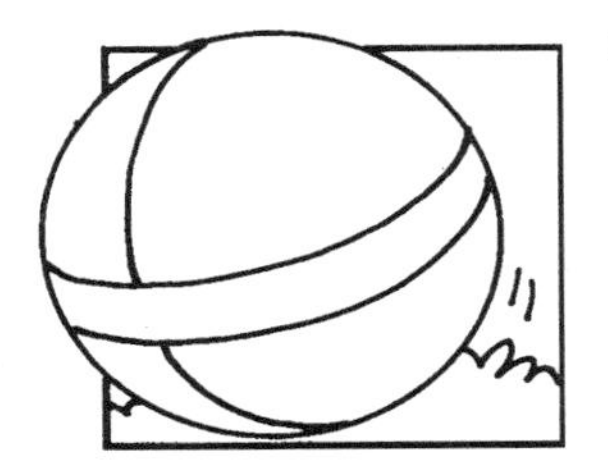

TRANSPORTATION

Games

A TRAIN GOES . . .

1. Hold a discussion with your children about the different means of transportation around the world. Have them think about the noises they hear during traffic. Talk to them about the ways that people and animals move.
2. Have your children imagine that they are going to change very quickly from one mode of transportation to another. They will have to act like each form of transportation, making the appropriate noises and movements.
3. Tell your children that they are trains, and that a train goes, "Chugga, chugga, chugga, chugga, chooo, chooo!" Encourage them to make wheel motions with their arms and shoulders to show that they are "chugging."
4. Now have your children imagine that they are kangaroos. Ask them how kangaroos get from one place to another. Then have them show you, and let them hop around the classroom.
5. Next, have the children pretend that they are airplanes. They can "vrroom" as they fly from the water table to the science center.
6. Continue this activity as long as you like, continually changing the animals and objects the children are supposed to be.

Additional Suggestions:
Car, boat, cat, dump truck, turtle, helicopter, bunny, fire engine, snail, steam shovel

Option 1:
Let the children decide what form of transportation they want to be. You might even hold a game of Transportation Charades!

Option 2:
Duplicate the transportation patterns (pp. 316-317), glue them onto tagboard, laminate, and cut out. Place the patterns in a hat and have each child pick one. Let the children take turns acting out their chosen vehicle.

TAXI
SUBWAY

TRANSPORTATION

Songs

I'm a Little Airplane
(to the tune of "I'm a Little Teapot")

I'm a little airplane
Watch me fly.
I can zoom across the sky.
You can hear my engine—
"Vroom" so loud,
While I zig-zag through the clouds.

I Can Ride My Tricycle
(to the tune of "Mary Had a Little Lamb")

I can ride my tricycle,
Tricycle,
Tricycle,
I can ride my tricycle,
Every single day.

Then I ride it home again,
Home again,
Home again,
Then I ride it home again,
And put it safe away.

Additional Transportation Songs
"She'll Be Coming 'Round the Mountain"
"Jingle Bells"
"Over the River and Through the Woods"

TRANSPORTATION

Mother Goose

Bumpety, Bumpety

A farmer went trotting upon his grey mare,
  Bumpety, bumpety, bump!
With his daughter behind him so rosy and fair,
  Lumpety, lumpety, lump!

A raven cried, Croak! and they all tumbled down,
  Bumpety, bumpety, bump!
The mare broke her knees and the farmer his crown,
  Lumpety, lumpety, lump!

The mischievous raven flew laughing away,
  Bumpety, bumpety, bump!
And vowed he would serve them the same the next day,
  Lumpety, lumpety, lump!

How Many Miles to Babylon?

How many miles to Babylon?
Three score miles and ten.
Can I get there by candle-light?

Yes, and back again.
If your heels are nimble and light,
You may get there by candle-light.

TRANSPORTATION

Mother Goose

This Is the Way the Ladies Ride

This is the way the ladies ride,
Tri, tre, tri, tree, tri, tre, tri tree!
This is the way the ladies ride,
Tri, tre, tri, tree, tri, tre, tri tree!

This is the way the gentlemen ride,
Gallop-a-trot! Gallop-a-trot!
This is the way the gentlemen ride,
Gallop-a-trot! Gallop-a-trot!

This is the way the farmers ride!
Hobbledy-hoy, hobbledy-hoy!
This is the way the farmers ride!
Hobbledy-hoy, hobbledy-hoy!

And when they come to a hedge—they jump over!
And when they come to a slippery place—
They scramble, scramble,
Tumble-down Dick!

Three Wise Men of Gotham

Three wise men of Gotham,
They went to sea in a bowl,
And if the bowl had been stronger
My song had been longer.

There Was a Crooked Man

There was a crooked man, and he walked a crooked mile,
He found a crooked sixpence against a crooked stile;
He bought a crooked cat, which caught a crooked mouse,
And they all lived together in a little crooked house.

TRANSPORTATION

Snacks

WHEELY GOOD SPAGHETTI

Children will "wheely" enjoy eating round pasta wheels.

Ingredients:
Wheel-shaped pasta, grated Parmesan cheese, spaghetti sauce

Directions:
1. Cook the pasta according to the instructions on the package.
2. Serve with tomato sauce and grated cheese.
3. Let children imagine the tiny vehicles that would use wheels this size!

FOOD TO GO

Ask children to bring their lunch or snack in a paper bag on this day. Or let them help make peanut butter and jelly sandwiches. Provide juice boxes or small cartons of milk. Let the children pack these lunches in paper sacks. Then have your class take their food "to go" on a picnic, either spread on blankets outside, or spread on a large sheet indoors.

Option:
Some paper stores sell Chinese restaurant-style boxes. Children can pack mini-snacks in these fun cartons and take them outside.

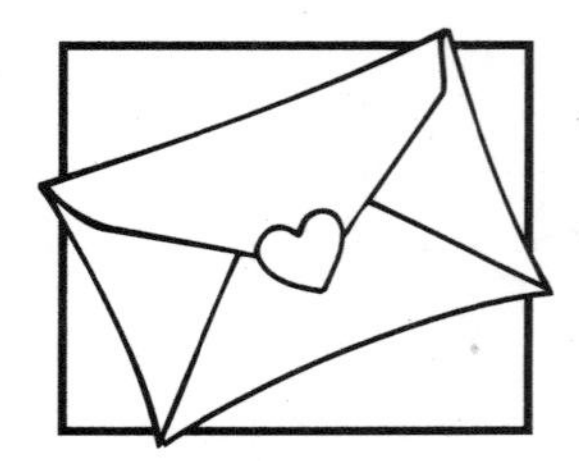

TRANSPORTATION

Letter Home

See-saw, sacradown.
Which is the way to London town?
One foot up and the other foot down,
That is the way to London town.
—Mother Goose

This month we are learning about many different types of transportation, from camels and cars to trucks and trolleys. If you own an interesting vehicle (a camper or pick-up truck, for instance), please bring it in (to the parking lot) for a special show-and-tell treat!

We are going to create an airplane in the classroom. We will be drawing pictures of what passengers see from up above, and we will take turns piloting our pretend plane. Any pilots, cabin attendants, or travel agents are invited to share their knowledge about planes.

We would also like to hear from truck drivers, race car drivers, sanitation engineers, firefighters, or other people with interesting stories about how they got from one place to another!

This month we need:

- old tires (bike, auto, truck)
- headphones (for our airplane pilot to radio the control tower)
- clean, empty juice bottles and aluminum cans
- shoe boxes (we're making a train!)

Thank you for your help!

August: Jobs

Whether children hope to be butchers, bakers, or candlestick makers, you can encourage them in striving toward their future occupation with the activities in this chapter. Invite a firefighter or police officer to talk to the children and display the equipment of the job. Or take a field trip to a local office building to explore the interesting environments of people at work: conference rooms, mail rooms, kitchens, escalators, and more! To introduce this unit, let the children help make ploughman's lunches to eat outside on a warm day.

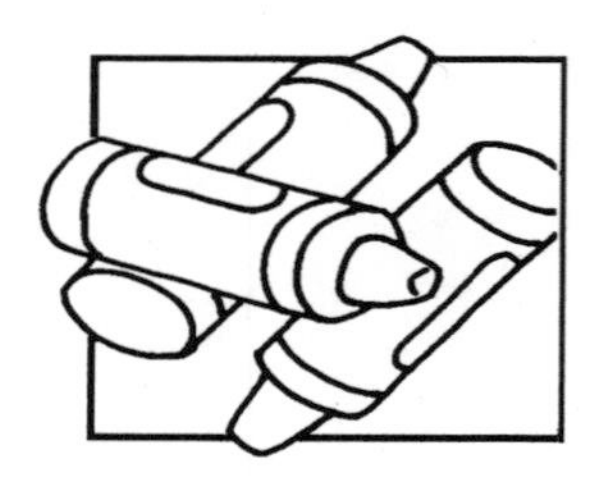

JOBS

Art Activities

WHEN I GROW UP . . .

This activity allows children to imagine working at many different types of jobs. Remind them that there are no right or wrong answers.

Materials:

People patterns (see "Family," p. 41), occupation patterns (pp. 325-327), construction paper, glue, scissors, markers or crayons

Directions:

1. Ask each child to think of two or more things they would like to do when they grow up. These could be jobs or hobbies.
2. Give each child a people pattern to cut out, decorate as him- or herself, and glue to a piece of construction paper.
3. Provide the assorted occupation patterns for children to sort through. Let them choose the patterns that correspond with things they would like to do, and have them glue these patterns around the picture of themselves.
4. Children can draw additional items around them, for instance, if a child wanted to be a race car driver, he or she might draw tires, cans of oil, and a race track to go with the glued-on car.
5. Post the completed drawings on an "I Want to Be . . . " bulletin board.

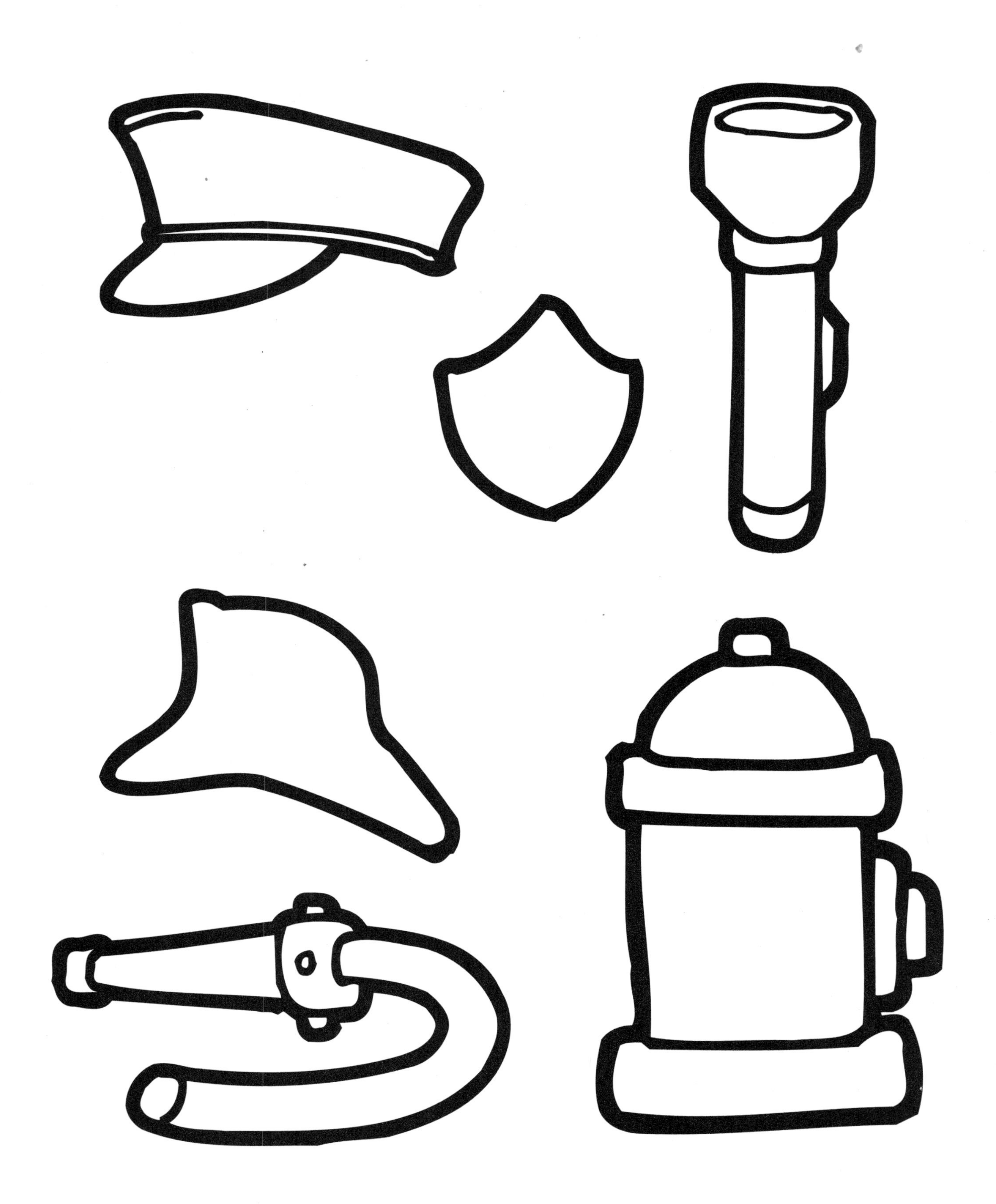

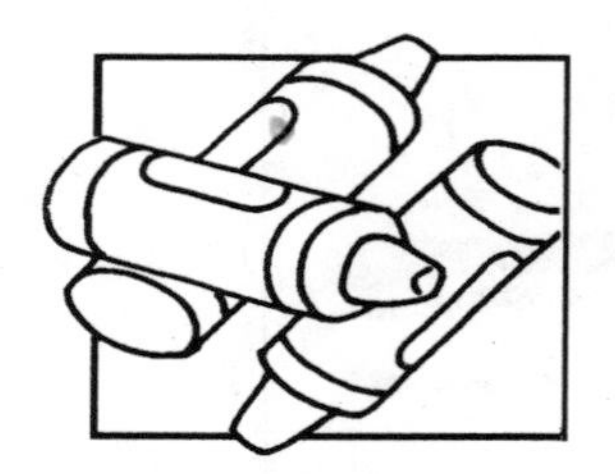

JOBS

Art Activities

MAKE A DESK

Many children like to play at going to work. This activity lets them make their own individual (and portable) desks for their "offices."

Materials:
Shoe box (one per child), construction paper, scissors, tape, glue, pencils, markers, note paper, rulers, stapler, small empty milk cartons or juice cans (with the edges covered in masking tape), colored Contact paper, wrapping paper, oak tag or tagboard

Directions:
1. Have the children turn their shoe boxes upside down. The bottom will be the top of their "desks."
2. Let children decorate their desks using construction paper and glue.
3. Provide note paper and pencils for children to use while "working" at their desks. They may want to staple a few pieces of paper together to make a pad.
4. Give each child a juice can or milk carton to cover with colored Contact paper, construction paper, or wrapping paper to use as a pen and pencil holder. (When desks are not in use, children can store their supplies inside the shoe boxes.)
5. Let children observe your desk and make any necessary additions to their own, such as rulers or paper clips. Children may also want to make desk blotters—provide oak tag or tagboard for this purpose.

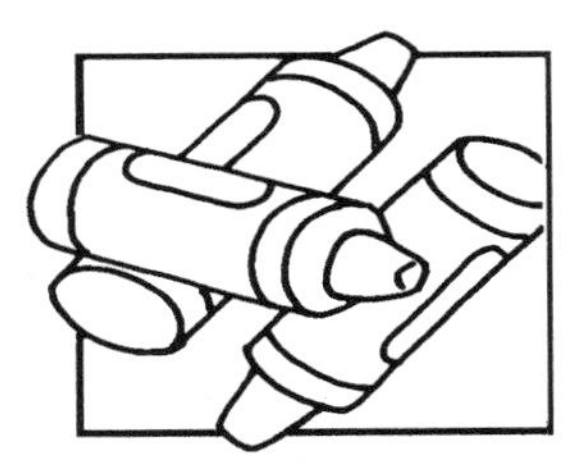

JOBS
Art Activities

TOOLS OF THE TRADE

Children can decide which tools of the trade to use in this painting, gluing, and clay modeling activity. Before you begin, spread out a variety of utensils, and have children guess what type of job would require their use.

Note:
All materials should be old and ready to be retired to the art center. Children will be using these items to mold clay and to paint.

Materials:
Clay in assorted colors, tempera paints in assorted colors, paper, glue, a variety of job-related items (spatula, egg beater, garlic press, screwdriver, measuring tape, ruler, pencil, note pad, movie theater tickets, used envelopes, paper clips, and so on)

Directions:
1. Let children decide whether they want to work with clay or paints.
2. Clay workers can choose utensils to mold and decorate their clay.
3. Painters can choose items to paint with and items to glue to their papers. Encourage the children to be creative, and paint or model using items they might not normally consider for the job.
4. Display the completed projects on a table with the job-related items in a basket nearby.

JOBS

Storytime

FEATURED PICTURE BOOK

***Charlie Parker Played Be-Bop* by Chris Raschka (Orchard, 1992).**
Charlie Parker was a great jazz saxophone player. This book tells the story of his music using sounds, such as "Be bop. Fisk, fisk. Lollipop. Boomba, boomba," that young children will easily be able to relate to. The music comes to life as the sounds and notes dance across the pages: "Boppitty, bibbitty, bop. BANG!"

ART EXTENSION

Have children study the drawings on the book's pages (especially the pictures of the notes and sounds, as opposed to the drawings of Parker). Ask the children to suggest the types of media used by Raschka to make the pictures.

Materials:
Watercolors, paintbrushes, paper, charcoal pencils (crayons or chalk may be substituted), recording of music by Charlie Parker

Directions:
1. Set up the book on an easel for children to observe. Open the book to the "lollipop," "bus stop," or "bibbitty" pages.
2. Put on one of Charlie Parker's recordings (perhaps "A Night in Tunisia") for the children to listen to while they create. Raschka was inspired by "A Night in Tunisia," the "be bop anthem" which helped make Charlie Parker famous. Let the children see if the music inspires them as well.
3. Provide an assortment of watercolors and black charcoal for children to experiment with. They can make colorful backgrounds and then draw charcoal scribbles once the paint has dried, or they can draw with the charcoal first and then use the watercolors to paint over their designs. They can also use the watercolors to outline or fill in charcoal drawings. Encourage originality.

JOBS

Storytime

MORE PICTURE BOOKS

Albert's Alphabet by Leslie Tryon (Atheneum, 1991).
Albert is the school carpenter in the Pleasant Valley school district. (He is also a duck.) One day, the principal sends Albert a note, requesting that he build an alphabet for the walking path on the school playground. Albert uses an assortment of tools and materials to complete this task.

Caps for Sale by Esphyr Slobodkina (Scholastic, 1940).
This is the story of a peddler who carries his wares on his head! He sells caps, and he keeps them well organized by color in a tall stack on his head. One day, he takes a nap under a tree. Before he goes to sleep, he checks that all the hats are still there. But when he wakes up, every cap is gone (except for his own). Who stole the caps, and how will he get them back?

A Chef by Douglas Florian (Greenwillow, 1992).
This book takes readers through a typical day in the life of a chef, from buying food at an open-air market to checking deliveries to planning the day's menu. The jobs of the assistant chefs, pastry chef, and waiters are also listed, as are the tools of the trade.

How We Work by Anita Harper, illustrated by Christine Roche (Harper & Row, 1977).
People work at many different jobs, in many different places, and at many different times of day. This book shows an assortment of occupations, including acting, teaching, boxing, farming, cleaning, and homemaking.

The Jolly Postman or Other People's Letters by Janet and Allan Ahlberg (Little, 1986).
The Jolly Postman does his job, delivering letters to an assortment of fairy tale characters, including Mr. and Mrs. Bear, the Wicked Witch in the gingerbread house, a giant, Cinderella, a wolf in grandma's clothing, and Goldilocks.

Miss Nelson Is Missing by Harry Allard, illustrated by James Marshall (Houghton, 1977).
Miss Nelson is the nicest teacher in the school, but her students take advantage of her and don't pay attention to their lessons. Then, one day, Miss Nelson disappears and Viola Swamp takes her place, laying down the law and loading children up with homework. When Miss Nelson reappears, the children have undergone a transformation. But where did Miss Nelson really go?

Simple Pictures Are Best by Nancy Willard, illustrated by Tomie de Paola (Harcourt, 1977).
The shoemaker and his wife have everything that they want. They have a garden, sunflowers, and a cat, and they play music together in the evenings. For their wedding anniversary, they decide to have their picture taken, but although the photographer insists that "simple pictures are best," the couple continue to add to the shot until a mild disaster occurs.

The Tailor of Gloucester by Beatrix Potter (Warne, 1903).
The tailor of Gloucester grows ill and cannot finish sewing the coat for the mayor's wedding. But as luck would have it, a troop of mice (who'd been rescued from the tailor's cat) pay the tailor back by finishing the coat, with the tiniest stitches and the most beautiful embroidery ever seen!

JOBS

Flannel Board

WHAT SHALL I BE?

One, two, three,
What shall I be?
I'll be a **teacher**,
And teach **kids** like me.
Four, five, six,
I'll get my kicks
As a great circus **clown**
With a big **bag of tricks**!
Seven, eight, nine,
What I'd like fine
Is to be a great **artist**
And draw a straight line.
Now we've reached ten,
Let's try it again.
We'll start at the top
And we'll work back again.
Ten, nine, eight,
Let's get it straight.
Whatever I'll be
I will be something great!
Seven, six, five,
As a **driver**, I'll drive!
And I'll race to the finish
In **car number five**.
Four, three, two,
I know what I'll do,
I'll be a **zookeeper**
And work at the **zoo**.
Now we've reached one,
And we're almost done.
Whatever we do,
Let's do something fun!

5

ZOO

JOBS

Discovery

CAREER DAY!

Many high schools hold career days and invite speakers to explain a variety of occupations to the students. You can set up your own career day by displaying throughout the classroom materials used in various jobs. Let the children move from one station to the next, trying out as many different jobs as they'd like.

AMAZING ASTRONAUTS

Provide books about space (planets, stars, comets, and so on), a pair of old headphones (for radioing back to Earth), space suits (jumpers), and "moon rocks" for future astronauts to study.

AWARE ARCHAEOLOGISTS

Set up a dinosaur dig in the sandbox or at the sand tables. You can bury a few plastic toys for the archaeologists-in-training to uncover. Provide sieves and small brushes for the children to use to carefully whisk the sand away from the buried treasure!

BLOCK BUILDERS

Architects, builders, and construction workers can hone their skills in the block area. Make sure that there are many different kinds of blocks for children to work with.

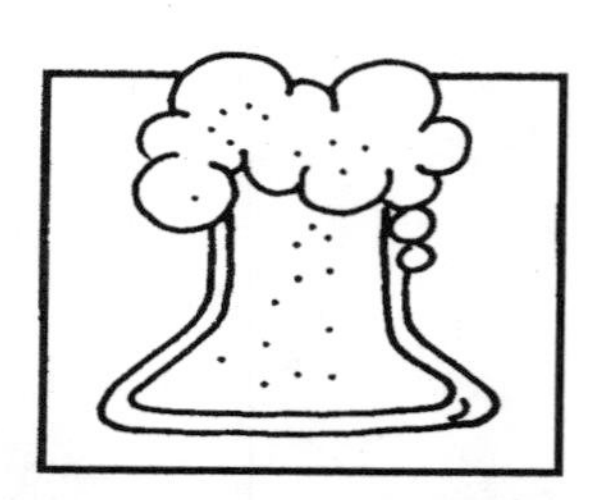

JOBS

Discovery

BUSY BUS DRIVERS

Bus drivers need hats, maps, transfers, and change (pennies). Set up a bus stop in a corner of the classroom, and encourage other children to join the bus driver in a hand-to-waist chain that drives along (indoors or out).

CREATIVE COOKS

Child chefs can help you make a snack. Or set up a food preparation area using plastic foods, plates, and utensils. Children can also make food from playdough to serve to other classroom workers.

DARING DOCTORS

Doctors-to-be can take care of sick dollies and teddy bears. Set up a special table with bandages, cotton balls, a stethoscope, and doll blankets.

FRIENDLY FIREFIGHTERS

Future firefighters can help you organize a fire drill and go over what to do in case of this type of emergency. If you have firefighter hats available, set them out, along with a hose (it doesn't have to be attached to a spigot), toy ladders, and a stuffed toy dalmatian!

JOBS

Discovery

GREAT GARDENERS

Provide shovels, seeds, watering cans, and a small plot of schoolyard or a window box or plastic tub filled with dirt. Encourage your gardeners to take good care of their seedlings, and make sure the young sprouts receive just enough water, sunlight, and TLC to grow into healthy plants.

MAKING MUSIC

Set out musical instruments, such as tambourines, drums, whistles, and bells, for children to use to create a Preschool Band! You might want to limit the number of children in the music corner to cut down on the noise level.

PAINTER'S PALETTE

Place easels, paper, tempera paints, watercolors, and paintbrushes in an area where future painters can practice. You might even set out a bowl with fresh fruit for children to use for a "still life" painting. Or ask a future model to sit for a portrait!

JOBS

Discovery

POTTER'S PLACE

Set up a clay corner on a table with clay and a variety of instruments (spoon, fork, chopsticks, garlic press) used by potters and other artisans.

PUPPETEERS-IN-PRACTICE

Set up a puppet theater (using either a large grocery bag with a window cut out, or a cardboard box). Provide hand puppets and finger puppets, and let the puppeteers practice before performing for the other preschoolers!

SERIOUS SCIENTISTS

Provide magnets, magnifying glasses, scales (and objects to weigh), water, and measuring containers for your serious scientists to experiment with and observe.

SUPER SANITATION ENGINEERS

Let all children have a chance cleaning up and recycling used materials. If possible, let them watch adult sanitation engineers at work.

JOBS

Discovery

TERRIFIC TEACHERS

Provide pencils, note paper, ABC blocks, rulers, tape, scissors, and other teaching tools for children to use in a classroom corner. They can practice their ABCs, make lines with their rulers, and create the day's lesson plan!

WEAVING WONDERS

Children can weave thin strips of construction paper through a construction paper "loom" (see the illustration). Set up a weaving area and provide many types and colors of papers.

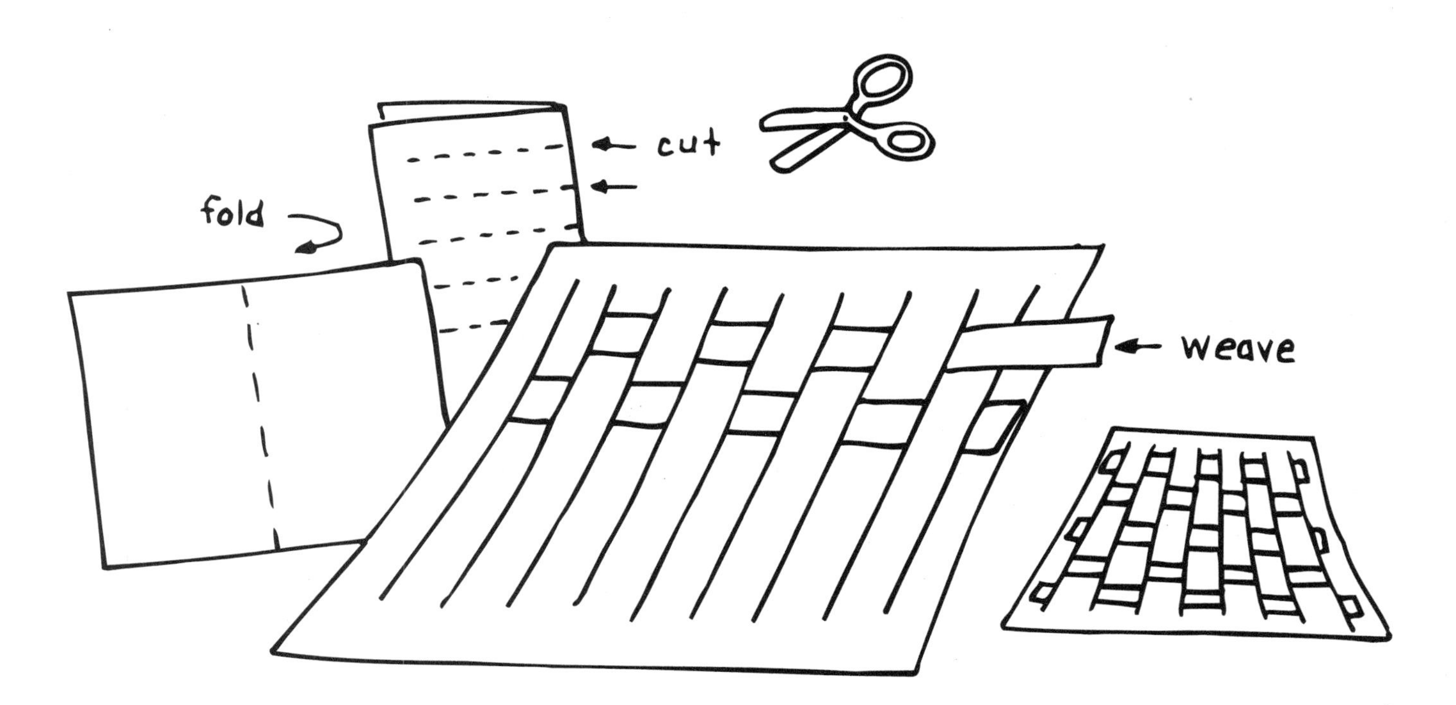

JOBS

Discovery

FIELD TRIP 1

Take a field trip to your school's office to view grownups at work. Children will want to check out the copy machine, the phone system, conference room, lounge, and so on. If possible, ask your receptionist, school nurse, and principal or director to discuss their jobs with your children. Make sure the children have time to ask questions.

FIELD TRIP 2

Visit your local children's library (or the children's section of your local library). Have a librarian talk to the children about his or her job. Let the children look at picture books and, in small groups, show them the filing system (either card catalog or computer). If possible, let each child get a library card with his or her name on it.

FIELD TRIP 3

Ask parent volunteers to come to the class to describe their jobs. Or, if possible, go on a field trip to where one or more of your children's parents work. Children are often especially interested in police officers, firefighters, pilots, drivers (bus, taxi, race car), chefs, and sanitation engineers. Some parents may be able to demonstrate their job in the classroom. For example, a cook could prepare a meal (with children's help), a librarian could read a story, an actor could read a page of a script, a tailor could show children how to sew a stitch, and a musician could play a song.

JOBS

Class Project

JOB FAIR

Choose the five most popular stations from "Career Day" to set up again in the classroom. Have the children help you organize the stations, setting out all of the necessary tools and materials.

On the day of the Job Fair, have children come to school dressed in the type of clothes worn by members of their chosen profession. Children who haven't decided what they want to be might want to dress up like one of their parents or guardians. Note: Have extra occupational clothing on hand for children who forget to dress up.

Display children's "I Want to Be . . ." artwork on bulletin boards above the career day stations. Also display the artwork made with the "Tools of the Trade."

At a designated time, have the children parade in small groups for each other. Children might try to guess the occupation of each of their classmates. If appropriate for the jobs chosen, let the children act out their future professions in a game of "Occupation Charades." At first, have the children mime their profession. If the rest of the class cannot guess an occupation correctly, then have the child miming add words to the act for extra hints.

If possible, have parent volunteers come to your Job Fair to speak about their professions and, if appropriate, their hobbies. For example, a chef might talk about cooking and about her SCUBA-diving hobby.

Place real tools in boxes or paper bags. Have children touch the objects (without looking) and guess what they are. Suggested items: hammer or screwdriver (carpenter's tools), spatula or wooden spoon (chef's tools), eraser or chalk (teacher's tools), telephone (receptionist's tool), keys (driver's tools), pen or notepad (writer's tools), book (librarian's tool).

During the day, sing some job-related songs, such as, "I've Been Working on the Railroad" and "Whistle While You Work."

JOBS

Dramatic Play

A HAT IS A HAT FOR ME!

In your dramatic play corner, set up a basket filled with occupational hats. You might include some of the following: football helmet, firefighter's hat, farmer's straw hat, swimming cap, police officer's cap, fishing hat, baseball cap, bus driver's cap, chef's hat, gardener's sun bonnet, fast food worker's hat, surgeon's cap, and so on.

THE MAGIC COAT

Bring in a special "magic" coat, and explain to the children that when they wear it they can become anything they want to be! The coat can transform them into a rock climber, a musician, a sculptor, a writer, a teacher, a superhero. . . . Hang the coat on a rack in the dress-up area, and remind children to take turns wearing it—and transforming themselves.

Encourage originality!

JOBS

Dramatic Play

THE BAG OF TRICKS

Many jobs require special tools. If you have play tools in your classroom, gather together those that fit particular jobs and place them in individual paper bags. For example, put a pad of paper, a pencil, and a press pass in a "Journalist's Bag." Place a badge, a microphone / walkie-talkie, and a blue hat in a "Police Officer's Bag." Place a roll of tape, a ruler, and a school book in a "Teacher's Bag." Set the bags on a table and let the children each choose one. (You may only have enough equipment for four or five children to participate at any given time.) Have the children pull out their tools and use them to pretend to be a worker in the particular field. They can play together as their new "bag" selves, or perform for the rest of the class and have those students guess what job they are doing. After children are done using the bags, they should put all of the tools back inside for the next child.

JOBS

Mother Goose

A Was an Archer

A was an archer, who shot in the fog,
B was a butcher, and had a great dog.
C was a captain, all covered with lace,
D was a driver, who drove in a race.
E was an esquire, with pride on his brow,
F was a farmer, and followed the plough.
G was a gamester, who had but ill-luck,
H was a hunter, and hunted a buck.
I was an innkeeper, who loved to carouse,
J was a joiner, and built up a house.
K was King William, who once governed England,
L was a lady, who had a fine hand.
M was a miser, and hoarded up gold,
N was a nobleman, gallant and bold.
O was an oyster girl, and went about town.
P was a parson, and wore a black gown.
Q was a queen, who wore a silk slip,
R was a robber, and wanted a whip.
S was a sailor, and spent all he got,
T was a tinker, and mended a pot.
U was a usurer, a miserable elf,
V was a vintner, who made wine himself.
W was a watchman, and guarded the door,
X was expensive, and so became poor.
Y was a youth, that did so love his school,
Z was a zany, a poor silly fool!

JOBS

Mother Goose

Hey Diddle, Dinketty, Poppety, Pet
Hey diddle, dinketty, poppety, pet,
The merchants of London they wear scarlet,
Silk in the collar, gold in the hem,
So merrily march the merchantmen.

Ifs and Ands
If ifs and ands were pots and pans,
There would be no need for tinkers!

Barber, Barber, Shave a Pig
Barber, barber, shave a pig,
How many hairs will make a wig?
"Four and twenty that's enough."
Give the barber a pinch of stuff.

Rub-a-Dub-Dub
Rub-a-dub-dub,
Three men in a tub;
And who do you think they be?
The butcher, the baker,
The candlestick-maker;
They all jumped out of a rotten potato,
Turn 'em out, knaves all three!

Rich Man, Poor Man
Rich man, poor man,
Beggar-man,
Thief,
Doctor,
Lawyer,
Merchant chief.

JOBS

Mother Goose

Old Mother Hubbard

Old Mother Hubbard
Went to the cupboard,
To get her poor Dog a bone,
But when she got there,
The cupboard was bare,
And so the poor Dog had none.

She took a clean dish
To get him some tripe,
But when she came back
He was smoking a pipe.

She went to the fishmonger's
To buy him some fish,
But when she came back
He was licking the dish.

She went to the baker's
To buy him some bread,
But when she came back
The dog stood on his head.

She went to the hatter's
To buy him a hat,
But when she came back
He was feeding the cat.

She went to the barber's
To buy him a wig,
But when she came back
He was dancing a jig.

She went to the grocer's
To buy him some fruit,
But when she came back
He was playing the flute.

She went to the tailor's
To buy him a coat,
But when she came back
He was riding a goat.

She went to the cobbler's
To buy him some shoes,
But when she came back
He was reading the news!

JOBS
Snacks

PLOUGHMAN'S LUNCH

Explain to your children that a ploughman was a person who worked in the fields, and that ploughmen brought their lunches to work with them. This snack is the traditional ploughman's lunch.

Ingredients:
Apple or pear slices, cheese slices, bread or crackers, pickles or relish

Directions:
1. Place all of the ingredients on separate plates on a low table.
2. Let children serve themselves, choosing from the apple or pear slices, cheese, bread or crackers, and pickles.
3. Children can make mini-sandwiches, layering a bit of each ingredient on the bread.

Other Job-Related Snacks:
- Mountain climber munchies (Gorp/trail mix)
- Shepherd's Pie (frozen pot pies—one small one will feed four kids)

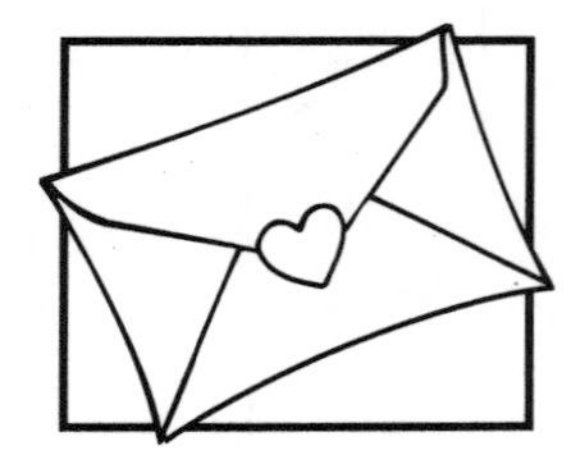

JOBS

Letter Home

Cobbler, cobbler, mend my shoe,
Yes, good sir, that's what I'll do;
Here's my awl and wax and thread,
And now your shoe is quite mended.
—Mother Goose

This month we are exploring our future and that ever-popular question, "What do you want to be when you grow up?" We will be trying out many different kinds of occupations in our classroom, and we hope to visit a variety of actual job sites.

If you would like to come and tell us about your job, we would love to listen. Or, if it's possible for our class to visit you at work, please contact me.

We will be dressing up this month in the garb of our future profession. Please join us on ____________ to take part in the festivities!

For our art projects, we need:

- shoe boxes
- small juice cans or individual serving milk cartons
- old uniforms and hats (for our dress-up corner)

Thanks for your help!

Resources

Lakeshore Learning Materials
2695 E. Dominguez St.
P.O. Box 6261
Carson, CA 90749

The Lakeshore catalog is filled with art materials, furniture, dolls, and more, including:

- Paper, crayons, paints, and pencils in people colors
- Sponges in animal and people shapes
- Glitter and sequins
- Multicultural baby dolls
- Plastic foods
- Career hats

You will find many of the books mentioned in our chapters in one of the catalogs below.

Gryphon House
Early Childhood Book Collection
P.O. Box 275
Mt. Rainier, MD 20712

Scholastic
P.O. Box 7502
Jefferson City, MO 65102

- Early Childhood Catalog

Environments
P.O. Box 1348
Beaufort, SC 29901-1348

The Environments catalog is filled with beautiful banners, wonderful wall hangings, creative carpets, and more. Themes include:

- The Arctic
- The Antarctic
- Ponds
- Deserts
- Prairies
- Forests

Mrs. Grossman's Paper Company

Spectacular stickers for a variety of subjects, including:

- Ocean (fish, octopus, crab, starfish, seahorses)
- Weather (clouds, rainbows, raindrops)
- Sky (sun, moon, stars, rocket ships, planets)
- Earth (leaves, flowers, trees)
- Animals (pets, wild animals, carousel horses, dinosaurs)
- Songs (musical instruments, musical notes)

You can find Mrs. Grossman's products at stationery supply stores or teacher stores.

ABOUT THE AUTHORS

Sarah Felstiner and Annalisa Suid met at Friends Nursery School in Palo Alto, Calif., when they were three years old. Since then, they have played together and collaborated on a number of creative projects, some of which appear in this book.

Sarah graduated from Yale University, where she received a Bachelor's Degree in Child Psychology. She has worked in preschools in the Bay Area and New Haven, Conn., and is currently a teacher at the Bing Nursery School of Stanford University. She teaches children aged two through five, and trains Stanford undergraduates in Early Childhood Education. Sarah has also presented at the National and State Conferences of the Association for the Education of Young Children.

Anna studied Art History and Early Childhood Education in Los Angeles, and is the author of a series of three environmental books for children in grades K-3: *Love the Earth, Save the Animals,* and *Learn to Recycle* (Monday Morning Books). She is currently at work on three new books on dinosaurs, space, and bugs.

Sarah and Anna, age 4